MW00638655

PET WHISPERER P.I

Books 4 - 6

MOLLY FITZ

Editor: Megan Harris
Proofreaders: Alice Shepherd, Tabitha Kocsis & Jasmine Jordan
Cover Designer: Lou Harper, Cover Affairs

WHISKERED MYSTERIES
PO Box 72
BRIGHTON, MI 48116

AUTHOR'S NOTE

Hey, new reader friend!

Welcome to the crazy inner workings of my brain. I hope you'll find it a fun and exciting place to be.

If you love snarky talking animals and crazy magical mishaps as much as I do, then I'm pretty sure you're going to enjoy the journey ahead.

This book is just one of my many brain-tickling adventures to come, so make sure you keep in touch to keep in the know!

I've done my best to make it easy by offering several fun ways to access sneak peeks of upcoming books, monthly giveaways, adorable pictures of my own personal feline overlords, and many other cool things that are just for my inner circle of readers.

So take a quick moment now to choose your favorite:

Download my app

Join my VIP reader group
Sign up for my newsletter
Kick off a cat chat on Facebook

Okay, ready to talk to some animals and solve some mysteries?

Let's do this!
Molly Fitz

To anyone who wishes she could talk to her animal best friend... Well, what's stopping you?

DOG-EARED DELINQUENT

Pet Whisperer P I

ABOUT THIS BOOK

Apparently I've been slacking on the job as a paralegal, even though the firm doesn't know that I'm secretly working as the area's premier Pet Whisperer P.I. to solve our toughest cases behind the scenes. Now they've hired an intern to "help" me manage my workload…

But what the partners don't realize is that they've let a nefarious criminal into our offices. Trust me, Octo-Cat can smell this guy's stink from a mile away. The worst part? I'm pretty sure he can talk to animals too… and he most definitely isn't using his talents to solve crimes and defend the innocent.

I've always wondered how that zap from an old coffee maker landed me with supernatural abilities. Now it's time to find out once and for all. Otherwise I fear I may wind up losing them–and my trusty talking feline sidekick–for good.

CHAPTER ONE

Hi, I'm Angie Russo, and my life is way harder than you'd expect for someone who lives in an old East Coast mansion. Well, it's not really my house— more like my cat's. After all, it's his trust fund that pays the bills.

It may seem like I've won the lottery but think again. Times are tricky when you have a talking cat bossing you around day-in and day-out.

Yeah, I said it.

My cat can talk.

As in, we communicate, have conversations, understand each other. I'm not sure how or why our strange connection works, only that it does. And as much as I wished I knew more, sometimes you just have to accept things at face value. It all happened so fast, too. I went to work unable to talk to animals, got zapped by a faulty coffee maker, got knocked unconscious, and when I woke up again—*bada bing, bada boom!*—now I'm talking kitty.

I've decided to think of it as a stroke of fate, because it really does feel like Octo-Cat and I were meant to find each other. In the past six months alone, we've worked together to solve three separate murder investigations. I guess that's why I'm considering my mom's advice and officially looking into starting a business. She's dubbed me Pet Whisperer P.I.—not because I want anyone else to know about my strange abilities, but because we needed some kind of excuse for me to take Octo-Cat around on my sleuthing calls.

After all, I wouldn't be much of a Sherlock without my Watson. Okay, *I'm* probably the Watson in our relationship. If you've ever been owned by a cat, then you should understand.

Regardless, I'll be the first to admit that my whole life changed for the better once Octo-Cat became a part of it. Before then, I was just drifting from one thing to the next. I'd already racked up seven associate degrees, due to my unwillingness to commit to any one major long enough to secure a bachelor's.

I guess you could say nothing ever felt quite like the perfect fit, but I kept trying anyway. I knew that somewhere out there my dream job was waiting… even if I didn't quite know what it was yet.

You see, greatness kind of runs in my family, and for the longest time I'd worried that particular trait had skipped right past me without a second thought.

My nan had followed her dreams to become a Broadway star back in her glory days, and my mom was the most respected news anchor in all of Blueberry Bay. My dad lived his dream, too, by doing the sports report on the same channel that featured Mom.

Now at last, after so much yearning, so much searching, wishing, and praying, I've found the career path that fits me like a glove—and that's private investigating. So what if I'm not getting paid for it yet? I probably could if I threw everything I had at getting my P.I. business up and off the ground.

But I'm scared of letting down the good people of Longfellow, Peters, & Associates. Oh, that's right. My favorite frenemy Bethany is the newest partner, and I am so proud of her. Between her and Charles, I know the firm is in the best possible hands, but quitting to pursue self-employment?

That's downright terrifying.

True, I'm only part-time at the moment, but the twenty hours per week I put in are really well spent. I know I'm making a difference, and yet…

Aargh. I've never had this much trouble quitting a job before. Why can't I just hand in my two weeks' notice and say, "See ya around?"

Maybe part of me still longs for the chance to see where Charles and I could take our relationship, provided he's willing to ditch his annoying realtor girlfriend. Or maybe I don't want to leave Bethany behind when we've worked so hard to overcome our differences.

It's also likely that I'm afraid of spending all day and all night at home with my crabby tabby for company. Nan lives with us now, too, but Octo-Cat reserves all his whining just for me. I mean, I guess it makes sense, seeing as I'm the one who understands him.

At the end of the day, life sometimes requires hard decisions.

Historically, I'm not so great at making them.

If I just give it a few more weeks, maybe the right answer will fall into my lap. Yeah, I like that idea.

Until that happens, though, I'll just continue to wait and pray I get the courage to ask for what I really need. First, I'll have to make sure it's actually what I want, and then…

Watch out, world! I'm Angie Russo, and I'm coming for you.

"I come bearing muffins!" I cried as I bounded into the firm ten minutes late that morning. I still had a hard time calculating my new commute, but I hoped that Nan's homemade baked goods would more than make up for my tardiness.

"Ahem," somebody cleared his throat from the desk near the door. *My* desk.

I whipped around so fast, I fumbled my beautiful basket of muffins and dropped them straight onto the floor. All of Nan's hard work was ruined in an instant. It was a good thing she enjoyed baking so much and probably already had another fresh batch ready and waiting at home.

"Let me help you," the stranger said, rushing over to offer assistance I most definitely didn't need. I watched him from the corner of my eye, still refusing to acknowledge this interloper's presence. From what I could discern, he was tall and gangly, with white-blond hair and thick, emo glasses.

"Oh, good," Bethany said, clasping her hands together as she strode toward us both with a smile. "You've met Peter."

"Peter?" I asked with a frown as the new guy stuck his hand out toward me in greeting. Looking at him straight on now, I saw he wore his dress shirt open with a t-shirt underneath that read *Awake? Yes. Ready to do this? Ha, ha, ha!* Charming. The disturbing top half was paired with wrinkly cargo khakis on bottom. Fulton and Thompson *never* would have let this fly in their days. Yeah, I knew the firm was mostly better off without them, but still couldn't we at least try to look like professionals here?

"You're Angie, right?" Peter asked, grabbing one of the muffins that had touched the floor and shoving it into his mouth with wide eyes. *"Mmm,"* he said pointing at it. "So good."

I disliked this guy more and more by the moment, but Bethany seemed so excited to introduce us that I forced a smile and shook his hand despite my better judgement.

"Peter's our new intern," she explained. "He's going to help you manage your workload."

"I don't need help managing my workload," I shot back, recoiling from Peter's grasp when he wouldn't let my hand go after the normal, polite period of time for a greeting.

Bethany frowned. "Not exactly true. It's been harder for all of us since you switched to part-time, but it's okay, because Peter is the perfect person to step in and smooth things out."

Yeah, me going part-time was the problem, and not the revolving door of partners we'd seen so far this year.

"What exactly are his qualifications?" I asked, regarding him coldly.

Peter popped the remains of that precious blueberry muffin into his mouth and mumbled, "I'm her cousin, and I work for minimum wage."

Bethany shot him a dirty look, finally showing me that he bugged her, too. That at least made me feel a little better about all this. "Really, Peter. You need to stop being so liberal about sharing your salary."

"Sorry," he muttered with a shrug that suggested he really couldn't care less about it.

Why was he here? I may not be the best paralegal in the world, but I was miles better than this guy. He probably didn't even have his degree. This was all wrong. I couldn't quite say why exactly, only that I hated everything about this Peter guy.

"Wait," I said, realizing something. "Your name is Peter Peters? You sound like a super hero."

"Or a super villain," he countered with another shrug and a strange, new smile.

"Anyway," Bethany said, glancing at her feet to make sure no errant muffin crumbs had attached themselves to her shiny patent pumps. "This is Peter's first day, which is why I asked him to come in a bit early. Can you help get him set up? Show him the ropes?"

"What kind of ropes?" I demanded. I didn't normally start my work day by playing babysitter to some annoying nepotistic hire.

No, right now, I was supposed to be in Bethany's office while she safely brewed me a cup of delicious, life-saving coffee. There was no way I'd touch another coffee maker as long as I lived, but I still enjoyed the extra jolt it gave me when someone else was willing to brave the brew master.

"Just the stuff you normally do," Bethany answered with a dismissive gesture, already turning to take her leave. "If either of you need me, I'll be in my office. I have client meetings most of the morning, but should be free around lunch time."

"Okay, bye," I said, turning to my new charge, resigned that I would have pretty much the worst work half-day ever.

He smiled after his cousin. "Too-da-loo!" he called, waggling his fingers, then turned to me. "Okay, so I'm ready to learn how to be you when I grow up," he announced.

He did not just say that!

Well, so much for turning in my notice. There was no way I could leave the firm with this bumbling oaf of a paralegal. If only we could cue a makeover montage in real life. I'd choose one of my favorite upbeat 80's pop jams, spend a few minutes reforming him, then call it done and move on. Real life never worked fast enough.

"Let's go set up your email," I said with a sigh, leading him back to my desk that we now seemed to be expected to share.

"Cool, cool. And when do I get my company-issued iPhone?" He bobbed his head, following after me like a lost little duckling.

"What? Why would we give you an iPhone?"

"Uh, hello. FaceTime." He twisted his hands and formed a rectangle about the size of a smartphone then looked at me through the gap.

And just like that, he went from simply irritating to downright terrifying. FaceTime was the same app I used to call my cat from work. Our senior partner, Charles, had found out when he was still brand new to the firm and bribed me to help him defend a client. Was it just a coincidence that this Peter Peters had alluded to it now?

Or did he know something that could get us both into very big trouble?

Oh, I did not like this. I did not like it one bit.

CHAPTER TWO

U nfortunately, the day only got worse as it went on. Peter met me with snark, indifference, or outright creepiness at every turn and quickly proved that he had zero of the necessary experience to do this job—*my* job. In fact, Peter grated on my nerves so much that I decided to go right over Bethany's head and appeal to our senior partner, Charles Longfellow, III. Surely he would see that hiring this guy was the worst kind of mistake?

Of course, things between Charles and me continued to be quite complicated. To start, I kind of, sort of, may have had some unresolved romantic feelings for him. We'd become close friends in the months since he'd joined the firm. It had all started when he discovered my ability to speak with Octo-Cat and then blackmailed me in order to help his client, Brock Calhoun the, um… other guy I kind of, sort of, may have had a bit of a crush on these days.

Still, despite the slight blackmailing, Charles was a consummate professional. It's how he'd managed to rise through the ranks at the firm so fast, and it was why I trusted him to do the right thing when it came to Peter. After finding a spot where his calendar was open, I barged straight into his office—so upset that I forgot to knock.

Oh, I wish I would have taken a quick second to knock!

"Angie," he said with a start, then cleared his throat and straightened his tie. It was the same tie Nan had bought him as a housewarming gift a month or so back—dark red silk with an intricate white paw print pattern that somehow managed to look both classy and kitschy at the exact same time.

His girlfriend, Breanne, untangled herself from his arms and glanced over her shoulder with a smirk. Her bottle-red hair clashed with Charles's tie, and everything else about her clashed with the rest of him, too. Of all the people in Blueberry Bay, I still couldn't believe he'd chosen to date *her.* They'd been wrapped around each other for months now, and I was beginning to suspect they may end up walking down an aisle before too long.

Granted, I hadn't known Charles much longer myself, but I still thought that he and I would have made a much better couple—a much more logical one, too. As each day passed, it looked less and less like I'd get my chance to find out what could be there. *Stupid Breanne.*

"I'll see you tonight. Okay, babe?" Charles said after several awkward moments passed between the three of us.

"I'll be waiting," Breanne gloated as she accepted his kiss, then sauntered past me, hips swinging. Have I mentioned how much I actively loathed her? Because it was a lot.

Charles sighed and sunk down into his leather desk chair. "What's up, Angie?"

"Sorry to interrupt," I answered, rubbing my index finger on my thumb to try and loosen a hangnail I'd been fighting all morning. It was a bad habit of mine—a nervous habit. Seeing Charles and Breanne's disgusting canoodling had knocked the speech I'd prepared clear out of my brain.

Guess I would just be speaking from my heart.

I closed the door behind me, then came closer and took a seat in one of the two visitor chairs angled across from his desk. "It's about the new person Bethany hired."

"Peter Peters?" Charles asked with a slight snort. "What about him?"

"I don't like him," I said plainly, hoping Charles would understand without me having to go into more detail. "And I don't want him here."

Charles sighed. "He didn't make the best first impression on me, either. But, unfortunately, we do need the help."

"Can't we find somebody else?" I whined, not caring how pathetic it made me sound. Charles needed to understand that this was so much more than bad first impressions.

Charles pinched his brow and fixed me with an exasperated stare. "People aren't exactly lining up to work here given, um… our recent history."

Oh, right. The small fact that the other partners continued to leave under less than savory circumstances. All the extra clout we'd picked up after our near-impossible win on the Calhoun case had quickly dropped by the wayside when…

Never mind, best to focus on our current problems instead of dwelling on the past.

"If we're really that spent, I could come back full time for a while." I enunciated each word while keeping careful eye contact. "Just until we find someone better than Peter, I mean."

Charles shook his head again. "I wish I could, but Bethany is my partner. We make decisions together now. If you just give Peter a chance, I'm sure he'll grow on you."

I rose to my feet and put my hands palm down on his desk, then leaned in as close as I dared. I wanted to slap him and kiss him in equal measure. *Stupid Charles.*

"I think he knows about me. About what I can do." I widened my eyes, refusing to so much as even blink until I was sure he understood.

"About you and," He gulped before continuing. "Animals?" When I nodded, Charles leaned back and let out a slow breath. "Well, that's not good."

I straightened to my full height once more. Whether or not we had a romantic connection, Charles and I had always seen eye to eye. I knew he'd get it. I knew he'd find a way to protect me.

That is, until he said…

"But it's also not possible. I'm sure it's all in your head."

"All in my head?" I demanded, throwing a hand on each of my hips. "You can't be serious!"

He glanced toward the far corner of the room instead of looking at me. "What do you want me to do, Angie? Fire him based on a suspicion? One that has nothing to do with what we actually do here, by the way."

I threw myself into his line of his vision. I was not just some problem that could be ignored. I was a real person and had a problem that demanded a satisfactory conclusion. "Yes, that's exactly what I want you to do," I practically shouted.

He cleared his throat again and shifted his gaze toward his keyboard on the desk. "Sorry, that's something I just can't do. Not without a valid reason to let him go."

I crossed my arms over my chest defensively and charged back toward to door. There were many things I wanted to say and do—chief among them quitting on the spot—but I simply walked out without another word.

I had to stop fast to avoid running straight into Peter who stood right outside Charles's office door, munching on a granny smith apple. "Trying to get rid of me?" he asked with a neutral expression, keeping his eyes fixed on the fruit in his hand. "That doesn't seem very welcoming."

"Why are you here?" I asked with a deep scowl.

Peter crunched into the apple again, and a spray of juice hit me on the cheek. He reached up with his thumb to wipe it away, but I jerked out of reach.

After swallowing everything down, he smiled and said, "Why do you think I'm here? It's to get close to you, Angie. To uncover your secrets and expose them to the world."

I took a step back, panic settling in my chest like a lead weight. I could scarcely breathe, let alone say anything in response to *that*.

Peter closed the distance between us and set a heavy hand on my shoulder. A smile broke out across his face and then he laughed. "Whoa, you really need to learn how to relax. Did you honestly just buy that garbage?" He shook his head as if dealing with an imbecile. "I'm here to make some money and help out my cousin. Okay?

I mean, seriously, Angie." He continued to laugh as he breezed his way past me back toward our shared desk.

I stood rooted to the spot as I watched him go. How much had Peter heard of my talk with Charles? And how much did he already know? Moreover, why?

And how?

If he was on to me, there had to be others as well. Maybe Peter was just some kind of henchman and the big bad had yet to reveal himself or his plan. I'd never hurt anyone, and I'd become much more careful when it came to concealing my strange ability.

If someone was on to me, then what could I possibly do to keep Octo-Cat and myself safe? And why would they ever want to hurt or scare us as Peter's mannerisms seemed to suggest?

Suddenly, it felt as if nowhere would be safe. That, even if I ran, there were people out there who knew, who would always know.

What was I going to do?

CHAPTER THREE

I couldn't escape the office fast enough that day. Physical distance, however, did little to calm my already frayed nerves. The whole drive home I kept looking over my shoulder, half expecting to see Peter following me in some kind of old junker. I knew I didn't have any real hard and fast proof, but still, something within me screamed that he was out to get me, that we were quickly headed somewhere bad.

Very, very bad.

Sure, he could have been some harmless and ordinary, run-of-the-mill weirdo whose goal was simply to score a few laughs at my expense. He totally could have been. And yet...

Ever since I'd gotten zapped by that old coffee maker and woken up with the ability to speak to Octo-Cat, my intuition had also been dialed up to at least a nine. I'd been wrong about some things, of course, but that was mostly when I let my personal feelings cloud my judgment. Whenever I stopped and listened to that still small voice, it led me straight to the answer I needed.

And right about now, that tiny voice was practically hoarse from shouting *beware* over and over again the past several hours.

As much as I hated it, this wasn't just about Peter moving in on my job and messing things up at the office. This was about keeping those I loved safe—and that now included the tabby cat who'd entered my life and turned it upside down again and again. How could someone I'd only just met already know the one very private thing I hesitated to share with anybody?

How could Peter have possibly figured me out when so few people knew what I could do and most of them were related to me?

I mean, Charles knew, but despite my disappointment in his response today, I trusted him not to tell a soul. Did that mean someone else at work had figured things out? Sometimes I slipped up and talked to my cat around others, but most people wouldn't just jump to the conclusion that we could communicate with each other. The normal thing would be to assume I'd gone wicked crazy. That didn't bother me since most days I was halfway there already.

I turned onto the secluded driveway that led to my huge manor house in the woods. The summer sun hung high in the sky, and my gardens were in full, beautiful bloom. In a lot of ways my life was pretty perfect—giant estate, wonderful family, cool cat, and a monthly stipend from his trust fund. So, then, why couldn't I just let this thing with Peter go?

"You look like you've had a rough day," Nan said, greeting me at the door when I entered our shared home just in time for a freshly prepared lunch. She and Octo-Cat both waited for me right in the foyer whenever I came home from work. Nan usually had a kind word and a hug. Sometimes, a joke.

Octo-Cat generally had a complaint. Today, he stretched out his toes, showing off his impressive claws, and moaned, "The sun is not bright enough today. It's hard to keep my schedule when my warm spot disappears halfway through the morning."

I shrugged off his concern, especially considering the sky had felt just as bright as ever during my return commute. "Sorry, nothing I can do about that."

I'd long debated getting him a heat lamp, precisely because of how often I heard this particular complaint, but that kind of felt like rewarding bad behavior. Ah, who was I kidding? It was just a matter of time before I'd ultimately cave. Heck, maybe I'd get him one for Christmas. Today, however, I had other things to worry about.

I took a long, appreciative sniff as Nan and I headed for the kitchen. Ever since we'd moved in together a couple of months ago, she'd taken it upon herself to cook up three square meals per day, finding a passion for the culinary arts a bit late in life but not lacking an ounce of enthusiasm nor, thankfully, talent.

"French onion soup," Nan revealed with sparkling eyes, which seemed to grow as she made this revelation. "Have a seat and I'll bring it right out."

I wanted to help, to give her a bit of a break, but she always pushed me right out of the kitchen and told me to hold my horses before they galloped away without me.

"What's got you so down in the dumps?" she asked, setting a steaming hot bowl before me, then returning to the kitchen to grab a second for herself. My nan always knew when something wasn't right. She had the gift of intuition, too, but I suspected that came more from being a mother than from a near-fatal run-in with a coffee maker or some other such mildly supernatural experience.

"They hired a new intern," I explained, pushing my spoon through the thick layer of perfectly melted cheese and allowing it to fill up with broth, then shoving it appreciatively into my mouth. *Mmm.* So good.

Nan smiled when she saw how much I enjoyed what she'd prepared. Rather than taking a bite herself, however, she folded her hands before her and said, "Well, I'm guessing we don't much care for this new person." That was another thing about my dear, sweet nan—she always took my side. She didn't even need to hear a single detail before she was ready to jump into the fray and fight for my honor. Heck, just a couple months ago, she'd hit a police officer multiple times for attempting to cuff me.

"We most definitely do not," I answered, preparing a second mouthful of gooey goodness, complete with onion and cheese this time. "Not only is he creepy, but I also think he knows about me. You know, about what I can do."

Nan shook her head and sucked air in through her teeth. "Well, that's not good. Not good at all." Finally, she dug into her soup, choosing to eat one of the broth-saturated croutons first.

"What are we going to do?" I asked after giving her a play-by-play of the awful day I'd had.

"That Charles deserves a good scolding," Nan said with a grimace. "After all we've been through together, he won't even stand up for what's right."

I shrugged and let my spoon clatter to the bottom of my bowl. "I don't know. Maybe I'm just being oversensitive about the entire situation."

"Hey, I didn't raise you to talk like that," Nan shouted so loud and so abruptly, it made me jump with surprise. "We don't discount or apologize for our feelings. We're not robots. Right?"

"Right," I agreed with a sigh. "Then what should I do about Peter Peters and all the weirdness?"

Octo-Cat hopped up onto the table and strode down the center line. As he did, loose hair floated off his body and a piece or two wound up in my soup. Guess that meant I was done.

"If I may," he said grandly, halting right in front of me and gesturing to himself with a paw. "I believe I have the solution to this problem."

"He says he has an idea," I translated for Nan, who smiled and waited for more. She loved watching the two of us talk, even though she needed a bit of help understanding Octo-Cat's side of the conversation.

"Not *an* idea," he corrected with a huff. *"The* idea."

"Well, what is it?" I asked impatiently. Sometimes his dramatics could be adorable, but this wasn't one of those times. I was far too stressed to sit and watch a show. I needed real-world solutions here delivered in a real-time fashion.

"You need to pull a stray cat on this guy," my tabby said plainly.

This, of course, meant nothing to me. "Come again now. What?"

"A stray cat. Not that I've ever been stray." He shuddered and flicked his tail. "But I've seen enough of them to know their modus operandi. They're free agents—strays—and most want to stay that

way. But a cat can get real sick of eating trash when Fancy Feast is
an option, you know? So, sometimes they have to make their eyes
big, raise their tails, and do the pretty meow when a human is
nearby. It hurts inside to fake it with a human—that much, *I do know*
from experience—but it's just a couple moments of cringiness to get
a full belly of food. Get it?"

I thought about this for a moment, ignoring the fact that he'd
probably just insulted me. His cat-based analogies often took me a
bit of finagling to truly understand, but they often did offer good
and surprisingly relevant advice. I recapped Octo-Cat's speech for
Nan, who seemed to understand instantly without even awaiting the
full translation.

She nodded her approval to Octo-Cat, then turned back to me
with a newfound fierceness burning in her eyes. "*Operation: My Enemy
is My Friend*'s an official go," she said in a low, husky voice that I
assumed belonged to her tough guy persona.

Still, no matter how much I wanted to find out what Peter knew
and, moreover, what he wanted, I wasn't sure I could find a way to
fake nice with someone I already despised so much.

Despite Nan's Broadway past, I hadn't inherited even one iota
of her acting talent. So then, how was I going to trick Peter into
revealing his motives here?

CHAPTER FOUR

I wish I would have been surprised when Nan showed up at my work the next day wearing an all-black satin gown and bolero jacket combo. She kind of looked like she was ready to attend an elegant society ball and then rob its hosts on her way out. She'd even done her makeup much more heavily than normal to match today's bold style. Yes, winged liner and a smoky eye currently topped off my grandmother's day-time look.

I knew she sometimes missed the glory days of singing, dancing, and acting her heart out on the Broadway stage, but sometimes she took her real day-to-day life in Blueberry Bay a bit far. I still fondly remembered how she'd donned a black and white checked bodysuit to accompany me to my driver's test, or how she wore a cap and gown of her own to my high school graduation. Her wardrobe probably stretched all the way to Narnia for all the crazy outfits she kept hidden away until they were needed.

Was I embarrassed? Nope, not one bit.

I loved my nan and was long past feeling the need to apologize for her eccentricities. They were just as much a part of her as her loving, generous heart, and I wouldn't trade either of those things for the world. Still, I did have to wonder what she had up her sleeve —or rather, her gloved arm—with this one.

"Hello, good people of Longfellow, Peters and Associates," Nan declared, strolling into the office like she owned the place. In her hands she clutched a sealed Pyrex dish, which she promptly uncovered to reveal freshly baked apple turnovers.

Of course—*apple* because I'd mentioned the creepy episode with Peter outside of Charles's office yesterday. What I couldn't tell was whether this whole display was meant as a power play or rather a way to ingratiate herself as part of our so-called *Operation: My Enemy is My Friend.*

With Nan, you just never knew what was going on inside that wonderfully whacky brain of hers.

"Hi, Nan," I said, rising from the small corner of the shared desk that I'd claimed as my own. "What are you doing here?"

Peter stayed seated but kept his eyes on us while offering up a cool, casual smile.

"Hello, dear." Nan gave me air kisses instead of a hug, further proving that she'd decided to play some kind of character role today. Even her voice sounded grander, surer, as it reached to the far edges of the room.

"Well, of course, you know how I'm planning that fabulous dinner party later this month. I'm testing out some gowns and some recipes ahead of time to lessen the burden of all the choices I'll have to make as we get closer to the big day." She paused and dipped her head, after tossing me a quick wink. "Now tell me. How do I look?"

She spun in a slow, graceful circle as if there was absolutely nothing for either of us to be embarrassed about. The thing that made her a great actress, I knew, was that she truly lived every single role. Granted, she was simply playing a farcical version of herself today, but that didn't stop her from owning it one hundred percent.

"You look beautiful," I said with a big smile. I may not have always agreed with her methods, but I had to admit that no one even came close to the space Nan occupied in my heart.

"Thank you," she said primly. "And, now, how do these taste?"

she added, shoving the open Pyrex dish into my face with a desperate, needy look.

I plucked one of the desserts from the top of the stack and took a nibble. "Absolutely delicious," I answered honestly after swallowing down the perfect mix of sweet and tart. Part of me wished she had discovered this newfound passion for baking when I was younger so I could've enjoyed these talents longer. My waistline thought differently, though. I'd already had to go up one pants size this month, and I was not keen to go up another.

Nan frowned and her voice dropped into a husky pout. "Oh, but you always say what I want to hear. I need an impartial opinion." She spun around again, this time searching the room as if she didn't know Peter was the only other person around.

"You there!" she called, erupting into a full, sparkling smile as her eyes landed on a watchful Peter. "Can I count on you to give me your honest opinion? There's a free dessert in it for you, if you agree."

Peter hopped to his feet and sauntered over to join us. "I was hoping you'd ask." Without waiting for any further invitation, he grabbed two pastries from the stack and ate them in giant, appreciative bites.

"So good," he smacked, his mouth still full. "You should definitely serve these at your party."

Nan frowned again. "But you haven't tried the other options. How do you know for sure that these are the best?"

Peter chuckled and took a third apple turnover. "If they're all this good, then you have nothing to worry about."

Nan placed one gloved hand on Peter's arm and the other on mine. "Oh, I know!" Her eyes sparkled with the promise of a new idea, even though I had no doubt she'd arrived at the firm with this exact script already written and memorized. "Would you mind stopping by later tonight to try some of the others and offer your expert opinion on which is best?"

Peter faltered as he shifted his weight from foot to foot. Today he wore a tight t-shirt that had a bowtie and shirt collar printed onto it.

He'd paired this with dark wash jeans and what I guessed was unintentional bed head. "Oh, I don't know if—"

"Please?" Nan begged, casting a pathetic shrug his way. "This party is so important to me. It might be the last I ever get to throw before God takes me back to the great dinner party in the sky."

Wow, she went there. She really went there.

"Oh, well. Sure, okay," Peter answered with a puzzled gaze that he quickly transitioned into a smile. "It would be my pleasure."

Nan perked up instantly. "Lovely. See you tonight, dear. Six o'clock?"

This whole time they spoke, Peter simpered at Nan and studiously ignored me. So, he only hated me, it seemed. At least I knew Nan believed me about his antagonism, even if my colleagues didn't.

He nodded now and took another two treats for himself. "Sounds like a plan."

"Excellent," Nan declared, then pushed the glass dish at Peter. "Why don't you keep these to remember me by? Just don't spoil your appetite for tonight." She reached up and pinched his cheek, then to my horror made a kissy face before letting go.

"Well, my dear," she said, turning back my way. "This gown may look divine, but it doesn't quite have the movement I need for an entire evening spent wearing it. Back to the boutique it goes!"

I nodded dumbly.

She glanced over my shoulder toward Peter and blew him one last kiss goodbye. "Now I must be off. Angie has the address. Toodles!" And just like that, Nan blew out of the office every bit as quickly as she'd entered.

I headed back to the desk while Peter slumped down into one of the thick armchairs in our waiting area, helping himself to yet another turnover. "That was weird," he said.

I shrugged. "That was Nan."

He studied the pastry in his hand, then widened his eyes and shoved it into his mouth. "She's fun. I like her."

I shot him a polite, fake smile, then tried to return my focus to work.

Peter, however, seemed in the mood for a chat. "It's really too bad you don't take after her," he informed me with a sigh. "We'd have a much better time at work if you did."

I pretended I hadn't heard him, but he kept talking anyway.

"You don't look much like her, either. Maybe you inherited something else from her. You know, besides personality and looks. Maybe some secret trait or talent. *Hmm?*" He chuckled and brushed his sticky fingers against his jeans. "I guess we'll find out tonight."

Indeed we would. Poor Peter had no idea he was walking straight into a trap. Nan may seem crazy on the surface, but she's the best sleuth I know. Her interrogation skills are also top-notch.

Not to mention, Octo-Cat and I would also be there and ready to pounce on even the slightest suspicion. It may have been easy for him to pick on me at work, but my house was my fortress and filled with everyone who loved me most. For all his faults, I knew Octo-Cat would also do whatever it took to protect me. Even all these months later, he still found new and terrifying ways to surprise me.

Peter Peters didn't stand a chance.

CHAPTER FIVE

Nan put me to work the moment I stepped through the door. She tossed me an apron and declared me in charge of mixing batter and rolling dough, the two tasks that were the most difficult to mess up, I noticed.

"It's all hands on deck. Only five hours until go time, and we have to make our ruse look believable," she explained with a curt nod. She'd changed out of her black satin gown from earlier and was now wearing a dainty crushed velvet number patterned with Chinese dragons. She'd replaced her smoky eye with a shimmering gold shadow and had contoured her cheeks like a Kardashian.

"I expect you to dress up, too, my dear," she explained while studying my unassuming floral dress with its giant, oversized belt and large hoop earrings as if it was the worst outfit anyone on earth had ever cobbled together.

Octo-Cat laughed between licks of his paw. "Being a human can be the pits, huh? A cat would never…" His eyes grew comically wide as his words trailed into oblivion.

I followed his line of sight to where Nan had been rummaging through the junk drawer. She now held out a red bow tie as she moved toward Octo-Cat with a broad, reassuring smile that only seemed to heighten his discomfort. "You, too, young man. We must all look our best tonight."

Nan then proceeded to fasten the bowtie to his collar with skilled and gentle fingers, but she may as well have been strangling the cat, given his over-the-top reaction.

"I am tainted!" he cried, shaking and twitching and throwing himself against the tile floor repeatedly. "Don't you know? I was born with all the clothes I'll ever need. So why add this? It's even the same color as that wretched dot! That's just taking things too far."

He heaved a giant sigh and fell over on his side when Nan had finished. I had to admit, he looked rather dashing. I did not, however, admit that aloud, or else I'd end up with cat puke in my bed.

Instead, I simply covered my mouth and tittered softly against my hand.

Nan smiled at our tabby approvingly. "Very handsome," she said in a way that was reminiscent of how she'd talked to Peter at the office that morning.

Octo-Cat continued to shriek and toss himself around the kitchen, pausing only briefing to shake his head and whisper, "*Et tu,* Nan? I thought you loved me."

"Chin up. It could be worse," I told him as I continued stirring and stirring until my hand cramped from the vigorous, repetitive motion.

"I don't see how," my cat told me, rolling onto his back and wiggling back and forth in an ill-fated attempt to shimmy loose of his adornment.

"Well, for starters, you're going to have to spend time with Peter tonight. Peter's the worst," I explained with a shudder as I placed the bowl back on the counter and flexed my hand. I would definitely be getting Nan a stand mixer for the next gift-giving holiday. Sure, they cost a lot, but it would be worth it to save my hands, and hers, too.

Nan popped a tray into the oven, but we had so many different dishes underway that I had no idea what was on it. "Now, Angie," she said, turning back toward me with a wagging finger. "If *Opera-*

tion: My Enemy is My Friend is to be a success, you need to commit to character."

"Hey, I never agreed to take on a character and, by the way, neither did he." I tilted my head toward Octo-Cat, who was too busy trying to find a way out of his collar to notice I'd just stuck up for him. *Figured.*

Nan tutted. "If you don't believe it, then how will our guest?" she asked, then grabbed my wrist and pulled me to attention. "It is an honor to have Peter with us tonight. We're friends, and as such, we tell each other things without hesitation."

"Like what he knows and how he found out?" I said drolly.

"Precisely," she said, punctuating the word by jabbing a dripping spatula at my apron. "But if you remain hostile, we won't get anywhere. Can you soften up a little so that we don't have to fall back on plan B please?"

"What's plan B?" I asked, biting my lip as I waited for the answer.

Nan let out a little laugh. "Well, we——"

"You know what? It doesn't matter," I interrupted. It would be easier if I didn't know too much ahead of time. I was a terrible actress, anyway. "I'm in. The sooner we figure out the deal with Peter, the sooner we can be done and rid of him."

"Now there's the sweet girl I raised," Nan said with a chuckle, returning to the other side of the kitchen to ice an enormous layered cake.

Octo-Cat flopped onto my feet, rubbing himself all over my socks until they practically changed color from all the shucked off fur. "I… can't… breathe," he exclaimed between gasps. "I think this is how I die!"

I bent down to pet him and slipped my fingers beneath his collar to make sure it wasn't suddenly too tight. "It's just for a little while," I assured him. "I promise we'll take it off the moment Peter leaves."

He sat up and swished his tail behind him as he thought. A scary smile stretched across his fuzzy little face. "So, if he were to leave sooner rather than later, I could have my freedom?"

I nodded emphatically. I had no idea how he intended to make that happen, but if agreeing meant he'd try to help tonight, then I was all for making a deal. "Yes, definitely. I don't want him around, either," I reminded my cat.

"Then our goals align." Octo-Cat returned to all four feet and blinked hard. "If you'll excuse me. I need to prepare."

I watched him trot away, then moved to wash my hands in the sink so I could get back to work. Nan didn't need to know about whatever Octo-Cat had planned. In reality, I didn't even know what he had planned, but I had no doubt it would be amusing—if not mortifying. It was starting to feel as if I didn't even need to do anything now that Nan and Octo-Cat both had grand plans of their own.

Once I'd done all I could to help in the kitchen, Nan ushered me upstairs and informed me that I would be wearing my red party dress with tiny white polka-dots that evening. Well, at least Octo-Cat and I would match for the upcoming festivities.

I bided my time, even going so far as painting my nails a shining ruby red, figuring that Nan would appreciate this small gesture of my commitment to the character. By the time I floated back down the stairs, Peter seemed to have just arrived. He stood inside the foyer with Nan, wearing the exact same outfit he'd had on earlier that day.

"Well, don't you look quite fetching," Nan said kindly as she studied the faux tux printed on his old T-shirt. "I love the irony of that ensemble. So clever."

Peter raked a hand through his messy hair and gave her a boyish grin, charmed as anyone who found themselves the subject of Nan's attentions.

Octo-Cat came racing down the stairs as well, a glint of determination shining in his amber eyes. "This ends now," he ground out as he passed me.

He walked straight up to Peter and rubbed against his legs while purring. Next, he transitioned to his hind legs and pawed at Peter's knees. He didn't do that for anyone. *Not ever.* Man, he must have been really desperate to get rid of that bowtie. I'd definitely have to remember that trick the next time I needed to trick him into doing something.

"He likes you," Nan said with a wink. "Why don't you pick him up?"

"I'm really more of a dog person," Peter said hesitantly.

"A dog person?" Octo-Cat asked in horror. *"Blech.* Gag me with a spoon. But, yeah, I can smell that canine stink all over this one. Totally not surprised."

Peter flinched, then cracked his neck on either side. "Should we go try the desserts? After all, that is why you invited me. Right?"

"Yes, dear. Come along." Nan led him toward the dining room while Octo-Cat and I stayed behind in the foyer.

"Was it just me, or…?" I began but let my words trail off. He'd flinched in response to what Octo-Cat had said. I was sure of it, and yet… there was no way. It was far too crazy to be believed.

"He reacted to me," Octo-Cat agreed. "I thought so, too."

"It was probably just a fluke," I said, keeping my voice low so as not to be overheard by Nan and Peter in the next room.

"But if it wasn't…" Octo-Cat shook his head and took a deep breath. "Now I'm just as curious as you are. Something's off about this one, and I'm going to prove it. C'mon, Angela."

He trotted off and I trailed helplessly behind, wondering what my cat could possibly have planned now and also wondering if Peter might really be like me. Did he get zapped by that old coffee maker, too?

I desperately hoped I'd have the answer by the time the evening was through, because if this big production didn't work, we probably wouldn't get another chance.

Peter already seemed on guard that evening. Had he finally realized that we might be on to him just as much as he was on to us? And if he didn't want to be found out, then why was he working so hard to push my buttons?

Was everything in my overworked imagination, or was my entire world about to change?

I honestly didn't know which option I preferred…

CHAPTER SIX

N an looked utterly beguiling in her getup for that evening. She'd even woven jade chopsticks through her hair in a fancy upswept hairstyle that complemented her angular bone structure quite nicely.

She often wore Asian-inspired garments, preferring their smooth, flowing lines to the more rigid structure of traditionally Western clothing. Between her style choices and my predilection for all things eighties, we really did make quite the pair.

I preferred eighties fashion simply because it was great fun. Nan, on the other hand, had done a brief tour abroad during the Vietnam War—not as a soldier, but rather an entertainer—and she'd fallen in love with everything about that part of the world. She'd managed to visit Japan, China, and Thailand over the years, too, and was greatly looking forward to the day when I'd finally agree to accompany her for an extended visit of all her favorite places. As for me, I wanted to get to know myself a little better before I ventured so far from home. Luckily, I was getting closer and closer to accomplishing just that with each passing day.

As loathe as I was to admit it aloud, Octo-Cat had made a huge difference in my life and had been a huge part of my recent self-discovery. I had a feeling I'd done the same for him as well. That was the thing about the people you loved— sometimes they made you crazy, but they would always be there for you in a pinch.

And this thing with Peter was the pinchiest situation we'd encountered yet. With the murders we'd investigated together, we at least knew what we were dealing with, what we were looking for. But with Peter? We now had questions on top of questions. As afraid as I was to discover where the answers may lead us, at least the three of us were firmly in this together.

Nan waited until Peter and I were seated at the table, then disappeared into the kitchen to plate up her sweet creations.

"Nice house," Peter remarked, twiddling his thumbs in front of him. "How'd someone like you manage something like this?"

"It's my house," Octo-Cat announced, jumping up onto the table and plopping his rear right in front of Peter. "And I don't think I want you in it."

"Don't mind him," I said, pretending that everything was as normal as could be. "He's just a bit suspicious of new visitors."

"Nice kitty," Peter said, reaching a hand toward the tabby.

"If you touch me, I bite you," Octo-Cat informed him with a low growl.

Peter instantly recoiled. Was it because of the growl or the words that preceded it? *Hmm.*

"Good human," Octo-Cat said in that condescending way I'd grown to love. "If you poke the tiger, you're going to lose some fingers. That's how the saying goes. Isn't it?" He tilted his head to the side and flicked his tail, keeping his unblinking eyes on Peter the whole time.

Peter laughed nervously. "So, Angie, how long have you been working at—?"

"Don't talk to her." Octo-Cat hopped back onto his feet and stared Peter down with his ears folded back against his head. "Talk to me. Who are you, and why are you such a jerk? *Huh,* big guy? You think it's nice to pick on my human?"

Peter leaned back as far as he could in his chair and looked toward me with large, pleading eyes. "Um, could we maybe put your cat somewhere while I'm here? I think I might be allergic."

"More like afraid," Octo-Cat said, then punctuated it with his signature evil laugh. I'd never seen Peter so shaken. Granted, I hadn't known him very long, but still, it really did seem as if he could understand what my cat was saying to him.

"Oh, don't worry about him. He's harmless," I said with a dismissive shrug.

Octo-Cat growled again. "Oh, she has no idea just how harmful I can be," he told Peter with a low rumble.

"Who's ready for some heavenly confections?" Nan sang as she floated back into the dining room with an artfully arranged silver serving platter, completely unaware of what Octo-Cat had been up to during her brief absence.

I widened my eyes as I moved them between Nan and the cat, trying to let her know that this was his show, but she didn't seem to get the hint.

"Bon appetit!" she cried, setting the tray between Peter and me.

"This looks amazing." Peter wasted no time in grabbing a rich puff pastry dessert and shoving it eagerly into his mouth.

"You want to know what's really amazing?" Octo-Cat asked, keeping his eyes trained on Peter. "My jokes. Seriously, I dare you not to laugh."

I selected a mini cheesecake bite for myself and smiled as I waited to see what would happen next. Octo-Cat's jokes were generally pretty terrible, but Peter didn't strike me as the type with a sophisticated sense of humor anyway.

"Okay, get this." Octo-Cat sat again, coming right up to the edge of the table so that Peter had to scoot back to avoid touching him. "What do you call a dog with a brain? Anyone? Anyone?" He paused and looked around. "No, nobody knows. Okay, I'll tell you— *a cat!*" He whooped and laughed hysterically while Peter attempted to make small talk with Nan.

I watched the whole thing in quiet fascination, smiling to myself as Peter struggled to maintain his composure. He certainly didn't enjoy getting a taste of his own medicine, the poor baby.

Octo-Cat yawned. "That one didn't get you. *Hmm,* okay. Well, I have lots more." He waited for Peter to take another bite before asking, "What's the difference between cat puke and a dog?"

Peter seemed to choke a little but recovered quickly.

"One's a slimy pile of disgusting excrement, and the other's cat puke. *Ha!*" Octo-Cat flopped over on his side and rubbed his back on the dining room table the same way he often did in the freshly cut grass outside. This was him luxuriating in the moment. He seemed to love taunting someone who deserved it.

I chuckled quietly, eliciting glances from both Nan and Peter.

"Everything okay, dear?" Nan asked, stopping the small talk she'd been making with Peter. I'd been so focused on the tabby's antics, I didn't even have the faintest idea what they'd been talking about.

"Yes," I answered quickly. "I just think it's funny how Octo-Cat invited himself along to the party. He seems to be really taken with you, Peter."

"Yeah, well." He cracked each of his knuckles and looked away.

"Tough crowd," Octo-Cat spat, pacing the length of the table once more. "Good thing I saved the best for last. Okay, who here knows why dogs can't tell jokes? No one? It's because they lose their minds whenever someone says *knock, knock!*"

At this, Peter snorted and then, at last, broke out into a full-fledged laugh. *Gotcha.*

I jumped to my feet and pointed at him. "I knew it! I knew you could understand him!"

Peter blanched and fumbled the dessert he'd been holding. "I don't know what you're talking about——"

"Oh, can it, honey!" Nan shot in. "The jig is up." I was pretty sure Nan didn't know what we were talking about, but it felt nice to have another ally on my side. She stood, too, and together we glared at Peter.

"Who are you, and why are you here?" I demanded.

"You invited me," he sputtered in equal parts confusion and irritation. "But if I'm not welcome anymore, I'll just go." He pushed his chair back and sped toward the door, but Octo-Cat leapt after him and sunk his claws into Peter's shoulder, hanging on for dear life as the lanky man tried to fight him off.

"Ow, what the…?" Peter cried as he spun and shook, but still Octo-Cat refused to let go.

"Say you can hear me," the cat hissed viciously. "Admit you understand."

When Peter said nothing, Octo-Cat sunk his claws in even deeper. Telltale droplets of blood appeared on his neck and dampened his shirt.

"Ouch! Fine!" Peter shouted. "I understand you. Now let go."

Octo-Cat hopped down and raced over to Nan, who'd taken a seat on our old Victorian couch while she watched this entire scene unfold. "Now that's the spirit," she told Peter. "And here I was afraid we'd have to tie you up before you'd willingly confess a thing."

"What do you want from me?" he asked, wiping at his wounds with a defeated scowl.

I crossed the room and stood before him with my arms folded over my chest. "What do *you* want from *me?* You're the one who started all this."

"I thought you might be like me," he explained in that whiny, nasally voice I'd come to hate over the last couple of days. "And, clearly, I was right."

I shook my head, refusing to admit anything. "So, why taunt me?"

"Why not? I was just having a little bit of fun."

"Need me to cut him again?" Octo-Cat asked, racing over to defend me.

Peter curled into himself defensively. "Please, no!"

"You need to tell me how you knew, and you need to do it now," I yelled, towering over him now.

Peter's voice came out muffled. "Or what? You'll sic your cat on me again?"

I tilted my head and smiled at Octo-Cat who bounced at my side, ready for more action.

"Actually, that's exactly what I'll do," I said, yanking Peter's arms away so that he'd look me in the eye again. "Now, are you going to talk or what?"

Peter shook his head. "Not here."

I nodded to Octo-Cat, and he took another step toward Peter. "You have the right to remain silent," he said. "And I have the right to defend the indefensible."

Indefensible? Ouch. I was pretty sure he was just quoting something he'd seen on his favorite TV show, *Law & Order*, but still.

"I'll talk. I will!" Peter cried. "I promise I will. It's just... it's not safe here, okay?"

Oh, Peter. How quickly he'd transformed from villain to victim.

"If not here, then where?" I demanded.

"If not today, then when? If not me, then who?" Nan chimed in, but was ignored by both of us.

Peter shoved his hand into his pocket and pulled out a black business card printed with silver lettering. "This is the address. I'll see you there Friday night. Around ten?"

"Fine," I said, yanking the card from him even though he seemed willing to give it freely. "And until then?"

"Just act normal at work. Not a word, I mean it." His eyes darkened for a moment, but he quickly shrugged it off. "So, if we understand each other, then I'm getting the heck out of here. Bye."

I watched in silence as he charged out of the house and sped off into the night.

"Well, that was interesting," Nan said after emitting a low whistle.

"Did you translate my jokes for her? They were some of my best yet," Octo-Cat said with another chuckle.

I just shook my head and wondered what Friday night would bring. I'd never met someone else like me, and frankly, I hated that the first other of my kind had to be someone as vile as Peter Peters. But now I was one step closer to figuring out why I could talk to animals, and maybe if I learned more, I could use my abilities more effectively. I could talk to more animals. I could solve more crimes.

Could Peter really have the answers I'd been looking for all this time?

Well, I'd know soon enough.

CHAPTER SEVEN

Friday couldn't come fast enough. Now that I knew there might actually be answers, I needed to hear them. My poor, tired mind was in overdrive trying to anticipate what Peter would say when we finally got the chance to talk things out.

Why could I talk to Octo-Cat and only Octo-Cat?

How could a quick zap from a faulty coffee maker land me with paranormal powers when the rest of the world carried on just the same as ever?

And how did Peter Peters factor into all of this?

I looked up the address he'd given me on Google Earth. It belonged to a squat brick building right in the heart of Glendale's tiny downtown area. Despite having lived in the area for my entire life, I'd never noticed that building before. Perhaps my eyes had always been drawn to the more colorful, vibrant storefronts, or maybe it was new.

I even drove past one day in search of clues and was disheartened to see a FOR LEASE sign taped inside the darkened window.

Right before I left work Friday, Peter pressed a folded-up Post-it note into my palm without offering a single word about it. I tried to act naturally, but the tiny yellow paper felt like it was burning a hole right through my flesh. Once tucked safely inside my car with the doors locked, I unfolded the note and read the single word that was written there: *Claw.*

Well, that made absolutely zero sense. I took a picture with my phone and texted it to Nan. *Peter just gave this to me. Any idea what it means?* I asked.

I waited for a few minutes. When her reply still hadn't come, I tossed the Post-it on my passenger seat and started my journey home. Nan often forgot her phone in various parts of the house and didn't realize it was missing until hours later. I could just ask for her feedback in person. After all, I'd be there soon enough.

At the stoplight, I glanced toward the note again. Maybe the trick was in how the word had been written rather than in what it said.

Only the note wasn't waiting on the passenger seat where I'd left it.

I did a quick scan of the floor, assuming it had fallen. *No.*

I groped under the seat, but the light turned green and the car behind me honked impatiently, forcing me to return my focus to the road.

The remaining minutes of my drive were grueling. Peter's note had to be somewhere. It just had to be. I needed to look harder to find it. It's not like it could have disappeared into thin air.

Then again, I was now living in a world where it was possible for at least two separate people to talk to animals. My reality had already warped and stretched into a vaguely unrecognizable shape. So, then, why couldn't a tiny piece of paper go poof when no one was looking?

Correction: when *I* hadn't been looking. Suddenly, I felt as if a million invisible eyes were staring directly at me, that I was the only one who didn't understand what had happened.

Paranoid. Vulnerable. But not crazy.

At home, I frantically searched the car. Still nothing.

I couldn't believe that Peter was making me wait until ten that night. Why had he even made me wait at all? Was this some kind of trick? Why hadn't I suspected so earlier?

Gullible. Naïve.

Nan found me less than half an hour into my search. "Lunch is getting cold. Granted, the cold cuts were already cold, but…" She stopped halfway down the porch steps and cocked her head to the side. "What are you doing, dear?"

"Looking for something," I mumbled, sweeping my hand beneath the seat for the one-millionth time. "Did you get my text?"

"What text?" she asked in obvious confusion.

I sighed. "Nan, you really need to start keeping your phone on you. What if there was an emergency and I couldn't reach you?"

Nan skipped down the rest of the steps and thrust her phone in my face. "You mean this old thing? Hasn't left my side all day."

I yanked it away from her and entered the top-secret passcode, *1-2-3-4*. That was probably another thing I should talk to her about when this whole business with Peter was put to rest. "Look, I sent you a picture of…"

I opened her recent texts and saw the conversation we'd had a couple days ago, but nothing since then. The text had sent, right?

"Dear, you don't look so good. Come inside and have something to eat," Nan suggested, as was her way.

But I was a woman on a mission. I brought my phone back out and checked my texts, checked my photo stream, checked the Cloud even.

Any indication that the Post-It note had ever existed had now also vanished into thin air. Why? It just said a single word with no context. It's not like it was something dangerous.

Wait, what *was* that word again?

It seemed that knowledge, too, had been plucked straight from my brain. I wanted to throw up as the realization hit me.

Nan put a gentle hand on my back and guided me into the house. "Eat," she commanded after pulling out my chair and pushing me down into it.

I did my best, but I just couldn't stop thinking about the note, about Peter, about everything. I couldn't wait any longer for answers. I needed to go now and hope that someone would be around who could explain all of this to me.

"I'm just going to go run a quick errand," I told Nan, not wanting to put her at risk in case we were dealing with something dangerous here.

Octo-Cat, according to his rigorously kept schedule, was now napping in the west wing of the house. That meant I could slip away without having to first explain to him why I preferred he not come.

Seizing my chance, I booked it downtown to the place I'd been fixated on all week. I hadn't tried to enter before, but now I found parking down the block and marched straight up to the presumably vacant building. A polite knock on the front door produced no results, nor did the frantic pounding that followed. I tried to peer in through the window, but everything appeared empty, dusty, uninhabited.

Was Peter just yanking my chain?

Sending me on a wild goose chase rather than giving me any real answers?

But then why the note?

It had seemed he wanted me to know about his ability—or at least to know that he knew about mine—but why?

I groaned in frustration and kicked the edge of the building.

"Come now, Angela. Try to control yourself," Octo-Cat said, appearing at my feet as if from nowhere. He yawned, then swiped a paw across his forehead.

"Where did you come from?" I asked, shaking my head in disbelief.

He looked bored with me already. "The car. Same as you."

No, something didn't make sense here. "We've never had a drive where you haven't clawed the heck out of my lap," I argued, crossing my arms over my chest and glaring at him. "How could you have possibly stowed away undetected?"

He shrugged his little striped shoulders. "You're improving your skills. I'm improving mine."

"Well, that's just great." And, under normal circumstances, it probably would have been, but I was too frustrated about all the non-answers floating around when it came to Peter, his Post-It, and now this building, too.

I pulled on the door handle, but it didn't budge. With another massive groan, I slapped the edge of the building and bit back a scream. Now my hand and my foot hurt from abusing this stupid brick façade, yet I was no closer to figuring things out than I had been before stupid Peter came to stupid town. Grrr.

Octo-Cat lay on the sidewalk with his face hidden beneath both paws. "You're embarrassing me," he ground out.

Great, great, great. I threw my hands up and charged down the block, back toward my car.

"Wait!" he called after me, running a short distance and then stopping at the alley. "We can still check the other sides, right?"

Darn it, he was right. I took a deep breath, then turned back his way.

Down the alley there was only a single door partially obscured by an overflowing dumpster. I lifted my hand and made a fist, but then hesitated. What would I find inside? Once I knew the truth, there would be no going back. Was I ready for that? *Really* ready?

"Well, go ahead and get it over with already," Octo-Cat said gently.

I knocked so lightly, the sound barely even reached my own ears.

But a voice immediately answered from the other side. "Password?" it demanded.

Password? Peter hadn't said anything about…

"Claw," I said before my brain had even finished connecting the dots.

The door opened.

CHAPTER EIGHT

The man who opened the door was slight and gangly with a massive array of freckles scattered across his pale face. Definitely not the type one would expect to see in the role of security for…

What was this place?

I squinted my eyes and strained to see in the dank lighting. The inside looked very much the same as the outside—all brick and *blah*.

"Who sent you?" the bouncer asked, guiding us down the long staircase. His eyes shone a beautiful shade of green I'd never seen before—and not just in nature, but had truly never glimpsed under any context.

"Peter Peters," I muttered, searching the big, empty space, but seeing nothing beyond the guard in front of me and Octo-Cat at my feet.

The guard shook his head and wrinkled his nose in a way that suggested perhaps he also didn't think much of Peter. "He's not due in until later tonight, but go ahead and have a seat if you want. You're welcome to have a drink while you wait."

I scanned the room again, wondering how I could have missed

something as large as a bar in my previous glance about. "Um, where?" I asked nervously when I was still only met by dust and dirt and cobwebs.

The guard jabbed me in the ribs playfully, but it still hurt. "Ha ha, good one."

I let out an awkward laugh, truly not knowing what I should say next. Should I ask how he knew Peter, or would it be better to inquire about how the door had just magically appeared in the alleyway earlier?

"Who are you, and what is this place?" Octo-Cat asked the guard, shifting his weight from one side to the other, clearly unnerved by the filth of our current surroundings.

Our strange host answered him directly. "I'm Moss O'Malley. Haven't you ever been to the lair before?" If you're keeping count, that's now at least three of us who could talk to Octo-Cat. I definitely wasn't alone, not anymore.

"Can't say that we have," I answered for the both of us, pointing at my chest emphatically. "At least *I* haven't."

"Me neither," Octo-Cat supplied.

Moss stiffened. "You did say Peter sent you, right?"

We both nodded, eager to learn more.

"What would that dog want with you two?"

I ignored Moss's strange choice of words and also the fact that he seemed to be edging back toward the stairs.

"That's personal, I—" I began.

"Clearly she can talk to animals, doofus," my very unhelpful tabby interjected. He lived by one simple motto: *when in doubt, add an insult.* That didn't seem to be a good plan right about now. We were both in over our heads with Moss and his strange lair here.

Moss's attention shot back toward me, and he sniffed. "But you don't see the bar over there?" He pointed a shaking finger toward the far corner of the room.

I followed with my eyes, but still saw nothing beyond the empty, dirty basement. "Well—" I began.

But before I could come up with a good excuse, Moss pushed

me back up the stairs with surprising strength. "Just forget you ever saw this place, okay?" he said after tossing both me and Octo-Cat into the alley. Next he did something strange with the fingers on one hand and then slammed the door shut before either of us could demand an explanation.

Octo-Cat twitched and flicked his tail. "That fool manhandled me. My precious coat is a mess!"

"What just happened?" I asked breathlessly, watching in disbelief as the outline of the door faded into the brick wall right before my eyes.

"A little help here?" Octo-Cat cried, and I crouched down to help straighten his fur.

"He… he scruffed me," my poor cat sputtered in tears. "Scruffed me!"

"I'm so sorry," I whispered, glancing back toward the door but finding that same unforgiving swatch of bricks where it had once been.

"Can we…" Octo-Cat let his words trail off and then sighed heavily. "Can we just head home? I need to be in my own environment for a while."

I still didn't know what had just happened. Would it have been different if we'd waited until ten like Peter had asked?

It was tough to say. We may have gotten more answers, but we also might have gotten ambushed. Moss hadn't told us much, but he'd made it clear that he also didn't much care for Peter. Maybe we should initiate *Operation: the Enemy of my Enemy is my Friend*. If Nan was here, that's surely what she would suggest.

But how could I get more out of Moss when I had no way of reaching him again? If I came back tomorrow, might I find the door again? Would Moss let me back inside? Or might a different guard welcome us to the lair? Would I be able to pretend I knew and saw everything?

Neither of us said a word on the short drive back home. As soon as I dropped Octo-Cat off at the manor house, I headed back into town to do some more reconnaissance on the mysterious underground lair. On my first drive through downtown, I accidentally passed it and had to turn around and track back.

It seemed a pretty silly mistake, one I'd probably made due to the fact my mind was still reeling from the earlier encounter with Moss.

I willed my brain to be quiet and focused hard, but still, I somehow managed to pass by it again.

Frustrated, I parked my car on the street in a sloppy parallel job, then went to search on foot.

An hour passed.

Two.

And still I could not find the lair again.

"I'm not crazy," I muttered to myself. "I'm not."

I checked in at home for dinner, then came straight back to town so that I could wait nearby for Peter. He said he'd be here at ten, that we could talk, and—most importantly—that he'd have answers.

People passed me on the street, shooting questioning glances my way, but I didn't care. I needed to know what was going on with me, now more than ever.

Nine o'clock came. *Just one more hour to go.*

Nine thirty.

Nine forty-five.

Ten came and went with no sign of Peter.

At five after, police sirens erupted in the quiet night. They grew louder and louder until the red and blue flashing lights were right upon me.

For a moment, I worried that I was about to be arrested for loitering, but the cop car flew right past me and stopped a couple blocks away. Now I had a choice to make—continue to wait for Peter or go investigate.

With one longing glance back toward where the lair should have been, I put my head down and jogged down the street to meet Officer Bouchard as he climbed out of his police cruiser.

"What happened?" I cried, short of breath despite the fact I'd only jogged a couple blocks. If only I could be in as good of shape as Nan. Maybe when this was all said and done, I could ask about accompanying her to that Zumba class she was always raving about.

My friendly neighborhood policeman just shook his head. "Got called about a robbery in progress, but the door is still locked and there's no sign of forced entry."

I peered into the lit up storefront, an upscale bridal boutique that folks from all across Blueberry Bay visited when they were ready to tie the knot. Nobody was inside. "Where did the robber go?"

Officer Bouchard shook his head again and turned to me. "You're on foot. That means you were nearby, right? Did you see anyone? Anyone at all?"

"No. Sorry." I frowned, wishing I had a different answer for him.

The officer let out a frustrated sigh and raked a hand through his overgrown hair. "Third time this week we've had a call like this. The security tapes always show up empty, but sure enough, the registers and safes are cleaned out. I'd say it was all for show—you know, insurance fraud—but it keeps happening. For the life of me, I can't figure out how."

I sucked in a shaky breath, choosing to keep quiet even though I had a sneaking suspicion the lair might somehow be involved with all of this.

I was well past beginning to suspect I wasn't the only one in Glendale with a super power. Yes, Peter I already knew about, but how many others stood hidden in plain sight as they went about their daily lives? My talking to animals was innocent enough, but what could others do? Could they make whole buildings disappear? Commit a burglary without leaving a trace? Murder someone without ever being suspected?

I gulped down the giant lump that had formed in my throat. "I'm sure there's a perfectly logical explanation," I told Officer Bouchard, praying my words would prove true, but also knowing that they wouldn't.

They couldn't. We were so past normal at this point, we weren't even in the same zip code.

Octo-Cat and I had taken on murderers more than once, but those were just regular, everyday people. Bad people, absolutely. But still *regular*.

What would happen when we found this mysterious new breed of magical criminal?

We wouldn't stand a chance…

CHAPTER NINE

Over the weekend, I spent some time reading news articles and social media posts about the recent rash of burglaries in downtown Glendale. Sure enough, the reports matched up exactly with what Officer Bouchard had told me. I also cruised through downtown a few more times hoping to spot the lair or to run into Moss again. Of course, that plan failed spectacularly.

"Why are you so bothered about this?" Octo-Cat asked me when we snuggled into bed Sunday night. "The building vanished and the mean scruffer guy went with it. They're not here anymore and thus…" He paused for emphasis and licked his chest. "Not our problem."

Maybe my cat didn't think all these strange goings-on were his problem, but I definitely considered them mine. Nothing bad would happen to him if people found out I could talk to him. I was the one in possible danger here, and it hurt that this failed to concern him.

Rather than sharing my hurt feelings, I decided to take a different approach to get him back on my side. "Aren't you at least a little bit curious about how a whole building could just up and vanish like that? Don't you want to know what happened?"

Octo-Cat lifted a leg over his head and began to lick parts that would be better tended to in private. "Curiosity killed the cat," he mumbled by rote. "And seeing as I only have five lives left, I'd rather not take too many chances."

It always weirded me out when he talked like this, and given Octo-Cat's flair for dramatics, it was hard for me to tell whether he was being serious or not. "Have you really died four times before?" I asked him quizzically. "I have a hard time believing that."

He lowered his leg, then stretched in a long arc with a satisfied mew. "It doesn't matter what you believe. All that matters is what's the truth. And whether you can do anything about it."

I contemplated this for a few moments. It seemed intelligent, even though it didn't satisfy my intense need to understand. "That makes sense," I said at last. "I know you're over it and everything, but do you have any idea what happened with the lair on Friday?"

"Sure I do." He rolled onto his back and wiggled around a bit. For all his complaints, he'd been doing a lot of that happy rolling about lately.

"Well," I demanded impatiently. "Are you going to keep it to yourself or will you just tell me already?"

He flopped back onto his side and twisted his mouth in a grimace. "I can tell you, but you're probably going to fight me on it."

"Why would I—"

"*Magic,*" he said, cutting me off mid-sentence.

Well, that was a bit surprising, but not altogether unexpected, given recent events. "Magic? Could you maybe be more specific, please?"

"*Mmm,* no. Probably not." He yawned and offered me a little shrug. "I don't really know more than that."

Honestly, the fact he knew anything at all surprised me. Now that I knew he had at least some intel, I was dying to hear more. I had to play this carefully, though. If I got too excited, my cat would punish me by simply walking away from the conversation until I got a hold of myself.

"But you say magic was involved?" I asked without making eye contact as I dragged my fingers across the soft comforter on my lap. "Does that mean you believe in magic?"

"Please refer back to my previous statement about belief versus truth," Octo-Cat answered drolly, then waited while counting under his breath. Was he actually giving me time to revisit our earlier conversation? His arrogance truly knew no bounds.

"Okay," I said, trying to hide my annoyance. "Please continue."

He nodded appreciatively. "Thank you. And, yes, magic *is* real. Although it's also very rare. And before you can ask, I know because some cats can see the traces it leaves behind. Not me, mind you. Just some other, less cool cats."

Unbelievable. I shook my head and suppressed a sigh. "So this whole time you've known magic is real and you've never said anything to me? You can spend hours telling me about your napping routine, but never once thought to mention magic?"

Octo-Cat stood up and arched his back defensively. "If you'll recall, I mentioned magic on our very first meeting. Back when you were still trying to figure out how we can talk to each other. You told me there's no such thing as magic, and so I dropped it."

I thought back to that day so many months ago, and... *he was right!* He was absolutely, unmistakably right. But he'd never been one to drop anything, so why would he have let something so important slip away?

Octo-Cat's golden eyes glinted as he studied me. "I know what you're thinking, and the answer is *no.* I don't think you should mess with this more than you already have. I've already gotten scruffed once. What further proof do you need that these guys don't play fair?"

"Am I...?" I hesitated. This was a hard question to ask, a hard possibility to come to grips with. "Am I like them?" I asked at last, my voice shaking.

Octo-Cat rolled over on the bed and laughed heartily. "Like them? What do you mean by that? Do you think you're some kind of wicked witch now just because you can talk to the great Octavius Maxwell Ricardo Edmund Frederick Fulton? Mind you, that's no small thing, but…" He broke apart in full-on laughter, rolling from side to side in glee.

My patience had more than grown thin by now. Once again, my cat had important information, information that I needed to solve a case. Yes, once again, he was being a brat about sharing it with me.

Finally, he sobered enough to say, "There's no such thing as witches or wizards, so drop those fictional stereotypes from your mind. Mmm'kay?"

"But—"

"But there *is* magic," he stated again. "I don't know much more, because I'm not someone who has any."

I pointed to myself, jaw hanging open. My lips simply couldn't form the words.

Octo-Cat shook his head. Magic or not, he clearly understood me. "And neither are you. Yeah, somebody's magical residue probably rubbed off on you or something. Hey, try not to look a gift cat in the mouth."

"So, what do I do?" I sputtered. My cat had just revealed a whole new hidden world, and my brain was racing a thousand miles an hour to keep up.

Magic was real. Who'd have ever guessed it? Certainly not me.

"You? *You* do nothing. Me? *I* do nothing. Just forget we had this talk, okay?" He jumped off the bed and left the room, thus ending the conversation. Why was he being so cagey? Did he know more than he was letting on? Would he be willing to talk if I tried bringing up the topic later?

Unfortunately, you just never knew when it came to Octo-Cat.

My only hope now was that Peter would be more forthcoming when I approached him tomorrow at work.

Peter beat me to the office the next morning and appeared deeply involved with something on his computer screen when I entered.

"Hey," I said halfheartedly by way of good morning. Something told me I'd do best to approach him like I would Octo-Cat. *Carefully.*

"Hey," he mumbled back without so much as a glance my way.

"What happened Friday night?" I asked casually as I made my way toward our desk.

Peter burst out of his chair and clapped a hand over my mouth, scaring the wits out of me in the process. "Don't," he warned before peeling back his fingers one by one. "Just don't."

"But I waited for you," I argued with a steely gaze. He could act weird all he wanted, but I wasn't going to be frightened off—at least not until I finally got the answers he'd been keeping just out of my reach.

He shrugged, returning to his normal disinterested affectations. "Yeah, well, something better came up."

"*Okay,*" I said slowly, pausing to take a slow, shuddering breath. If I lost my cool, we'd get nowhere. Whatever game Peter was playing, I needed to play it, too. "Can we try again some other time?" I asked sweetly.

"Stop acting like a scorned lover," he spat. "It isn't flattering."

"But—"

Peter raised his hand and made the same odd gesture that the bouncer at the lair had made just before the door disappeared. I watched, mesmerized.

It made me feel happy—no, not happy, *content.*

Good.

Satisfied.

Ahh.

Someone cleared her throat from across the room, and I turned toward Bethany with a goofy smile planted on my face.

"Angie, a word in my office, please?" Despite the kindness of her words, she did not sound happy. Didn't look it, either.

"What's going on with Peter?" she demanded after I'd eased the door shut behind me.

I shrugged. My body still felt light, my mind fuzzy. It took me a little bit to come up with an answer.

Then I remembered.

Peter. I hated that guy.

"He's annoying, and I wish you hadn't hired him," I said with a scowl. All my earlier elation was now gone.

Bethany regarded me suspiciously from behind her desk. "Anything else?"

This was it. Someone was finally willing to listen to my misgivings when it came to Peter Peters. Only I couldn't exactly remember what they were.

Bethany tapped her fingers on the desk and raised one perfectly groomed eyebrow. "Well?"

"Nothing specific," I said, wondering why it seemed all my recent memories had fallen clear out of my brain. "I just don't like him."

A smile washed across her face, replacing the anxiety that had been there only seconds earlier. "Good," she said, and then, "Thank you, Angie. That will be all."

I had no idea what was going on or why the conversation bothered me so much. Why did my head still feel like it was full of cotton?

Maybe I was coming down with some kind of cold.

Or maybe Peter…

No.

No way.

I felt like the answer lay just along the edges of my mind, but no matter how I strained, I couldn't break through the barrier to retrieve it.

Maybe the inevitable had finally occurred.

After months of talking to my cat, I'd now completely lost my mind once and for all.

CHAPTER TEN

"How was Peter today?" Octo-Cat asked over lunch. Normally he slept straight through our afternoon meal, but today Nan had prepared a tiny saucer of clam chowder for him, too, so that he could join us at the table.

My day up until that point had been completely unremarkable, which made it all the more unnerving that my cat seemed to expect me to share some wild, juicy gossip. "Fine," I answered slowly, still not knowing what else he expected me to say. "Why are you asking about Peter?"

Octo-Cat stopped lapping his soup and stared at me aghast. Droplets of cream clung to his fur, but he didn't seem to notice—or at least not to mind. "What do you mean *why?* Remember his visit here? Our trip downtown to the lair? Any of that ringing a bell for you?"

"The lair…" That sounded familiar. Didn't I…? "Oh, right!" I shouted as it all came rushing back.

"What's the lair?" Nan asked from her spot at the head of the table.

"How could you forget?" Octo-Cat cried as he continued to

study me with a worried expression. "It was seriously all you could talk about this weekend!"

I dipped my spoon into my soup and watched the steam rise before me. "Today was weird," I said at last. Then to Nan, "The lair is what was at the address Peter gave me. Or, at least it was, until it disappeared."

"And you were talking about it all weekend but didn't once mention it to me?" She seemed hurt and intrigued in equal measures. It wasn't easy to upset Nan, which meant I felt extra crummy whenever I managed to do so.

"I'm sorry. I didn't think it was safe, but I can't exactly remember why," I tried to explain, but kept coming up short.

"Wow, they really did a number on you," Octo-Cat said with a low growl. "I didn't think it was worth investigating, but if they're working this hard to mess with your memory, maybe it is."

My memory? Is that why my brain had been so fuzzy today? In a way it made sense, but people couldn't really just make someone forget—at least not outside the movies. "You think they wiped my memory?" I mumbled as Octo-Cat's eyes continued to bore into me.

"Uh, yeah!" he cried with an agitated swish of his tail.

"Who's they?" Nan asked gently.

I looked to Octo-Cat for the answer.

"Magic folk," he spat in disgust.

"Magic?" I asked with a start. Had we already discussed this? Was I again forgetting something important?

"Magic!" Nan shouted in delight. "Has magic finally come to Blueberry Bay?"

Now we both zeroed in on Nan. "You know about magic?" I squeaked. Had I been the only one in the dark here?

She laughed it off. "No, but I'd like to. It sounds fun."

"No," I snapped at her. "Please don't get involved in this one, Nan. I'm begging you."

She crossed her arms over her chest and stared me down. "Fun or not, where you go, I go. This time, it just so happens to be fun. Now catch me up."

Or really, really dangerous, I mentally added as my stomach did an impressive series of somersaults.

Octo-Cat guided me through the events of the past week, both to refresh my stolen memories and so that I could share with Nan. As he recounted each detail, I instantly remembered them in full. How strange that I hadn't been able to recall anything without his guidance.

"So," Nan said, rubbing her hands together as she prepared to sum things up. "Peter can talk to animals, too. There's a magic club downtown that can disappear at will, and someone is using magic to rob the shops downtown blind. Is that everything?"

"What do you mean is that everything?" I asked. Where earlier my brain had felt light and fuzzy, now it felt heavy from the burden of all this information slamming into it at once. "It's an awful lot all on its own."

Nan stood abruptly and headed toward the foyer.

"Where are you going?" I sputtered. *Dizzy.* I needed to lie down, but I also couldn't let Nan walk into a dangerous situation all on her own.

Luckily, the next thing she said was, "We need to go shopping."

"What? Why?" I rubbed my temples to try to get the blood flowing to my brain again.

Nan appeared completely unbothered by this strange turn of events— rather, she appeared to be genuinely excited. "I don't have any good outfits for a stakeout, and I doubt you do, either."

"A stakeout?"

"Yes, that's what I said. Now, are you coming or what?"

Nan and I went to Target and bought new outfits, complete with nondescript black skull caps for each of us. She even bought Octo-Cat a tiny black bandana, which I knew for a fact he would despise.

The rest of that evening was spent baking and putting together a custom stakeout kit that included board games, blankets, audiobooks, and other random items meant to help pass the time. I mostly just tried to stay out of the way while Nan prepared for our upcoming adventure.

When night fell, she popped onto her feet, narrowed her gaze, and said, *"It's time."*

Honestly, between Nan's spy movie obsession and Octo-Cat's legal drama TV addiction, I was burnt out on this stakeout before it even began. Hopefully it would actually lead to some helpful new information—but I wasn't holding my breath.

"We'll take my car," Nan declared. Her little red sports car was less than discreet, but arguing would get me nowhere, seeing as she'd already committed to whatever role she planned to play tonight. Maybe a silver-haired female James Bond? I guess that made me the bimbo sidekick.

We parked downtown and sipped on matching thermoses filled with hot chocolate. Octo-Cat complained heartily from his place in the tiny, cramped backseat.

"Watch for anything suspicious," Nan instructed in a cautious whisper, even though no one was around to hear either of us. "Keep an eye out for anyone nosing around the lair or entering one of the shops after closing time," she further clarified.

"How long are we going to stay out here?" I asked with a yawn.

"As long as it takes," she answered, her jaw set with determination. "We can sleep in shifts if we have to."

Well, that didn't sound fun at all. Hopefully our magical crooks would reveal themselves quickly so we could go home and snag a proper night's sleep.

Time passed slowly as Nan recounted the plots of all her favorite action flicks. Downtown Glendale slowly stilled as the businesses shut down for the night and people headed home. Other than the odd stray dog that galloped past, no one came or went. *Nothing happened.*

That is, until something did.

A clanging alarm sounded just down the street, and bright lights flooded the darkness. I recognized the jewelry store at once. Nan wasted no time reversing more than a half dozen parking spots bringing us to idle right in front the shop with the triggered security system. Despite the alarms and the lights, I couldn't see anyone inside.

Officer Bouchard showed up a few minutes later, sirens blaring just as they had Friday night. "You again," he said upon spotting me.

"It's a coincidence," I said, putting my hands up in mock surrender. "I promise."

"We were on a stakeout," Nan said, setting her mouth in a firm line.

"We just wanted to help," I said quickly. "See if we could catch the robber in action."

"And you brought your cat with you?" he asked, spying Octo-Cat through the open car window.

"I'm just really attached to him," I said between clenched teeth as Octo-Cat preened in my peripheral vision. "But I didn't see who broke in."

"The owner's on the way," Officer Bouchard explained. "But I think it's best that you clear out before he gets here."

Nan tapped her temple and smiled up at the handsome policeman. "Smart," she said. "We're the only witnesses, so naturally he'll suspect us."

I glanced back toward the lair and thought I saw a dark figure disappear around the alley. I wanted to go investigate but couldn't make Officer Bouchard any more suspicious of us than he already was.

As a compromise, I ducked my head back into the car and spoke in a low hush. "Octo-Cat, I saw someone or something by the lair," I whispered. "Can you go check it out?"

"On it," he said, sneaking out through the open window that faced the street.

"Thank you for your time, Officer," Nan cooed, shameless flirt that she was. "I know you're very busy and important, and it always feels nice when you take a little extra time out from your day for us."

"No more stakeouts," the cop called after her as he walked away. "You hear me?"

Nan gave a salute, then sank into the driver's seat.

I pressed the button to roll up the front windows and then whispered, "Stall for a few minutes. Octo-Cat is checking something out for us real quick."

Nan made a great show of fumbling her keys and taking inventory of the various supplies and activities she'd brought for our big stakeout. When at last Octo-Cat climbed back through the window, she gave a friendly wave and then peeled off into the night.

"What was it?" I asked my cat.

"Nothing," he said as if he still had a hard time believing it. "Absolutely nothing at all."

How could we have missed everything when it had happened right before our eyes?

It seemed the only thing our stakeout had accomplished is making me even more afraid of the magical forces that had taken hold of my hometown.

CHAPTER ELEVEN

The next morning I woke up to Nan wearing a velour jogging suit with the word *sassy* written across her tush. A matching pink sweatband pushed her gray curls out of her face, and she held a metallic purple water bottle clutched firmly in one hand.

"The stakeout continues?" I asked, wiping the sleep from my eyes.

She stretched her arms overhead and then bent to touch her toes. "I'm sure I don't know what you're talking about," she answered with a wink while stretching both arms to one side and then the other. "I'm just headed into town to do a little exercise. Keeps me young and spry."

"Well, don't forget to take the cat with you," I said, doing my best to hide the smirk that slithered its way across my face. "His harness is on one of the hooks in the laundry room."

I finished getting ready for work, and Nan and I had a quick breakfast together before saying goodbye. Octo-Cat, however, flatly refused to speak to me—the harness being one of the few things in this world he hated more than dogs. His irritation aside, Nan really did need his help on her investigation. A leashed-up cat might make her a bit of an inconspicuous character, but her snooping would have been obvious even without the cranky feline partner. At least now she'd have a second set of eyes and ears to help her out.

As for me? I had to go all by myself to face Peter yet again.

Fortunately I, too, had an operative planned for that day. It definitely wasn't like me to keep forgetting, so I grabbed the digital voice recorder Nan liked to use to record her monologues, popped in a pair of fresh batteries, and tucked the device into the corner of my bra. Once at work, I'd turn it on and record everything that happened that day. I mean, nobody could tamper with my evidence if they didn't know it was there, right?

God bless my giant boobs. Usually they were just a pain in my back, but today they'd finally serve some kind of actual purpose. Maybe James Bond had more than one reason for keeping all those ample-bosomed sidekicks around, after all.

Whatever happened next, I was ready. We all were.

That morning, Peter arrived at the firm before I did, a fact that didn't quite feel consistent with the rest of his personality, now that I thought about it. I said hello, then slipped into the bathroom to power on my recorder.

"Did you have a good night?" I asked Peter conversationally when I returned to settle into our shared desk.

He groaned and shifted abruptly in his chair to face me. "I know you saw me, so cut the BS. What part of drop it don't you understand?"

"Drop what?" I asked casually. Meanwhile, my heart thrummed inside my chest. Was I close enough to the truth that he'd finally tell me what he knew?

Apparently not, because his expression grew venomous as he said, "Just back off, all right?"

I folded my arms across my chest in defiance and spun toward him in my twirly office chair. Our knees were less than an inch apart as I leaned even closer and captured Peter with my most determined glare.

"You're the one who pushed me first. Why would you do that if you didn't want to talk about…?" I paused for a brief moment before settling on, "Um, what we have in common."

He curled both hands into fists, and for a second there, I truly thought he might punch me. But then he sighed, released some of the tension, and whispered, "This is not the place to have this conversation."

I had him on edge. That had to count for something. Heck, maybe if I pushed a little harder, he'd teeter right over, yelling all his secrets on the way down.

I refused to let him intimidate me. Instead, I jabbed a finger in his chest and ground out, "Maybe not, but you stood me up last time we tried to meet somewhere else, and I'm done taking chances."

"I didn't stand you up," he practically shouted, then took a deep breath and worked hard to compose himself once more. "I didn't stand you up. You're the one who broke the deal by showing up early and bringing the cat with you."

The first crack in his composure had appeared—*pry, pry, pry!*

"Yeah, so what?" I said, keeping my eyes fierce, determined. "There's nothing wrong with my cat."

Peter laughed bitterly, then pulled his shirt aside to show the deep claw marks from Octo-Cat's attack last week.

"Fine, okay." I had to fight hard to keep my smirk at bay as I studied the still-red skin. "So, let's start again."

"No," Peter said, turning his chair away from me and pretending to focus on the computer. I could still see him watching me from the corner of his eye, though.

I reached across and shut off his monitor with a humph. "Yes," I insisted.

"If I'd have known you were this much trouble, I never would have—" He stopped abruptly, catching himself before he could get to the climax of that particular sentence.

"Never would have what?" I demanded, leaning even closer. His cloying cologne filled my nostrils, and we were now so close I could have kissed him if I wanted. Not that I'd ever want anything more from Peter than a few answers.

"Forget it," he said, his voice shaking as his face began to turn the same shade of red as the claw marks on his chest.

I poked him again, showing him that I couldn't simply be brushed aside with broken promises and non-answers. "Yeah, you tried to make me forget, didn't you? But I'm not as pliable as you think I am."

"Will you just shut up?" Peter squeaked, his eyes widening in obvious terror. After clearing his throat, he leaned in close and whispered in my ear, "Stop prying into my secrets. Otherwise, I might just have to share yours with all of Blueberry Bay. You got me?"

I nodded slowly, not knowing whether he was bluffing or dead serious but also preferring not to find out. It didn't matter, though, because he did that wavy finger thing under the desk and suddenly I just didn't care anymore.

It wasn't until I got home that evening that I remembered about the digital recorder I'd stashed in my bra. Thank goodness for my tendency to whip that thing off the moment I stepped through the door.

"Did you get some good scoop during your walkabout?" I asked Nan when I found her putting the finishing touches on lunch in the kitchen.

She rolled her eyes, but smiled. "Nothing yet, but we'll be back out there tomorrow."

Octo-Cat huffed. "Maybe she will, but I'm done. Please tell me you got something out of Peter today." He looked up at me with huge pleading eyes, and I wish I had a better answer for him than *I don't remember.*

"I have this recording," I said, holding up the small item I'd palmed after finding it in my bra.

"Oh, goodie!" Nan cried. "The perfect dinner theater." She tilted her head to the side and let out a chuckle. "Only for lunch."

I laughed, too, and flipped on the recorder, hoping I'd managed to catch something good. Thankfully, it was only a matter of minutes before Peter's and my conversation from earlier that morning played back through the tiny speaker.

Some of the words were drowned out by the rustle of my shirt fabric, but the message still came through loud and clear. Peter knew that I knew something, and he was terrified of me finding out anything more.

"All right," Octo-Cat said following Peter's final whispered threat. "I'm taking the lead on this one."

"Wait. What do you mean?" I sputtered. Octo-Cat had never taken the lead before, and the fact he wanted to now scared me worse than anything I'd seen yet. "What's your plan?"

He sat before me on the table, flexing the claws on one of his front paws and staring at them with delight. "I'm sure you already know that cats are great at everything. And, lucky for you, I'm even greater than most cats. But do you know what I'm greatest at?"

I shook my head, hoping he would just get on with it. Octo-Cat considered himself the greatest genius and talent of our time, so he could literally be talking about anything right about now.

"Stalking my prey," he answered with a sinister smile. "I smell a rat, and you better believe I'm going to make him my dinner."

I continued to stare blankly at Octo-Cat, not sure whether he was done or what he'd even meant by the things he'd said so far.

He sighed and rolled his eyes. *"Peter.* I'm talking about Peter."

"You're going to eat him?" I ground out, trying so hard not to laugh.

"No, it's just..." The tabby groaned. "I was going for a poetic moment there and you kind of ruined it. Can you please get with the program already?"

"Yes, sorry," I murmured, then waited as he went through his entire speech again. When he got to the part about smelling a rat and making it his dinner, I brought a hand to my chest and pretended to swoon.

"My hero," I said overdramatically.

Octo-Cat smiled proudly. "And don't you forget it."

Oh, of all the things I'd forgotten lately, this was one thing I'd never be able to erase from my memory—no matter how much I might want to.

Whatever his plan, I just hoped that my cat—*my hero*—would be safe.

CHAPTER TWELVE

That evening Octo-Cat sent me out for a bit of last-minute shopping. He'd requested an Apple Watch, of all things. Now, if you think people can be snobby about their preference for Macs, multiply that by one hundred and you'll have a good sense of how devoted my tabby was to his particular electronics brand of choice.

Sometimes I regretted ever giving him that iPad.

Of course, I had to drive to the next town over to reach the closest big-box electronics store, and I may have gotten laughed at by the employee who'd been assigned to help me.

"You want an Apple Watch for your cat?" he asked incredulously for the third time that conversation. Seemed he thought I was too stupid to understand the question.

I decided to offer a bit more of an explanation to help get us past the whole laughing and customer-shaming episode. "Yeah, I need to attach it to his collar so I can track where he goes when he's outside."

"And it has to be Apple?" he asked, gasping for air between laughs. "There are way cheaper options that are made specifically for pets."

My brow pinched in frustration. Clearly, this man had never been owned by a cat. *The poor oaf.*

"My cat really prefers Apple products whenever possible," I answered quietly, hoping that we wouldn't attract any other clueless employees before my purchase was made. "Can we please just hurry?"

"Yeah, sure. There's a slight problem, though." He stopped laughing and offered me a piteous expression. "The current generation of Apple Watches have to be tethered to a phone in order to work long range."

"Meaning?"

"Meaning it won't work for what you want," he explained somewhat impatiently.

I glanced around the emptying store. Soon closing time would be upon us, which meant I needed to make a relatively quick decision. I could cater to my cat's ego—or to his safety. You may think the correct choice would have been obvious, but it was a harder decision than you could possibly imagine.

"Okay, show me the pet GPS units," I decided aloud.

The worker smirked as he led me over to a glass case at the end of the aisle where we'd been standing this whole time. I chose the one that looked most like it could be an Apple product and pointed to where it sat inside the display case.

"Ooh. Great choice," the worker said with a nod of affirmation. "It's our best reviewed model."

"Yeah, that's great," I said dismissively before lowering my voice and saying, "I'll slip you a twenty if you can help me with something."

He put both hands up and took a giant step back. "I hope you're not trying to bribe me so that I'll steal from my store." He lowered his voice, came back beside me, and leaned in close. "Not saying I won't do it. Just that the price has to be right."

"What? No." I searched around for the security cameras, which were of course trained right on us. "I already told you, my cat is really committed to Apple products. So, do you maybe have a left-over sticker or something we can use to cover up the real logo and replace it with Apple's?"

His eyes widened with surprise. Yup, he'd definitely never been owned by a cat. "Um, maybe," he mumbled as he glanced around for an escape route.

"Listen, I know I sound crazy. I promise I'm not." I smiled, hoping he'd see just how harmless I really was. "Not that it even really matters," I continued quickly. "Can you please just help me make this look like an Apple product?"

After a little more back and forth—and ultimately raising the bribe to forty dollars—the worker agreed to help. By the time I was done, I had a passable new accessory for Octo-Cat that I decided I'd tell him was the new Apple Pet. I stashed the instruction manual in my glove compartment and tossed the box in the trashcan outside. I'd just tell him it was the floor model, that we'd gotten the very last one.

He'd like that, the whole exclusivity of his new toy.

Sure enough, my cat was overjoyed when I presented him with his new collar charm that evening. "The Apple Pet. Wow," he cooed. "It's even more beautiful than I ever could have imagined."

"And you're one of the very first to get one," I added, ignoring the fact that he'd probably be the only cat ever with this particular Frankenstein of a GPS tracker.

Nan helped us test it out by watching the tracker on her phone while I drove Octo-Cat around for a few minutes. When we returned she showed me the exact path we'd driven mapped out on her phone. It looked like everything was in place for his big solo mission.

"Be safe," I said the next morning, unable to resist the urge to give him a big hug and a kiss between his ears.

"Angela, really," he ground out while wriggling free of my arms. "The Apple Pet offers the latest state-of-the-art technology. Combine that with my superior intellect, agility, and stamina, and we'll have this case solved by sundown."

I almost felt bad lying to him but knew he'd do better thinking he had Apple on his side. The plan was for him to drive with me to work that morning and then hang around outside the office, hidden among some bushes. Later, he'd slip into Peter's car when he came out at the end of his shift and secretly accompany him to wherever he decided to go that evening.

I personally hoped it would be the lair.

Nan and I both had the app on our phones so that we could follow Octo-Cat's location, and I'd also told him that I would pick him up at midnight, no matter where he was or what was happening at the time. I refused to leave him unassisted for the entire night, especially since Peter appeared more than a little bit unstable judging by all the interactions I'd had with him so far.

"Are you sure?" I asked him one more time as we pulled into the tiny parking lot outside the firm.

The determination in Octo-Cat's gaze didn't waver. "Of course I'm sure. You need me."

"Yes," I repeated. "I need you. So, please be careful and make sure you come home safe."

"Angela, I…" His voice cracked and he bowed his head, then he dragged his sandpaper tongue along my hand in a quick show of affection that practically melted my heart.

"Nothing of this later," he whispered while waiting for me to open the door and set him loose.

I was too stunned to say anything more as I watched him trot away and take cover in the greenery around my office.

After a deep, calming breath, I headed into the office and fought back my urge to start checking the app right away. Nan had eyes on him, too. He would be okay.

Of course, Peter came into work late for the first time since I'd known him. Those forty-odd minutes of thinking our plan would have to wait another day just about killed me, too. When Peter finally did show up for work, he studiously ignored me, even going so far as to pop some earbuds in as an excuse not to talk to me.

Well, that suited me just fine.

I waited as patiently as I could for my half-shift to end, then raced home and sat with Nan as we both watched the unblinking dot that represented Octo-Cat's location on our phones.

"Oh, it's moving!" Nan shouted later that afternoon while we were both enjoying a cup of hot tea with homemade cookies to top off the light snack. Sure enough, the little dot had left the office and was now crawling down Main Street.

I glanced at the time displayed on the top of my phone screen. "But it's too early," I protested. "Peter is supposed to work until five."

"Not today, it seems," Nan said with a half-hearted shrug. Her eyes, however, shone with excitement as she watched the little dot continue its journey.

In fact, we both fell silent as we tracked the dot along the screen. It turned down a series of side roads before finally coming to a stop.

"Zoom in," I told Nan. "What address is that?"

She clicked the dot, and the app gave us the exact street and house number.

"That must be where he lives," I said, taking a quick picture of the screen in case we needed this information for later. "Good to know for future."

"What if he just does a Netflix and chill?" Nan asked, worry lining her aged forehead.

"Who told you about Netflix and chill?" I asked in horror.

Nan waved a hand dismissively. "One of the guys at Bingo. He said it's what all the kids are doing these days. I'm glad you'd rather read than rot your brain with all that TV."

I nodded and hid a smile behind my hand. It was best that Nan stayed innocent as long as I could keep her that way.

Unfortunately, it looked like she was right—at least when it came to what she assumed she'd meant earlier. The dot remained idle for hours. Poor Octo-Cat must have been going out of his mind just sitting there and waiting for Peter to do something skeezy.

I yawned more than once, wondering if Nan and I would have to take shifts to watch the unmoving dot until it was finally time to go and retrieve Octo-Cat at midnight.

How unthrilling and—even worse—unhelpful.

I had all but declared today's mission a bust, when suddenly the dot began to move again.

CHAPTER THIRTEEN

"They're headed downtown!" I shouted, recognizing the path after the dot took a few sharp turns and swung back onto Main Street. I grabbed my phone and rushed toward the door, not even taking the time to slip my feet into my tennis shoes properly.

"I'm coming, too, dear," Nan insisted in that sugar-sweet way of hers as she floated over.

"No way," I insisted right back, albeit with far more hostility. "We need you at home base in case there's any trouble. Keep watching that dot!" I called over my shoulder as I slammed the door shut behind me and made a beeline straight to my car.

If Peter and Octo-Cat were headed toward the lair, then I wanted to be there, too. I kept my phone hooked in its holster and watched the GPS app the entire time I drove. Luckily, Peter made a pit stop, which meant I miraculously managed to beat him downtown. I parked around the corner and then hid myself beside the dumpster in that same alley I now knew led to the magical lair.

I watched breathlessly as the blinking dot approached my location.

Closer, closer…

They should have been right upon me now, but I could see neither Peter nor Octo-Cat. Instead, a humongous pit bull burst into the alley and charged straight toward me. I was so shocked by his sudden arrival that it took me a second to realize his sharp and shiny teeth held something clenched between them.

My cat!

Oh my gosh, this abnormally large dog was carrying Octo-Cat by the scruff of his neck, and he looked mad. Tough, too.

"Please, Mr. Dog," I said, my voice squeaking even though I wanted to appear as strong as possible in that moment. "Please don't hurt us."

The dog locked eyes with me and growled a warning.

I froze in place the way the Girl Scouts had trained me to do in case of a wild animal attack. Would this dog bite me? Kill me? And why was he still clinging so tight to my cat?

The door to the lair opened and the menacing dog hurled Octo-Cat down the stairway. A sickening crack followed as Octo-Cat hit the ground below. *No!*

"Get in there. Now!" someone growled at me. The voice sounded like Peter's, but it had to belong to someone else, right? Maybe Moss stood nearby just out of sight.

I still couldn't move, although now I was more afraid for Octo-Cat than for myself. Was he okay after that savage fall? What did the dog want with him? And how did it know about the lair?

"Angela!" Octo-Cat cried from the distance. "Angela, don't! It's a trap!"

Oh, Octo-Cat! He was okay. I wanted to cry for joy, but I still couldn't move.

"I said get in there!" the voice came again, and then the pit bull head-butted me down the staircase. The door slammed shut and disappeared. Even if I finally got my wits about me, I couldn't have escaped if I wanted to.

The pit bull stood seething with rage at the top of the stairs. "I knew you would be trouble," he said. This time I knew for sure the voice had come from the dog. It was speaking to me, much in the same way Octo-Cat did. But how? How was I understanding him? And why did he sound so much like Peter?

Octo-Cat lay across the room just a few feet from the far wall. He struggled to stand but fell back on his side with a gasp of pain.

"Thought cats were always supposed to land on their feet?" the dog taunted us in Peter's voice once again.

"That's a low blow and you know it," Moss said, appearing suddenly from the shadows. "What's got your fur in a twist?"

"Caught one of yours creeping about my territory," the pit bull answered with a nod toward Octo-Cat. "Figured I'd bring him here and let you deal with him, seeing as he's one of your kind."

Moss tensed, then narrowed his eyes and stared the dog down. "I'm not doing it this way. Show yourself."

I whipped my face back toward the dog, but not fast enough to see whatever transformation had occurred. Now it was Peter who stood crouched on all fours exactly where the dog had been. My eyes bulged and strained, trying desperately to find a way to explain what they'd just seen.

"Take a picture," Peter said with a wry smile. "It will last longer."

A picture? That wasn't actually a bad idea. I still had my phone clenched in my hand from tracking the GPS app, so I raised it toward Peter and—

He slapped it right out of my hand. "Seriously? Ever hear of sarcasm?" he demanded, curling his lip in disgust.

"Okay, enough!" Moss cried, yanking me away from Peter with surprising strength and lifting me up high so I dangled right in front of his face. "*You.* I've met you before. Didn't you say Peter was the one who invited you here in the first place?"

I nodded slowly, not breaking eye contact. Although I was still terrified, I knew I stood a better chance of eliciting sympathy from Moss than from Peter. Could I somehow convince him to let us go without further harm? I had to try.

"Yes, yes!" I shouted. "He told me to come here last weekend, but then he didn't show up!"

Moss sucked air in through his teeth. "That's bad form, dog. Really bad form." Turning back to me, he said, "I thought you were one of us. Why are you hanging out with *him?*"

"One of…"

"He's a cat," Octo-Cat informed me with a wheeze. "I thought I smelled it on him the first time we met, but I didn't know that people could, could…"

"Become animals?" Peter asked, changing into a dog again so quick I still couldn't tell how it was done. He rounded on Octo-Cat and raised his hackles. "Not so tough now are you, big shot?"

"Hey!" I cried, straining to break free so I could defend my poor, injured kitty. "Leave him alone!"

Moss groaned and set me back on my feet. "You know the lair is neutral territory," he said to Peter. "So knock it off already."

When I glanced back toward Moss, he'd transformed into a stunning long-haired cat with those same ethereal green eyes.

"Can you two please stop doing that?" Octo-Cat whimpered from his place on the floor. "It's making me dizzy."

"Are you okay?" I hurried over to him, then knelt down to lift him into my arms.

Octo-Cat allowed me to cradle him to my chest, which he'd never done before.

"I'm fine," he croaked. "Just down a life is all."

Seeing the intense worry that, no doubt, filled my expression, he let out a dry chuckle. "Hey, don't look so worried. I still have almost half of them left. Just give me another few seconds here and I'll be back to fighting form."

"No," I whispered, pressing my forehead to his and fighting against the hot tears that threatened to spill. "No more fights. This stops now."

"Or what?" Peter asked with a sneer as he observed Octo-Cat's and my tender moment with thinly veiled hatred.

"I said knock it off already!" When Moss hissed, it sounded like air being let out of old tires. "We agreed to work together when it came to Glendale."

"Then she's a threat to us both," Peter spat, human again and with his arms crossed tightly against his chest.

Moss studied me with a frown. "Well, what do you want me to do about it? Lock her up and let the council decide?"

Peter gave one emphatic nod. "Yes, that's exactly what I want you to do."

"Fine," Moss said, returning to his human form faster than a snap. He picked me up and pushed me into the corner of the room. I tried to charge after him but was stuck behind some kind of invisible barrier.

"How do you like the fishbowl?" Peter asked with an evil smile I wanted to slap right off his cruel face. If I hadn't liked him before, now I outright hated him. I would never be able to forgive him for hurting my best fur friend.

"We still don't know who sent her or why, so maybe we should stop antagonizing her until we get some answers," Moss pointed out, though he sounded unsure of the words even as he spoke them.

"What's going on?" I cried, still clutching Octo-Cat tightly to my chest. My tears had broken free now and drove down my cheeks in hot trails.

Moss bit his lip, then turned to Peter. "We at least need to remove the glamor if we're going to hold her here. Too long without it and she'll go crazy. You know that, Peter."

"Fine." Peter snapped his fingers and that old, dank basement suddenly transformed into a posh underground club. Finally, I could see why they called it the lair. Cherry wood paneling lined the walls and the floor had been laid with marble. Sure enough, Octo-Cat and I were in a fishbowl just as Peter had described. The tiny room that imprisoned us was made of glass on two sides and hard wall on the others.

I jumped back to my feet and pounded on the thick glass. "Let us out!" I screamed.

"Not a chance," Peter said with a sinister laugh. He was definitely enjoying this way too much. Had this been his plan all along? But why go to such lengths to steal my crummy paralegal job?

"We can't let you go just yet. Not until the council decides," Moss said with an apologetic shrug.

Again with the council? Who were they? And what would they decide?

I looked past Moss in a frantic search for some kind of escape route. That was when I realized we had an audience.

CHAPTER FOURTEEN

The lair appeared to be a boy's club. I didn't spot a single woman among the spectators, although I supposed any of the many cats or dogs could have been female. I sank down in the corner where the two wood walls joined together and tried not to look intimidated by the night's bizarre turn of events.

After nursing his wounds a bit longer, Octo-Cat slipped out of my arms and began to pace the length of the glass. "Chin up. Don't let them see you break," he instructed, almost as if he'd been imprisoned before. I'd definitely be asking about his kittenhood once we were free of this whole mess.

"What happened when you were with Peter?" I asked quietly, hoping nobody else would be able to pick up on our whispered conversation.

"Oh, Angela. It was all my fault." He turned to me suddenly, immense sorrow reflecting in his normally steady amber gaze. "Everything would have been fine, but on the drive downtown, Peter took a turn really fast and I couldn't help it. I-I-I-I yowled!"

My cat now blubbered in earnest as if realizing for the first time ever that he wasn't actually perfect. *The poor thing.* This entire experience had to be as life-altering for him as it was proving to be for me, perhaps even more.

Octo-Cat tried to keep a stiff upper lip as he continued, but broke down at several points in his story. "He slammed on the brakes and dragged me out by-by-by my scruff, then threw me in the trunk for the rest of the drive. I m-m-made a plan to leap at him and go for the eyes when we stopped, but it wasn't hi-hi-him that opened the trunk. It was the other him."

The dog. I still couldn't believe Peter could change into that pit bull at will. This was the stuff of fairytales, and honestly, it didn't belong in my picture-perfect little coastal town.

"Did you learn anything good?" I asked as I watched my cat continue to pace back and forth. I hated how worked up he was, but also found myself quite relieved that he was moving and talking like normal again.

"Not until we got here," Octo-Cat answered with a sigh. "But I'm afraid I was so out of sorts after I c-c-crashed down the stairs that I missed most of it. And…" He sniffed hard, then tried again. "And!"

He broke down into incomprehensible sobs once again. His shoulders heaved with distress as he struggled—and failed—to get the words out.

"It's okay," I cooed, tapping my fingers softly on the ground to call him to me. "You can tell me anything. It's not going to make me love you any less."

Octo-Cat trotted up to my side, then turned his face away and mumbled. "My new Apple Pet took a lot of the impact and it-it-it… it shattered, Angela!" he finished at last.

"Oh, Octavius," I said, using his full first name to help remind him of who he was. I hated seeing him so broken up like this. "Please don't worry about that. In fact, if it makes you feel better, that wasn't an Apple at all."

He turned back toward me, his eyes wide now for a different reason—complete and unadulterated horror. "*What?*" he demanded.

Oh, no. I was in such a rush to help him that I hadn't thought about how this particular revelation would impact me. I should have just kept my big mouth shut. I guessed now that the cat was out of the bag, though…

"It wasn't Apple," I said again, trapped by the intense scrutiny of his angry gaze. Now I was the one who had a stutter. "Apple Watches n-n-need to be tethered to a phone to work out of range, and I w-wanted you to be safe, so—"

"Angela!" he shouted, then evened his voice out and went into full-fledged lecture mode. I hated lecture mode. It meant that he was too angry to even insult me now. "If you'd gotten me an Apple like I requested, none of this would have happened in the first place."

"That's not fair," I shot back. The way he'd described being discovered by Peter had absolutely nothing to do with any failings of the GPS.

He pressed his ears back flat against his head and stooped toward the ground. "I can't believe you let me think that *I* could have been the one to mess things up so royally. How could you let me doubt myself like that?"

I hung my head, properly chastised. "I'm s-sorry."

"Sorry isn't good enough, Angela," he said with a small tutting noise. "If you would've followed my very simple, very clear instructions, we wouldn't be in this mess."

At least as I felt worse, he appeared to feel better and better. Perhaps we'd even each other out. "Fine, it's all my fault. Happy?"

Octo-Cat shook his head again, slowly this time. "I thought I'd trained you better."

"You can catch up on my training later," I promised with a giant, unhappy sigh. "Right now we need to focus on finding a way out of here."

"Well, that's easy," he said with a quick shrug.

I scrambled to my feet. "Great! Then tell me."

Octo-Cat deadpanned as he revealed, "There isn't one."

"Great." I let myself sink back to the floor before realizing that maybe I shouldn't just take his word at face value here. "What makes you so sure there's no way out?"

"Magic," he answered matter-of-factly.

"I thought you said you couldn't see magic."

"I can't, but I think maybe now I can feel it a bit." He flexed a paw demonstratively. "Can't you?"

"Well, I…" I closed my eyes and focused on my breathing, trying to see if I felt any different than I had before we'd entered the lair. I gave it a good try, but ultimately came up short. "Yeah… no," I said pathetically, wondering if my cat's newfound ability might be all in his head anyway.

Octo-Cat growled and flicked his tail. "Even so, we just saw one human turn into a dog and another into a cat. We saw this place appear out of nowhere and then get an insta-makeover from dirty dungeon to swanky night club. I think it's safe to say we're in magical territory now."

He had a definite point.

"But what do they want with us?" I mumbled, watching Peter as he laughed and joked with a small group of people I'd never seen before.

"I don't know." Octo-Cat was back to pacing while Peter paused and looked toward me, victory dancing across his face.

I refused to let him win, especially since I didn't fully understand the stakes. "How did Peter even find out about me in the first place?"

"I also don't know that."

I swallowed hard, then asked the toughest question of all. "Are they going to kill us?"

Octo-Cat paused and looked at me over his shoulder. "Well, they already killed me once, although I don't think that was intentional."

"Did you really die back there?"

He nodded grimly. "It was my fifth time."

"How did you die the other four times?" I asked, having always wondered about this. If we couldn't break out of our magical prison, then at least we could pass the time learning more about each other's pasts. It seemed we were always so caught up in our current adventures that we rarely had time to stroll down memory lane side-by-side.

Octo-Cat plopped down, facing me, and I could tell I was in for a good story that would hopefully take my mind off our current predicament. "Well, the first time was at the beach. I—"

One of the glass panels slid to the side with a swish, cutting off what I was sure would be a riveting tale. Perhaps Octo-Cat would be willing to tell it to me later.

The cat version of Moss slipped through the opening, and the moment he'd crossed the barrier, the glass wall slammed shut again.

"What's going on?" I pleaded, remaining seated so that I was closer to eye level with both cats. "Are you here to help us?"

Moss sat by the glass, leaving a large distance between us. "I can't say for sure, but maybe."

"Maybe what? Maybe you'll help us?" I crawled over to him on my hands and knees, and laughter rose from outside the fishbowl. I didn't care about our audience, though. I only cared about getting help, and Moss still seemed our best chance at that happening.

"Yes," he answered, looking down his nose at me as I scrambled closer. "But first, I have some questions."

"He's going to interrogate us," Octo-Cat translated, even though I didn't need the help. "Just like in the order part of *Law & Order.*"

Moss smiled, and that small gesture put me at ease. He really was a very pretty cat—not that I'd ever admit that aloud near Octo-Cat.

"Yeah, well, things work a little different when it comes to the council," he said, still smiling although something in his expression had changed.

"Different how?" I asked, raising an eyebrow. Slowly, the fear was returning. What did they have planned for us? And how could we get them to change their minds? I no longer much cared about decoding my abilities. These were the new questions I desperately needed answers to.

Moss chuckled, his green eyes boring into mine.

I paused in my tracks and waited for the big reveal.

Finally, Moss stopped laughing and informed us, "For starters, we're not the good guys."

I gulped hard, but nothing I did made me feel any better.

We'd been captured, and by a shape-shifting magical gang that seemed to show little regard for the rules.

If we died down here, would anyone ever even know?

I was suddenly so thankful that Octo-Cat's tracker had broken. At least I knew now that Nan would be safe.

Even if we weren't.

CHAPTER FIFTEEN

"Who do you work for?" Moss demanded, turning back toward me sharply.

A cheer rose up from the club. I blinked in horror as I noticed close to a dozen people and animals crowd in toward the glass, each vying for the best spot. *Oh, great.* Octo-Cat and I had become the unwitting stars of some kind of twisted, magical reality TV program.

"We ain't telling you nothing!" Octo-Cat shouted, then spat dramatically on the ground. This antic earned him a few polite chuckles from the audience.

"Actually, there's nothing to tell, seeing as we don't work for anyone," I explained, quietly willing Octo-Cat to ignore the lure of this momentary fame and let me handle things. "Unless Longfellow, Peters, and Associates counts," I added with a forced calm.

"Peters," Moss said, rubbing his chin with a paw. "Interesting."

"Not *that* Peters," I corrected with a quick glance toward the audience. Peter stood just on the other side of the glass, watching with a disturbing hunger in his eyes. "Bethany Peters. She's nice."

"They're all the same, sweetheart," Moss said with a chuckle.

Did he know Bethany? Was Bethany—*gasp*—like him? How could that even be possible?

And why did it feel like everyone else was playing out some kind of old-timey movie? Even Octo-Cat had stars in his eyes now that he realized we had an audience.

Me? I just wanted to get home safe and put this whole ordeal behind me. If it meant never learning the truth about my abilities, then so be it. I'd rather be alive than informed.

"Are you really working with the dogs?" Octo-Cat asked, then spit on the ground again. When nobody laughed this time, his expression fell.

"Will you just stop spitting?" I demanded with an exacerbated sigh. Now I was equal parts annoyed and terrified. I'd much preferred being tied up or held at gunpoint as I had in my previous misadventures. At least then I'd known what I was up against. Here, everyone was crazy and unpredictable, super-powered and spry.

I definitely didn't like my odds, being that I appeared to be the only semi-sane, semi-normal person around.

"You can talk to him," Moss pointed out, narrowing his eyes at me as he tilted his head sideways toward Octo-Cat. We were getting nowhere fast, seeing as Moss wanted to revisit all the previously established facts.

"Yes, but you already knew that," I said, raking my hands through my hair in frustration. "Also, why does it even matter? Obviously, everyone here can talk to him, too."

"Who sent you?" Moss demanded yet again.

I glowered at him as I explained, "You've already asked that, and I've already explained that nobody sent me. Well, except Peter."

"Are you a double agent?"

A low *ooh* swept through the crowd. Apparently, this was a very important question. Too bad I didn't have the slightest idea how to answer it.

"What? I really have no idea what you're talking about."

"Shift," Moss demanded, looking from me to Octo-Cat and back again.

"Um, we can't." I rolled my eyes to show him how ridiculous I found this whole thing.

Octo-Cat spit on the ground again and said, "No can do, fuzz."

Oh, jeez. I had really thought he'd remain silent after his last joke was met with zero applause. I already knew the more he spoke, the longer this would take. Luckily, Moss seemed more interested in me than in my cat.

"Shift," Moss said again, raising a threatening paw with claws fully extended.

I didn't even flinch. "I told you I can't," I said through gritted teeth.

Moss apparently did not like this answer, because he hurled himself at my face and sunk his claws into my cheek.

Peter's voice rose above the others as pain exploded on my cheek. "How do you like it now that the tables are turned?"

Blood dribbled down onto my shirt, but I was too scared to focus on the pain. "You can torture me all you want, but I don't have a different answer to give you," I said through gritted teeth.

"Nobody attacks my human and lives to tell the tale," Octo-Cat shouted, surging forward to tackle Moss.

"Stop!" I screamed at them both. Octo-Cat couldn't take a beating so soon after losing that last life. As noble as I found his choice to defend me, this was one fight I knew he'd lose.

"Just stop!" I begged Moss whose teeth were now at Octo-Cat's throat. "I'll tell you everything I know. It's not much, but I'll tell you."

Octo-Cat backed away, hackles fully raised, his tail so poofy he looked more like a long-haired breed than his usual tabby self.

"Excellent." Moss dragged his claws across the cold marble floor as if to remind me he could still do considerable damage, should we step out of line again. "Now, which one of you is magical?"

"Neither," I answered, throwing my hands over my face defensively. "I never even knew magic existed until this week, and I couldn't even talk to him until about six months ago."

Moss came closer and stood on his hind legs. He pressed his

front paws against my chest and peered into my face as he asked, "What happened six months ago?"

"I got zapped by a coffee maker," I answered breathlessly. My cheek had begun to throb from his earlier attack. More than mad, it made me scared.

"And when she woke up, we could understand each other," Octo-Cat finished for me.

"That's rather anti-climactic," Moss said. His voice now had the slightest hint of a twang. If he'd had an accent before, he'd done a wonderful job hiding it. I wondered if the fact it was coming out meant he was every bit as flustered as I felt.

Perhaps Octo-Cat and I could still win this yet.

"But you can't shift?" he asked for what felt like the millionth time in the span of just a few minutes.

I shook my head so hard it hurt. How could I make him—and the others who were still watching hungrily—believe me once and for all? *"No,"* I said with as much emphasis as I could assign to the short, little word. "And I can't do that memory thingy, either."

"The memory… Oh." Moss laughed a full-belly laugh, and the room joined in. "So, you're a normie?" he asked at last, wiping tears away as he fought off the final throws of laughter. Octo-Cat had never been able to produce tears on demand. I wondered if Moss could because he was really a human.

"If that means a normal, ordinary person, then yes," I told him with a stony gaze.

Moss nodded toward Octo-Cat. "And him?"

I nodded again. "Totally normal."

"Excuse you," Octo-Cat hissed, stomping over to join us. "I'm anything but—"

"Shut up!" I shouted at him. This was not the time for that overblown ego of his.

"What are you hiding?" Moss demanded, turning toward Octo-Cat but still watching me from his peripheral vision.

"Nothing. I swear."

He studied Octo-Cat for a moment before breaking out in an

unfriendly smile. "Ah, I get it," he concluded. "He's just your average, everyday cat with an unfailingly high opinion of himself."

I let out a breath I hadn't realized I'd been holding in. "Yes. Exactly."

"So, somehow you got hit with magical resonance," he continued.

I couldn't tell whether it was meant to be a question or not. "Sure?"

"And that's why you don't show up on any of our tracking systems," he continued. "You're a non-magical entity with a single magical ability."

I nodded along. This explanation certainly made sense, seeing as I was sure about only two things here—one, I wasn't magical, and two, I could talk to Octo-Cat.

A collective gasp sounded from the crowd. Why did they find me so interesting, especially when they could all do such extraordinary things themselves?

"Does that happen often?" I asked, suddenly desperate to understand more.

Moss shook his head. "No, it really doesn't. This started six months ago, you say?"

I pumped my head in agreement. Finally, someone would tell me the answers. I could feel them bubbling just beneath the surface. Peter hadn't helped me, but Moss would. I just knew it.

"That's worrying," he said.

"Why?"

"If you were a true magical person, you would have been born that way. If you were hit with some magical residue, it should have faded within twenty-four hours."

"So, what am I then?" I asked as my heart hammered away inside my chest.

"That depends," he said with a thoughtful expression.

"On?" I was so close to begging him for more. Couldn't he see how desperately I needed to know?

"Your cooperation," he answered with a pensive gaze.

Nobody said anything for a few moments until Peter appeared at the edge of the glass. "You're either big trouble," he said with a scowl.

"Or our greatest weapon," Moss finished, his eyes now shining with an evil joy.

"No, no, no. I don't want to be a weapon," I argued, shuffling backward until my back was flat up against the wall.

"What about me?" Octo-Cat asked. "Am I a weapon, too?"

"You?" Moss laughed and shook his head. "You're just an ordinary, everyday tabby cat."

CHAPTER SIXTEEN

O cto-Cat took several steps back until he bumped into the glass. *"No,"* he whispered over and over again. "No, it's not possible."

The crowd roared with laughter but, despite their glee, I could tell my cat was hurting. Badly.

"Don't listen to them," I pleaded, pushing myself to my feet so I could go to him.

He flinched at my touch, then bounded out of reach. "Don't," Octo-Cat said sadly, refusing to look at me.

"Always with the dramatics," Peter said, stalking in on all fours to join us inside the fishbowl. He waved one arm in a circle and the glass turned into a shiny opaque surface, cutting off both the sights and sounds from outside.

"We're alone now," Peter confirmed, sitting down on his haunches. His great tongue lolled from the side of his open maw in clear anticipation.

"It would be easier for me to talk to you if you were human," I said, clenching my eyes shut tight as I turned away. A part of me still didn't want to believe that any of this was happening.

"Have it your way," Peter said coldly.

When I opened my eyes again, both he and Moss had returned to their human forms while Octo-Cat remained turned away and sulking in his corner.

"Now are you going to cooperate or what?" Moss asked, his green eyes taking in my every move.

"Or would you rather do this the hard way?" Peter asked. Apparently, we'd returned to their previous good cop, bad cop routine. But I wouldn't be fooled this time. Moss had already admitted that neither of them was good, and thus it stood to reason that neither of them would help us out of the kindness of their hearts. They wanted something, and I just hoped it wouldn't be too high a price to pay.

I bit down hard on my lip as I watched them watch me. And then I couldn't take the studied silence any longer. A million questions weighed on the tip of my tongue, and I let the first few spill out into the open air. "What do you want from me? And if you're not the good guys, then who are you? Are you going to let us go?"

Peter puckered his lips unattractively and made a condescending tutting noise. "So many questions when you won't even answer our one simple request."

"Cooperate," Octo-Cat murmured from across the room. He had his forehead pressed to the wall as if that was the only way he could remain upright. I'd never seen him like this. Not even close. At this point, I knew I needed to do or say whatever it took to get us out of here, to get him help.

"Fine," I answered, keeping my gaze on that poor forlorn tabby to remind myself why I was suddenly so willing to assist my enemy. "What do you need from me?"

"Money," Peter said with a smirk. "Lots of it."

I faltered at this. After all this hocus pocus nonsense, were they really only after my money? "I-I don't have much at present, but if you'll allow me to make monthly payments, I can—"

"Not from you," Moss amended. "But *rather by way* of you."

That's when all the pieces began clicking into place. Finally, I could see the picture for what it was. "The robberies downtown," I murmured, unsurprised that this gang would stoop so low but somewhat disappointed in myself for not figuring it out sooner.

Peter licked his chops even though he was still in human form. "The first several were easy, but the jewelry store has a magic-sensing alarm."

"That's why you couldn't get in the other night," I said. And that's why we'd seen those dogs running back and forth through town during our stakeout. All of it, everything fit together so neatly, and Moss had just delivered the tidying bow.

"Hey, try not to judge us too harshly," the cat shifter said with wide eyes. "It was invisible, so we didn't know it was there until it was too late."

Oh, I was judging them all right, just not for this reason. "How did you get into the other stores?" I asked, emboldened by the thrill of this new information.

"Glamor," Moss said simply as if this one word answered every question. I thought I recalled reading about glamor in one of the fairy books I'd enjoyed as a kid, but that was back when I hadn't known that magic could be real, that it could also be dangerous.

It explained so much now that I thought about it, though. How the dingy basement had transformed into our current surroundings, how Peter had tampered with my mind on more than one occasion. Was that how they changed into their animal forms as well?

I wanted to know more, but more than that, I just wanted to be free.

"I don't see how I can help," I said, raising my fingers to my mouth and chomping at the nails to offer myself some sort of small comfort.

"Well, that part's easy," Moss said, stretching from side to side. "We have the code for the human alarm, and you're not magic so you won't trigger the magical one."

"Won't they catch me on the security camera, though?" I wondered aloud.

Moss shook his head. "Not if you send in the cat."

"I don't want to steal," I argued. Couldn't they see that I was a good person? That, despite the fact that I may have once absorbed some magical resonance, I was nothing like either of them?

That was when Peter snapped at me, lunging closer. "Do you want to live?"

If Moss hadn't caught his arm and pulled him back, I have no doubt he'd have attacked me.

"Just do it, Angela," Octo-Cat mumbled into the wall. "It's too late for me, but you can still save yourself."

Oh. My heart broke for him all over again. He was right. I needed to stop dawdling. I could still save us both—and I would.

"When?" I asked, licking my lips.

A giant smile slithered across Moss's freckled face. "Tonight."

"And then you'll let us go?" I asked, watching him closely for any sign that he might be lying.

"Yeah, you're really of no use to us beyond this one thing," Moss said with a quick, reassuring nod.

"But if we run into another magical alarm, we just may call on you again," Peter added afterward.

I crossed my arms over my chest and pouted. "I don't want to be at your beck and call."

"Do you want everyone to know your crazy little secret?" Peter asked, cracking his knuckles so that I would look at his strong fists.

I bit my lip to keep from speaking. I had wanted to keep my ability a secret, but now it felt like the lesser of two evils. If the only thing Peter had over me was threatening to tell, then maybe I should just tell everyone myself.

"Fine," I said through clenched teeth as I motioned toward Octo-Cat. "I'll do it, but first he and I need some time alone."

"So you can plan your escape? No way." Peter transformed back into the dog and bared his teeth at me.

Moss put his hand on top of the pit bull's head. "You go. I'll stay and supervise."

Peter continued to growl, and Moss smacked him upside the head. "They may not be magic, but they're still cat people. It's best I handle this. Now get."

Peter whimpered as he shuffled away with his tail tucked

between his legs. I would have laughed at the sight if I hadn't still been so scared.

"I don't get it," I said to Moss, once the opaque glass closed again. "If you hate each other so much, then why do you work together?"

He sighed as if he didn't like it much more than I did. "It's part of the truce that the council enacted many years ago."

"Who is this council you keep talking about?"

"The court that governs the magic world," he answered, unbothered by all my questions now that I'd agreed to help carry out their robbery and Peter had left us on our own.

"The good guys?" I asked hopefully.

Moss nodded. "Yes, the good guys. Bad guys, too, though. In our world, they work together."

I shook my head, unable to understand. "But that doesn't make any sense."

"Maybe not to you, but if the magical world is to survive, we need perfect balance in all we do. The good with the bad. The light with the dark. The fact with the fiction."

"The cat with the dog?" I asked, cracking a smile.

"Indeed," Moss confirmed solemnly.

I thought this over, and it did seem to make sense, even though Moss and Peter's world obviously worked differently from the one I knew. "Could you maybe give us a few moments to talk this out?"

We both watched Octo-Cat who still had his forehead pressed against the cold wood of the wall.

"He needs me," I explained, keeping my eyes trained on my depressed feline companion the entire time. "And he also needs a pep talk if you want him to have any part of this."

Moss situated himself in the other corner of the room, then looked to the side and mumbled over his shoulder, "Go ahead."

I walked over to Octo-Cat and sat down beside him. "Rough day, huh?"

He let out one sarcastic laugh, then quickly fell silent again.

"They don't know you, Octavius. Not like I do." I begged him to understand, to not let them break him. He'd been through so much before—too much for this to be the thing that finally brought him down.

"They said I'm ordinary," he choked out.

"They're wrong," I said firmly, stroking my hand across his fur.

"They can do such amazing things, things I never even dreamt of before," he explained, still unwilling to meet my eyes.

"But you can do pretty amazing things yourself. And without any magic to push you over the top."

Finally, he turned toward me so that his cheek rested against the wall. "Are you saying their magic is a cheat?"

"Yes," I said with a huge smile. I loved when he helped to fill in the blanks for me. I could convince Octo-Cat of anything just so long as I appealed to his special brand of cat logic. I bobbed my head in continued agreement. *Definitely.*

He sniffed and cautioned a glance toward Moss. "If they're cheating, then they have to be disqualified."

"You're right," I said. I wasn't sure what game we were talking about but figured it must be the competition for best cat in the room or something. "They should totally be disqualified."

At last, a small smile played across his lips. "And if they're disqualified, then I'm the winner by default."

"The best cat in the entire world!" I said without missing a beat.

He stood and pushed himself away from the wall. "Okay, Angela. I'm on board."

We locked eyes and smiled at each other—partners, friends, and now co-criminals, it seemed. "Let's do this," we said in unison.

CHAPTER SEVENTEEN

W e were held in the fishbowl for a couple more hours while everyone waited for peak criminal hours to approach. Nan must have been going crazy with worry. I could only hope we'd be back to her soon.

First, we just had to commit one teensy, little burglary, then Octo-Cat and I would be home free. Once Octo-Cat was feeling like himself again and ready to help, Peter walked us through what he expected of us, step by excruciating step.

Apparently, this plan had been in the works for quite some time. It made me wonder if Peter would have abducted us, had we not followed him downtown to begin with.

The burglary would go down like this...

I'd enter through the back door with the key they'd filched and had copied earlier that week. Next, I'd deactivate the alarm with the code they'd give me, then open the door for Octo-Cat who would slip in and begin knocking all the jewelry from the cases out onto the floor.

When he gave his signal, I would rush in wearing a crazy green bodysuit that covered everything, including my face, and Octo-Cat would stand guard while I shoved our bounty into the oversized purse the good folks at the lair had provided me with.

Once I returned to the street, one of them would use their glamor to hide me from view—apparently that was easier to do with me already wearing a walking green screen get-up—and we'd all run back toward our underground hiding spot. As soon as Moss and Peter confirmed that I'd completed the job to their satisfaction, they'd wipe our memories and release us back to our ordinary, everyday lives.

This, of course, was provided that everything went perfectly.

And also that Peter wouldn't trick me into helping him again in the future. And, well, I trusted him just about as far as I could throw him.

Oh, how I hated everything about this night.

Mr. Gable, the old man who owned the jewelry store, had always been kind to me whenever I'd passed him on the street. He'd even helped to pick out the heart-shaped locket my parents had purchased as a gift for my eighteenth birthday. Whether or not he had the right kind of insurance to deal with getting robbed blind, he still didn't deserve for this to happen.

No one did.

Now, obviously, Mr. Gable had to be magical, too. Otherwise he wouldn't have known to add a magic-seeking alarm to his store's security system. And that made me wonder... could he transform into an animal, too? Use glamor to hide both thoughts and things?

The old shopkeeper had been a part of this town for as long as I could remember, and it unnerved me to think that magic had always been so close by without me ever even suspecting it. So, was he one of the good guys or the bad guys? And did it even matter which side he ascribed to if the two opposing teams always worked together anyway?

I felt so lost in this strange, new world.

I really just wanted to get back to my normal life as soon as possible.

By the time, Moss returned to let us out of the fishbowl, I was ready to do whatever they said if it meant freeing ourselves faster. Octo-Cat was in a better mood now and actually seemed a bit excited about the mission that we'd been forced into carrying out.

"I've always suspected they call it cat burglary for a reason," he quipped as Moss joined up with Peter, and together they escorted us toward the jewelry shop.

I wanted to run but knew it would be useless. We didn't have a level playing field here, and the only way I could emerge safely from this situation was to do exactly as I had been told.

"Are you ready?" Moss asked, tightening his hold on my arm as we peered around the corner. "You understand the plan?"

Peter gripped my other arm just as tightly. I would definitely have bruises the next morning, provided it ever came. "If you try any funny stuff, we'll know. And I promise that I will personally make your life a living hell after that."

I nodded glumly. "Understood." I did not doubt the sincerity of that particular statement. Peter had been gunning for me ever since that first awkward morning in the office. Probably even before then, too.

"The cat stays with us until you've deactivated the normie alarm," Moss said. "Got it?"

Octo-Cat struggled underneath Moss's arm but had no words of encouragement to offer me as I readied myself for action.

"Yes, I've got it," I said with an angry stare.

Finally, both Moss and Peter let me go and shoved me down the alley.

The little metal key burned in my palm, the only witness to my sad fall from grace. These people had hurt me and my cat. They'd hurt others, and still they weren't finished. They'd probably never be finished.

Was it really worth continuing that chain of destruction and greed?

And what if I did everything they said, but they kept us prisoner, anyway?

Anything was possible, I supposed. Nothing was guaranteed in life, especially when working hand-in-hand with such unsavory characters. Still, I had to at least try to get myself home in one piece. After all, it wasn't just me they held captive. Octo-Cat was firmly in their clutches as well, and he definitely wouldn't be able to take four more lifetimes of being told he was nothing special.

I'd reached the door now. This was really happening, and it was happening now. The key slipped seamlessly into the lock, and I sucked in a deep breath as I twisted the knob open. Inside the doorway, the alarm sounded with a warning chirp. I had ten seconds to punch in the correct code, just as Peter had instructed.

I closed my eyes and saw the numbers appear before me. Feeling my way around the pad, I found the first number and pressed it inward.

With another deep breath, I punched the second digit. I opened my eyes again. I could do this. I was doing this. Doing something bad didn't make me a bad person, not when I'd been threatened and tricked into helping commit this crime.

I was halfway through my first task. Just two more buttons and only a handful of seconds left.

By the time I pressed the third button, my hairline had moistened with sweat. My breathing slowed not because I was calm, but because every single inhalation became more and more difficult to take. My head spun and vision blurred as I regarded the keypad before me.

Only one more digit, then this—or at least *this part*—would be over.

I raised my index finger, trying not to focus on the way it shook as I moved it toward the array of buttons.

I closed my eyes and pressed it down hard…

On the panic button.

An ear-piercing siren sounded overhead, but I made no effort to get away. *Let them find me here.*

A voice sounded over the speakers, but I was too clammed up to say anything. I only hoped that Moss and Peter hadn't punished Octo-Cat for my insubordination, that he still believed in himself enough to fight back.

It only took minutes for a battle-ready Officer Bouchard to arrive on the scene. When he saw me waiting with my hands held in the sky, he took a step back in surprise. "Angie. What are you doing here? Did you see who broke in?"

I nodded stoically. "Yes, me."

"You?" He stopped to scratch his head and wrinkled his nose. "That's not possible."

"I willfully entered with this key." I tossed the illegal copy his way.

He pulled it closer with his foot but didn't bend down to pick it up. "Then why did you hit the panic alarm?"

"I didn't have a choice," I sobbed. "They threatened me and my cat."

"I figured it was something like that," Officer Bouchard said, worry lining his brow. "Put your hands down. I'm not going to arrest you."

I took a deep breath and let my hands fall to my sides. Tears had snuck up on me again. But I didn't care about me. More than anything, I was desperately worried about Octo-Cat. Had I just signed his death warrant by refusing to play along with the magic-folks' devious scheme?

"Who made you do this, Angie?" the officer asked kindly.

I took a deep breath. This was it. Peter had promised to make my life hell. What he didn't know is that stooping to his insidious level would have done the exact same thing. I'd never be able to live with myself knowing I'd done something so wrong. Whether or not he wiped my memory clear, my heart would always know that something was wrong.

This was the time to make sure that the bad guys went down for their crimes. Even if Officer Bouchard didn't understand the full extent of how they'd carried out the burglaries downtown, I hoped my testimony would be enough to get them arrested—and punished.

"Peter Peters and Moss…I don't know his last name," I told him, my voice clear and sure as a bell.

"It's okay, Angie," he said, placing a comforting hand on my shoulder. "You're safe now."

Maybe I was, but I still had no idea what had happened to my poor cat.

CHAPTER EIGHTEEN

Officer Bouchard gave me a ride home in his cruiser, seeing as my captors had relieved me of both my phone and my car keys. When we pulled up, Nan raced down the porch steps and pulled me to her chest.

"I was so worried," she sobbed into my hair, then reared back and hit me on the chest. *"Never, ever* do that to me again."

"Thank you, Officer," I said with a small yet appreciative smile, even though inside my heart was still broken. Every minute that ticked away without me knowing the location of my best feline friend only broke it further. It had been nearly an hour since Officer Bouchard found me with my hands up inside of Mr. Gable's shop. After I'd given him Peter's name, he let me search the downtown area far and wide while he called in the new lead.

Sadly, despite my frantic searching, Octo-Cat was still nowhere to be found.

"Where's Octavius?" Nan asked, leading me inside with one arm draped across my shoulders.

"I-I-I don't know," I sputtered.

"Oh, dear," she said, her mouth pressed in a thin line. "First tea, then you can catch me up on everything."

I waited on the couch while Nan tended to the kettle. A short while later, she pressed a mug of hibiscus tea into my waiting hands.

"For strength," she said, settling in beside me on the stiff couch. "Now go ahead whenever you're ready, dear."

I'd held back in sharing the full details of my story with Officer Bouchard, but with Nan, I spared no detail. By the time I reached the part where I'd decided to inform the authorities rather than give in to Peter and Moss's demands, Nan wore a giant grin.

"I'm so proud of you, dear one. You did everything right." She hugged me to her side and pressed a kiss onto my forehead.

"But Octo-Cat," I argued, feeling like the worst pet owner in the entire world.

Nan waited for me to look up at her, then said, "You and I both know he's no ordinary cat. He's resourceful and smart, and don't forget that he's also tough as nails."

I sniffed as the one person I loved most in this whole wide world soothed my tears. She would never even dream of lying to me. If she said Octo-Cat was going to be okay, then I knew he'd somehow find a way to get home again. We would find him, or he would find us. I simply couldn't accept any other outcome.

With great difficulty and a good deal of support from my nan, I finally headed to bed. Of course, Nan entered my tower bedroom several times throughout the night, making one ridiculous excuse after the other as to why she'd stopped in. It made me feel better, though, knowing she was there, that she'd always be there.

Even if Octo-Cat wasn't.

I hardly slept a wink, thinking every sound I heard might be Octo-Cat coming back to me. By the time the sun rose, I'd driven myself mad with worry.

A couple hours into the day, Nan came into my room with a mug of coffee and a freshly baked scone and sat beside me petting my hair as she spoke. "I already called in sick to your work, and I figured since you're so sleepy, I can be the one to drive us around as we continue the search."

"Thank you, Nan," I managed around a deep yawn. I tried to

stand but fell back toward the bed in exhaustion. My limbs simply felt too heavy to move all on my own.

"Sit for a spell," she instructed, tucking me back beneath the covers. "Finish your breakfast, and while you do that, I'll start calling around to all the local shelters."

She headed back toward the stairs, but I called for her to stop.

"Stay," I pleaded. "I don't think I can be alone."

"All righty, then." Nan nodded, settled herself at the end of my bed, and whipped out her cellphone. "We'll find him," she promised again as she placed a call to the first shelter on her list and waited through the rings.

One by one, the shelters all said they hadn't found our cat yet, but they would call if he turned up. With each failed outreach, my heart splintered even further. I needed to know that he was okay, that my rash decision hadn't cost him everything.

Once Nan had finished calling every shelter in the region, she placed her phone in my hands and said, "You should keep mine until you can get a new one. You need it more than I do."

I nodded and finished the coffee with a giant gulp, then tried to stand again. This time I didn't fall. Progress, at least.

"Let's get out there," I told Nan, reaching for the handrail to guide me safely down the stairs. "I can't wait another moment."

That was when the phone rang.

In my excitement to answer, I dropped it down the stairs.

Nan raced after it and managed to answer before the caller hung up. She faced me with wide, animated eyes as she spoke.

I stood at the top of the stairs and waited, trying not to get my hopes up too much.

A giant smile filled Nan's face as she said, "Yes, that sounds like our guy. We'll be there on the first ferry over."

She hung up and held the phone out to me as I raced down the stairs, stumbling as I went but not clumsily enough to fall. "Did somebody find him?"

Nan nodded brightly. "A small vet's office on Caraway Island of all places.

Caraway Island? How would he have gotten there? I know he

wouldn't have braved that kind of swim, and the public ferry stopped running after eight o'clock.

"Someone definitely took him out there on purpose," I said through clenched teeth. "And I'm pretty sure I know exactly who did it."

"Oh, dear." Nan hummed a beat, then said, "Where are your priorities? First, let's bring our fella home, and then we can make sure those crooks pay."

We had to wait a solid hour for the next ferry, but the trip out to Blueberry Bay's only local island was a quick one at least. The vet's office wasn't hard to find, either.

"We scanned his microchip and called right away," one of the techs explained. Thank goodness I had updated the information to include both my number and Nan's after I'd officially adopted him. Otherwise they would have gotten a dead number that belonged to his dead former owner. I also wondered whether my phone was still active and if the bad guys still had it with them.

"Where is he?" I asked, glancing around the small office anxiously. "Is he okay? I can't wait to see him!"

Nan and I held hands while the tech returned to the back and then re-entered with a struggling Octo-Cat held in her arms. "He's got a bit of an attitude, this one," she said with a laugh.

"Octo-Cat!" I cried with relief. Yes, *cried*. I was crying yet again, but I was also far too happy to be embarrassed by it. "I missed you so much!"

He let me pick him up and even purred as I cuddled him to my chest.

"You had us really worried there, old boy," Nan said, giving him a scratch beneath his chin.

"Meow," he told her with a loving gaze. Nan always had been one of his favorites.

We thanked the vet and headed back to the parking lot. I couldn't wait to get the full story from Octo-Cat. As soon as we were all safely tucked within Nan's little red sports coupe, I placed him on my lap and said, "Tell us everything!"

He didn't answer; instead, he appeared tense as he stretched his head up carefully to peer out the front window.

"Octo-Cat," I said with a nervous laugh. "Stop being weird. We were so worried about you. I'm sorry about everything that happened, but I'm just so glad you're okay."

"Meow," he said sullenly.

"Hey, I know you're probably mad at me right now, but please, can you at least tell us what happened after the jewelry shop last night. You know, for Nan's sake?" I waited breathlessly. If he wanted to yell kitty curses at me, I would dutifully sit here and take it. After all, this was my fault. I deserved the worst.

Octo-Cat tilted his head to one side and meowed again.

That was when I realized the worst had already happened.

My cat could no longer understand me.

The magical residue that Moss had told me about had finally worn off. I'd lost the one thing that made me special, and with it, the best friend I had ever had. Something important in me had died, and I'd need a miracle to get it back.

Surely, there had to be a way.

I couldn't accept any other outcome.

We would fix this, Octo-Cat and me. We would fix everything.

Failure was simply not an option.

CHAPTER NINETEEN

When we made it back home from our trip out to Caraway Island, a familiar Lexus sat waiting for us in the driveway. I'd seen it pretty much every day for the better part of the year and had no doubt that it belonged to Bethany, my frenemy turned boss.

I'd really thought we'd made great strides in our relationship. That is, until she hired Peter and refused to listen to any of my concerns.

She sat waiting in one of the rocking chairs Nan had added to the front porch earlier that summer. When we pulled up, she stood but didn't take any strides forward, instead waiting for us to join her on the porch.

"Take him inside," I told Nan, handing Octo-Cat off to her. I was afraid to leave him alone since we'd picked him up. True, he'd lost his voice and not a limb, but the associated pain cut deeper than I could have ever imagined. I wondered if he knew, too.

"Come with your nan-nan, you sweet kitty boy," Nan cooed as she disappeared into the house. Although she understood that he and I had lost our special connection, Nan had never been able to talk to him, anyway. As far as their relationship was concerned, everything was perfectly normal. I knew he'd be happy with her. He'd always held a special place in his heart for Nan.

But without our ability to communicate, would he still hold one for me? I couldn't think like that. We'd find a way to fix everything. I had to believe in that, had to believe in us.

"What do you want?" I asked Bethany with a frown. I was both too exhausted and too devastated to play nice. I was also still more than a little miffed that she had been the one to bring Peter into my world.

"I'm assuming you heard about my cousin," she said, sitting back down and crossing her ankles like some kind of grand duchess.

I joined her by taking a seat in the other rocking chair, mostly because I was too weary to keep standing on my own. "What about him? That he got arrested? Or that he's responsible for the string of burglaries downtown? Oh, maybe you mean the fact that he can turn into a dog!"

Bethany sucked air in through her teeth. Her light blonde hair blew gently in the breeze, and she sat with one of her suit jackets draped across her lap, though it was far from chilly. Under any other circumstances, this would have been the perfect summer afternoon. As it was, though, this had become my own personal hell.

Just as Peter had promised if I pulled anything funny.

"Did you know?" I demanded of Bethany. "Did you know about all of this?"

She hung her head and nodded. "Yes, but I never thought he would hurt you, Angie. You have to believe me."

"I thought we were friends," I said coldly. Her betrayal stung. I couldn't pretend that it hadn't.

"We were," she insisted, looking like she wanted to say something more, but stopping herself. She sighed and added, "Still are, I hope."

I crossed my arms over my chest and refused to answer her either way. So much had already been taken from me that day. As much as I didn't want to lose anything else, I also didn't know if I'd ever be able to forgive Bethany for the things Peter had done. They never would have happened if she hadn't hired him in the first place or if she would have listened when I shared my concerns.

"Why are you here?" I demanded, not caring that my voice sounded cold and uncaring—or that she was technically my boss now.

"To help," she said softly. "And to explain a few things."

I made a dismissive motion with my hands. "Well, go ahead and get it over with, then."

"I hired Peter because I thought having an honest job would help him. I never meant for you to get hurt." She said so quickly it took me a moment to process. *"Please,* if you believe nothing else I say today, believe that."

I considered this but kept quiet, waiting for her to offer more. I wasn't sure any explanation would ever be enough, but at least someone was finally giving me answers without threatening or hurting me in the process.

"I knew he'd been hanging out with some less than savory characters, but I had no idea just how deeply he was involved. I had hoped it wasn't too late to save him, but apparently I was wrong." Most of the women I knew would cry to gain sympathy, but not Bethany. She remained stoic to the bitter end. Always had.

"Did you know about the magic?" I demanded.

"Yes," she said emphatically. She clenched her eyes shut then admitted, "Because I have it, too."

I stared at her with my mouth hanging open rather impolitely. Of course she did. They were cousins, after all. "Do you use it to rob people, too?" I asked with a snort.

"No," she insisted, shaking her head. "I don't use it at all."

"What about the essential oils?" I mumbled, thinking back to all of the strangeness Bethany had exhibited since I've known her. As far as I knew, she was perfectly normal other than her obsession with mixing and matching scents each morning. "Are those your potions or brews or whatever?"

I laughed bitterly at this, but Bethany remained firm.

"I'm not a witch," she told me. "Mostly because witches aren't real."

"How can I believe you, though? Up until a few days ago, I didn't even know that magic was real." I paused a moment to let that sink in. "Where does it end? How do I even know what's real and what's made up now?"

"You can't," she said sadly. "And I'm sorry that you've been pulled into this world. I never wanted that for you."

"Then what were you doing this whole time?" I couldn't take her at face value. Not anymore. I'd seen too much to ever trust anyone at their word again. "Were you lying in wait until the timing was right?"

She looked truly pained, but only a small part of me cared. I'd been hurt, too. Burned. Damaged beyond repair.

"Just trying to live a normal life, the same as you."

"But you're one of them," I reminded her.

"Not all magic people are bad."

"Peter's bad."

"Yes," she confirmed with a sigh. "I wanted more for him, but I was too late to help."

We sat in silence for a few moments as the wind blew the overgrown blades of grass in a wave across my front lawn.

"Have you ever wondered why you can talk to your cat?" Bethany asked, her eyes full of unshed tears. She was still too tough to cry. That was another thing about us that was irreconcilably different.

I cried freely. Why even fight it anymore? "You know about that?" I asked, too exhausted to be shocked by anything now.

She nodded, then raised the suit jacket from her lap and tossed it to me. "Do you recognize this?"

"It's one of your ugly blazers."

"I'll let that slide, because I know you're hurting right now," she said, waiting.

I fingered the cool fabric, releasing the scents of juniper and lemon into the air.

"Do you remember wearing it?" she pressed again.

I thought back to one of the many times Thompson had forced

me to borrow clothes from Bethany to appear more presentable when an important client visited the office.

And that was when the final piece of this week's horrible puzzle settled into place. "Ethel Fulton's will reading," I said.

"Yes," she said with a nod of affirmation. "Do you understand what happened now?"

"The magical residue Moss mentioned. That was from you?"

She nodded again. "It was in my blazer. The electric shock strengthened it, transferred that energy to you."

"But I'm not magical," I said with a huff.

"No, not fully. Usually resonance disappears quickly. The fact yours didn't is my fault, I'm afraid."

I turned to her with a hundred questions begging to be let out. A single word escaped my lips. *"Why?"*

"I already told you, I don't practice magic. The energy has nowhere to go. A lot of it has built up over the years, packed in tight. That zap uncoiled all of it and created a reaction."

"But I can't mess with people's minds or use glamor or change into an animal." I felt so incredibly small and helpless as I reminded her of all the things I couldn't do. Ever since I'd gained the ability to speak to Octo-Cat, I'd thought of myself as having superpowers. What a joke. There were real super humans out there in the world, but sadly, I wasn't one of them.

"You got a small but powerful dose from that jacket," Bethany explained, watching me carefully. "The cat got it, too."

I searched her face while she struggled to find her words.

"He was close by and somehow it created a bond between you. I don't know why you only got the one ability or why it hasn't left you yet."

"Oh, but Bethany," I said, once again crying for all I'd lost. "It has. Octo-Cat and I… We can't talk anymore."

Then I realized something wonderful. "Can you fix it? Can you make things how they were again?"

Bethany bit her lower lip and sucked a deep breath in through her nostrils. "I don't use magic," she said again. "But for you, I'm willing to try."

CHAPTER TWENTY

"The cruel irony is that the less one practices magic, the stronger she becomes," Bethany explained as we settled into my home library side-by-side. Octo-Cat sat on my lap, but I'd asked Nan to sit this one out. As much as I loved her, I felt this moment needed to be private.

"It's all part of the great balance," Bethany continued as I stared at the trees swaying in the gentle winds outside. "It helps to keep the power-hungry from becoming too powerful. Keeps the magic world hidden and safe."

"Moss mentioned some of this," I said, nodding along as I recalled my time in the fishbowl.

"As I already said outside, the fact that I'm a non-practitioner makes my magic abnormally strong," Bethany continued. "But I'm not an expert in harnessing it. I can try to transfer some of it back to you, but it might not work." She swallowed hard. "You could also get hurt."

"It's worth the risk," I said without hesitation, petting Octo-Cat as I spoke. "I'm ready."

"Our best chance at getting this to work right is to recreate the scene at the will reading as closely as possible. That's why I brought you the jacket." She nodded toward the blazer which sat crumpled in my lap, then picked up the reusable cloth shopping bag she'd brought inside with her.

The moment I saw what came out of that bag, I jumped to my feet in sheer terror. "Keep that thing away from me!" I screamed as I stared at the old office coffee maker, refusing to so much as blink until it was safely put away. It had almost killed me the first time, and I didn't doubt it could finish the job today.

"We need to recreate what happened that day," Bethany reminded me. "I'm sorry, but it's the most surefire way to get this to work."

I shivered violently as I regarded the evil appliance. Could I do this? Could I face this deep-seated, albeit very rational, fear and live to tell the tale?

Octo-Cat meowed and rubbed himself against my ankles. When I reached down to pet him, I found that he was purring. He gave me a sandpaper kiss, then jumped back into the window seat and rubbed his head against the coffee maker, keeping his eyes on me the whole time.

I smiled despite my fear. "If he believes this will work, then so do I. Um, do you mind if I close my eyes first?"

"Do whatever you need to do," Bethany said, situating the coffee maker near the closest outlet. "I took the liberty of fraying the power cord some. Thought it might make for an easier electrocution."

Oh, joy.

Octo-Cat mewled again. He believed in me, believed in us. I'd do anything to protect that even if it meant walking head-first into danger—which, apparently, it did.

Bethany put both hands on my shoulders, and I felt a warm, pleasant sensation transfer from her to me through the blazer. "Are you ready?" she asked, pulling her hands away.

I nodded, clenching my eyes tight as she guided me toward the coffee-making death trap. Octo-Cat stayed at my side every step of the way, and when I couldn't find the cord with my eyes still closed, he pushed my hand in the right direction.

There was only one thing left to do.

With a deep breath—one I hoped wouldn't be my last—I picked up the power cord and jammed it into the outlet. When the burst of electricity shot through my body, I collapsed and fell unconscious with a smile.

"Angie? Angie? Are you okay?" Bethany asked, cradling my head in her lap as I came to.

"What happened?" I asked. My mind felt… fuzzy.

"Did it work?" she asked excitedly, disregarding my question entirely.

Bethany helped me sit up, and I glanced around the room. We were at my house in the library I had claimed as my own special sanctuary. But why?

Octo-Cat approached me carefully, almost as if he could catch whatever I had. "Yuck," he said. "You still smell like that basement."

Tears filled my eyes and suddenly I remembered everything. "You can talk," I said, sobbing freely.

Bethany cheered and pumped a fist in the air.

Octo-Cat shook his head in amazement. "Of course I can talk. I've always been able to talk. But now you can listen again. Oh my whiskers, I have so much to tell you."

"It worked," I sobbed. "I'm magic again."

Bethany placed a gentle hand on my shoulder. "I think you've got it all wrong. Don't you see? You're not magic, but the bond you two share is."

"This sounds like an episode of the *Care Bears,*" I quipped.

"*My Little Pony* would be the more recent reference," Bethany said with a shrug. "But sure, *Care Bears,* yeah."

I gave her a tight hug despite the fact sarcasm simply dripped off her. "Thank you so much for helping us."

"Hey, don't get too friendly there," Octo-Cat warned as he wrinkled his nose in disgust. "She's a dog, too."

"You're a dog? Like Peter?" I asked.

She nodded. "I can become a pit bull. I did it a few times in my school days to scare bullies away. *Bully breed*, indeed," she said with a dry chuckle.

"So what happens now?" I wanted to know.

Bethany sighed and looked toward the door. "Unfortunately, I need to go."

"Okay, but I'll see you at work tomorrow, right?"

She shook her head. "I have to leave Glendale, I mean. Now that magic has been exposed, it isn't safe."

I'd be sad to see Bethany leave but understood her position. "What about Peter and Moss? Are they going, too?"

"Peter's coming with me just as soon as I bail him out. Moss, on the other hand, will… Well, he'll be around for a while."

"Why? What happened?"

"Peter turned Moss in to the cops so that he could plea out of felony charges."

"Figures," I scoffed, thinking of neither man-animal fondly now that the worst was over.

"I'm taking him to Georgia. It's kind of like the magic capital of the world."

"Atlanta?"

"No, a much smaller town called Peach Plains."

"Can you do me a favor before you go?"

"I'll help however I can, but remember, my magic isn't very focused."

"Can you do that memory thing on me?" I begged her to understand. This was the only option for me now.

Bethany stared at me in confusion. "Why would you want that?"

I shrugged even though I'd already made up my mind and knew I wouldn't be changing it any time soon. "I liked the world better when it made more sense. If the magic is leaving, anyway, then I think I'd rather not remember it."

Bethany thought about this for a second before nodding her

agreement. "But you do understand that you also won't remember why you can talk to your cat? And that if anything ever goes wrong again, you won't know who to turn to for help?"

I considered this, but it wasn't enough of an argument to sway me. "We've become good friends. Haven't we, Bethany?"

Bethany smiled at me and gave me a quick hug. "Of course."

"Then just check in on us every so often. Make sure we're okay."

"I can definitely do that," she promised. "Now, before I try this, you're sure you want to forget all of it?"

"All the magic stuff, if you'd please."

Bethany raised one hand and made the whirling hand gesture I'd seen both Peter and Moss use before. Soon I wouldn't remember any of it.

I watched her fingers dance gracefully before me. Bethany had always been so delicate and dainty. It was pretty hilarious that she could secretly turn into a pit bull. I liked knowing that, even if it wouldn't last much longer...

"There," Bethany said, blinking at me curiously. "How do you feel now?"

"A bit light-headed," I answered, wondering why I suddenly felt so dizzy. "Can we open up the window and get some air flowing through here?"

"Sure," she said, kneeling down on my cushy window seat and cranking the glass open. Funny, I couldn't even remember asking her over, let alone what we'd discussed during our visit so far.

"Ahh, what a beautiful day it's turned out to be," Octo-Cat said, inhaling the sweet summer air.

We both stuck our noses out and took deep, contented breaths. I closed my eyes and let the sun kiss my face. What a perfect day it had been. I couldn't remember much about it, but knew I was happy—and also that I was blessed beyond measure.

"What's that cat doing?" someone asked from so close it startled me.

"Do you think he's going to eat us?" another voice wondered aloud.

"Stop asking questions and fly away to safety," a third said.

I opened my eyes just in time to see a trio of gulls launch themselves off the roof.

I desperately wanted to ask Octo-Cat if he'd heard them, too, but Bethany still stood nearby and she didn't know our secret.

I knew one thing for sure, though. Those birds had talked…

And I'd understood every word they'd said.

THE CAT CAPER

Pet Whisperer P I

ABOUT THIS BOOK

What's even worse than having a snarky talking tabby as your best friend?

When he inexplicably goes missing…

Octo-Cat is gone, and all the evidence suggests that he was taken on purpose. With the growing number of people the two of us have put behind bars, it's no surprise that someone's out for revenge.

But how will I ever manage to solve this particular crime without the help of my partner?

The only other person who might be able to help me just relocated to Georgia. But I'm desperate enough to try anything, including exposing my secret to the whole of Blueberry Bay. Anything to bring him home safe.

Oh, Octo-Cat. Where have you gone?

CHAPTER ONE

My name's Angie Russo, and I'm a cat person. Lately, that is the most important thing about me.

Not that I'm a part-time paralegal and also a part-time private investigator. Not that I live in a giant East Coast manor house or that my quirky nan is one of my best friends. Not even the fact that I've managed to rack up seven associate degrees due to my academic indecisiveness.

Nope.

The most important thing about me is definitely the fact that I have a cat.

But he's not just any ordinary feline, mind you.

He talks. *A lot.* As in hardly ever shuts up.

And if you think your cat is demanding, just imagine what my life looks like.

I have to feed him a particular brand of food in a particular flavor in a particular Lenox dish and at very particular times of the day. He also only drinks Evian. I've tried to trick him in the past to save on this ridiculous expense, but—I kid you not—he knew the difference. And, boy, did I pay for that one.

In all honesty, I can spare the expense, though. You see, my cat also has a trust fund—a big one. His previous owner was murdered, and it was by pure dumb luck that he and I ended up together. That is, if you can call almost dying at the hands of a faulty coffee maker "luck."

I mean, I do.

I love my life and would change very little about it. I do plan to quit my paralegal gig soon to pursue detective work full-time. Naturally, my cat would be my partner in that operation. He watches so much *Law & Order* that he practically has an honorary degree in criminal justice, and he's got claws that he isn't afraid to use when we find ourselves in a tricky scrape.

Other than his sometimes gratuitous violence and over-the-top television addiction, he has plenty of other unique skills that make him an indispensable partner, too. First, there's the fact we can communicate. Obviously, no one ever suspects that the curious-looking feline across the way is actually listening in on their conversations.

When you add Nan to the mix with her background in Broadway and knack for creating colorful characters and then flawlessly bringing them to life, we have quite the little operation.

So, go ahead and eat your heart out, Scooby Doo.

If you're wondering about me and who I am outside of being a cat owner, I'll make this real simple for you: I'm the Velma of the group. I love researching, learning, wrapping my mind around any and every puzzle that comes our way.

I have a near-photographic memory and a knack for mnemonic devices, but lately my brain has been a tad less reliable than I'd like.

Usually, I remember everything without fail. Ever since this new guy Peter Peters started working at the law office, though, things have definitely gotten a bit fuzzy. I hated that guy almost instantly, and I'm pretty sure he has something to do with the fog that's taken up residence in my head… But I just can't remember why.

Lucky for me, he'll be leaving the state very soon. Unluckily, he's taking his cousin Bethany, a former partner at the same firm, with him. She was a good friend, and I'll definitely miss having her around. Still, I get the fact that she needs to be there for her family

—even if this particular member of her family is the creepiest guy I have ever met.

Honestly, it's probably time for me to quit, anyway. Well, just as soon as I work up the nerve to let down my secret crush by handing in my two weeks' notice. I've had the hots for our senior partner, Charles Longfellow, III, ever since he moved here from California and began working his way up the ranks at our firm. He's only a few years older than me, a legal prodigy and also someone who's had a few lucky strokes like I have—so no judgment, please.

I'd probably have bitten the bullet and asked him out already, but he has a girlfriend now. By the way, I hate her, and not just because she's standing in the way of what I'm convinced could actually be true love, but because she's mean and bitter and has never shown me an ounce of kindness in our entire acquaintanceship.

At least she's not a murderer, although I did suspect her of a double homicide a few months back. We solved that one, though, and got both her and her brother off the hook. We also solved the murder of a prominent senator who used to live right next door.

And as ready as I am to hang up my sign as a full time P.I., I'd much rather be chasing white-collar criminals around town than the homicidal maniacs I've been dealing with as of late. Because that's the thing about murderers: they're dangerous with a capital *D*. It stands to reason that eventually one of them is going to want revenge on the crazy girl and her cat that got them arrested in the first place.

I just hope I'm ready when karma comes calling…

I almost ran straight into Nan when I returned home from work that sunny afternoon.

"Look what I made for you today in my community art class!" she cried, completely unbothered by the fact I'd almost knocked her into the antique stained-glass windows that flanked either side of our front door.

I took one giant step back and studied the sizable metal sign she held between her aged hands.

"Pet Whisperer, P.I.," I read aloud, then grabbed the thing to take a closer look—and almost dropped it as soon as the heft transferred to my hands. "Oof, this is really heavy!"

Nan shook her head and tutted at me. "Well, it's not made of paper, dear."

"What kind of art class are you taking, anyway?" I said as I appreciated how the various scrap metals had come together to create something new and beautiful.

"It's a little bit of everything—sculpture, welding, landscapes, still-lifes, nudes." She winked at that last one, and I had no doubt that this meant the nudes were her entire reason for signing up in the first place.

"Sounds like a good time," I said with a laugh. My nan was always finding something new and exciting to occupy her time. Apparently, this included advertising my closely kept secret to all of Blueberry Bay.

Nan caught me studying the sign with a nervous expression and explained, "It's for your business, dear. Seeing as I'm your assistant, I figured I'd make myself useful."

"But we haven't even officially opened yet," I argued. I loved Nan and was excited she wanted to help, but the added pressure didn't make this big career transition any easier on me.

"Yes, you really do need to get on with it already," my grandmother told me as she furrowed her brow in my direction.

I groaned even though she was one-hundred percent right about this. "Okay, but I don't want people to know I talk to animals, remember?" That was the other weird thing about the last couple weeks.

My memory was a bit fuzzy, but also my mind seemed to be more open. I still didn't know how I could talk to Octo-Cat, but lately I'd been able to hear other animals besides him, too.

First there were the birds on the rooftop, then a curious squirrel in my garden. I'd even managed to listen in on a great big buck I'd startled in the woods outside our manor house. My ability to understand other animals was touch and go, and also a brand new complication in my already crazy life.

It had always been Octo-Cat and only Octo-Cat, and I really didn't know how I felt about becoming a full-on Dr. Dolittle these days. If word spread among the animal kingdom that I could understand their needs, would they all start swarming me with their legal problems?

I was way out of my depth here, considering I was just a paralegal and had no great passion for the law—other than choosing to uphold it most of the time in my day-to-day life.

"Where's Octo-Cat?" I asked, craning my neck to glance up the grand staircase but not finding him at the top. Normally, he liked hanging out up there this time of day because it was when the skylights dumped lots of warm sunlight in that exact spot.

"He's around here somewhere, I'm sure," Nan answered dismissively as she took the sign back from me and studied it with a huge, self-satisfied grin on her face.

"When did you last see him?" I asked, checking his other favorite nap spots. Maybe the sun wasn't following its normal, predictable pattern today. Perhaps cloud cover had interfered. I knew my cat well enough to know he hadn't voluntarily changed his routine.

Something was off, and the sooner I figured out what that was, the better I'd feel going into the rest of the day.

Nan came over and gave my shoulder a little squeeze. "I watched an episode of *Criminal Intent* with him during my mid-morning tea. That was only a little more than two hours ago. I'm sure he's fine, dear."

But I wasn't. Not at all.

I'd already lost him briefly a couple weeks ago, when he'd ended up on Caraway Island as if by magic. I still had no idea how he'd gotten out there or why I couldn't remember going with Nan to pick him up. All I knew is I needed to find my cat, and I needed to find him now.

"Help me look for him. Would you?" I asked Nan.

She nodded and tucked the metal sign away in the closet, then together we conducted a thorough search of both the house and the yard.

"Well, that's strange," Nan said, scratching her forehead. "Maybe he's just out for a walk and lost track of time."

Again, this was not how my cat operated. If I so much as tried to sleep in an extra minute, I'd get an earful about how disappointed he was in me. He did use his cat door as Nan suggested, but he never strayed far.

At least not until today.

A swatch of white appeared at the bottom of the driveway, and I watched as the mail truck drew closer and closer.

"Beautiful day, isn't it?" the mail lady, Julie, trilled as she rummaged through her sack. "A light load today," she said next as she handed me a stack of mail that had been folded together using a thin rubber band.

"Thank you, Julie!" I called after her, biting my lip as I quickly flipped through the junk mail, bills, and solicitations.

But then I found an unfamiliar envelope, one that had no return address and was addressed simply to *"Octavius" Fulton*.

Yes, to my cat.

I swallowed hard and tore it open without even the slightest moment's hesitation…

CHAPTER TWO

The date at the top of the letter had already passed two months ago. Not a good sign. Not good at all.

"What is it?" Nan asked as I quickly scanned the legalese before me.

"It's..." I took a deep, shaky breath in an effort to avoid either screaming or breaking down in tears. "It's an arbitration notice."

Nan's face loomed closer, concern pinching at the edges of her mouth. "An arbitration for what?" she huffed with clear outrage.

After a deep, painful swallow, I forced my eyes to focus on the page and read the entire letter from top to bottom before I spoke again. "The other beneficiaries of Ethel's will are disputing Octo-Cat's inheritance."

"Oh, dear," Nan said with a disappointed shake of her head.

"If he wants to contest, he has to appear in court by this Friday. Otherwise his agreement will be implied, and the arbitration will go forward." Even as I spoke the words, I couldn't quite believe them. Why was this happening now? Or ever for that matter? It's not like the others had gotten cut out of the will. Ethel had loved her cat dearly and wanted to make sure he lived the rest of his days comfortably. Knowing Octo-Cat as I did now, I totally understood.

It wasn't exactly cheap to fulfill his demands for Fancy Feast, Evian, fine china, Apple products, and—oh—a giant East Coast manor house.

I folded the letter back into thirds and sighed, pinching the bridge of my nose to stave off the rapidly building headache. "Nan, if this goes forward, he could lose his trust fund. We could lose the house. We could even lose him."

I would not cry. Crying wouldn't fix this. It wouldn't bring Octo-Cat home. I needed to suck those tears that threatened to spill back in and approach both situations with a clear head.

Nan placed a hand at the small of my back and guided me back toward the house. "Well, we'll just have to find him by Friday, then," she ground out. "Failure is not an option."

My cat had only been missing for a few hours, tops, but already I was terrified for him. He'd be devastated if he lost his inheritance and I could no longer afford to maintain his lavish lifestyle and expensive tastes. Worse still was the fact that he could be lying hurt in a ditch somewhere, and I didn't even know where to look.

Nan motioned for me to sit on our massively uncomfortable antique Victorian couch. "You wait here while I make tea," she instructed softly. "The hit of caffeine will help wake up our brains. We'll solve this. Yes, we will." She hurried out of sight, singing to herself as she went.

That just left me sitting on my own in our large, empty living room. I hated it. Octo-Cat should have been there, complaining about something, questioning my life choices, or telling tasteless jokes that no one else found funny.

While I worked hard not to let fear cloud my normally rational brain, Nan continued to sing loudly from the kitchen. Apparently, she'd already composed a ballad about our mighty victory over catnappers and arbitrations. I had no idea where she found the energy.

Could a catnapper really be to blame for Octo-Cat's sudden disappearance? It was certainly a possibility, given how unlikely it would be for him to wander off on his own. But who would want to take my crabby tabby, and why?

Nan's gray, curly head popped out of the kitchen. "Yoo-hoo, Angie dear!" she called, waving at me.

I lifted my head and attempted a smile that wouldn't come.

"Why don't you give our good friend Charles a call? May as well update him on the situation and see if he can help." As soon as she'd said her piece, Nan disappeared from view and the singing started up again.

Charles. Would he know what to do? Nan seemed to think so, and the three of us had made a pretty good team more than once before. At the very least, he'd be able to walk me through this arbitration notice and help me formulate a plan for escaping unscathed.

The phone felt heavy in my hands. Placing this call meant admitting that something was wrong. That Octo-Cat was really missing. Could I maybe pretend for a few blessed minutes that everything was still okay? Would that be selfish of me? Stupid?

"Don't dilly-dally, dear!" Nan trilled from her place in front of the stove, then switched to singing in a different language. I assumed Korean, given her newly discovered K-pop infatuation.

Not even the deepest breath I could muster filled my lungs with the strength I needed to make this call, to speak these dreaded words aloud. But I did it anyway. I did it for Octo-Cat.

"Angie, everything okay?" Charles answered after a couple rings. He was still at the firm, of course. He'd been putting in long hours ever since Bethany had put in her resignation notice. With her moving away to start a new life in Georgia any day now, that left Charles as the sole partner at a law office that had seen a veritable revolving door of attorneys these past several months.

Hearing his voice so full of concern, of kindness, set off the tears I'd already been struggling to hold back. "Charles, he's gone!" I cried. "Octo-Cat is missing, and we can't find him anywhere."

Charles sucked in a deep breath, then said, "I'm sure he just found a great new napping spot and will wander home when his belly starts rumbling."

The way he rushed through this explanation proved that Charles didn't believe those words. And neither did I. We both knew my cat too well to believe he had willingly altered his routine.

"There's also this arbitration thing," I added, knowing I should probably re-open the letter and read the exact wording. But I was already far too tired, too emotionally spent to read that horrible thing again.

"What?" Charles's voice came out low, hostile almost. "Who's requested an arbitration with you?"

"Not me," I corrected with another deep, weighty sigh. "Octo-Cat. And it's the other recipients of Ethel's will."

He was silent for a few moments as he contemplated this newest development in the everyday traumas of Angie Russo. "Don't let that add to your worry," he said at last. "For now, just focus on finding Octo-Cat. He can't be far. Besides, we both knew that the will would probably be contested eventually despite Richard's best attempts to prevent that from happening. You'll have a chance to contest the dispute before the arbitration goes ahead, too."

"Yeah, but the deadline's Friday," I said glumly. So far, I'd managed to avoid going to court for any personal matters. The only reason I'd ever stepped foot in the county court before was to offer on-the-spot assistance for the lawyers from my firm. Usually, Charles.

He balked at this. "Friday? But that's nowhere near enough time."

"Yeah, I know." I traced the intricate paisley pattern on the couch with my index finger, letting my vision go blurry but still refusing to let any tears fall. With a sniff, I informed Charles that, "The letter has a few different postmarks on it. Looks like it originally went to my old rental and then got turfed back as undeliverable until they finally found my forwarding address."

"But they all know exactly where you and Octo-Cat are," he protested. Charles had always been the sort to wear his heart right on his sleeve, and as such, I could tell that he'd become angry. *Real angry.*

I nodded, even though he wasn't there to read my body language. "I know that, too."

We both sighed in unison, and then I asked the question that had been plaguing me ever since the letter first arrived. "Do you think they sent it to the wrong place on purpose?"

"Of course I do," he growled. I could hear something slam down on his end of the line. "It's still okay. We'll find Octo-Cat in no time at all. Meanwhile I'll start putting together your grounds for contesting the arbitration, and we'll show up on Friday ready to kick some serious complainant butt."

"Thank you. You always make me feel better." That was Charles for you. He never hesitated to offer his help when I needed it, and that was a big part of the reason why he'd become my closest friend since he relocated from his home state of California in favor of the scenic Blueberry Bay region of Maine.

"Want me to stop by after work to help you look for Octo-Cat?" he asked me after a brief pause. "I could finish up early and offer a second set of eyes. Or third, rather, since I'm sure Nan's already on the case."

I let out a weak laugh. He knew us too well. "Actually, I kind of could use a change of scenery. We've already been searching for hours, and he's clearly nowhere nearby."

"Want to come over to my place, then?" he asked without even the briefest hesitation.

"Yes, please," I trilled.

Now that Charles was on the case, I knew everything would be okay. I had to believe that, because the alternative simply broke my heart.

If Octo-Cat were here, he'd no doubt yell at me to toughen up and do what needed to be done. And that's exactly what I would do to bring him back home—and to make sure we kept him here, right where he belonged.

CHAPTER THREE

Charles invited me to come over for a quick dinner and epic brainstorming session at six thirty that evening. When I showed up at six thirty-three, however, the house stood dark and empty. Assuming he'd gotten delayed at work, I decided to let myself in using the key he kept stashed in the garden around back. At least it was a better hiding place than Nan's preferred placement under the front door mat. It's a wonder she never got burgled even once in all her seventy-ish years of life.

"Hello!" I called as I pushed my way inside, just in case Charles was in the shower or something and hadn't heard me knock.

Nothing.

I shrugged, then made my way to the kitchen. The least I could do is set the table, since I assumed he'd be bringing takeout home with him. Neither of us were great cooks, but thankfully I had my newly awakened culinary genius Nan to make sure I always had something yummy on my plate. It was both a blessing and a curse, considering I'd grown at least one pants size in the months since she'd discovered this new passion of hers.

I marched through the house, turning on some lights as I went, knowing Charles preferred to keep the curtains drawn for some odd reason. It still felt incredibly odd, though—seeing the house that I'd grown up in now set with all of Charles's sparse, manly decorations. Nan had decided to sell her former home and move in with me when I gained possession of the big manor house we both resided in now, which meant putting this one on the market.

It all worked out kind of perfect in the end, considering Charles needed something a bit more permanent than the Cliffside Apartments, where he used to live. Cliffside was also host to a vast percentage of Glendale's criminals—or, at least the ones that got caught. Based on my own unique experience as of late, the more money a person had, the more likely they were to kill somebody to protect it.

Some people were just never happy, and I vowed never to let myself become one of them.

Feeling a bit more at home now, I grabbed a pair of plates from the cupboard by the stove, then turned to head back out to the dining room and almost jumped right out of my skin at the horrifying sight before me.

"Oh my gosh," I cried, fumbling the plates in my shock, but thankfully not dropping them. "You scared me!".

Yes, it seemed I was no longer alone. Charles still hadn't put in an appearance, but his two Sphynx cats had appeared in the doorway and stood contemplating me with twin sets of glowing eyes. How had I forgotten about them?

"Hello, Jacques and Jillianne," I said with a friendly smile. Hopefully, they couldn't see that I was internally screaming at that moment. J and J, as Charles had taken to calling them whenever discussing the cats as a pair, had no hair but lots of wrinkles on their exposed skin. If you try to picture what a brain might look like if it grew four legs, a tail, and a pair of glowing eyes, then you'd have a pretty good idea why I was so startled at the initial sighting of these two.

The larger of the animals—Jillianne—stepped toward me. "A prince, a princess, and a paralegal walk into a kitchen. Which didn't belong?" she said, allowing me to hear one of the famous Sphynx cat riddles firsthand for the very first time. After all, it was only very recently I'd gained the ability to talk to anyone of fur or feather other than Octo-Cat.

Jillianne flicked her tail and narrowed her eyes when I didn't immediately answer. "Oh," I sputtered, suddenly feeling as if I were a contestant in the final round of Jeopardy—and that I'd just bid all my money without having the slightest idea what the answer might be. "Is the answer the paralegal? Um, because I'm here by Charles's invitation, I swear!"

I raised my hand and crossed my heart, hoping it would reassure the suspicious felines. It did not. Little Jacques arched his back and let out a dry, hacking hiss.

I took two giant steps back and put out my hands before me. "Don't you remember me? I took care of you, when..." Probably best not to bring up their recent trauma involving the untimely murder of their first owner. "I helped solve the case and get justice for the Senator. Remember?"

"Angie?" Charles's voice sounded from the other room followed by fast approaching footfalls. "Are you talking to J and J?" he asked when he'd made it to the kitchen. "I thought you couldn't do that."

Oh, crud.

I crossed my arms and scowled at him. "How is it that you are always the one to randomly discover all my secrets? Seriously, how?"

"Lucky timing?" he offered, lifting Jillianne into his arms and giving her a kiss on her forehead. And let me tell you, that cat went from threatening my life to contentedly purring within a matter of seconds.

I let out a giant, happy sigh. Well, at least I was safe now. I was also never going to let myself into Charles's house with the spare key ever again.

"So..." Charles said, drawing the single syllable into several long beats. His green eyes bore into me, and I found myself trapped in his gaze. "You can talk to all animals now? Because this development would have come in handy when we were working the Calhoun case."

"Shut up," I grumbled, trying and failing to look away. Even when he was irritated with me, Charles's expression still held so much kindness. "You still won. And yes. I can talk to other animals now. I have no idea what changed or why, and I'd prefer to keep it hush-hush for now, please."

"Do you hear that?" he asked the black hairless cat in his arms using an adorable baby voice. "She thinks we're going to share her secret. Yes, she does."

It was strange how hot I found it watching Charles baby and dote on his creepy cat. Obviously, my crush was never going away, no matter how many times I accidentally walked in on him kissing his horrible girlfriend, Breanne. Regardless of his bad taste in... well, many things but especially girlfriends... Charles was the best guy I knew. Bar none.

He proved that further by coming in close and rubbing a calming hand on my shoulder. "We're going to find Octo-Cat, and we're going to dismiss this arbitration. Everything is going to be just fine."

The friction from his touch gave me a little thrill that I quickly worked to stuff down. He was my friend, my boss, the most inappropriate choice possible. Not for me, at least not right now.

I let out a weary sigh. It had been such a long day already.

Charles set Jillianne back onto the floor and searched my face for a moment. "You do believe me. Don't you?"

"Yes," I said without hesitation. Even though I didn't know what the future might one day hold for the two of us, I knew Charles would take care of everything going wrong in the present. I also knew that one way or another we would all be okay. Unfortunately, I didn't know what it might cost us in the meantime.

"What's the real pot of gold at the end of the rainbow?" the smaller spotted cat, Jacques, asked me from his spot on the kitchen floor. Apparently, he wasn't as good at riddles as his companion, which is why he typically let her speak for the both of them.

Still, I couldn't help but wonder what the answer to this one might be. Was it important? Would it somehow help me find my missing cat?

"Do you know what the pot of gold at the end of the rainbow really is?" I asked Charles as I rolled one of my hangnails beneath my thumb—a disgusting nervous habit I'd given up on trying to overcome.

He blinked at me a few times, then burst out laughing. "I don't know. A bowl of cereal. Weird question."

I looked back toward Jacques, but he'd retreated back into the bowels of the house. Was he just messing with me, or had he tried to share something important?

Perhaps I'd never know.

CHAPTER FOUR

"I hope you're in the mood for some fried chicken," Charles said at the same moment I spotted the red-and-white containers stacked in the center of the table. "It seemed comfort food-y," he added with a grin as the two of us moved into the dining room.

"It smells so good," I cooed. Then I remembered the one time I'd attempted to bring fast food chicken into the house while living with Octo-Cat. He'd claimed the greasy smell bothered him so much that he'd swatted the still-full bucket off the edge of the table, sending wings, thighs, and drumsticks cascading across the dusty floor and rendering my dinner plans obsolete.

That guy. He always did love making a scene.

Charles studied me carefully as he scooped a giant heap of mashed potatoes onto his plate. "What's up?" he asked softly.

"Just thinking about him," I admitted, returning to that sad, anxiety-filled place inside of me. "Do you really think he's okay?"

"Angie, look at me," Charles demanded, his stern expression brooking no argument. "That cat of yours could probably survive a nuclear holocaust if he wanted to. You know, he's kind of like a cockroach in that way. Nothing stands in the way of him and what he wants, and I guarantee he wants to get home to you. And he will. Okay?"

"Okay," I mumbled. Should I be offended that he basically just called my cat a cockroach? Octo-Cat certainly wouldn't like that comparison if he were here. But he wasn't here, and I was beginning to worry we'd never find him—especially not in time to make his court date.

Charles gave me a few minutes alone with my thoughts, but the whole time his gaze didn't waver from my face. "Tell me you believe me," he said at last.

"Yes, yes, I believe you," I hurried to assure him. In some ways I did, but in others? It was hard to keep the faith when I had no idea what we were dealing with. "It's still hard, though," I added, unable to hide the emotional turmoil that raged on the inside. Had I somehow caused this? If so, I would never forgive myself.

"Eat," Charles commanded, motioning to my plate, where the salty pile of comfort food still sat untouched.

Even though I knew Charles was just trying to help, my stomach churned at the sight of it. I twisted my face into a grimace and leaned away from the table, trying to gain at least a little distance from the nauseating aroma before me.

My thoughts immediately turned back to Octo-Cat. "Do you think he has access to Evian and Fancy Feast wherever he is? What if he's starving or dying of thirst? What if—?"

"Okay, that's it," Charles said firmly as he set his fork down and pushed his plate to the side. "You're officially not allowed to talk until you get something in your stomach."

"But—" I argued, unsure of how I wanted to finish this particular sentence. Luckily, I didn't have to.

"But nothing," Charles huffed, folding his arms in front of him. "While you eat, I'll do the talking. Got it?"

I sat, staring at him with a furrowed brow, which elicited a deep sigh from Charles.

Both his voice and expression softened then. "C'mon. I'm trying to be a good friend here."

Even though my gut still roiled with anxiety, I obediently picked up a chicken leg and smiled at Charles with wide eyes before taking a large, juicy bite. Instead of feeling worse like I'd feared, something like relief settled over me. Maybe I really was hungry, after all.

"Thank you," he said with a quick nod in my direction. "Now, we have a couple of big issues to address. Let's start with the arbitration, because I'm assuming it will be easier for you to focus on your dinner while I'm yammering on about the boring stuff."

I gave him a thumbs up and waited to see what he'd say next.

"Like I said before, we should have Octo-Cat back by then, which means it probably won't be a problem for us." He held up his hand to silence me before I could even begin to offer another argument.

"*However,*" he continued emphatically. "Just to make sure all our bases are covered, I'll stop by the county court tomorrow to request a continuance. Meanwhile, I shouldn't need much to prepare your argument against the arbitration. Ethel Fulton made her will very clear in regard to how she wanted her assets divided and who she most wanted to see benefited by them. And while she was certainly the most generous with Octo-Cat, she didn't cut any of the family out, either."

He paused to take a quick drink from his glass of tap water. Funny how my cat had more particular tastes than the senior partner at my law firm. "Now, they might argue that Octo-Cat and his monthly trust fund payments should have remained with one of the members of their family, but that won't be a problem, either. We have lots of evidence that you're a fantastic pet owner. Many witnesses who would attest to that fact as well."

I pushed my plate aside, already having eaten all I could stomach for the time being. I did feel better in some ways, but in others nothing had changed. And now my head swam with all the new information Charles had provided about how we were going to fight this arbitration.

"Well, maybe I *was* a fantastic pet owner," I murmured with a frown. "But now my pet either ran away or was stolen right out from under my nose."

Charles waved his fork at me, sending a small lump of mashed potatoes soaring half way across the table. We both stared at the spot where they'd landed for a moment without saying anything.

"We're going to find him," he promised again. "And you know how you're going to do it, right?"

I lifted my eyes to his with what I assume must have appeared to be a blank expression, when inside my head was reeling with all the places we had yet to look, all the things that might have possibly gone wrong in the meanwhile.

"Um, hello!" he cried, waving his hand between us with a flourish. "You can talk to other animals now. That's huge!"

"J and J weren't exactly thrilled to see me," I hedged. Even though I could talk to other animals, I hadn't done much of that yet. I was still learning, and there was so much I needed to figure out, given that each species seemed to have its own personality, lingo, and set of social guidelines. Heck, I was still figuring out Octo-Cat more and more with each new day, and now I had an entire world of creatures I knew very little about. It wasn't as if I had anyone I could ask for advice on this particular issue, either.

"Not them," Charles said with a dismissive chuckle, referring to his two moody felines. "I'm sure there are at least a dozen forest animals that regularly hang out in your yard or in the woods by your yard. Maybe one of them saw something."

"Oh my gosh, you're right," I said, suddenly eager to get home again. Even if I didn't know exactly how to act with them, at least I had my words. At this point I'd try anything—risk almost everything —to find my missing friend again.

Charles simpered at me. "Do you feel better now?"

I knew I wouldn't feel better until I had Octo-Cat safe in my arms again. Granted, he would probably scratch me like crazy, considering how hard I planned to hug his furry little body once I found him again. Even the sting a of fresh wound would be welcome right about now. Anything to prove that my cat was still here and that he didn't blame me for his sudden disappearance.

Actually, even if he did blame me, that would still be okay. I'd have to work harder to make sure nothing like this ever happened again.

"Thanks for talking me off the ledge," I said as Charles began to clear our plates from the table.

"No more ledges for you," he said with a laugh. "You hear me?"

I knew he was just joking, but still I couldn't promise anything. If Octo-Cat needed me to walk a tightrope a hundred feet off the ground, I would jump at the chance to do it.

Anything to bring my number one guy home safe and sound…

CHAPTER FIVE

Nan was nowhere to be found when I returned home from Charles's place. Her little red sports coupe was missing, too, which led me to assume she was out widening our search radius.

Now that the twilight hour had set in, the animals who normally scampered and flittered around my yard had all tucked in for the night. Some of the forest creatures were most definitely nocturnal, but I felt uneasy going into the dark woods without backup. Instead, as much as it pained me, I decided to head to bed early so that I could also wake up early to resume my search.

"Wherever you are," I whispered, hoping somehow, some way Octo-Cat would hear or would at least know I was thinking of him, "I hope you're okay."

The next morning, I dragged myself out of bed at the first sign of dawn. The animals were up, and I needed to be as well. Nan's little red sports coupe was back in front of the house, but she herself wasn't up yet. She had, however, left a long and very detailed note for me on the kitchen counter:

. . .

M y dearest dear,
I know you are eager to find our missing buddy, but make sure you grab a bite to eat first. Scones are in the ceramic container on the opposite side of the fridge. I also brought home some of those cold coffees that taste like chalk in case I'm not up early enough to make the brew.
As for the search, here are all the places I checked last night...

What followed was a lengthy list of almost every place in Glendale. No wonder Nan was still in bed. She must have been out all night. Yet still, she hadn't managed to find "our missing buddy." More and more it was looking like foul play had been involved, and that made finding him all the more urgent. I grabbed one of Nan's scones and a chilled coffee shot from the fridge, planning to eat while I searched the woods.

Or rather *interrogated* the local woodland creatures.

Outside, the sun was bright and warm like a reassuring hug. Hopefully, the animals would be every bit as accommodating as the weather.

Then we might really get somewhere.

A little chickadee sat on the porch railing, tilting its head to the side as it studied me.

I stopped in my tracks and plastered on my best smile. "Hello, there," I said around a very full mouth of scone.

The short, fat bird quickly became a tall, thin bird as it rose on its tiptoes and stretched its neck high in alarm. "It speaks!" he cried.

I nodded and swallowed down my food before speaking again. "My name's Angie, and I was wondering if you could help me with —" My words fell away once the chickadee flapped its wings furiously and darted away without so much as a backward glance in my direction.

Well, then. It seemed clear I would need to find something a little less skittish than a bird. I already knew from my limited experience that almost everything seemed to set them off and send them flying away. Definitely not the most useful as far as witnesses went.

Leaving the porch behind, I made my way toward the edge of the forest that edged my property on three sides. Once there, I stood stock-still and listened to the morning chorus all around me. Much of it belonged to a cacophony of various birds singing in the trees, but I'd already decided that I'd only be questioning them as an absolute last resort.

A chittering sound came from above, and sure enough a hyper brown squirrel jumped from one branch to the next, singing a peppy little tune that seemed to be about all his favorite kinds of nuts.

"Oh, what a beautiful day for eating an acorn," he belted out, then hummed a few beats before continuing his song. "Hey, it's always a great day to enjoy a walnut!"

"Hey!" I called in his general direction. I didn't know much about squirrels, but they definitely didn't seem to be the shyest of creatures. Perhaps I could use that to my advantage now.

The squirrel immediately stopped singing, stopped moving, stopped everything as he took me in with his shiny, black eyes.

"I heard you like nuts," I said, formulating my plan right there on the spot. "But do you like peanut butter?"

He sniffed the air with giant, exaggerated motions. It practically looked as if his nose would fly straight off his face. A second later, he zagged to the side and scampered down to the base of the tree. "Do-do-do you have peanut butter?"

"That depends." I crossed my arms and tried to appear to look both bored and non-threatening.

Luckily, Mr. Squirrel wasn't up on the latest human bribery techniques, because my hesitation to answer his question only made his eagerness grow. "You dooooo have peanut butter. Don't you?" He closed about half the distance between us and sniffed at the air again.

"My name's Angie. I live in that house back there," I informed him, hooking a thumb over my shoulder in the general direction of the manor house.

The fuzzy rodent before me nodded vigorously. "I'm Maple. I live about three trees back and five to the right." Now that part of the squirrel's energy was being used to nod, its voice came out squeakier but also less hurried. Different. This was the point that I realized Maple was most likely actually a girl.

I didn't know how to politely ask, so I just did my best to avoid any gendered language as our conversation proceeded. "I'm trying to find my friend," I explained. "If you can help me with that, then there's a whole jar of peanut butter in it for you."

Maple's eyes grew even wider as she scrambled straight up to me and put both of her furry little hands on the toe of my shoe. "Really? A whole jar?" she asked almost reverently, unwilling to take her eyes off me for even a second.

"Yup," I confirmed with an earnest smile. "But I need help figuring out where my friend's gone first."

"Do you mean the other human? Or maybe the cat?" Maple reached one small hand up and scratched at her head. "I don't think there's anyone else in your drey is there?"

"The cat," I said with a nod. "And how do you know so much about my... drey?" I stumbled over the unfamiliar word, assuming this must be what a squirrel called its family.

"I like to watch you sometimes from my tree," Maple answered unabashedly. "Sometimes I even climb up onto the roof to get a closer look. You're a funny trio, you three are."

I couldn't tell whether that was meant as an insult or some kind of strange compliment, so I just said, "Um, thank you?" It was a bit creepy that Maple had made a habit of peeping in on us, but I tried to let that go—especially if it led to information we could use to recover Octo-Cat.

"You are very welcome," the squirrel said, sniffing at the air yet again. "Peanut butter?"

"First cat, then peanut butter," I reminded her.

"Oh, I'm so hungry, just thinking about all that gooey, melty nut butter, but I promise I will try my very best to help!"

Clearly, it was going to be difficult to keep my new squirrel friend on task, so I'd need to be quick and to the point with my questions. First, I needed to give her a little background on the situation.

"Octo-Cat went missing yesterday during the late morning or very early afternoon," I explained. "We've been looking everywhere but haven't been able to find him. We're wondering if maybe someone took him. Did you see anything unusual happening around here at that time?"

"Unusual? Hmmm." Maple grabbed her tail and began to brush through it with her fingers. Her eyes darted from side to side as she thought. "The big buck was here. You know the one with lots of pointy parts on his antlers? He was hanging out near the edge of the forest, which I thought was weird since he usually likes to stay hidden. And my friend, Willow, said she saw the old human taking a nap in the sun."

"Nan?" That definitely didn't sound like my active, vibrant grandmother, but who else could it be?

"Sure, I guess so." Maple put her hands out to either side in an approximation of a shrug. "I don't blame him, since sleeping in the sunshine is so nice. The only thing nicer is nuts—especially peanut butter. Do you still have some you wanted to give me?"

"Nan's a she, by the way," I said with a small chuckle. "Don't worry about it, though. I know it can be hard to tell with humans. And, yes, I have that jar of peanut butter I promised you. But do you think maybe you can help me out with something very important, Maple?"

She spun in a slow circle, searching the woods around us. I looked, too, but didn't see or hear any other animals nearby.

Maple turned back toward me with her mouth ajar. "Didn't I do that already?"

I had to make fast on my peanut butter promise. Otherwise I'd lose the opportunity to get anything else from my first animal informant. "Yes, which is why I'm giving you the first jar of peanut butter. I'll give you another if you can ask around the forest and see if you can learn anything—anything at all—about what might have happened to my cat."

Maple saluted me, then ran off shouting into the forest. No idea where she learned that particular gesture or how screaming to all the animals at once was going to help anything, but I could at least keep up my end of the promise.

Now I knew that at least some of the animals kept a close eye on my house and family. Did that mean one of them saw what happened yesterday?

I returned home to raid my pantry for a fresh jar of peanut butter, hoping that when I returned, Maple might have more to tell me.

Each moment that passed by without my cat's safe return had become agonizing for me, and I wasn't sure I could last another night without knowing he was safe.

Oh, Octo-Cat, where have you gone?

CHAPTER SIX

E ven though I'd barely been out for half an hour, I returned home to find Nan both wide awake and wearing a full face of makeup. She also wore a lace-trimmed blue sundress that hit at the knees, which she'd paired with hot pink tights and big dangling earrings.

"Hey, good morning. What are you all dressed up for?" I asked, eyeing her suspiciously as I clicked the door shut behind me.

"Dressed up?" Nan asked with a small frown as she scratched at her collarbone. "Are you sure? I was worried it makes me look too much like an old fogey."

I widened my eyes and shook my head. Nothing about Nan's ensemble aged her in the slightest, but I also knew better than to argue with her when it came to fashion. We both had a special flair for it but tended to prefer very different styles.

"The lace, dear," Nan explained. "Doesn't it feel a bit old-fashioned to you?"

"I think you look nice," I offered with a smile and shrug as I sat to join her. "But I still don't know why you're all dressed up."

"Oh, yes. Well, that nice young man, Brock, called and said he was coming by to do a bit of work." Nan shimmied her shoulders and giggled—actually giggled.

This was weird. Even for her.

And especially for so early in the morning.

"He prefers to be called Cal now," I pointed out. "You know, short for Calhoun."

Nan studied her reflection in the antique mirror that hung near the doorway. "Ah, so he does."

"But none of this explains why you felt the need to dress all…" I stopped just short of saying *flirty* and let out a big gasp. *Of course.* "Nan, you don't have a new crush, do you?"

She waved her hand and rolled her eyes, but the blush that now painted the apples of her cheeks was unmistakable. "Oh, pish posh. I don't think it can be categorized as a crush if I never plan on making a move. Besides, silly, I've already decided he's for you."

"For me?" I shrieked. "You can't be serious!"

"He's single. You're single. You get along. I don't see what the problem is…" A wicked smile lit up her face. "Unless you have romantic inclinations for another fella?"

Sure, there was no denying that Cal was an attractive man and somebody I got along well with, too. But to think about dating at a time like this? No way. Not until Octo-Cat was back home, safe and sound.

I groaned and cracked my neck to either side. "This is not the 1800s, nor is it the Deep South. We live in twenty-first-century Maine, Nan. And I can find my own boyfriend when I'm ready. Right now, I'm a bit more concerned about finding my missing cat, thank you."

Nan remained completely unperturbed by my protestations. "Still no reason to pass up a perfectly good opportunity when it just so happens to present itself," she said. "Besides, you say you can find your own boyfriend, but you haven't. Let your poor old nan help. By the way, is that what you're planning to wear?"

"That's it!" I shouted, throwing both hands in the air and marching right past her. "I'll meet Cal outside, and you can make yourself scarce. Preferably by continuing the search for Octo-Cat."

Even though I knew it was a touch overdramatic, I slammed the door shut behind me and practically ran straight into the handsome handyman on the other side.

"Oh, sorry," I murmured as I tried to edge my way past him without losing my footing or brushing up against anything I shouldn't. I found myself even more aware of his good looks than normal now, thanks to Nan.

Cal's brow furrowed in sympathy. "Is everything okay?"

"Just peachy," I said, giving a thumbs-up and tossing him a wink for good measure. Ugh. Why was I always embarrassing myself?

Cal stretched his hand across the back of his neck and glanced down toward the porch. "Your nan called me a little bit ago and said you needed help installing a sign for your new business." He glanced up again and his dark eyes locked with mine. "I didn't know you were starting up your own business. If you need any advice or anything, I'd be happy to help in whatever way I can."

Nan had said Cal called himself, but seeing as he had no reason to lie about things, I had to wonder why Nan would have intentionally misled me. What was she playing at, and why now?

"Thanks, Cal. That's…" I stopped and cleared my throat, otherwise it felt like I might legitimately stop breathing. "That's really nice of you. I'll definitely let you know if I need any help."

He rocked back and forth on the balls of his feet and glanced awkwardly toward the door before finally asking, "So, um, where's the sign?"

"Oh, just a sec. I'll go in and grab it real quick. Be right back." I raced inside, clicking the door shut behind me so that Cal wouldn't try to follow. The last thing I needed was an added layer of embarrassment from Nan. I was doing a mighty fine job of that myself, thank you. I grabbed the metal sign and stepped back outside, where I handed it to Cal.

He laughed as he studied it. "I'm guessing your nan made this."

"Yup." I stared at the door, praying that Nan wasn't planning on bursting through it anytime soon.

"So you're opening a… what exactly?"

"A private investigation firm." I bit my lip while he continued to stare at the sign with a furrowed brow.

"And you're a pet whisperer now?" His eyes snapped up and locked with mine.

I took a step back and forced a laugh. "It's just a cute name Nan and my mom came up with."

"So you don't talk to animals?" he asked, raising an eyebrow now. He didn't appear judgmental, just curious. Still. I really would have preferred a different name for my new firm.

I shook my head so hard, I practically got whiplash. "No, ha! Don't be silly!"

"Too bad," Cal said after making a gentle clicking noise with his tongue. "I think it would be interesting to hear what they had to say."

"Yeah," I said with a laugh. "I'm sure it would be. Especially considering my cat turned up missing yesterday, and I'm worried sick about him."

"Octavius, right?" he asked. "I remember that guy. Do you need any help searching for him? It should only take me a few minutes to hang this sign, and then I have the rest of the day free."

I took a deep breath, suddenly feeling much better about Cal's visit. Nan was only trying to help expand our search team. All the flirty stuff was just her way of adding a bit of dramatic flair, but not really the point. "Thank you, Brock—I mean, Cal. That would be really nice, if you're sure you don't mind."

A curtain rustled in the window, and I saw Nan poke her head into view wearing a giant, naughty grin. I, of course, shot her a death glare. Whether or not her heart was in the right place, sometimes her tongue ran away with her. Sometimes I needed to put my foot down, to remind her that meddling with my life wasn't an appropriate—or appreciated—hobby.

Less than a minute later, Nan flung the front door open and pushed her way between us on the porch. "Did I hear you're going to help us search for our sweet missing kitty?" she cooed, batting eyelashes so long I had to wonder if she'd applied fake lashes—or at least several extra coats of mascara.

"Yes, of course," Cal answered, fixing her with a charming smile. I don't think I'd ever met a single person who didn't immediately adore my nan. It was kind of like her own personal superpower.

"Oh, goodie," she cried. "Angie and I need all the help we can get. We are so worried about our little guy."

"Think nothing of it. It's my pleasure," Cal assured us both just as another vehicle pulled up the driveway and stopped in front of our manor house.

Well, Nan and I were certainly popular this morning. I, of course, recognized the dusty black sedan right away. Sure enough, Charles parked quickly and then hurried over to join us on the porch.

"Nan," he cried. "I came as soon as I got your text. Is everything okay?"

Nan floated over to give him a hug hello, smiling at me as she did. Would every eligible bachelor in Blueberry Bay show up at my house this morning? Ugh, I sure hoped not.

Exactly two thoughts flittered through my mind then as the four of us stood awkwardly together on the porch.

One, I definitely regretted teaching my grandmother how to text.

And two, I was going to kill her.

CHAPTER SEVEN

E veryone except for Nan seemed a bit uncomfortable during our impromptu porch meeting. This was made incredibly clear by the fact that no one said anything for several moments.

"Are you okay?" Charles finally asked Nan again, seeing as she hadn't given him a clear answer upon his arrival. "Your text worried me."

"Oh. I'm fine, dear," she responded with a grandmotherly grin. "I'm just so worried about Octo-Cat. You know how it is. He didn't come home last night, and poor Angie is sick with worry, too. We could both really use some help and a friend through this trying time."

Well, that at least was true. I pumped my head in agreement. "Sorry to call you out of work," I muttered by way of apology.

"That's okay," Charles said, placing a hand on my shoulder and giving it a quick squeeze. "This is important."

Cal shifted his weight between his feet and took a small step back. "Hi, Charles," he muttered.

"Brock," the other man said, clamping a hand on his shoulder now, too. "Good to see you, man."

Things seemed more than a little awkward between them,

despite the fact that Charles had gotten Cal acquitted of a double murder charge not too long ago and had been dating Cal's twin sister for the past several months to boot.

Was the sister thing what made them so tense around each other? And if so, might that mean trouble in paradise? Most importantly, though, why was I so darned happy about that possibility? I needed to quit daydreaming and get back to focusing on finding my lost fur friend.

"I do have a bit of bad news, unfortunately," Charles said just then, looking from me to Nan and back again. "I exchanged some emails first thing this morning, and needless to say, we can't get a continuance for the arbitration."

"Which means?" Nan prompted as she rolled her hand at the wrist impatiently.

Charles sighed. "We need to find Octo-Cat and find him fast. That's the only way we'll be able to contest, and believe me, you'll want to contest."

"Wait," Cal said as he lifted his hands in apparent confusion. "The cat is the one who needs to go to court. Not the two of you?"

"The cat," Charles informed him, "is the beneficiary, so yes, he does need to be present."

Cal grabbed my hand and gave it a friendly squeeze, then said, "Don't worry, Angie. I'm sure we'll find him today, and if we don't, how hard could it be to find a lookalike to take to court in a pinch?"

My jaw dropped open, and I was too agitated to speak. I wanted to rip my hand away from anyone who would suggest such an awful solution to our problems.

Then Cal burst out laughing. "Sorry, just trying to lighten the mood with a bit of humor. I guess that joke flopped and flopped bad."

"It was a big ol' belly flop," Nan told him with a wink. "Why don't you come with me, Cal? We can buddy up for the search. Charles, are you fine escorting Angie?"

I saved my breath rather than try to explain to Nan that I didn't need an escort for this—or really anything else. It would be nice to spend some time with Charles, to have a partner in the search, especially since I was now losing hope at a depressingly rapid clip.

"We can pick up where we left off last night, or at least by doing what we talked about. Come with me," Charles said, motioning for me to follow him toward the woods.

The woods!

"Just a second," I called, darting back into the house and straight past Nan and Cal as I dashed toward the pantry. I found an unopened jar of peanut butter and grabbed it for my new squirrel informant, Maple, making sure to hide it from view as I passed Cal. No need to invite any awkward questions if they could just as easily be avoided.

"Have a craving?" Charles asked with a sarcastic smile when I returned to him.

Heat flooded my cheeks, but then I remembered that Charles knew everything, and I had absolutely nothing to be embarrassed about. "Let's just say I owe a squirrel a favor," I said, making a clicking noise as we fell into step beside one another.

"A squirrel, huh? Did he have any good leads for you?" He asked this as if it were a completely normal and rational development, and I loved him for it.

"*She*, and not really. But I've asked her to be my eyes and ears in the forest, provided she stops thinking about peanut butter long enough to pay attention to anything else."

Charles chuckled. "Maybe we need to find you a different animal helper. Who do you think would be good at playing detective?" He raised his hand to his chin and rubbed it while making a funny face. He even took on a fake British accent as he ran through the possibilities.

"How about a bird, darling? Or a deer, my dear? Ooh, maybe a mountain lion!" He lost his phony accent on that last one, but I was still ridiculously charmed by him.

"Ha, ha," I said, willing my heart to stop beating so hard against my rib cage.

Charles bumped his shoulder into mine and sent that poor, overworked organ of mine galloping off at full speed again. "No, really. Who should we be looking for?"

"Well, the birds won't talk to me. Way too skittish," I informed him, still very much aware of how closely we walked beside each other. "I'm not sure what else is in the forest, and I've never talked to any of them before, so I just really don't know."

"C'mon," he said, extending his hand to me as we reached the edge of the tree line. "Let's go find out."

My pulse quickened as I took his hand. I knew he was just being gentlemanly, but at the same time, I'd been carrying a bit of a torch for the guy for the past several months. He didn't seem to have the slightest clue I felt how I did, given that he had a girlfriend and I was the one with the ace sleuthing skills.

But still. Still! My heart whomped wildly as I searched the trees and ground for any animal who might be willing to talk to us.

"Let's go deeper," Charles said, tugging me along.

"I've heard there are bears here if we go deep enough." A shiver ran through me as I imagined coming face-to-face with the most fearsome predator in all of Blueberry Bay. For some reason, bears didn't strike me as the type to talk through their problems—especially not with a meddlesome human such as myself.

"I ain't afraid of no bears," Charles said in a sing-song voice. "Boy Scouts taught me how to take care of that."

I couldn't hold back the laugh that bubbled to the surface. "Ran into lots of bears in California, did you?"

"Tons," he confirmed, giving my hand a quick, playful squeeze.

A twig snapped several feet away, and our eyes both zoomed to the location. A light brown doe stood ramrod straight and perfectly still, her dark eyes boring into mine. I could feel her fear, sense the internal debate that raged within her as she tried to decide whether it would be better to stay frozen or make a run for it.

"We're not going to hurt you," I whispered evenly, but that was enough to send her zigzagging through the trees and out of our view.

"I won't hurt you!" I yelled after her. "I won't hurt any of you. Please won't somebody talk to me?"

Another twig snapped nearby. The leaves rustled under the weight of some kind of creature approaching us quickly from behind.

Charles stretched his arms out and blocked me with his body in a move so sudden it almost seemed as if he hadn't needed to think about it at all.

"Are you sure you're not afraid of bears?" I asked, trying to lighten the mood even though I was still more than a little frightened myself. I'd been caught off guard in these woods before, and a strange man had grabbed hold of my arms and covered my mouth. Obviously, I'd lived to tell the tale, but I didn't trust my chances if Charles and I really did run into the infamous Blueberry Bay bears.

Everything fell quiet.

Charles and I both waited in silence.

And then a blur of brown burst into view.

"Is that my peanut butter?" Maple squeaked, jumping from tree to tree in excitement and leaving me to wonder how one little squirrel had managed to make so much noise.

"Yes, it's yours," I said, squatting down to offer the jar. "But first I want to know what you found out for me."

Maple bolted toward me, stopping just short of my knees. "About what?"

"Um. About my missing cat?"

"Your cat is missing. Oh, no!"

I hoped squirrels weren't good at reading human emotions, because my disappointment was most definitely evident in that moment. Had Maple really forgotten everything we'd talked about already?

"Here," I said with a sigh as I unscrewed the cap of the peanut butter and handed the jar to the forgetful little squirrel. "Take it. It's yours."

Charles and I both watched as Maple pushed the peanut butter onto its side and rolled it away with a series of euphoric squeaks and shouts.

"C'mon," I said. "I don't think we're going to find what we're looking for out here."

I hated to admit defeat, but I also hated wasting time when Octo-Cat needed me. What was the point of explaining the situation to Maple when she would just forget again the second we said goodbye?

Maybe I should try to find that buck. If it meant getting my cat back, then it would be worth the risk…

CHAPTER EIGHT

"Back so soon?" Nan asked when Charles and I trudged into the house an hour after departing. Even our brief outing, however, had seemed to take forever. Charles had insisted we give our forest investigation a solid effort before calling it a total bust. But even he could see we weren't making any progress, despite the fact he couldn't talk with the animals himself.

"Yeah," I grumbled, kicking my shoes off by the door. "We accomplished absolutely nothing. How'd you guys fare?"

"I sent Cal home," Nan said with a dramatic sigh, anger flitting across her normally controlled features. "He lost at least ten points in my book when he suggested we find an Octo-doppelgänger. Talk about a terrible idea!"

Well, I couldn't disagree with her there. Joke or not, what Cal had said hurt us both, and it would have enraged Octo-Cat had he been around to hear it.

Nan now sat alone in the living room with a giant sheet of poster board sprawled across the floor in front of her. A row of colorful Sharpie markers lay nearby, and she clutched an angry-looking red one tightly in her hand.

"What are you doing?" Charles asked, moving in for a closer look.

"And where did you get all these crafting supplies?" I added as I trudged along after him.

Nan kept her attention on the spread before her as she explained, "I always keep a stash nearby. You never know when you're going to need to papier-mâché or pottery wheel your way out of a disaster."

"Oh, yeah. Well, of course," I said, making sure Charles caught my giant eyeroll. I loved Nan dearly, but sometimes her priorities seemed a bit out of whack—like deciding to play matchmaker when we had a missing cat to find.

She lowered the marker to the bright yellow poster board and began to write while she mumbled, "I'm gathering all the facts we have so far in one place and all our suspicions, too. Consider this poster board command central. Now, look here. Red is for the things we know for sure. Blue is for the things we aren't quite sure of yet."

"And black?" Charles asked as he reached for the last marker.

"Black are ideas we've already eliminated. Things we know for sure aren't true," Nan said, bobbing her head as she continued to write in large, looping letters, then stopped to yank the Sharpie away from Charles. "That's mine, thank you very much."

"Nan…" I warned. Even though she had raised me, sometimes I felt like the mom in our relationship.

Charles just laughed it off. When he'd finished, we both stood in silence watching as Nan completed her project.

"Okay, kids. It's time to get serious here," Nan said a few minutes later after she'd finished making her list and recapped the final marker.

"What do we know so far?" I asked. The poster board had remained depressingly light on text, showing just how far we had yet to go.

Nan straightened up tall and folded her hands in her lap. "Octo-Cat is missing. *Fact*," she began. "He disappeared between the hours of ten and one yesterday. *Fact.* He may have been taken against his will. *Suspicion.* A letter also arrived yesterday announcing the arbitration thingy. *Fact.* It could be related. *Suspicion.*"

"I don't see any black," I said, doing my best to read Nan's teeny tiny handwriting on the bright poster board but coming up short. "What have we been able to rule out?"

"Nothing yet," she announced with a frown. She spun the black marker between her fingers, and I could tell she desperately wanted to use it for something.

"Chin up," Charles said, gracing us both with a mega-watt albeit super-fake smile. "We're making progress. Even if it feels slow."

"Oh, let's make a list of all the places we've checked," Nan shouted with glee and began to push herself up off the floor.

I placed a hand on her shoulder and shook my head. "You already gave that to me this morning with your note. Remember?"

"Yes, but it's not on the poster board with all the other case info yet," she moaned.

"Hang tight. I'll go get it for you." I decided to just go with whatever Nan wanted in this case. At least she was getting us organized. All I'd done so far was go in circles around the forest, making myself both dizzy and frustrated in the process. I was also down one jar of peanut butter.

After retrieving the note from the kitchen, I read Nan the list of places she'd checked last night. She chose a green marker to note the places we'd already explored. Finally, the poster board began to look a little fuller, although I suppose that wasn't exactly a good thing. It meant we were running out of options.

"We'll find him," Charles assured everyone for what felt like the hundredth time that morning, and while I appreciated his optimism, I also kind of wished he'd just keep quiet already.

"Did you ask the neighbors?" he asked us.

Nan clucked her tongue. "Of course we asked the neighbors. That was the first thing we did yesterday afternoon."

"Well, what about—?" Charles began, but was cut off by the unexpected buzz of our electronic cat door lifting open in the nearby foyer.

Could it really be? Had he come home all on his own?

"Octo-Cat!" I cried, pushing myself to my feet and stumbling as fast as I could toward the door. His cat door had been programmed to open whenever it sensed the little chip on his collar, which meant it could only be Octo-Cat trotting through the door now. I began to cry softly as tears of relief pricked at my eyes.

Maybe he had just stayed out too late, or perhaps he'd strayed too far and then had a hard time finding home again. Oh, he had some major explaining to do, that kitty boy of mine.

I thrust a hand on my hip as I took the last few steps toward the door, ready to go full-on angry pet parent on his furry behind.

I turned the corner, and sure enough, the first thing I saw was that familiar striped tail of his. It seemed puffier than usual, which meant that he was also upset and scared.

Next I spotted a pair of fat gray haunches, which definitely did not match my brown tabby's fur. That's when I realized it wasn't Octo-Cat making his triumphant return. No. Instead, we had an imposter.

But how? How could it have possibly gotten inside without the special collar that interfaced with the pet door?

I was still puzzling over this when the creature turned around and stared at me from deep, masked eyes. A raccoon!

In one hand, he held Octo-Cat's broken collar and in the other an empty can of Fancy Feast. Where had this intruder come from, and why did he have my cat's things?

"You have some serious explaining to do!" I shouted, realizing too late that my anger may cause him to flee. Despite my anger and fear in that moment, this raccoon was our best lead. I had to play nice, even though I wanted to keep screaming until I got the answers I craved.

The raccoon wasn't afraid of me in the slightest. He held tight to both items and then stood on his hind legs, tilting his head to the side as he studied me. "Did you just talk?" he asked with a quizzical expression.

A brief moment of silence passed between us. I could feel Nan and Charles at my back, but neither said anything as the three of us stared the trespasser down.

Suddenly, our raccoon visitor burst out laughing in a high-pitched, squeaky giggle that immediately grated on my nerves. "Aww, you can talk! That's so cute!"

I hated to think what might have happened next had Nan and Charles not each grabbed one of my arms and held me back. It would have been a very low moment, indeed, if I'd gotten into a fight with a raccoon—especially since I was pretty sure that I would have lost.

CHAPTER NINE

I rounded on the beady-eyed intruder. Perhaps I should have been afraid of rabies or some other random infection, but in that moment I was just too angry to care about anything other than finding some answers. "Why do you have my cat's collar?" I demanded, unwilling to back down.

The raccoon bared his teeth, then took far longer than I would have liked in deciding whether he wanted to talk to me or to bite me.

"Octavius Maxwell Ricardo Edmund Frederick Fulton is his own animal," he said at last, enunciating each word carefully. "He can't be owned by you or anyone else."

Whatever answer I'd expected, it had most definitely not been this. "You kn-n-now him?" I stuttered, dropping to my knees so that I could look the animal in the eye.

He laughed nervously, all his bluster having disappeared in an instant. "Know him? No! I wish I knew him! Even to be standing in his home right now is such a tremendous honor. I can't even begin to—"

"You broke in," I snapped at him in frustration. "There's no honor in that."

The raccoon hung his head and wept. I couldn't tell whether his tears were fake, but this ring-tailed bandit definitely gave both Nan and Octo-Cat a run for their money in the drama department. No matter what I did or where I went, I was always surrounded by thespians.

"Enough blubbering," I blurted out, more than ready to get on with it. "Tell me who you are and why you're here. Are you some kind of weird Octo-Cat fanboy?"

"He prefers his full name, I'll have you know," the raccoon actually had the audacity to correct me. "And I'm not just some random fanboy." He shook his head adamantly, then bared his teeth again in a creepy smile that sent me stumbling backward to put a bit of distance between us. "I'm his biggest fan. Numero uno, baby!"

There weren't many moments in my life when I'd done an actual facepalm. This, however, was one of them. "I didn't know house cats could have fans," I admitted, still in utter disbelief.

The raccoon shot forward and positioned his face mere inches from mine as he cried, "He's not just any house cat, lady! He is the ultimate in animal sophistication."

Okay, it was probably time to move the discussion to finding out whether he had any leads as to where Octo-Cat had gone, but I desperately needed to know how my cat had landed himself such an enthusiastic follower. "Why do you like him so much? How did your, um, fandom get started?"

The raccoon stood higher on his haunches and swept his hand in front of his face theatrically. "It all started one dark and starry night. I was going about my business as usual, spying on some humans, raiding some trash cans, you know, the works. When lo and behold, I found something new and shiny. It caught my eye right away. Not just because it looked valuable, but because the smell… Wow, what an aroma!"

He scooped the empty Fancy Feast can he'd brought in with him up from the floor and held it out to me. "It was the most succulent delicacy I'd ever tasted in all my life, and then to find that each day there was more! Wow, I was the luckiest trash panda in all of Blueberry Bay."

I had to fight hard not to explode with laughter. "Did you just call yourself a tra—you know what? Never mind. Go on."

"Well, naturally, I needed to learn more about from whence this heavenly food had come. So I started to watch. Observe, if you will. And that's when I first saw Octavius. Being the intelligent creature that I am, I realized the food was his and that I was feeding off mere scraps. Made me wonder what other wonderful things he knew about, so I watched some more. Soon I'm learning about Evian and Apple, sun spots, and a million other amazing things. Naturally when I found his collar here, I knew it was the ultimate king piece for my collection. And in I came to see what else I might find or if— for the love of the great raccoon in the sky—I might actually get the chance to meet the great Octavius."

"What's your name?" I asked skeptically. For the first time since Octo-Cat had gone missing, I was actually glad he wasn't around to hear this. I'd always assumed his ego couldn't get any larger… until now.

The raccoon set the empty can of cat food back onto the floor and attempted to place Octo-Cat's collar around his neck. With another off-putting, sharp-toothed smile, he asked, "Would it be too much to ask you to call me Octavius? If I could pick any name that's the one I'd choose. Definitely."

"Yes, definitely way too much." I needed to be firm with this one, else we'd never get anywhere. At least he seemed smart and like he'd remember our conversation after the fact. Perhaps he'd even want to help. "What's your actual name?"

He pouted a lower lip and looked down at his feet. "Pringle."

Okay, that was adorable. So why did he seem embarrassed by it?

"Nice to meet you, Pringle. I'm Angie." I reached out and shook his paw, and the raccoon knew just how to return the friendly gesture. He was definitely smart and definitely familiar with human and cat customs alike.

"So, Pringle. How'd you get a name like that?" I'll be the first to admit this little guy had me enamored—hopeful, too.

"Well, *Angie,*" he began with zero hesitation. "It's a long story, but basically when my mother was carrying me and my littermates,

Pringles were her number one favorite trash snack. Me being the first born, Pringle became my name. Hey, actually it's not that long of a story, after all. There you have it. The end."

I allowed myself a small laugh before regaining my composure and sharing a bit of information I knew my new friend would not like. "Okay, Pringle. Thanks for the back story, but I've got bad news. Our dear Octavius has gone missing. It's been close to twenty-four hours now, and we have no idea where to find him."

The raccoon lifted both of his tiny black hands to his face and gasped. "Octavius, noooo!" he shouted. "You were far too young and perfect to meet such an untimely end." Pringle then fell backward in a mock faint, and I wondered if he might also be watching a bit of television on the sly when he spied on us during the day.

"Hey. No, none of that!" I cried, nudging him until he sat back up. "Not dead! Why do you jump straight to dead?"

Pringle's eyes widened and began to shine with gaiety. "Then he's alive! Our dear Octavius is alive!"

When I nodded my confirmation, he jumped at least a foot in the air and pumped his fist enthusiastically. What an odd little creature.

"Stop jumping to conclusions and just listen, okay?" A smile snaked across my face when I realized exactly how I could get through to the hyperactive raccoon. "Octavius depends on it. Actually, he depends on you."

"You had me at Octavius," he said, taking a bow, although for the life of me, I didn't know why. "And now you have my rapt attention."

I nodded. "Good. Come meet the rest of the Octavius fan club, and we'll catch you up."

"I'm still the president, because I'm the number one fan," he said, eyeing Charles and Nan with a newfound aggression as we approached.

"Of course you are," I assured him. "You are definitely his biggest fan. I don't think any of us are going to challenge you for that honor."

Pringle smirked as if he'd just won some hugely desirable prize.

Charles waved hello to the newest member of our party. Nan held up her poster board, and I caught the raccoon up on everything we knew so far. Could his passion be the key to cracking this case wide open?

Oh, I sure hoped so.

CHAPTER TEN

Pringle paced from one side of the living room to the other. Half the time he walked on his hind legs, and the other half he hobbled along on all fours. The entire time, however, he talked and talked... and talked.

I barely had time to translate for Nan and Charles before he'd cut me off to continue with his monologue.

"Whoever took Octavius, we're going to make him pay. We're going to make him pay big." The raccoon pounded his tiny black fist into his open palm for emphasis. "I won't rest until he's brought home safely. I won't eat a single—Actually, okay, I'm going to have to eat. A raccoon's gotta keep his strength up if he's going to rescue his cat pal from clear and imminent danger."

"Um, excuse me?" I said, raising my hand to draw Pringle's attention my way. "Have you ever even met Octo-Cat?"

The raccoon sighed and heaved his furry shoulders. "Not yet, but I assume you'll introduce me once he's home again, yeah?" His eyes grew wide, and for a brief moment he stopped pacing and started shaking instead. I assumed it was with excitement.

Although I was tempted to reach out and pet him, I didn't know how he'd take to such an intimate gesture. "I can promise he'd love nothing more than to meet the president of his own personal fan club," I said with a huge grin. "Thank you for being so willing to help us with this."

Pringle stretched on his tiptoes and spread his arms out wide as he boomed, "Of course. This is what I was put on this earth to do. Octavius is a legend, but he's not yet ready to be a memory. He must live another day to inspire animals both near and far." The raccoon pounded his fist on his chest and then kneeled and bowed his head reverently.

Not knowing what to do, I patted him between the ears and said, "Thank you for your service."

He lifted his head but kept his fist held firmly to his chest. "It is an honor to serve him. What is my first assignment?"

Uh-oh. Had I just unwittingly knighted a trash panda?

I blinked hard at the creature who remained kneeling before me. This whole scene would have been hilarious if I weren't so worried about Octo-Cat.

Pringle cleared his throat. "Lady Angela, my assignment?"

"Oh, oh, yes." It took me a second to snap back to reality. So what if the creature before me was half-medieval knight and half-screaming fanboy? He had pledged his service to finding Octo-Cat. We now shared a passion and a cause. Hope sprung anew as I racked my mind for a list of tasks I could give Pringle to keep him busy.

"I need you to talk with the other animals around the forest. Find out if they saw or heard anything that could be useful. After night falls, come back here and keep an eye on things around the house. If you see anything suspicious, be sure to let us know."

"On my honor." Pringle gave me one last lingering look before racing back out through the cat door and, presumably, setting to work.

"Hopefully he'll be more successful than we were," Charles said, reminding me that I wasn't alone. Sometimes when I got deep into a conversation with an animal, I forgot about the humans nearby.

"If nothing else, at least it will keep him busy," I said with a shrug.

Nan flipped the poster board over and uncapped a purple marker. "Now, dear. I know this won't be easy, but it's time we discussed you a bit more. Or more specifically, who might have it out for you."

A fresh wave of panic bubbled inside me. "Do you think someone kidnapped Octo-Cat to get back at me?"

"Well, it's not like he had any enemies of his own, so I guess it's a possibility." Charles scooted up to me and wrapped an arm around my shoulder. I laid my head on his chest and tried not to feel as if I'd somehow signed my best fur friend's death warrant. When it came right down to it, though, we had no proof he would ever come home again—or that he was even still alive.

"Now, dear. Who hates you most in this world?" Nan asked, completely oblivious to the emotional river that raged within me. She was never one to use a gentle word when a stronger one would do.

Hate, wow. There were people out there who actually hated me. That was, indeed, a tough pill to swallow.

"But also knows you well enough to know that taking your cat would be a huge punishment," Charles added softly.

"Oh, excellent point," Nan said with a giggle. She spied Charles's hand on my shoulder and tossed a wink my way, enjoying this whole mess far too much for my liking.

"Hate's a really strong word," I hedged as I shook free of Charles's arm. Immediately the cold took his place and sent a shiver rushing down my spine.

"It's a strong feeling, too," Nan agreed. "I know it's hard to think about, but I'm almost certain the folks you put in prison aren't too happy with you about that."

I got up and walked across the room, then sank down onto the sofa with a groan. "Okay. First of all, I didn't put them in prison. Their crimes did that. And second, they're *in prison.* How could they have possibly taken Octo-Cat even if they'd wanted to?"

"She's right," Charles told Nan, and they let out matching sighs. It was eerie how well we all knew each other and had even started to pick up some of each other's mannerisms. "We may be working against a two-man operation here."

"Or a two-woman gig. Girls can be bad, too, you know." She seemed to take perverse pride in this observation. Now that was a really messed-up form of girl power.

"That Peter guy who worked with us briefly certainly didn't like you much," Charles added, referring to Bethany's creepy cousin who had worked as a paralegal at our firm. We'd even been forced to share the same desk. I was definitely happy he'd moved down to Georgia, putting a comfortable number of miles between us.

"Yeah, and didn't another fella get fired after you complained about sexual harassment?" Nan quickly interjected. "Brad, was it?"

"Yes and yes, but both those guys were skeezy," I whined. Was my proud feminist grandmother really giving me a hard time about standing up against inappropriate advances? Unbelievable.

"Brad sexually harassed everyone and should have been fired a long time before I finally complained about him. And by the way, I'm not the only one who complained, either. Meanwhile, Peter seemed to have it out for me from day one. Thank goodness they're both gone now."

Nan frowned and fiddled some with her markers. "I'm not trying to upset you. Just trying to help bring our buddy home."

"Look. I can see we're not really getting anywhere with this line of questioning, so let's back it up," Charles said, jumping graciously to my rescue.

"Yes, and Angie seems quite worked up now, too." Nan came to join me on the couch and placed one aged hand on my knee.

"It's not fun making a list of people who despise you," I told them both. It seemed like this day just kept getting worse and worse. "You should try it and see."

"Oh, nobody dislikes me." Nan fluffed her hair and wiggled in her seat. "I'm just a quirky old grandma."

"Uh-huh." I smirked. At least we'd moved on from compiling our Angie's-worst-enemies list.

Charles came over and sat on my other side. "More and more

this looks like it must be tied to Ethel Fulton's estate and somebody who was unhappy about how the inheritance was doled out."

"He's right," Nan said, leaning back into the hard antique cushion. "The timing is too suspect to be anything else."

"And we're sure he didn't just wander off on his own?" Charles raised one eyebrow and waited.

"No way," Nan and I cried in unison.

He pressed his lips in a thin line and made a *harrumph* sound. "Then that narrows our pool considerably. Since Ethel used our firm for her will, I should be able to get a copy. You'll have to catch me up on all the key players and what we know about them so far, though, since this all happened before I moved to town."

"Should we call Officer Bouchard and let him know?" Nan asked. She'd had a crush on this particular member of local law enforcement for close to a year now. Jeez. Between me and Nan, we were crushing on practically everyone in our small town. Not that either of us ever went out on any dates, but still.

Charles shook his head and frowned. "Let him know what? Unfortunately we haven't got any proof."

"You know what that means, then." Nan pressed down hard on my knee and pushed herself back onto her feet. "We need to go find some."

CHAPTER ELEVEN

Nan stayed back at the house while Charles and I headed to the law firm so we could grab a copy of Ethel's will along with a list of its beneficiaries.

"There are like thirty people on this," I said with a sigh as I ran through the lengthy legal document a second time. "How do we know which one took Octo-Cat?"

"Let's make a list of addresses and last known contact info," Charles suggested, pulling up a fresh document on his laptop. "Then we can probably eliminate anyone out of state and take things from there."

"I'm going to see what I can learn about our suspects on social media, too." I fished my phone out of my pocket and waved it between us with a mischievous grin. "People are amazingly transparent when they think nobody is paying attention. Maybe we'll find out who's unhappy about the will or having money problems. Someone's gotta have a clear motive if we dig deep enough."

"I like how your mind works. Have at it," Charles said before turning his full attention toward his computer.

We passed a few hours in this way. I took a page from Nan's book and placed color-coded marks next to each name on the list of beneficiaries, depending on what we learned about that person and how likely it was they might be our catnapper.

"The blue checkmarks are for those people I remember seeing at the will reading," I explained once we'd both completed our research. "Gosh, that feels like it happened forever ago."

My life had changed astronomically since that day. I still remembered coming into the office and getting hounded by Thompson for not having on suitable attire. I borrowed a jacket from my friend Bethany, even though we weren't quite friends yet at that point, then I got electrocuted by the coffee maker, woke up able to speak with Octo-Cat, and—boy—things really escalated from there.

Now I had a talking cat for my best friend, lived in one of the swankiest manor homes in the entire state, and was on the verge of opening up my own private investigation firm.

That is, once I got up the nerve to hand in my resignation notice to Charles.

I swallowed hard and continued walking him through my list of suspects. "The black X means either their profiles are set to private or I couldn't find them. I drew a red circle next to the names of people I thought seemed suspicious or like they could kidnap a cat."

"But almost everyone has a red circle," Charles pointed out with a chuckle that sent a knife straight through me.

"Hey, don't laugh. This is serious." I glowered at him until he quieted down.

"You're right. I'm sorry."

"What did you find?" I asked, hoping desperately that he'd narrowed down the pool a little better than I had.

"Well, only a handful live nearby, so they're probably our most likely suspects." He turned his computer toward me so I could see the list of names and addresses, which appeared to be organized by distance with those closest to us up at the top.

"Great," I said, rising to my feet, ready to go. "Print that out for me, and I'll swing by to check them out now. Wait, actually, I'll just grab a picture real quick."

I picked up my phone and navigated to my camera app, but Charles pushed his laptop lid down with a click.

"No, you won't," he said, keeping his hand firmly on the laptop as he waited for me to back down. Ugh, he was so irritating sometimes. "Whoever took Octo-Cat will definitely recognize you and probably Nan, too."

"So, what?" I demanded, stomping my foot like the overdramatic teenager I once was. "I'm just supposed to do nothing?"

A smile lit up his handsome features, putting me at ease. "I didn't say that. I'll go and check things out myself."

I couldn't help but smile. I loved how he'd taken real ownership in this case, too. "Great, let's go," I said, reaching toward the laptop so I could snag a photo of those addresses.

Charles held up an index finger and wagged it at me. "No, Angie. You're not coming. Trust me with this, okay? I want him back just as much as you do. I'm not going to mess this up. But I do have a court appointment this afternoon, so I'm not going to be able to check out these leads until after work."

I hung my head and tried really hard not to sigh. I knew he was right, but it didn't make the waiting any easier. "Thank you," I murmured at last with great difficulty.

"You're welcome," Charles said. "Now, c'mon, let me take you back home. Maybe Pringle will have discovered something helpful while we were gone."

One could only hope…

Of course, Pringle hadn't found anything worthwhile in my absence and neither had Nan.

"I wonder what Ethel would have thought of all this hullabaloo if she were still alive to see it," Nan drawled over dinner that evening. She'd busied herself by cooking up a storm in the kitchen, so dinner was a strange yet satisfying combination of dim sum, gnocchi, and empanadas.

"You would never kill me to get to my fortune," Nan asked as she bit into a steamy dumpling and trained a wary eye on me. "Would you?"

I dropped my fork and stared at her, slack-jawed. Luckily, I'd just swallowed a mouthful of pasta, otherwise it would have fallen straight down onto the table. The things my nan said sometimes!

"Kidding," she sang with a merry little titter. "Still, though. Poor Ethel. Betrayed by those she loved most, both in life and in death. She only wanted her beloved feline companion to live out the rest of his days in comfort, but that, too, has created difficulty. The old broad just couldn't win."

She shrugged and took another bite, chewing thoughtfully as we sat in silence. I understood why we were talking about the late Ethel Fulton, but it still made me tremendously sad—especially since in some ways, I was living her life now, or at least in her house. To think, even though Ethel had died with lots of money, it was clear she'd been missing some important things in life.

Like love, family, respect.

Nan said nothing more about it, but the woman I'd seen only at her funeral last year remained solidly at the front of my mind. I owed it to her to make sure her cat maintained his lavish lifestyle, that he was brought home safe and sound. So what if other people didn't exactly understand?

I did, and this was my job. It was also something I cared deeply about and would fight to put right again.

Octo-Cat was coming home, no matter what it took.

Thankfully, updates from Charles started coming in via text shortly after we'd finished dinner. He messaged after each visit he made to one of Ethel's heirs. At first his messages came relatively close together since he was visiting those who lived in our own Glendale, but eventually they became fewer and farther between.

I lay in bed with my phone beside me, eagerly awaiting each one.

Until I fell asleep.

I dreamt of the early days with Octo-Cat, back when we lived in that tiny rental he hated and were still finding our way around each other. I revisited all my favorite memories—like giving him his very own iPad and eating grilled shrimp together, the day the paperwork came in and I officially adopted him. We'd lived through so many important moments together and had so many more that were yet to come.

We'd caught killers and thieves. We could catch a catnapper, too.

The happy memories quickly gave way to the scary ones. To high-speed car chases and ominous staircases, visiting a friend in maximum security and staring straight into the eyes of someone who wanted me dead.

A bang sounded from across the room, and I jumped into a sitting position before I'd even had the chance to fully wake up. The image of a shiny pistol flashed behind my eyelids. I'd been threatened by a gun more than once this past year, and—

BANG!

It was coming from the other side of my closed door.

No, it *was* my closed door.

Someone was knocking on it as if their very life depended on me answering and answering fast.

"Nan?" I called as I padded hesitantly over.

"Open up! Open up!" a familiar squeaky voice shouted. "There's been a development."

I flung the door open, and in came Pringle.

He clambered right up onto my bed, blinking hard when I flipped the light switch on. "Ahh, I'm blinded by the light," he said, rubbing at his eyes. "Doesn't that thing have a dimmer?"

"Sorry." I switched off the overhead and turned on my bedside lamp. As I came closer, I noticed that he had a piece of white paper with small colorful blocks pasted on one side.

"Where'd you get that?" I asked, pointing.

"That's what I'm trying to tell you. Someone just slipped this under the front door. I came running, but I wasn't fast enough to see the person's face. Definitely a human, though. Definitely a human. *Here. Take it.*"

My hands shook as I took the paper from Pringle's outstretched paws.

"It's a ransom note," I said in disbelief as I looked over the hasty arrangement of letters that had clearly been cut out from a magazine. "Why go to all this trouble? Why not just type what they wanted to say?"

"Clearly somebody has a flair for the dramatic," Pringle said, baring his teeth and rolling his eyes. "So, what's it say? Huh? Huh?"

I moved the paper closer to the light and read, "You don't belong here. Give up the house, or I kill the cat."

I gasped and dropped the letter as if I'd been burned.

"No way, no way, no way!" Pringle shouted as he jumped on my bed. "Nobody threatens Octavius and gets away with it. What do we do now?"

"I don't know," I answered with a sob. "They didn't give us any directions or tell us a place to send our response."

I'd give them the house if that's what it took, but how? I felt more helpless than ever as I stared into Pringle's dark eyes, praying he had the answer.

CHAPTER TWELVE

"C'mon," I told my raccoon accomplice after several moments of tense silence passed between us. "Let's go get you some Fancy Feast."

I took a picture of the ransom note with my phone and forwarded it to both Charles and Nan, then headed for the pantry to prepare a late-night snack for both me and Pringle. I'd already made it about halfway down the stairs when I realized he wasn't following me.

Instead, Pringle stood at the top of the narrow stairway with giant, glistening tears in his dark eyes. "Fancy Feast? For me?" he crooned.

I smiled at the sweet but bizarre forest creature. "I can also throw in some Evian if that helps to sweeten the deal."

Pringle scampered down the stairs as fast as his four feet could carry him and attached himself to my leg in what I assumed was a grateful hug. "This is the best day of my life," he whispered into my plaid pajama pants. "The very best day."

"Just wait until you meet Octavius," I said with a chuckle, picturing the scene unfold—the look of unadulterated joy on Pringle's face, the likely irritation on my cat's. "I have a feeling he's going to love you," I said anyway. It was true; once Octo-Cat got past the raccoon's enthusiasm, he'd love having someone in his life who appreciated him as much as he appreciated himself.

Pringle stopped in his tracks but quickly started moving again. I absolutely loved how easy it was to make his day. Once I prepared a late-night meal of Fancy Feast and Evian for him—served on disposable dishes rather than Octo-Cat's preferred Lenox set—and grabbed a granola bar for myself, I went to wake Nan with news of the ransom note.

Before I could reach her bedroom, however, my cell phone buzzed in my hand. The call came from a number I didn't recognize, which seemed especially odd this late at night.

Could it be the catnapper calling to talk terms? I'd happily pay whatever he wanted if it meant getting my cat back.

"Hello?" I asked, a quiver of anticipation racing through me.

"Angie, why didn't you call me earlier?" The speaker sounded quite angry, so it took me a moment to place her.

"B-B-Bethany?" I stuttered, finally recognizing my friend's voice. "Where are you?"

"Peter and I made it down to Georgia earlier tonight, and Charles just called to catch me up on everything that happened since we left. First tell me, are you okay?"

"Yeah," I lied for some reason. I'd grown to love Bethany, even though our relationship hadn't always been an easy one. Still, as much as I trusted her, I didn't want her to know how destroyed I was by this latest turn of events. She didn't know my secret, and I planned to keep it that way.

"Do you have any idea who could have wanted to take Octo-Cat?" I asked, my voice shaking.

Bethany didn't hesitate in her response. "Clearly, this has something to do with Ethel's will. Remember how angry everyone was that he got anything at all, let alone that huge trust fund?"

I'd already been thinking along these same lines myself, but there was a part of it that still made absolutely no sense to me. "Yeah, but that was months ago," I added. "Why act on it now?"

She hummed a few beats, then asked, "How long has it been since you moved into Fulton Manor?"

"A couple months," I mumbled as I slipped one of my fingers into my mouth and began to bite at the scraggly fingernail. "Think that has something to do with it? I did get this ransom note that specifically mentions it."

"Of course the house has something to do with it," Bethany exploded after I caught her up. "There's one thing that doesn't quite make sense, though. If the catnapping was supposed to keep you from contesting the arbitration, then why send a ransom note at all? I mean, without Octo-Cat's monthly stipend, you wouldn't be able to afford the house and would have to give it up, anyway. Right?"

I groaned, suddenly feeling like I might pass out. "Thanks for reminding me of just how much is at stake here. But yes, I can't afford my mansion on a part-time paralegal's salary. This isn't House Hunters." My joke fell on deaf ears.

"I'm thinking," Bethany mumbled without giving me even a pity laugh.

"Like thinking you might know who did it?" I chanced. It killed me that I hadn't been able to figure this out yet. Was I missing something big due to my panic? Could my shrewd and logical friend catch something I hadn't been able to?

"Not yet," she answered with a sigh. "But I do know the Fultons a bit better than you do. I may be able to connect some of the dots if I puzzle over this long enough."

"Anything you can do would be very helpful," I said politely. "Thank you, Bethany."

"Hey, I owe you one, anyway." Now she let out a little chuckle. I had no idea what she was talking about, though.

"You do? Why?"

"Um, never mind," she said with another nervous laugh. "Gotta go. Bye!"

Well, that was weird. Bethany was right about one thing, though. The arbitration notice and the ransom note did seem at odds with each other. The note might even establish grounds for delaying the arbitration a bit longer. Could the catnapper master-mind really be so shortsighted?

Charles would know better than me.

I glanced at the tiny digital clock on my phone. It was just past twelve thirty. Since I knew Charles regularly burned the midnight oil, I decided to try giving him a call.

"Hello?" a woman's voice answered coldly.

"Oh, um, Breanne?" I chanced a guess. It gutted me that she had answered his phone at this hour.

"Who else would it be? And why are you calling my boyfriend in the middle of the night. *Hmm?*" Well, apparently, it bothered her just as much that I had reason to call so late at night. Charles was my friend before he was ever her boyfriend, though, and I was willing to bet I knew him better and cared for him more.

"Give me that," I heard Charles say before presumably yanking the phone free of his girlfriend's hands.

"Sorry," I muttered. "I didn't mean to interrupt anything."

Charles sucked air in through his teeth. "You're not interrupting. Breanne just stopped by to say a quick goodnight since we're not going to be able to see each other tomorrow."

Yup, uh-huh. Likely story.

Even though I myself was a twenty-eight-year-old virgin, I knew how the world worked. It made me want to throw up everything in my stomach, but still I understood.

"Charles!" Breanne hissed from the other end of the call. "I haven't got all night to wait around here."

"I've gotta go," my friend said, and he even sounded a little sad about it.

"Bye," I whispered after he'd already disconnected the call.

"Humans are weird," Pringle informed me as he waddled his way over to my side.

"We are," I agreed. "But raccoons are kind of weird, too."

He laughed and used his hands to groom himself following his decadent feast of canned cat food. "You've got that right."

"Do you think he's okay out there?" I asked, not bothering to clarify who I meant.

"Listen, babe. I can't live in a world that doesn't have my boy Octavius in it. You better believe he's okay and that whoever did this is gonna pay—and pay big-time."

I reached over and stroked Pringle's fur. If I closed my eyes, it almost felt like he was my missing friend. Instead of purring, he made a soft chattering noise.

"You know," he said after a while. "I've been thinking that perhaps we should start planning Octavius's welcome home party now. That way we're ready whenever he turns up."

"That's a good idea. Why don't you think it over and then get back to me with what we need?"

"It would be my pleasure." Pringle showed me his toothy, slightly scary smile and then hobbled out through the cat door to begin his preparations.

I clutched the ransom note to my chest and sent up a prayer for Octo-Cat's safe return. There were so many people—and animals— who loved him, who missed him, and needed him home.

CHAPTER THIRTEEN

I couldn't sleep for the rest of that night. Instead, I hung out in the living room with all the lights off as I watched the yard, hoping our mystery ransom note writer might make a second appearance.

I must have nodded off at some point, because the next thing I knew, Nan was pressing a warm mug of coffee into my hands and telling me to "Sit up and catch me up on whatever it is I missed."

"What? Oh." I struggled to straighten myself on the stiff couch, but everything hurt. If the catnapper had made another appearance last night, then I'd surely missed it. Darn me and my biorhythms.

"Someone slipped this under the door," I informed Nan after finding the letter on the floor near my feet and handing it to her.

She clucked her tongue and shook her head. "Well, someone isn't playing very fair. Are they?"

Suddenly, I couldn't keep it in any longer. I'd tried so hard to be strong, and for what? My stiff upper lip wasn't bringing Octo-Cat home.

And so I cried.

Nan took my coffee mug away and set it on the end table, then wrapped me in a hug and made soft shushing noises.

"Do you think they'd really do what they're threatening?" I sobbed, letting all my worry and anxiety overtake me at last. "That they'd kill Octo-Cat?"

Nan stroked my hair as she spoke. Her words came out soft but determined, true. "In my many years on this earth, I've learned one very important lesson, and I've learned it more than once, I'm afraid."

She sucked in a deep breath, and I pulled away from her embrace so we now sat face-to-face.

"Crazy people will do anything if they think it will help them reach their crazy goals," she said sagely.

This was not the answer I'd wanted to hear.

Nan reached forward and brushed her wrinkled fingers against my cheek, picking up a tear on one of her fingertips. "I've learned another thing, too. People will do anything to save their own hides. And I bet that goes for cats, too. Don't count that cat of ours out yet. He's a survivor."

"Yeah, and he still has four lives left. At least according to him," I added with a sad chuckle, pressing my face against her soft sweater and allowing it to offer some measure of comfort in this painful moment.

"That he does," Nan said as she squeezed me with surprising strength. One day I endeavored to be as fit as my nan. Just maybe not today. "So what's the plan? What do we do next?"

I'd had a lot of time to think about our next steps as I staked out the living room last night. Ultimately, I realized that even if the forest animals didn't know what had happened to Octo-Cat, they might still be our best chance of finding him again. Whoever had taken him probably didn't know I could speak with animals, so they wouldn't be on the lookout for my special crew of furry helpers.

"I know that look," Nan said with a huge, relieved grin. "You already have it all worked out. So go ahead. Catch your dear old nan up."

"I haven't worked everything out yet, but I do have a pretty good idea," I said, twisting my back to try to rid it of the kinks I'd developed last night. "C'mon, I'll tell you all together."

We both slipped on shoes and charged out of the house toward the forest. Nan didn't even question it. Perhaps a part of her already knew what I'd decided.

Maple found us as soon as we reached the tree line. "Hey, it's the peanut butter lady!" she cried from her perch on a low tree branch. "Hi, peanut butter lady!"

I bit my lip and widened my eyes, then exchanged a look with Nan while waiting for Maple to calm down enough to talk to her.

"Hi, Maple," I said with a quick, friendly wave. "My name's Angie by the way. You know, in case you forgot. Have you seen Pringle around this morning?"

Her little squirrel nose twitched and then she hopped onto another nearby tree branch. "Pringle!" she screamed. "The peanut butter lady needs you! Maybe she has more peanut butter to give us."

Maple raced back toward the thick tree trunk and scampered down to the ground at lightning speed. "Do you have more peanut butter?" she asked, pushing both hands down onto my shoe again and again, almost like she was performing CPR on my toes.

"I might," I answered in a sing-song voice. "But first bring me Pringle, please."

"Roger that!" Maple bounded into the woods, leaving me and Nan waiting at the edge of the forest.

"What did that cute critter say?" Nan whispered once Maple was out of view.

I chuckled. Despite her faults, Maple was growing on me as well. If she actually managed to carry out this plan and help us get Octo-Cat back, then I'd make sure I hooked her up with free peanut butter for life. "She wants peanut butter," I explained, "and everything she says pretty much traces back to that one thing."

Nan gasped affectionately. "Oh, then why didn't we bring some with us?"

I shook my head and kept my eyes focused on the trees before us. "Believe me, I've already made that mistake once. As soon as she has her peanut butter, she forgets everything else in the world. I need her to focus long enough to help with our plan. She can have her treat after."

Sure enough, Maple appeared again and zipped past us, running back toward the house. "Be right back!" she cried in an excited squeak.

We watched as Maple approached our front porch and then stopped right in front of it. A big gray fluffball climbed out from underneath and blinked in the sunlight.

"I didn't realize he lived so close to us," Nan said as we both watched the wily squirrel lead the dazed raccoon over to us.

"Neither did I," I grumbled. He must have chewed a hole somewhere to get under there, and I was not happy about the unexpected damage to my already hard-to-maintain house.

"Blessed morning, Lady Angela," Pringle crooned once he and Maple had made their way back to us. So we were still doing the whole medieval thing. Okay.

Even though I preferred reading mysteries and true crime, I'd worked my way through enough fantasy novels to emulate his grandiose speaking patterns.

"And good morrow to you, Sir Pringle." I paused and gave a quick curtsy. Oh, brother. "We come to you today with a most noble quest."

"Why is the peanut butter lady talking all funny?" Maple squeaked but was quickly shushed by the raccoon who was still doing his best to remain in character.

"Yes. Octavius." Pringle confirmed his understanding with a nod.

"It's time we brought him home. Are you and your squire up to the task?" I shifted my gaze toward Maple. As flighty as the little squirrel had proven to be, I was hoping Pringle could do a good job keeping her in line. We'd need both animals to carry out my plan.

"Might I choose my own squire?" Pringle asked with a faltering grin. I couldn't say I blamed him. The raccoon appeared to be of near human intelligence, while the squirrel… well… She sure was cute!

"Goodly Maple will serve you well," I said with a curt nod, then brought one hand up to my mouth and whispered, "Besides, I happen to know she'll do anything for peanut butter."

The squirrel's ears perked up at this, but she remained blessedly quiet.

Pringle bowed his head, whether in defeat or humble acquiescence I couldn't quite say. But he said, "Then reveal your plan to us, and we shall make it so."

Okay, it was show time.

Let's hope my harebrained plan was enough to bring our boy home safe.

CHAPTER FOURTEEN

N an and I sat down cross-legged in the grass, and the two animals settled down across from us.

"Okay, here's what I'm thinking…" I said, then launched into a winded explanation of my new plan.

"Oh, we should get a pet GPS tracker," Nan added. "I've heard, uh, good things about them." She beamed at me as if I'd just crowned her Ms. Maine. Weird.

"Sure, we can pick one of those up this afternoon," I conceded. It was a good suggestion, but also pretty high tech for a woman who'd only just begun to send and receive text messages.

"Also get some peanut butter while you're out," Maple suggested rather unhelpfully.

"First results, then rewards," Pringle scolded his squirrel squire. Yup, this raccoon was definitely a keeper.

I reached out and gave him a high five, and thanks to his constant human surveillance, Pringle knew just what to do. He may have worshipped Octo-Cat, but he clearly knew more than the idol of his affections.

"That's right," I said, exchanging my goofy grin for a granite jaw and narrowed eyes. "Nothing is more important than bringing Octo-Cat home. Nothing. Not even peanut butter."

Maple gasped.

Pringle cheered.

Nan looked confused but still quite enthusiastic. "What's my role in all this, dear?" she asked, once everyone had quieted again.

This was the tough part. I didn't technically need Nan to carry out my plan, but I knew better than to exclude her.

"You'll keep running command central, and you can help me stay awake tonight, too. Also wardrobe. You're definitely in charge of wardrobe."

She appeared pleased by this. "I'll make cocoa and call the guys."

Ugh, not this again. Why couldn't she have become obsessed with my lack of a love life some other time? It's not as if I were newly single. It had always just been me against the world.

I shook my head emphatically. "The guys? *No.* We don't need Cal and Charles for this."

Nan elbowed me in the ribs. "They're nice distractions, though. Eh?"

I just rolled my eyes rather than dignify her ill-timed match-making efforts with a response. "Does everyone understand what they need to do?"

"Yes," Nan and Pringle said in unison. Both looked ready for action.

Maple, however, raised her tiny brown hand. "Um, I forgot," she squeaked meekly.

"It's okay, kid. Come with me and I'll catch you up." Pringle stood on all fours and motioned for the squirrel to follow him back to his under-porch apartment. It looked like we were done playing knights of the round table now—and for that, I was very thankful, indeed.

"I do love a good stakeout," Nan confided in me as we made our way back to the house. "You get the GPS tracker, and I'll head to the supermarket to pick up some snacks and drinks for our little get-together tonight."

I stopped walking and stared at my grandmother. "Are you really going to invite the guys? This isn't exactly a social event. At least it shouldn't be."

Nan traced her way back to me and wrapped me in a hug. "I know that, dear, but it helps to have good friends by your side when the going gets tough."

Well, I couldn't exactly argue with her there. "Okay," I said, hoping I wouldn't be too embarrassed by whatever she had planned for the evening.

Then again, this was Nan we were dealing with…

Of course I was going to be embarrassed.

Our stakeout party began at ten that night. Pringle had explained the plan to Maple at least a couple dozen times, and they'd even run test drills both with and without the pet GPS.

Charles and Cal came over right at ten, taking care to hide their vehicles around back. Our entire plan hinged on the ransom note writer coming back that night, and we needed him to assume that the house lay quiet and empty, which meant our party was now taking place in the pitch dark without even a candle to light the room.

We kept our voices low, too, as we whispered and conversed with each other. The whole thing was strangely intimate. We all wore comfortable black sweats—provided by Nan, of course—and sipped warm thermoses of hot cocoa—also provided by Nan.

"Are you sure the person is going to come back tonight?" Cal asked from my left.

"He has to, since he didn't leave any way for Angie to get in touch," Charles answered from my right.

They both sat close enough for me to feel their body heat as it crashed into mine. It didn't escape my notice that these were the two most handsome men I knew now—or had ever known, really. One had brains for days while the other was all brawn. Both had huge hearts, but there in the dark, without their good looks to distract me, I knew there was only one man my heart craved.

And he was the one who was already taken.

Because that's how my life worked. Darn.

"Are you nervous?" Charles whispered in my ear.

"More excited than nervous," I answered, wondering if he felt little zips of electricity jump between us, too.

His phone buzzed in his pocket. We were so close that I felt the vibrations, too. "It's Breanne," he said, pushing a button to send the call straight to voicemail.

A small, petty part inside me did a cartwheel. He was choosing me over her. At least for this. At least for right now.

Around eleven thirty, a sound from outside drew everyone's attention toward the window.

"*Shhh,*" I reminded them all. "We have to hang back, stay out of sight, and trust in the plan now."

"Yes, the plan will set us free," Nan whisper-yelled.

Poor Cal still didn't know I could talk to animals. He thought the plan involved high-tech video cameras and a sophisticated booby trap. Little did he know that one nocturnal raccoon was watching carefully from his spot beneath the porch, and one forgetful but lithe squirrel was already equipped with a GPS and ready to hurl herself into our mysterious catnapper's car the moment the raccoon gave the okay.

Sure enough, a few minutes later, Pringle charged through the cat door to alert us that the plan was underway.

"C'mon, Cal. Why don't you help me in the kitchen?" Nan guided him away before he could set sights on the newly arrived raccoon visitor holding a second ransom note between his paws.

"Good work, Pringle." I grabbed the note and patted him on the head, then Charles and I burst out into the night. We'd already agreed that he would drive, and I'd navigate by following the tiny tracking dot attached to Maple, who had already stowed away in the car and was now being driven to who knew where.

As curious as I was, I didn't even glance at the new ransom note. Instead, I focused on following that blinking dot, hoping it would take us to Octo-Cat and end this whole terrible ordeal once and for all.

Charles drove effortlessly as I called out each turn. We weren't far behind the catnapper now. Soon the three of us would come face-to-face, and I'd be able to demand answers to my many, many questions.

"This is weird," Charles muttered as we pulled into a sleepy suburb. "I know someone who lives here."

"Yeah, well, Glendale is a pretty small town. Most of us do," I said, staring at the phone so that I wouldn't miss a single beat.

"Charles," I shouted in excitement. "The dot stopped!"

This was it. We were getting our boy back, and we were getting him back now.

"Where?" he asked, a darkness I didn't understand overtaking his features.

"Just a few driveways ahead. Looks like it's the—"

"Yellow Cape Cod?" he asked at the same time he pulled into the driveway and transitioned us to park.

"Yeah, how'd you know?" I asked in shock. Was he just a good guesser, or—?

"This is Breanne's house," he revealed with a low growl from deep in his throat.

Uh-oh.

CHAPTER FIFTEEN

I jumped out of the car before Charles even had time to put it fully in park. I caught up with the red-headed realtor on her porch step and yanked on her purse strap until she was finally forced to turn around and face me. "Where's my cat, you…? You… You… *Breanne!*"

"Don't touch me," she snapped back, foisting her designer purse from my grip.

Oh, I wanted to do a whole lot more than touch her. I wasn't really a slapper, but I would have happily ground her expensive, showy purse into the mud. I only held back due to the urgent need to get to my cat. Was he inside? Had Breanne had him this whole time? So many questions.

"Where is he?" I boomed, taking great satisfaction in how rattled my nemesis looked in that moment. If I kept pushing, she'd crack, easy. "Give him to me right now and nobody gets hurt."

She took a step back and pressed herself against the door. "What are you talking about?" she ground out, looking at me as if I'd gone crazy even though all of this was most definitely her fault and not mine.

I took a step closer and got right in her face, so close I could smell her cloying perfume. Gross. "Don't play dumb. I know it's you who's been slipping ransom notes under my door. We followed you here, too. Didn't we, Charles?" I turned back toward my friend, who remained standing by his car, seemingly unable to speak.

"Let me in!" I screamed. "Let me in right now!"

But Breanne stood firm with both arms crossed over her chest. "No. Go away!"

Thankfully, Charles finally snapped out of whatever funk he was in and marched right over, then stepped around us and pushed the door open.

"How could you?" he asked his horrible, no-good girlfriend, but I didn't stick around to hear her answer.

Once inside, I began to shout for my cat at the top of my lungs. But even after tearing through the entire house, I still couldn't find him. "Octo-Cat! Octo-Cat! Are you here? Come out! It's safe!"

When no answer came, I rounded on Breanne once more. "Where is he? Why did you take him? How could you?"

"I don't have your stupid cat, and I don't owe you anything," she answered with a sniff and looked away, almost as if she might feel a little guilty. Yeah, right. I was most definitely not buying that.

"I think you owe me some answers, though," Charles interjected. "Did you really steal Angie's cat and send her threatening letters? Why would you do that?"

"You both need to calm down," she muttered through clenched teeth. "I don't have the cat. Okay?"

"Sorry. I'm not buying it. You delivered the letters. We caught you in the act," I exploded.

Breanne narrowed her gaze, looking past Charles so she could focus all of her venom and hostility right on me. "Fine. I'll admit it. That was me. But I'm not the one who wrote them."

"Who did? Stop stalling, and tell me what you know," I demanded. Why wouldn't she just come out with it already? It's not like either of us treasured spending time together, and this was serious.

Breanne shook her head. "I don't know." She took a step back when Charles stepped back so that we now stood side-by-side. Now we were united against her, and that seemed to break her. Apparently, she'd expected him to take her side in all this.

"How could you not know?" I couldn't see Charles's face as he spoke, but his disappointment came out loud and clear. "Why would you ever agree to be a part of this? And then to not get all the answers?" He cleared his throat before continuing. "I thought you were smarter than that, Bree. Kinder, too."

"I didn't," I spat.

Breanne had never liked me, and I'd never liked her. I wasn't surprised she'd want to hurt me, but it did startle me that she was involved in this terrible thing. Breanne had absolutely no link to Ethel Fulton's estate, so why would she even get involved in the first place?

"It's not a big deal," Bree cried. "So, seriously, calm down. You know my income has been down ever since my brother was branded a murderer. So when an anonymous client turned up and promised me a big commission in my future plus a generous cash infusion now, how could I say no? It's not like I'm hurting anyone. We were just trying to spook you out of that house of yours."

"You threatened to kill my cat!" I shook with rage now that I had someone to blame but still had zero idea where my cat might be.

"No, I didn't do that. I didn't write the letters. And seriously, who would kill a cat? That's taking things a little too far." She seemed to be losing steam by the minute but still wouldn't admit she'd done a single thing wrong.

"But extortion is just fine," Charles grumbled as he narrowed his eyes at Breanne. "Really, Bree. I thought I knew you."

"You do know me, which is why I thought you'd understand," she pleaded. "You know how hard things have been lately."

"But you're working through that," he argued. "Honest work. Not blackmail and threats." Despite my anger, it struck me as a bit funny that Charles was berating his girlfriend for blackmailing me when he'd done the same thing to get my help on a difficult case. Granted, he never would have actually hurt me. Breanne, on the other hand...

"No," she insisted. "I'm trying to, but not succeeding. And you know why? Everyone thinks my brother's this monster, even after he was acquitted, and it's all her fault." She raised a shaky finger toward me. If looks could kill…

Charles put his hand on my shoulder. "She helped me get him acquitted. How have you conveniently forgotten that little part of the story?"

Breanne shrugged. "Her mother, though. That news anchor woman. She's the one who convinced all of Blueberry Bay that Brock was guilty, and even after he was proven innocent, they've had a hard time changing their minds. Oh, and don't think I've missed the fact that you're trying to steal my boyfriend right out from under my nose."

"Jeez, what is wrong with you?" Charles yelled. "Angie and I are just friends. And that doesn't even really matter anyway, because you and I are officially through."

"Charles, baby. Don't be like that," Bree begged, approaching him with hands raised in supplication.

He turned from her and strode toward the front door. "I'll wait for you in the car," he informed me before disappearing outside.

"Do you really not know who was sending the letters?" I asked gently. As much as I hated Breanne, she had just been dumped and seemed pretty upset by it. Besides, yelling at her wasn't getting any of the answers I needed, but maybe a bit of kindness would.

"I really don't know," she said with a sniff. "Now please… Just… Just go away."

I studied her for a moment before finally turning away and following Charles outside. I found him behind the wheel of his car with this head down and tears spilling down both cheeks. "Are you okay?"

He sat up straighter and cleared his throat. "I should have known better. I've been so stupid."

"I'm sorry," I said, because it seemed like the best response given the situation. "Do you want to talk about it?"

"Honestly," he said, pulling the car back out of the driveway. "I kind of want to forget it ever happened. I can't believe I wasted so many months of my life on her."

I found myself torn between wanting to be a good friend to Charles and wanting to scream *I told you so* from the top of my lungs. I'd always known Breanne was a bad egg, but I'd never known just how rotten she'd become, never would have suspected she'd go to such drastic lengths to make my life miserable.

"I'm so sorry she did this to you," he said, keeping his eyes glued firmly to the road ahead. "I wanted to find Octo-Cat before, but now it feels like it's my duty, like somehow this is partially my fault. I know I'm a big part of the reason she hates you, and it's up to me to make things right."

"Charles, none of this is your fault."

"It feels that way, though."

I put a conciliatory hand on his forearm. "I accept your help, but not because you owe me anything. Thank you for being such a good friend."

We drove back to my house in utter silence. Had Charles meant it when he told Breanne we were only friends? Or had he also been harboring a secret crush on me all these months?

I pushed these questions from my already overcluttered brain. Only one question mattered now, and it needed all our focus…

Where was Octo-Cat?

CHAPTER SIXTEEN

B ack at my house, Nan and Cal were waiting for Charles's and my return with every light on the main floor at full blast.

Cal popped to his feet when we entered. "Did you find him?"

"No," I said, accepting a fresh mug of cocoa from Nan, who was clearly enjoying her role as stakeout hostess.

"Did you find who was leaving the notes?" she asked with large eyes.

"Yeah, we did." I bit my lip, not wanting to be the one to break this news to Breanne's twin brother, especially since she'd used his unfairly earned bad reputation as an excuse for getting involved in her shady dealings.

"It was Breanne," Charles answered for me. His voice brooked no arguments. I'd never seen him so livid about anything in all the months I'd known him.

"You mean, your girlfriend?" Nan looked from one man to the other and frowned. "And your sister?"

"She's my ex now," Charles said with a sigh.

Nan didn't even try to hide her happiness at this news. She even wrapped an arm around me and squeezed me to her side. "Good. She wasn't right for you anyway."

I about died when she shot me what she must have assumed was a surreptitious wink.

Charles saw it plain as day, but at least it made him smile.

Cal, however, seemed to be the most upset of everyone. "Why would she do something like that?" He sank down onto the couch and dragged both hands through his hair. "Oh, wait. It's because of me. Isn't it?"

"It's not your fault you got framed for murder," I pointed out gently.

"It sure feels like it, though."

"Charles is blaming himself, too," I said. "But, believe me, this is nobody's fault except Breanne's."

"Okay," Nan shouted, drawing everyone's attention to her. "Enough with the pity party. We have work to do."

"What work? We reached a dead end with Breanne. She says she doesn't know who was paying her to drop off the letters." Charles paced around the living room like a caged lion ready to pounce.

"I'm going to go talk to her." Cal rose to his feet and marched toward the front door. "Call me if you need me."

The door slammed shut, and we all took a collective breath in.

"Charles, look at me." Nan walked right up to him and stood on her tiptoes in an effort to bring her face closer to his.

He stopped pacing, the pent-up energy visible in the bulging veins that had risen to the surface of his neck and forearms. This was killing him.

"I know you're feeling down in the dumps right about now, but you and that woman were never right for each other anyway," Nan said firmly. "So, stop mulligrubbing, and fire up that big, beautiful brain of yours again. We're going to need it to bring our kitty boy home safely."

"Maybe we didn't get anywhere with Bree," I told Charles much gentler than Nan had just spoken to him. "But that doesn't mean we're at a dead end, either. We still have the list of beneficiaries from Ethel's will, and you only checked out the local ones, right?"

He nodded but said nothing. I briefly wondered whether he was holding back tears or shouts. Maybe both.

After grabbing his hand in mine, I gave it a reassuring squeeze. "Then I say it's time we take a little road trip. If someone needed to pay Breanne to drop off those letters, chances are they don't live close enough to do it themselves."

"I'll stay here with the animals in case anything else goes down at mission central," Nan volunteered.

"Charles?" I asked. "I know you're having a really hard time with all of this right now, but I could really use a friend by my side. Are you in?"

He dropped his gaze toward the floor and nodded as if a hundred-pound weight was pushing down on his neck. "I'm in," he groaned.

I wrapped my arms around Charles and gave him a tight hug. "Thank you," I murmured. "But first before we go, we need to make a quick stop off at the twenty-four-hour market and swing back by Bree's real quick, too."

He studied me in horror. It seemed our opinions about Breanne finally matched, although I hated the circumstances. Unfortunately, we didn't have much of a choice as to whether or not to return to her house that night.

"I'm pretty sure we forgot Maple there," I admitted with a flippant shrug, even though I was beating myself up about having left a man—*er*, a squirrel—behind on our mission. "I figure we should come prepared with an apology and peanut butter, thus our other stop. C'mon, let's go."

G iven that our stakeout party had started at ten that night, neither Charles nor I had slept recently. Still, I doubted either of us could have grabbed even a few winks if we'd tried—not with all that was weighing on our minds. Instead, we grabbed a case of the cold espresso drinks—the ones Nan always said tasted like chalk

—from my fridge and set off on our next great fact-finding adventure.

"Who should we pay a visit to first?" Charles asked once we'd made it to the main road that ran through our tiny town of Glendale.

"Ethel's niece, Anne," I said definitively, pointing to her name on the printout Charles had given me. "She gave off definite creepy vibes when last we met."

"Creepy as in catnapper creepy?" Charles asked with a lopsided grin. He adjusted his hands on the wheel and settled back in his seat. Now that we'd rescued Maple from Breanne's house and moved past that portion of our night, he seemed to be returning to his normal relaxed self.

"Creepy as in she was on my short list of murder suspects creepy." I then filled him in on my various run-ins with the eerie older woman.

"Definitely creepy," Charles agreed. "So she really broke into Ethel's house?"

"Yup, but seeing as I'd also broken in, I decided to let that one pass." I began to fiddle with a hangnail absentmindedly. Even though Charles and I were back to our usual easy banter, something important had changed. Now I was wondering what every glance, touch, and word meant, whether it might imply that he felt how I did.

I pinched the skin on my wrist to force myself to focus on finding Octo-Cat rather than finding out what Charles may or may not feel for me.

Luckily, he had to keep his focus on driving, which meant he missed all the weirdness I was serving up in the passenger seat beside him. "But you said she was there to scout out antiques and other valuables she wanted to keep for herself, right?"

"Yeah, and if Octo-Cat and I hadn't showed up to stop her, I'm pretty sure she would have taken it all."

"That's what she said." Charles suppressed a boyish chuckle, and I gave him a playful slap over the center console.

"C'mon. We're both grown-ups here."

Charles broke out laughing again.

"I'm going to let that go, since it's already been a long night and we're just getting started," I said graciously. "Anyway, yeah, my gut says it's Anne. Nobody else really left much of an impression, to be honest."

"Well, then I guess we're headed into Boston. At least we'll beat the morning rush."

We both surveyed the darkness ahead as I plugged Anne's address into the GPS on my phone. "It's almost a four-hour drive," I whined.

"It could have been worse," Charles said with a shrug. "Ethel had family as far away as Oregon. Now there's a drive."

"What do we do if it's not Anne?" I wondered aloud. "Where do we go next?"

He reached for my hand and held it in his. "We're not going to think like that. Just focus on finding Octo-Cat and bringing him home. The in-between details aren't important. And if your gut is saying Anne did it, then that's what I believe, too." He raised my hand to his lips and gave my knuckles a quick kiss before letting go.

Despite the fact that this small gesture of kindness sent my heart cartwheeling and my stomach loop-de-looping, the feel of his lips on my skin did more than any anti-anxiety pill ever could. Charles believed in this, believed we could do it.

And now so did I.

CHAPTER SEVENTEEN

I couldn't have slept even if I'd wanted to. Anticipation at finding my long-lost feline friend gripped one side of me, and excitement for this private time with Charles grabbed hold of the other.

For so long I'd wished that he would just break up with Breanne already, and now he had. Might he also see that it had always been the two of us who were meant for each other? I'd tried to put my feelings for Charles aside for months now, but nothing ever worked.

He'd defended Cal against that double murder charge with everything he had. He accepted my ability to speak with animals and never made me feel weird because of it. He'd taken in two homeless, traumatized cats after they'd accidentally killed their owner. He'd just always been there, always been good and kind.

"What are you thinking about?" he asked me now.

I yawned to buy myself some time. "Just sleepy."

"You better not fall asleep on me," he teased. "Your shift is coming up soon."

"Pull over. I'll take it now." Driving would be a nice distraction from all the thoughts fighting to take center stage in my mind.

Charles glanced toward me, then back to the road. "You sure about that?"

"I'm awake, I promise. But if it makes you feel better, I'll shotgun another one of these coffee things." I picked up one of the small blue and brown cans and gave it a good shake.

"Okay, but after that you're cut off." He turned up the music and shuffled through a few songs before landing on one of my favorite '80s hair metal jams.

"It's a myth, you know," I said while bobbing my head along to the heavy, soul-filling beat.

Charles stopped singing along with the track and risked a quick glance my way. "What is?"

I shrugged. "That too much caffeine will either stop your heart or make it explode." As it was, my heart was still beating wildly like a caged animal rattling against its bars. No amount of coffee would change that, either.

It was all Charles, my dream guy. Heaven help me.

When the song ended, Charles put away his air keytar and pulled onto the side of the road so we could switch seats.

"Are you sad?" I asked him when a slow jam took over the speakers and he had to put away his air keytar for a second time. "About Breanne?"

"Angry, more like." He flipped through his playlist again, and this time chose something hard, angsty, and most definitely not from my favorite musical era.

"Do you think you'll forgive her? That the two of you will get back together?" I yelled over the shouty, migraine-inducing music.

He took the hint and lowered the volume. His eyes stayed firmly fixed to my profile as he asked, "Do you think we should?"

I felt a flush rise to my cheeks and hoped he didn't notice. "No," I answered honestly.

"Yeah. Neither do I," he said, crossing his arms and leaning his face against the cold glass of the window with a sigh. "We were never really right for each other anyway."

"Then why'd you stay together so long?"

Yeah, I was most definitely being nosy, but I also needed to know where things stood, and Charles seemed more than willing to share.

Plus we had a lot of time left to kill before we reached Anne's Boston-based bungalow.

"That's a good question," he answered after a short pause.

When I glanced over toward him, his eyes were closed, and he wore a subtle smile on his face. "You don't have to answer, if you don't want," I offered, hoping like heck he wouldn't accept.

He sighed and shifted in his seat, his brow furrowed in a pained look. "I think I was just lonely after having moved so far away to start my new life in Blueberry Bay. I was trying to put down roots."

"Like with the house and the cats," I suggested. *See, there are other ways to build a life. No Breanne Calhoun required.*

"Yeah, and the firm. I never thought I'd make senior partner so fast or that we'd have so much turnover with our associates. It's kept me very busy. Perhaps too busy to really pay attention to what was going on with me and Breanne."

Well, this was a fresh, new perspective. "What do you mean?"

"I guess that it was just easier to keep dating her, to maintain status quo, you know?"

"No," I answered honestly. "I really don't."

He took a deep breath and squinted over at me for a moment before pressing his eyelids shut once more. "I always liked spending time with Breanne. I know she hated you, but she was always nice to me. I enjoyed being with her, and that was the crucial part. I enjoyed it. It was nice. Fine. Not something I craved. I never counted down the hours until I could see her again. I never let it distract me from work or anything else I had going on in my life. She filled a hole in my life, but didn't overfill it, I guess."

"That's what she said," I muttered when I sensed the mood was getting too serious.

Charles chuckled softly but stayed on topic anyway. "Maybe I was unfair to her, letting it go on as long as it did. I'd feel guilty if I weren't so furious about what she did to you."

"Don't worry about me," I said. "I'll be just fine."

"I know you will be. You're the strongest person I know," he said softly as another rush of heat flooded my cheeks.

Was now the time I should confess how I felt about him?

It seemed he had just offered me the perfect segue, and this was the first time in our relationship I actually could share my feelings without it getting in the way of a shared case at work or having an angry girlfriend to answer to. We were both free to explore what had been there between us from the very start.

Now was as good a time as there had ever been. I needed to be brave. This was it…

"Charles…" I mumbled, glancing over toward him. There was so much that needed to be said.

But now wasn't the time, seeing as Charles was fast asleep.

I'd never been great at city driving, but luckily we reached Boston before the sun even had its chance to rise for the day. I woke Charles right around the time the GPS informed me we had five minutes left in our drive.

"Why'd you let me sleep so long?" he exclaimed with a groan.

"It seemed like you needed it," I said with a smile. I'd been so close to revealing everything, all my secret longings and wishes. Thank goodness he had nodded off and saved me—saved both of us—from myself. I needed to focus on Octo-Cat right now. We both did.

Charles straightened in his seat and slapped his cheeks a few times to wake himself a bit more. "So, what's the plan?"

Luckily, I'd had a lot of time to think things over as I drove with only Charles's eclectic playlist to keep me company on the long, lonely road. "I thought you could be the one to approach her. Make some excuse about the estate and the arbitration. Use a lot of legal terms, and I'm sure she won't question you."

He nodded, then rubbed the sleep from his eyes. "Okay. Then what?"

"Get her to invite you inside. Excuse yourself to use the bathroom. Then see if you can find him."

"That's a good plan, but…" He sighed and stretched his legs out in front of him, then turned back toward me. "Don't you think it will be suspicious that we're doing all this before six a.m.?"

"Yeah, probably," I admitted. It looked like we'd just fallen into a hurry up and wait trap. I hated those.

Charles seemed unbothered by the inconvenient hour. He smiled over at me and asked, "Don't you think it would be better if we grabbed some breakfast first and then came back at a more reasonable hour so we can sell our story better?"

"Yeah, probably," I agreed.

His smile widened, and he pointed at a big, bright diner sign just down the road. "Then, c'mon. Let's load up on eggs and bacon. My treat."

I nodded and turned into the parking lot, wishing we would have timed this a little better but happy we were at least making some form of progress.

Charles held open the door for me, which was a small thing but felt monumentally huge. "Ladies first," he said.

And I blushed.

Me and my stupid crush.

CHAPTER EIGHTEEN

Breakfast was slow, leisurely, and full of unspoken angst on my part. At around seven thirty, Charles handed the waitress his credit card and asked if I was ready to head over to Anne's place.

Oh, was I ever.

"Thanks for the hot meal," I mumbled shyly. "I needed that."

He looped an arm over my shoulders as we made our way through the mostly empty diner. "No thanks needed between friends."

Friends, right.

"How do you think Octo-Cat will react once we find him?" I asked, once again trying to pull my head back into the game we were actually playing here.

Charles smiled and widened his eyes. "My money's on one very grateful kitty. There may even be licks and scritches involved."

I giggled as he held the door open for me on the way out. "I'll take that bet, because I'm pretty sure he's going to demand a proper meal and then chastise us for taking so long to find him."

"Oh, c'mon," Charles said, joining me in my laughter. "Of course he's going to be grateful. Why would he complain after all we've been through?"

"First agree to the bet," I insisted, not making eye contact with him as we crossed the parking lot. "Twenty bucks?"

"You're on." Charles slid behind the steering wheel, and I climbed into the passenger seat. "Now explain yourself, Russo."

"Let's just say that I'm the only one who can actually understand him, and well… I might just censor out his catittude when translating for you and Nan." I just couldn't stop smiling. I missed Octo-Cat and his grandiose way of doing absolutely everything.

"Wait!" Charles shifted in his seat and faced me head-on. "Has he been saying awful things about me all this time? And here I had no idea."

I laughed again. It felt so good to laugh. Almost like Octo-Cat was here with us now. "Not lots of bad things. He does call you UpChuck, though."

"What a bratty cat!" Charles cried. "First, let's get him home safe and sound, and then I'm going to come up with an equally disgusting nickname for him."

"You've got it," I said between laughs.

Oh, I couldn't wait to see how this played out.

We reached Anne's bungalow about five minutes later. We were early, but some of the neighbor kids were already milling around at what appeared to be the local bus stop.

"I'll wait here. You go ahead." I gave Charles a little push, then watched as he marched confidently up to Anne's front door, briefcase in hand. Despite the five o'clock shadow and noticeable bags under his eyes, he certainly looked the part of a lawyer visiting on official estate business.

Let's just hope Anne would buy it.

He pressed the doorbell and waited.

When nothing happened, he pressed again.

"Maybe it's broken," I texted rather than calling out, just in case Anne remembered me and chose to hide for that reason alone. "Try knocking."

Charles knocked several times, but nobody came. If Anne was inside, she clearly refused to answer the door.

I scrambled out of the car and joined Charles on the porch.

"Open up, Anne Fulton!" I shouted into the hard wood of the door. "We know you're in there!"

"Um, excuse me," a woman's voice called from the next condo over. "Are you looking for Anne?"

Well, it looked like I wasn't the only one with ace detective skills around here. Charles and I both backed down off the porch and came to join the woman where her yard met up with Anne's.

"Yes," he said with a nod in greeting. "We're from the firm representing her late aunt's estate and have some very important developments to discuss."

The woman frowned and shook her head. "I'm so sorry. You just missed her. Well, missed her by a few days actually. She's on vacation this week. I've been collecting her mail and watering her flowerbeds. Can I take a message for you?"

"Thank you, but that's all right," I said, forcing a smile. It wasn't the neighbor's fault that Anne was nowhere to be found. It was, however, her fault that we couldn't break in to explore the premises.

"Do you know what day she left?" Charles asked intelligently.

"Tuesday morning, bright and early."

"Great, thanks. You've been a huge help," he said with another nod to say goodbye.

I followed him back to the car. Neither of us spoke until the neighbor woman gave us one final wave and walked back into her condo.

"The timelines match up perfectly," he said, his hands shaking with excitement. "Anne left Boston early enough to take Octo-Cat. For all we know, she's had him this whole time."

"Do you think she's hanging out somewhere in Blueberry Bay?"

"Call Nan. She'll know what to do on her end. We can discuss the rest on our way back home."

Sure enough, Nan picked up on the first ring, then immediately launched into her plan of attack once I'd caught her up on what had gone down in Boston. "If that wretched woman's staying anywhere near here, I'll find her. I have the perfect costume for this role."

"What role?" I asked.

"Why, of the forgetful but well-intentioned elderly aunt, of course. Nobody ever suspects the little old lady, you know. They'll hand over her room number in a heartbeat, and when I find her, I'll—"

"You'll wait for me and Charles," I interrupted. "Promise me, you'll wait for us."

"Fine. I'll find her and then I'll stake things out until the B team can arrive."

"So we're the B team now?" I asked with a chuckle.

"We can't all be the A team, dear. Now get that man to drive fast, so we can bust in on the bad gal and take back what's ours."

After hanging up with Nan, I turned to Charles with a giant grin and asked, "How fast are you willing to book it back there?"

He pressed down a bit harder on the accelerator, and we were off.

I felt confident we'd find Octo-Cat before the day was through, but I still had questions. Mainly, if Anne was staying locally, why would she have hired Breanne to hand-deliver her ransom notes? And also, why do all this now when the arbitration for Ethel's estate was already scheduled for tomorrow?

Charles didn't have any good answers, either, which meant the best we could hope for was a crazed confession when we caught Anne red-handed later that morning—or afternoon, depending on the traffic we had to fight coming back home.

We were still a couple hours outside of Glendale when Nan called. I put the phone on speaker so Charles could hear, too.

"The eagle is in the nest!" she shouted into the phone. "I repeat, the eagle is in the nest!"

"Does this mean you found Anne?" I asked, hope rising in me like a shiny, Mylar balloon floating toward the ceiling.

Nan giggled. "Of course we found her. We are the A Team, after all."

I let out a giant, relieved sigh. We were so close to bringing our boy home. Something about what Nan had said didn't quite make sense, though, so I asked, "Awesome, so I just have two questions. Where are you, and who else is part of that "we" you just mentioned?"

"Um, just a second, dear." Nan's track pants swished, and a moment later she explained, "Sorry, I wanted to get a bit of privacy for this part. I'm with Cal and his sister."

"You're with Breanne?" I growled, immediately tensing up all over again. "Why?"

"Relax. I know we hate her, but she's the one who found out where Anne was staying and led us straight to her."

Charles sent me a panicked glance, and I made a gun out of my thumb and index finger and pointed it at my head with a grimace.

"Are you ready for the address?" Nan asked. Apparently, we were done talking about both Breanne and Anne now.

I agreed. No more talking. It was time for action.

I jotted the address down and made Nan promise to text it over, too. Apparently, Anne had taken a motel room in the nearby town of Cooper Cove. And we'd be there in less than two hours.

"You got that twenty bucks ready?" I asked Charles. Soon I'd be collecting on our little bet, but even more importantly, soon I'd have my cat back and would finally be able to figure out why he was taken in the first place.

This was it. Everything was about to go down.

Anne didn't stand a chance.

I was one angry cat-mama, and I was coming for her.

CHAPTER NINETEEN

C harles and I made it to that dingy motel in Cooper Cove in record time. When we arrived, we found Nan waiting with the Calhoun twins in the parking lot. Nan and Charles sat together in Nan's sports coupe while Breanne sat parked a few spots away, flipping through a giant stack of papers in the driver's seat of her luxury SUV.

The moment Charles and I pulled into that parking lot, everyone scrambled out of their cars and rushed over to join us.

Cal gave me a huge hug. "Welcome back," he said with a charming grin.

Breanne tried to hug Charles, but he was having none of that.

"Let's do this!" Nan let out a battle cry and led the charge up the outdoor staircase and toward motel room number twenty-six.

The rest of us followed like obedient little ducklings.

We found the room, third on the right, after exiting the narrow stairway. Charles nudged his way to the front of our pack and banged on the door. "Open up," he called, his voice much deeper than usual. Maybe to sound more intimidating. Yeah, because that was the way to get her to voluntarily open the door.

"Are you sure Anne's even in there?" I asked. A frustrating sense of déjà vu had already begun to set in. What if this was Boston all over again?

"Anne? No," Nan admitted with a look of determination that didn't waver. "The catnapper? Yes."

"How…?" I began. My voice shook just as much as my hands in that moment.

Cal generously explained the situation to Charles and me, who were now both utterly confused. "So hang on a sec. Here's what happened. First off, Breanne felt really bad about her role in all of this, so she agreed to help."

"It's true. I did. *I do.*" Bree placed a hand on Charles's arm, but he ripped it away.

"I'd prefer to hear this from your brother, thank you very much," he grumbled, refusing to even look at his recent ex.

Cal waited until I nodded for him to go ahead. "Well, um, Bree sent an email since that was the only form of contact she had for the ransom note writer, and basically, well, she said that the plan had worked and that you had agreed to give up the house, Angie." The poor guy seemed so nervous. It was obvious he didn't like being the middleman in this lovers' spat, and I couldn't say I blamed him.

When Cal hesitated again, Breanne took over the recap. "I told the person that I had the preliminary paperwork and that we needed to meet face-to-face in order to move on with the next phase of the plan. About an hour later, I was sent this address and room number."

"Have you been inside yet?" I asked, glancing back toward the closed door.

"No, we were waiting for you," Nan said. "We wouldn't have solved the case without you."

"Yes, unfortunately, we've been here for quite a while now," Bree snapped, focusing all her hostility on me now that Charles had made it clear he didn't want to have anything to do with her. "So can we please just get this over with already? I have other things to do today, you know."

"Like delivering more ransom notes?" Nan quipped, laughing at her own joke.

It may not have been the most mature decision, but I couldn't resist giving her a high five for that perfect joke.

Bree scowled at both of us, reminding me how serious this situation was.

"She's not answering," I muttered, staring at the cheap motel door and wishing I had the power to see right through it. "Why is she not answering?"

Nan cleared her throat and held up one pointer finger. "Housekeeping," she called out happily, giving the door an upbeat series of knocks.

The door in front of us remained closed, but the one to the next room opened a crack and a middle-aged man peeked his head out. "Housekeeping?" he asked us with a confused expression.

"They just went inside another room. Looks like you've got a bit of time to make yourself decent," Nan said with a flirtatious wink.

"Wait," I cried just as the door was closing the last bit of the way.

The man nudged it open a few inches and stared at me curiously.

"Did you happen to run into the woman who was staying in this room? We were supposed to get together today, but she's not answering."

He shook his head. "Sorry, no. I just got in last night."

Click. The door closed again.

"Oh, this is ridiculous," Breanne groused. "C'mon," she told Cal, grabbing his arm and pulling him along. "We'll go check with the front desk. You can all stay here."

Nan, Charles, and I waited in silence. What was left to say? Octo-Cat might be in the room, but he might also not be. It was like Schrödinger's cat but without the box and hopefully without the dead cat, too.

Thankfully, it only took five minutes for the twins to return.

"The occupant checked out," Cal explained with a sad shake of his head. "And we were so close, too. I'm sorry, Angie."

Nan patted Cal on the bicep. "That's okay, dear. Did they give us a name?"

"No, they wouldn't," Bree seethed. "Some ridiculous code of privacy or something."

Angry tears burned at my eyes and throat. "Now what?" I screamed at the closed door.

Charles and Nan hugged me from either side, which apparently was enough to send Bree tip-tapping out of there on her impossibly high heels. "It's been swell," she said, waving as she walked away. "Keep me posted. Or, you know, don't. Whatever."

"What a piece of work, that one. You know I never did much care for her," a smooth, haughty voice informed us from below.

"Not now, Octo-Cat," I murmured. "We have to figure out what we're going to do next."

Wait… Was that…? *Oh!*

My head snapped up, and I ran to the edge of the outdoor hallway so fast I practically tumbled straight over the edge.

"Watch it there," Charles cried, looping his arms around my waist and catching me just in time.

But I didn't care about the fact my crush held me tight or that I'd almost fallen a full story. All I cared about was the blurry, brown-and-black-striped figure that sat in the small courtyard below, regarding me irritably.

"You know…" Octo-Cat said slowly, his way of making sure I understood. "I've been gone for three whole days. That's three whole days drinking tap water and choking down store brand cat food. *Three days* without my iPad or cat door. Do you know how much I've suffered? Honestly, Angela, what took you so long?"

I choked on a sob and jabbed Charles with my elbow. "Give me twenty bucks," I said, holding out my hand.

"Are you going to take me home now?" Octo-Cat demanded. "I'm not stepping a paw on that dirty cement again, and I've had more than enough of an adventure for this week, thank you very much."

I wiped my nose on the back of my arm and ran down the stairs. When I reached Octo-Cat, I scooped him up into my arms and squeezed him to my chest.

"Gross!" he protested. "I just finished my mid-day ministrations, and now you've gone and wiped your germs all on me. Unhand me, you filthy human. Unhand me right now."

I set him back on the grass and laughed like a crazy person. I didn't care what anyone thought. This was one of the very best days of my entire life. Octo-Cat was here, and he was no worse for the wear—no matter what *he* claimed. I did wonder, though…

I stared into his glinting amber eyes as I asked, "How are you here on your own? Where's the person who took you?"

My tabby jumped up onto a nearby bench seat and waved his paw around dramatically. Whatever he was about to say, it was sure to be entertaining and to overexaggerate his importance. Ahh, it was so good to have him back.

Octo-Cat smiled as he launched into his harrowing tale. "Well, she was leaving in a hurry a couple hours back. She tried to take me with her, but I let these babies out, and—"

Schwink. His claws popped out in all their menacing glory.

"Let's just say I won that particular fight." He laughed in that favorite villainous way of his.

"You said *she.* Do you know who took you? Was it a woman?"

He shrugged his adorable little kitty shoulders. "It was definitely a person I've seen before. I'm pretty sure it was one of Ethel's relatives, and I am at least sixty percent sure the person was a female."

I patted him between his ears. "Good work." He still had a hard time telling humans apart, but he was getting better. Slowly but surely, he was getting better, and he was back with me where we belonged.

"Um, Angie?" Charles said, approaching with Nan and Cal at either side. "We can still make the arbitration, if you want to—"

"Let's do it," I said.

Now that I had my best friend at my side, there was no way I would let anyone hurt him ever again. We were back together, and that's how we would stay.

CHAPTER TWENTY

"I object!" Nan cried when the five of us burst into the county court roughly twenty minutes later.

The nearest clerk waved us over to her window behind a thick layer of plexiglass. "Hello, there. What are we objecting to today?"

Charles pushed himself in front of Nan. "Hi, yes. We're here for the arbitration hearing regarding Ethel Fulton's estate."

The woman nodded her permed head and continued to smile brightly at all of us. "Oh, lots of folks have come in for that one. Room B-2. You're right on time. Good luck."

Before we could stop her, Nan ran down the hall and flung open the door to Room B-2. "I object!" she cried.

The rest of us ran after her and popped in a second later.

"Longfellow," the person who sat at the front of the room said, fixing Charles with a stern look. "Control your client, and do it now."

We all sat in the back of the room, careful not to make direct eye contact with any of the other heirs. I did a quick scan and saw that Anne was nowhere to be found.

Drats! I still desperately wanted proof that it had been her, and I wanted to make sure she understood the lengths I would go to in order to protect my cat from any future shenanigans on her part.

"Now," the arbiter said, "there have been several challenges to the will of Ethel Fulton, particularly in regards to one Octavius Fulton. Is he here today?"

"Yes, your honor." I rose to my feet with my furry friend in my arms, not sure whether I was addressing the arbiter correctly since this was all a huge first for me.

"Let me guess. Octavius is the cat. Isn't he?" the man asked with a bored expression.

"Yes, but Ethel loved him like a son and wanted to make sure he was cared for in the manner to which he'd grown accustomed," Charles explained.

"I can see that." The arbiter flipped through the copy of the will in front of him and cracked his neck to either side. He glanced up at us again a few minutes later with a tight-lipped smile. "There are precedents for this. Ethel could have left the entire state of Maine to her cat for all I care. It's not up to the court to question that. So, why are we here?"

"The house," a scratchy voice wheezed from near the door.

Everyone turned, and I about lost my lunch when I saw who was standing there.

Anne Fulton was every bit as frumpy as I remembered. Her gray hair had been cut short, and her arm was freshly bandaged but still bleeding heavily.

"Is that your work?" I whispered to Octo-Cat.

"You bet it is," he answered proudly, then narrowed his gaze on Anne and let out an impressive hiss.

"The house wasn't specifically in the will," the arbiter said.

"Maybe not," Anne said, keeping a great deal of distance between us as she approached the front of the room. "But somehow the cat's still managed to inherit it."

"Actually, the house is mine," I said.

"And mine," Nan added.

"My clients purchased the house from the open market. Their

ties to Ethel Fulton's estate are irrelevant," Charles added helpfully. *My hero.*

"I agree," the arbiter said. "Anything else to contest?"

Nobody said anything, but Nan wore a giant, sappy grin. Octo-Cat had hopped into her lap, and she was petting him with slow, leisurely strokes—just the way he liked.

"Then the terms of the will stand as written," the arbiter said. I expected a gavel to bang, but it didn't. Oh, well.

We remained seated until all the Fultons had shuffled out of the room. I was sad to see that my old boss, Richard, hadn't been able to make the trip up from Florida, but happy that this was finally over.

Only Anne remained behind.

"I know it was you," I hissed.

Octo-Cat backed me up with a hiss of his own, too.

"Why did you take my cat?" I demanded, gripping the edges of my chair so I wouldn't be tempted to charge straight up to her and give her the beat-down she deserved.

Anne didn't even look sorry. "That's my aunt Ethel's cat. He should have stayed in the family after she'd gone."

"Him or his trust fund?" Nan shot back. "Because judging by that open wound on your arm, our dear Octavius doesn't want anything to do with the likes of you."

"You can't prove anything," Anne spat. "And you can't do anything, either. So I took a cat for a few days. It's not like I committed murder."

"You're walking on really shaky ground," Nan warned as Octo-Cat jumped off her lap and trotted over to the villainess of the hour.

"I'm going to get that house," Anne mumbled, then grabbed her injured arm and fled through the door right as Oct-Cat was getting ready to take a fresh swipe.

Nan and I exchanged a quick glance, then she tucked her arm into Cal's and said, "C'mon, you handsome thing. I want to thank that kind lady who helped us when we first arrived."

They left through the same door Anne had. Now only Charles, Octo-Cat, and I remained in the arbitration room.

I sighed and laid my head on Charles's shoulder.

"I'm glad you got him back," he said.

"Me, too."

"Are we going home now?" Octo-Cat whined, waiting for some-body to open the door for him. "I'm absolutely dying for some Evian."

"Soon," I said after making a brusque hushing noise.

Charles shook his head. "Is he seriously complaining again?"

"Yup," I answered with a chuckle, pulling myself back into a full seated position.

Charles turned in his seat to face me more directly. "Well, now that he's back, there's something I've been meaning to say to you for a while now."

I gulped hard as blood rushed through my veins. He had some-thing to say.

Did that mean…?

Was he finally going to…?

Would we…?

He placed a hand on each of my shoulders and tried to hide his widening smile. "Now I don't want you to take this the wrong way, but…"

"Yes?" I asked, lowering my eyelashes to show him I was ready for his kiss. Heck, I was pretty much ready to marry him on the spot, and we were already at the county court. *I do. I do!*

"Angie," he said softly, then waited for me to re-open my eyes. "You're fired."

My heart dropped all the way down to the floor. He was supposed to kiss me, not fire me!

Charles pressed his forehead to mine, and his warm breaths landed near my nose. "I told you not to take it the wrong way. I'm doing you a favor here. Actually, I'm doing both of us a favor."

"Come again now?" I mumbled, wishing I had something more intelligent to say in that moment.

"I've known you wanted to quit for weeks now. Maybe months. What's stopping you?"

"I didn't want to let you down," I admitted.

He tucked a stray tendril of sandy brown hair behind my ear. "You could never let me down, but I don't want you putting your dreams on hold because of me, either."

He was so impossibly close that it made it hard for me to focus. I still wasn't sure exactly what was happening and whether or not I should be happy about it.

"You're a great P.I., and it's time you went into business for yourself. You can't do that if you're still spending half your days at Longfellow and Associates, so… You're fired."

"Thank you?" I said, guessing at the appropriate response. There may have been precedents regarding Ethel's estate, but what was happening between me and Charles right now was completely and totally new.

He laughed softly. "Don't thank me. I'm doing this for selfish reasons, too."

"Oh?" I asked on a soft exhale. Still so uneasy about how close we were. Still wanting that kiss.

"Yeah, because when I was your boss, I couldn't do this."

I sucked in a deep breath, but before I could let it out, Charles's lips were on mine. Oh my gosh, I was kissing Charles!

And it was everything I'd ever dreamed it would be.

"Humans are disgusting," Octo-Cat complained, taking a swipe at my arm. Thankfully, it was much gentler than the number he'd done on Anne.

Charles laughed as he pulled away. "Let me guess, he didn't like that."

"Yeah," I admitted. "But not because he's jealous, because he thinks it's gross."

Charles rolled his eyes, which just so happened to have happy sparkles in them at the moment. "Whatever, cat. I know you call me UpChuck behind my back."

"Boys, boys," I said, smiling so hard that the corners of my mouth hurt. "You're just going to have to find a way to share."

I stood, and Charles immediately laced his fingers between mine, leaving Octo-Cat to follow behind on foot.

"I can't believe you're choosing to focus on this needless

romance when you should be focused on getting me Evian as soon as humanly possible," my cat grumbled predictably.

I scooped him up in my free arm and held him as we walked out of the courthouse. "When we get home, there's someone very special I want you to meet."

"Ugh, why? I'm so tired," he whined.

"He's the president of your fan club," I revealed, picturing how insanely happy Pringle would be to meet his idol.

"Can I be the president of your fan club?" Charles asked, giving my hand a squeeze.

I pretended to think about this for a moment. "I don't really need a fan club, but you can be my boyfriend. That is if you—"

Charles stopped walking, pulled me close, and kissed me again.

I took that to mean he agreed.

CHIHUAHUA CONSPIRACY

Pet Whisperer P I

ABOUT THIS BOOK

My crazy old Nan loves making decisions on a whim. Last week, she took up flamenco dancing. This week, she's adopted a trouble-making Chihuahua named Paisley. This wouldn't be much of a problem were it not for the very crabby tabby who also lives with us.

Man, I never thought I'd miss hearing Octo-Cat's voice, but his silent protest is becoming too much to bear, especially since we just opened our new P.I. business together.

Things go from bad to worse, of course, when Nan and I discover that someone has been embezzling funds from the local animal shelter. If we can't find the culprit soon, the shelter may not be able to keep its lights on and those poor homeless pets won't have anywhere to go.

Okay, so I just need to find the thief, rescue the animals, and save the day—all while trying to find a way for Octo-Cat and Paisley to set aside their differences and work together as a team. Yeah, wish me luck…

CHAPTER ONE

Hi, I'm Angie Russo, and this last year has been quite the wild ride for me. Yes, it's been exactly one year since my entire life changed for the better.

Sure, I've come face-to-face with a lot of dangerous characters lately—murderers, kidnappers, creeps, you name it—but I wouldn't trade my life for anyone else's.

Here's the deal… It all started at my former job as a paralegal.

A wealthy old woman had just died, and her heirs had gathered at our office for the official will reading. I was instructed to make coffee, and, well, that was the last time I ever attempted such a dangerous feat.

You see, I got electrocuted and knocked unconscious. I woke up with a wicked fear of coffee makers—oh, and also the ability to talk to animals. At first, I could only talk to this one cat named Octavius Maxwell Ricardo Edmund Frederick Fulton. He was one of the primary beneficiaries of his late owner's estate, and I now call him Octo-Cat for short.

Long story short, he told me the old lady was murdered and begged me to help him catch the killer. We did, and we pretty much became best friends in the process. Now he lives with me, and I oversee his care and also his generous trust fund.

And because I accidentally made an open-ended deal with him when I needed to get him to wear a pet harness, we now reside in his former owner's exquisite manor house. Yes, a ten-dollar neon green harness ended up costing me a cool million.

At least most of the money was my cat's, anyway.

Yeah. A lot has happened over the last year. My cat and I solved three more murders together. He got catnapped. I finally quit my paralegal job so we could open up a private investigation firm together, and oh, yeah… I got a boyfriend!

My nan might be even more excited about that one than I am. She'd been trying to matchmake me for years, and now that she's finally succeeded, she's not quite sure what to do with herself.

Yes, she continues to bake up a storm in the kitchen and take her community art classes, but lately she's also been flipping through new hobbies like they're going out of style. There's been flamenco dancing, learning Korean as a second language, even Pokémon Go. She claims Pikachu understands her on a spiritual level. Personally, I don't get it.

My mom and dad are busy with their jobs as Blueberry Bay's local news anchor and designated sports guy. Nan and I have them over once per week for a nice home-cooked meal. Did I mention my grandmother and I live together?

It's not weird. She's not just the woman who raised me, but she's also my best friend and the most amazing person I know. She even helps with Octo-Cat's lavish demands and rigorous schedule.

And between the two of us, we keep him dining on only the seafood flavors of Fancy Feast and drinking Evian from his favorite Lenox teacup.

Most recently, he's demanded a brand-new iPad Pro. His reasoning? That he needed a professional upgrade to go along with our new business venture. Never mind that he uses his tablet primarily to play various fish tank and koi pond games.

He's given his old device to the president of his fan club, a raccoon who lives under our front porch. His name is Pringle, and he's a pretty all right guy most of the time. Octo-Cat definitely enjoys having a fanboy to support every single decision he makes, including his regular criticism of me.

It's true. Octo-Cat complains a lot, but I also know he loves me tons. That's why I'm planning a special evening to celebrate our petaversary. I'm not sure he remembers, but after tonight he will.

I can't wait to see the look on his little kitty face when he sees what I have planned for him. Let the games begin!

It wasn't easy hiding my party preparations from Octo-Cat, but so far he hadn't managed to catch on. Rather than cooking something myself, I asked Nan to pick up some grilled shrimp and lobster rolls from the Little Dog Diner in Misty Harbor. It's a bit of a drive, but worth every mile.

Nan would be returning any minute, which meant it was time for me to wake the guest of honor. I found him sleeping in his five o'clock sunspot on the western side of the house. "Wakey, wakey!" I cried in a sing-song voice he loathed.

"Angela," he groaned, "haven't you ever heard that you should let sleeping cats lie?"

"I'm pretty sure the expression is—you know what? It doesn't matter. C'mon, I have a surprise for you."

Whoa, close one. I almost used the word dog in a sentence. That little slipup would have ruined our whole night, but I caught myself just in time.

"A surprise?" he asked, yawning so wide that his whiskers overlapped in front of his nose. "What is it?"

"You'll see. C'mon." I patted my leg and motioned for him to follow.

But he sat his butt back down on the hardwood floor and flicked his tail. "Tell me, or I'm not coming," he demanded.

"Octo-Cat, can't you just—Ugh, fine. Today marks one year since we first met. Do you remember that day?"

"So you mean it's been one year and one day since Ethel died?" he asked, raising his eyebrows and staring me down.

Oh, I didn't think of that. I hoped he wouldn't be too sad to celebrate.

"I'm just giving you a hard time," he said with a cruel laugh, trotting over as he shook his head. "Happy anniversary, Angela. I'm glad you're my human."

Footsteps sounded on the porch. I hadn't even heard Nan pull up, but now she was here, and we could officially begin our little party. I'd asked my boyfriend, Charles, to wait a couple hours before he turned up, since he and Octo-Cat didn't get along particularly well as of late.

I secretly loved that my cat was jealous of my boyfriend but hoped that he'd eventually get over it.

"Nan?" I called when Octo-Cat and I reached the bottom of the stairs, but she still hadn't entered. Padding over to the door, I twisted the knob and—

A wagging ball of black fur pounced into the house.

"I'm here! I'm home! Oh, boy. Oh, boy. Oh, boy!" the little dog cried, then immediately squatted and peed on the welcome mat.

I turned to Octo-Cat, who stood on the last stair with his back arched and his tail at full-blown puffball status. "Angela, what is this?" he screamed, unwittingly drawing the dog's attention over to him.

"A cat! A cat! Oh, boy! Oh, boy! Oh, boy!" The dog, who upon closer examination appeared to be a Chihuahua, bounded right up to Octo-Cat and pressed his nose to the cat's butt.

Octo-Cat hissed, growled, swiped with his claws, and sent the little dog shrieking away.

Yipe! Yipe! Yipe!

"What's all this commotion?" Nan asked, charging into the house, spotting the little black dog and scooping the poor, whimpering baby into her arms. "Okay, fess up. Who hurt my Paisley?"

"Nan…" I pinched the bridge of my nose to stave off the rapidly building headache. "Why is there a dog in our house?"

"This is Paisley. Yes, she is," Nan cooed in a baby voice, and the

Chihuahua licked her cheek, the horrible, scary cat and the pain he'd inflicted apparently forgotten. "She lives here now."

"Oh, heck no!" Octo-Cat shouted from his spot on the stairs. "I thought we were celebrating me tonight, not taking a visit to the ninth circle of hell!"

"Nan," I said trying to make peace before everyone lost their cool. "We can't have a dog here. Octo-Cat hates dogs."

"Hatessssss," Octo-Cat hissed, then growled again.

"He hates me?" the shivering little dog asked. "He doesn't even know me. I'm Paisley, and I'm a good girl."

Nan continued to talk in a goochie-goo voice, keeping her eyes glued to the mostly black tri-color Chihuahua in her arms. "Well, I saw this little girl at the shelter and right away she stole my heart. What was I supposed to do?"

She looked up and narrowed her eyes at me. "Was I supposed to let her stay in that cage all by herself? Or, Heaven forbid, let them put her down when the shelter got too full?" She covered Paisley's oversized ears and frowned at me.

"No, I mean..." I sputtered. "No, of course you couldn't do that." Ack, I was such a softie.

"Octavius is just going to have to get used to his new housemate, because I'm not taking her back," Nan said in a way that made it more than clear that this topic was not up for discussion. "C'mon, baby, let's go outside and meet the forest creatures."

Once Nan and Paisley were safely outside, I searched around for Octo-Cat so I could both explain and apologize on Nan's behalf.

But he was nowhere to be found.

Crud, he was never going to forgive me for this one.

CHAPTER TWO

I found Octo-Cat at last in my bedroom, where he was crouched under my bed, his wide amber eyes glowing in the darkness. When I flopped down on my belly to get a closer look, he emitted a low growl that made me jump in my skin.

"Go away," he added in a rumbly, somewhat terrifying voice.

"That's not fair," I enunciated as if scolding a petulant child. "Might I remind you that I was just as shocked by that as you were."

I searched my brain for the right way to spin things, the way that would make him understand. Unfortunately, all logic tended to go out the window whenever Octo-Cat was unhappy—and today's unhappiness had already reached a record-breaking level.

With great difficulty, I managed to put a happy-go-lucky smile on my face as I said, "But, I mean, if you think about it, it kind of makes sense. Right? We have each other, and now Nan has a best fur friend of her own, too. Isn't that nice?"

"No," the tabby replied stubbornly and turned his face toward the wall.

I hated that he was this upset, but there was nothing I could do without him being willing to at least meet me partway. "Will you at least come out for our petaversary?" I begged, practically whined.

Octo-Cat turned toward me again; his eyes still held that eerie glow as he considered my request. "I'm not coming out," he said at last. "But if you bring my shrimp and my Evian here and promise not to let that dog in, I shall consider sharing the celebratory meal with you in our private quarters. *Privately.*"

I couldn't help but sigh. "Are you really not going to leave the room at all?"

He flicked his tail, waking a cloud of dust and pet hair that rose from the carpet in a sickening flurry. Wow, I really was not a good housekeeper.

If Octo-Cat noticed the filth, he didn't seem to mind—not when he already had much bigger fish to fry. "Not until that interloper is gone," he informed me with another hiss. "Need I remind you that this is MY house?"

"No, you needn't." It felt strange using Octo-Cat's overly refined language, but he often listened better when I did. And right now, I needed him to understand that controlling Nan was every bit as difficult as trying to control him. Both were so stubborn about the things they wanted that we would have no choice but to find some kind of compromise to the Chihuahua situation.

I sighed again. "However, given your stance, it would probably be best if I brought your litter box up here as well. I'll be back in a little bit."

After pushing myself back into a standing position, I left my tower bedroom, careful to latch the door fully behind me. As much as I didn't want to trap Octo-Cat inside, I was also incredibly worried about what might happen to Paisley if she nosed her way in there. She was half his size at most and clearly didn't have an aggressive bone in her whole body.

My cat on the other hand?

He had a whole skeleton's worth.

I found Nan in the kitchen setting out a pair of dog bone-printed ceramic bowls for Paisley in a spot just to the left of the pantry. "Sorry about Octo-Cat," I muttered, ignoring the fact that he would be upset that the dog's bowls were so near his stash of Fancy Feast.

"That cat was mean," the Chihuahua whined as she rubbed at the fresh claw wound on her nose.

"He didn't mean to hurt you. He's just difficult sometimes," I offered with what I hoped was a reassuring smile.

The little dog jumped up and pawed frantically at my leg, wiggling her whole body as she cried, "Hey! Hey! Hey! Did you just talk? Do you know how to talk? You're a very good, very smart girl!"

I bent down and scooped her up, and Paisley immediately set to licking my face as if it were covered in gravy or bacon grease or some other irresistible treat. "Yes, I can talk to both animals and people," I explained. "I don't know why, though. It's kind of just the way things are. Would it be okay if I talked to you?"

Paisley wagged her tail so hard her entire body shook, then she broke apart into a shivering fit. Whether she needed a sweater or some anti-anxiety medicine, I couldn't say for sure. The shivering continued as she jumped into an excited monologue. "I've always wanted my own humans, and now I even have one that talks! The other dogs back at the shelter won't believe it! When are they coming for a visit? Or, oh! Maybe they could move in with us, too. This house is plenty big, and there are lots of dogs that need homes."

I laughed at her enthusiasm, even though her reminder of all the homeless pets that had remained behind following Nan's impromptu adoption of Paisley made my heart feel heavy. "I'm sorry, Paisley. I wish I could adopt all your friends, but I already made a promise to take care of my cat the best I can, and he would be very upset if we filled our house up with dogs."

As soon as I set Paisley back on the floor, she curled up against my foot and pouted. "He's a very mean kitty."

"Yeah, he kind of is, but he'll grow on you, I promise. And I bet you'll grow on him, too. He just needs time to get used to having you here. It's a very big change."

"It's a big change for me, too." The little dog ran in a circle to indicate the giant manor in which she now lived. "At the shelter I had to share a cage with two other dogs. It was very crowded. That's why I thought we could give some of the others a home, too."

Three to a cage?

I hadn't spent much time at the local animal shelter, but from what I remembered, we'd never had an overcrowding problem in the past. Maybe things had just been a bit different for Paisley than the others due to her extremely small size.

I already felt guilty about not being able to adopt more animals. Thinking of them now all cramped together made me feel that much worse. Maybe a few volunteer shifts or a small donation were in order, both to help them out of a potentially tough spot and to ease my guilty conscience.

"Hey," I said, crouching down so that Paisley and I were at closer to the same level. "How would you like to visit the shelter with me tomorrow? You can say hi to your friends, and I'll see if there's anything we can do to help them find new homes."

Paisley let out a high-pitched cry and began to shake furiously once again. "You're not making me go back. Are you?" the dog yelped. "Because Nan said this is my home now."

This poor thing. No wonder Nan had been charmed enough to bring her home.

"Oh, sweetie. I promise I wouldn't do that to you. Nan's right. This is your home now, and nothing's going to change that."

Paisley stood on her hind legs and reached her paws up my leg. "I love you, new mommy," she said. "This is the best day of my entire life."

My heart swelled at the Chihuahua's confession of love. It had taken me almost dying at the hands of a gun-toting psychopath to get Octo-Cat to even admit he liked me. Yet Paisley had only needed a single short conversation to forge the deepest of bonds. As much as I adored my Octo-Cat, it sure felt nice to be appreciated rather than insulted.

Hmmm. Maybe I'm not as much of a cat person as I once thought.

Of course, I immediately felt guilty for thinking that even in passing. It was our petaversary, after all, and I'd promised my feline overlord freshly grilled shrimp by way of celebration.

It was time to leave Nan and Paisley to celebrate their own

adoption day together while I did my best to ease the poor, put-out kitty that sat waiting for me in my bedroom tower.

I closed my eyes tight and wished that one day we could all be one big happy family. I didn't have a candle to blow out and it wasn't anyone's birthday, but I hoped the special wish magic I'd grown up believing in could save us now.

Honestly, we were going to need a miracle to get my stubborn cat to change his heart when it came to the poor, shivering dog that needed us.

Just in case, I said a quick prayer, too.

One way or another, we would find a way to all live peacefully together.

After all, we didn't have any other option.

CHAPTER THREE

W hen I returned to my room with grilled shrimp and Evian for both Octo-Cat and myself, I found him sitting on my pillow flicking his tail pensively.

The moment he saw me, he popped to his feet and began to pace the length of the mattress. "Well, did you talk some sense into Nan about the unappreciated monstrosity she has wrought on our house? On my house?" He didn't even look at me as he spat each word. If he had, I'm sure my face would have given away everything he needed to know.

"Umm, a little," I hedged, trying hard not to sigh yet again. "Mostly I talked to Paisley, though, and she is really happy to be here."

Octo-Cat stopped pacing and stared at me with open disdain. "And I'd be really happy for her to *not* be here."

I let out a groan and sunk down onto the bed beside him. "I know change is hard, but——"

The tabby diva lifted a paw and shook his head. "I'll stop you right there. If you're not for me, then you're against me. And thus..." He paused and sighed heavily. "I bid you good night, Angela."

I watched helplessly as he hopped off the bed and crawled back beneath it. "Hey, I didn't ask for any of this, either," I called after him.

But Octo-Cat refused to respond.

"We can't just send her back. From what Paisley told me, the shelter is already pretty overcrowded, and that's not a very nice way for her to have to live, especially when there's a family who wants her. *Our* family."

He still said nothing to acknowledge me or my arguments.

"You can't just ignore me," I huffed, throwing myself back onto the bed in resignation. "How are we supposed to solve our cases if we're not talking to each other?" I asked while studying a smudge on the ceiling.

Octo-Cat didn't answer, which was probably for the best regarding this last point. The truth was even though we'd opened Pet Whisperer P.I. for business more than one week ago, we still had yet to book our first case.

If I could do it all over again, I might have rejected the kooky name that Mom and Nan had saddled us with. Around Blueberry Bay, calling yourself a pet whisperer pretty much guaranteed that folks thought you were crazy—or worse, a fraud.

And I was neither, thank you very much.

Maybe if I started a website or took out an ad, business would pick up a bit. My boyfriend Charles had already offered to refer business from the firm our way when he or one of the associates needed extra help. I'd originally rejected his offer, preferring to either succeed or fail totally on my own. Now, however, I was starting to wonder if I was being too stupid, too proud. If I could help people, do what I loved, and get paid for it, then who cared how I came about my clients?

"Can we please talk about this?" I begged my still fuming cat.

"You already know where I stand on the matter. When you decide to join me, then I'll decide to talk to you," Octo-Cat mumbled in that horrible patronizing tone I loathed.

"Fine, then you can spend our petaversary alone." Even though

I knew he wasn't going to answer me, I still stormed off and slammed the door.

Of course, I hated to leave my kitty companion like that, but being together at that moment was, unfortunately, creating more problems than it was solving. Maybe with a good night's sleep, we'd be able to start this conversation fresh in the morning.

Maybe.

But until then, I just couldn't take any more fighting.

And so I set his food and water on the floor, went to retrieve his litter box, and then moved my bedding to one of the spare bedrooms so we could both have a bit of time to cool off. Once I'd settled in, I shot Charles a quick text to let him know not to come over that night and went to bed several hours earlier than I'd planned.

Happy Petaversary to me!

The next morning, I woke up feeling refreshed and much less irritated than I'd been the night before. The moment I left my temporary quarters, Paisley raced over to lick my ankles and tell me about the great adventures she'd had touring the estate with Nan.

"There are so many great places to pee! So many!" she gushed as I reached down to scratch her between her adorable oversized ears. "I love it here! It's like a paradise for dogs! I can't believe I get to live here now! I love my new life! I love you!"

I chuckled to myself while she zoomed off again. She ran in such fast, tight circles that soon she was almost completely out of breath from the exertion of it all. When Paisley slowed down and approached me again, her tongue lolled from the side of her mouth and she panted heavily, smiling up at me with unmistakable affection.

"I'm glad you like it here," I told her. "Nan and I will do everything we can to make sure you love everything about your new life. Hey, by the way, do you still want to go to the shelter with me for a quick visit today?"

"Oh, boy. Oh, boy! Oh, yes! Yes, please!" the little dog trilled, running another manic lap before returning to me once more.

I laughed again, something I could tell I'd be doing lots of now that Paisley was a part of my world. "I don't think they're open yet, but let me check their hours online and find out when they do."

Paisley followed me up the stairs and toward my bedroom—the bedroom where I just happened to know that one very crabby tabby would still be sitting by his lonesome and bemoaning his bad luck.

I stopped so abruptly that the eager Chihuahua bumped into my lower leg. "Um, I'm sorry, but Octo-Cat is going to be upset if you come in with me. Would you mind waiting outside for me? I promise to come back very soon."

The little tricolor dog plopped her butt down on the top stair and wagged her tail furiously. "I will be a good girl and wait, because that's what you said to do!"

Well, that was an entirely different response than I ever would have received from Octo-Cat. Oh, a pet owner could most assuredly get used to this. I wiped my face of the smile that had just spread from cheek to wicked cheek and quietly let myself into my cat's self-imposed prison.

"Octavius?" I called out, using his preferred name in the hopes it might earn me some sorely needed brownie points. "Are you in here?"

"Of course I'm in here, Angela," he growled from beneath the bed. "But I also smell that the dog is out there."

"Oh, Paisley? She's not coming in. I—"

Just then, the door burst open and an exuberant Paisley bounded through the door and rushed straight under the bed. "I heard you call my name. I'm a good girl. I'm coming to you!" she called as she shot past me in her renewed pursuit of her new cat roommate.

"Betrayal!" Octo-Cat cried, shooting past me and bolting down the stairs in a whirlwind of fluff and attitude. "Betrayal of the highest order!"

Even from all the way up here, I heard his electronic cat flap beep and pull open from the foyer.

Paisley at least hadn't given chase. Instead, she stood proudly at my heels, beating a steady drum with her small black tail against the floorboards. "Did I do good, Mommy?" she asked.

I didn't have the heart to tell her no. "You did good," I hedged. "But next time, wait until I say *come*. Can you do that?"

"Yes, Mommy. I surely can do that! You're my best friend, and I love you!" With this said, she began licking my toes and didn't stop for at least three whole minutes.

Okay, fine. So maybe I was starting to find her enthusiasm *a little* annoying…

CHAPTER FOUR

Paisley and I trotted into the Glendale Animal Shelter around lunchtime. A pudgy older woman greeted us from behind a battered oak desk tucked into the corner of the entryway at the very moment we arrived.

"Welcome! Welcome!" she crooned. Then, shooting her gaze toward Paisley, she cleared her throat, dropped it a few notes, and said, "Hey, I recognize you, little dog. You aren't bringing her back. Are you? Was something wrong at home?"

Paisley scuttled back to cower behind my leg, shivering violently as I'd already come to realize was her way whenever anything either upset or excited her.

"No, of course not!" I assured them both. "We're just here for a little visit is all. Actually, is there someone I can speak with about maybe putting in some volunteer hours?"

The other woman's entire countenance lit up at this. "Oh, how lovely! Yes, yes, let me just take you back to our Community Outreach Coordinator's office so the two of you can have a little chat."

I nodded my agreement, then followed her through a set of double doors into the behind-the-scenes area of the shelter.

Paisley pranced alongside me, stopping frequently to sniff at the air or press her quivering nose to the floor. "It all smells exactly the same as it did yesterday," she mused. "Oh, can you believe it, Mommy?"

I could believe it; I could believe it very easily but chose not to say anything that might dampen the little dog's spirits. Instead, I held my tongue as our guide led us down a long, narrow room filled wall-to-wall on each side with floor-to-ceiling kennels. Sure enough, many of the dogs were housed several to a cage, just as Paisley had described the night before.

"Hey, Chihuahua! What are you doing back in this awful place?" a black Labrador mix called after us, then pushed his snout through the metal caging and whined.

"Haha. Just visiting!" Paisley cried happily. "I have two new humans. This one even talks," she added, referring to me as we continued to follow the front desk volunteer deeper and deeper into the shelter.

"It talks?" a fluffy little dog asked in a high-pitched voice. "Really?"

"*Really*. And it's a girl, so say she. That's the polite thing to do." Paisley followed up her answer by nudging my leg with her cold nose. "Hey, Mommy. Say something to our friends!"

I coughed and widened my eyes at Paisley, giving my head a subtle shake that I sincerely hoped she would understand. She was still very new to our home and didn't yet seem to understand that I couldn't exactly out my ability in front of unknown humans. I'd have to explain how everything worked once the two of us had some privacy. Hopefully, she wouldn't be too embarrassed by my unexpected unwillingness to perform my neat human trick for the other shelter dogs.

"Here we are," our guide said brightly, rescuing me from that disappointed look on my sweet doggo's face. "You'll find Mr. Leavitt straight through that door."

"Thank you," I said, reaching out to shake the woman's hand.

"My name's Pearl," she offered with a friendly smile. "And it's my pleasure to assist. I'll be just up front, should you have any questions for me before you go. Good luck!"

I watched Pearl zoom away, somewhat confused by the fact that she'd wished me good luck. Didn't places like this always need a steady stream of volunteers?

The dogs behind us began to bark in earnest. I tried to understand what they were saying, but too many voices mixed together for me to make out any single thread. Suddenly, I felt very anxious as I raised my fist to knock on the office door before me.

"Come in," someone—presumably Mr. Leavitt—called.

I scooped Paisley into my arms, then pushed the door open. At the same exact time, the fluorescent lights overhead flickered on, off, on, and then at last off again. The long room filled with kennels fell completely dark and silent, but the small office before me had a steady stream of sunlight wafting in from the large row of windows along the back wall.

"Hello," I said shyly. "If this is a bad time, I can come back later."

The man behind the desk glanced up at me with a welcoming grin. Shockingly, he appeared to be about my age—late twenties, maybe early thirties. For some reason, I'd expected someone far older. Maybe it was the fact that the gray-haired woman I'd just met had chosen to refer to him as a Mr.

He stood and extended a hand in my direction. "You mean the lights? Nah, that happens all the time. Come on in all the way, take a seat, and tell me what I can do for you." His blue eyes shone as our hands made contact, and I swear I felt a tiny spark jump from his skin to mine.

I didn't find Mr. Leavitt particularly attractive, but there was something about him that was inescapably alluring. If this whole Community Outreach Coordinator gig fell through, I'm sure he'd have a long and prosperous career in Hollywood, D.C., or even the boardroom. He'd fit in easily anywhere charisma was valued and rewarded.

"I know this guy," Paisley said from atop my lap after I'd taken a moment to get settled in one of the padded chairs opposite Mr.

Leavitt's desk. "He'd play with us sometimes. And he brought lots of people by to visit. Sometimes they would play with us, too."

I patted the dog's head instead of answering her directly. Keeping my hand there, I directed my attention back toward the only other human in the room. "As you can see, my Nan and I adopted this sweet little girl from your shelter. And, well, we're just so happy to have her that I wanted to pay it forward somewhere."

Mr. Leavitt nodded and folded his hands on the desk before him. "Pay it forward? How so?"

"Could you use any volunteers? I kind of have a way with animals." Of course that was the understatement of the year, but there was no way I was telling this guy the truth about my hidden abilities.

"That's very kind of you, Miss...?" He paused and flashed me a disarming grin.

"Russo," I offered, hating that heat was now rising to my cheeks. "Angie Russo. Hi."

He winked and leaned back in his chair, putting me at ease once more. "As I was saying, that's very kind of you for wanting to help. You probably noticed we're a bit overcrowded at the moment."

I nodded again. "Yes, that's why I thought I could help."

The lights flickered again, illuminating a small lamp on the edge of Mr. Leavitt's desk. He studied it for a moment, then frowned thoughtfully. "We're just as overcrowded with volunteers as we are animals. But I'm afraid it may not be enough."

My heart dropped straight onto the linoleum floor beneath my chair. "Is everything okay?" I whispered, wishing the sensitive little dog in my lap didn't have to be here for whatever came next in our conversation.

Mr. Leavitt offered an even wider smile than before. "Of course, everything's okay. At least it is for now. Just a bit of growing pains, if you will. You see, at present, we have more animals and more staff, but not more money. It makes covering all our expenses a bit tricky, but we'll manage. We always do."

Was I actually being dismissed? Had Mr. Leavitt somehow

decided that my help wasn't good enough? That rankled me and suddenly made me desperate to contribute in any way I could.

"That's good to hear, but still I'd like to do something," I argued, giving him my best, most placating smile. "Would a donation be better than volunteering right now?"

He shook his head and let out a low sigh. "Oh, no, no, no. You don't have to do that. I wasn't trying to suggest——"

I chuckled as I fished around in my purse for my checkbook. Mr. Leavitt was obviously a proud man, but this was a community shelter, and I was part of said community. I owed it to the animals to make sure they had enough to eat, drink, and keep a roof over their heads. "I know you weren't, but I'm already here anyway and I want to help," I said with a shrug.

"Well, if you insist, then it would be wrong of me to say no. Thank you so much for being willing to help these wonderful animals."

Mr. Leavitt told me the information I needed to fill out my check and then accepted it with an outpouring of gratitude. "You're a good woman, Angie Russo. I can tell this little one is very lucky to have landed a place in your home," he said, scratching the mostly black Chihuahua in the center of her forehead.

And for once I didn't argue. Paisley was lucky to have us. I knew that better than ever now that I'd seen the alternative. Now, if only there was something more I could do to help the others who hadn't yet found their forever homes…

CHAPTER FIVE

After writing out the check for my donation, Mr. Leavitt showed me around the shelter and detailed how my gift would help the residents there. I left that afternoon about a thousand dollars lighter and feeling fantastic about it.

It was nice to use my money for something good. Not that it wasn't great to keep Octo-Cat stocked on all the specialty water, gourmet cat food, and new Apple technology his little kitty heart desired, but this time I was helping dozens of animals in need rather than catering to the spoiled whims of a single pampered pet.

I couldn't stop smiling the whole way home.

During that drive, Paisley and I also had a little talk about what I could and could not do in front of other people.

"So you can't talk to animals when other humans are around?" the Chihuahua summed up from her precarious perch on the passenger seat.

"Bingo," I sang with a huge smile of confirmation, then added, "Unless, of course, it's Nan, Charles, or someone else we're close to. Got it?"

"Got it," she barked, taking a quick moment to stare at me in admiration before putting her front paws up on the windowsill and basking in the fresh breeze blowing through our tiny vehicle.

Back at home, we found Nan listening to showtunes while slathering a tall layer cake with light pink buttercream. "Is that the Hamilton soundtrack?" I guessed, suppressing a laugh when I drew close enough to hear my seventy-year-old-plus grandmother rapping about the founding of our nation.

"That Lin Manuel Miranda is so talented, and so cute, too! If I were thirty-five years younger or he were thirty-five years older, I'd have a half a mind to take off half his clothes and—"

I was quick to shove an index finger in each ear so that I wouldn't have to listen to the rest of that sentence. "Nan, that's way more than I ever want to hear about that."

She chuckled and shook her head. "Hey, I may be old, but I'm not dead yet!"

I simply gave her a hug and changed the topic. "Yeah, um, right. So, uh, anyway... Has Octo-Cat come out at all today?"

Nan shrugged as she continued work on her towering bubblegum-colored confection. "Not that I've seen. How did things go at the shelter?"

A vision of all those poor caged animals sitting in their dark cages flashed through my mind, eliciting a sad sigh. "I made a donation, but I wish there was something more we could do to help. It's really crowded in there, and they even lost power while I was visiting."

"You don't say," Nan remarked, biting down on her lip and then spinning the cake before her to make sure it had been fully frosted.

"I wish I hadn't," I admitted. "What brought you into that place to begin with? Did you know they were struggling when you went in to adopt Paisley yesterday?"

Nan took off her apron and washed her hands in the kitchen sink, then dried them on an embroidered tea towel. "I sure didn't, and the lights at least stayed on while I was there, but I did notice the fact that they had more dogs than kennels to put them in."

"So what made you decide to adopt a dog yesterday then?" I

took advantage of her quiet thoughtfulness by grabbing a spoon from the drawer and snagging a spoonful of buttercream to taste.

Nan rolled her eyes playfully and followed me out toward the living room where we both claimed our favorite spots in the large sitting area filled with uncomfortable antique furniture. "Oh, I didn't decide," she revealed once we were both settled in our seats. "I just did it."

"Yup, that sounds about right," I said with a chuckle. I loved my nan dearly, but it was true that she did first and thought later—if at all. "Well, you picked a good one in Paisley. She's a real sweet girl."

"Of course I did. And of course she is," Nan clucked like a proud mother hen. "Was there ever any doubt?"

"Not at all."

We made some tea, then chatted for a bit about our plans for the week. Nan was hard at work developing new recipes for her upcoming book. It wasn't a cookbook, but rather a memoir that would be enhanced with half a dozen of her favorite custom recipes. She was also working on some kind of secret art project that she planned to convert into the book's eventual cover, but I wasn't allowed to see that until it was ready.

I had originally planned to work on rustling up some new business for Octo-Cat's and my new private investigation firm, but now it seemed I'd be spending every waking hour serving as mediator for our two pets as they learned to live in harmony.

"Would you be okay with chicken parmigiana for dinner?" Nan asked with a quick glance toward her new Apple Watch. Octo-Cat's zeal for all things iTech had spread to me and Nan, too. "We have another couple of hours yet, but it wouldn't hurt to thaw the meat a bit first."

As a proud American of half-Italian descent, I was always up for a hearty pasta dish—and everything Nan cooked tasted like Heaven to my untrained taste buds. "You know I love your chicken parmigiana," I answered without hesitation as I stretched my arms overhead and let out a happy moan in anticipation of that night's meal.

A loud crash followed by the sound of something fragile shattering on the ground sent us both scrambling to our feet.

"What was that?" Nan shrieked.

"Sounded like it came from the kitchen. C'mon."

We both rushed in and found little Paisley sniffing a broken pile of china. No, Lenox! Oh, this was not good!

"Was that one of Octo-Cat's teacups from Ethel?" I shouted, a wicked headache already brewing beneath my temples.

Nan bent down and picked up a shard. "Judging from the floral pattern around the rim, why yes. Yes, it is."

"Did you do this, Paisley?" I asked after kneeling down to speak with the dog at her level. "Did you accidentally knock this down?"

"No way. I would never do that!" she barked, wagging her tail affectionately. "I would never break Mommy's or Nan's things."

I believed her. Not just because I knew she wanted to keep us both happy, but also because it didn't seem possible that she'd be able to jump onto the counter, push off the teacup, and then jump back to the floor without managing to hurt herself.

"Do you think Octavius broke his own cup in protest?" Nan asked, shaking her head in disappointment.

"It seems like something he might do, but he's been locked in my bedroom the whole day. Remember?"

Nan reached one hand up to scratch her head. "Are you sure you didn't leave a window open or something?"

"Pretty sure," I said, even though I couldn't really be sure of anything at the moment, at least not as far as he was concerned. "But let's go check and see if he's still in there."

"Can I come?" Paisley asked, trailing after us excitedly.

"No, he doesn't——" I began, but then quickly amended my answer. "You know what, Paze? Yes. Yes, you can come."

"Oh, joyest of joys!" the Chihuahua sang, racing up both flights of stairs as fast as her diminutive paws could carry her.

"You do realize that the cat is going to be furious with you," Nan pointed out with a naughty grin.

I shrugged. "Yeah, well, maybe I'm furious with him, too," I muttered, then took a deep breath and pushed the door open.

CHAPTER SIX

We found Octo-Cat sitting on the corner of my bed and staring unhappily into the void. A flurry of striped hairs danced in the sunlight that filtered in through the nearby window. Just looking at the scene made me have to sneeze… and so I did.

"Why so loud?" my cat moaned in response to my *achoo*, turning toward me with a sneer on his scrunched face.

"Kitty friend!" Paisley cried as she charged toward the bed and took a giant leap upward. All that momentum wasn't enough to propel her tiny body onto the mattress, however, and she rammed into the side of the bed head-first.

Matters also weren't helped by Octo-Cat's decision to take a clawed swipe at her. "Hey, you punk! Let's get one thing straight. I am not your friend," he growled and flexed his claws, ready to take a fresh shot at the poor, misguided pup.

"That's enough, you two!" Nan hurried across the room and grabbed an animal with each arm. "Let's play nice here. After all, we're a family."

Paisley strained to reach Octo-Cat across the short distance, barking happily as she cried, "Brother, brother, brother!"

Octo-Cat mewled demonically, twisting furiously until he at last wriggled free of Nan's embrace.

As for me? I laughed and laughed hard.

Which only made my cat that much more livid with the lot of us. "Why are you bothering me?" he whined. "Go away."

"We were wondering if you knew anything about what happened in the kitchen." I studied him carefully for any glint of recognition.

If Octo-Cat knew anything, though, he didn't give it away. His face remained an unreadable mask—well, at least behind the thick layer of disdain. "What happened in the kitchen?" he asked with a yawn that smelled like two parts Fancy Feast and one part cat butt.

Oh, boy.

Maybe he actually didn't know. Maybe I was about to break his poor, aggrieved heart all over again. I thought back to the first time one of Ethel's heirloom teacups had broken, remembering his utter despair and the touching funeral that had followed.

"Are you going to tell him about the broken teacup, or should I?" Nan asked me with one raised eyebrow.

So much for putting things delicately.

"*What broken teacup?*" the tabby asked after a sharp gasp, struggling to speak each word with his crackly, suddenly oxygen-starved voice.

"I'm sorry," I said, and I really did mean it. "It was one of Ethel's. We were all in the living room, when—"

"Enough!" he shouted, turning on me so quickly, I took a reflexive step backward. "It was the dog, and you know it!"

I shook my head, unable to tear my eyes away from the enraged feline. "We thought that at first, but she can't reach the counters."

Paisley yelped. "I'm sorry about your teacup, brother!"

"You know, she's not that much bigger than a rat. It wouldn't be so hard to snap her neck," Octo-Cat said through gritted teeth.

"That's a very bad cat!" I yelled. "How dare you say that about your new sister?"

"She is not my family, and she never will be. Get her out of here if you know what's good for her… or for you."

Paisley let out an ear-piercing chain of shrieks and wouldn't stop.

"There, there, dear one," Nan sang softly while I glared at my cruel cat companion. It was one thing to be upset, but quite another to threaten such violence.

"Stop looking at me like that," he rasped with a weighty flick of his dark tail. "You're the one who's forcing my paw, and can't you see I'm grieving my poor, sweet teacup here?"

Nobody said anything as we all stood around my tower bedroom awkwardly. Paisley at least stopped crying, though.

"Get out of here! Go! Leave me in peace!" the distraught tabby shouted at last.

I knew he was upset, but I still couldn't believe how quickly he'd gone from simply irritated to threatening murder. It was moments like this that made me question whether my life was really better with him in it. Of course, I knew it was silly and that hunting was part of a cat's nature, but still... How could he be so cold-blooded about it all?

"Fine. We're going," I mumbled, then led Nan and Paisley from the room. "Next time we see you, I hope you'll be a bit more welcoming."

"Well, that didn't exactly go as planned," Nan whispered in my ear once we'd shut the door firmly behind our small party.

"No, it really didn't."

We trod down the stairs side by side.

Nan carried Paisley in her arms, not unlike a little baby. "What now?" she asked.

"It looks like we'll be adding to our teacup cemetery in the back-yard. Other than that, I don't know. We both know he can hold a grudge for a long time, and we also know that Paisley isn't going anywhere. I guess the only thing we can really do is wait the situation out. And maybe keep a close eye on Paisley while we do." I hadn't repeated Octo-Cat's murmured threats to Nan, and I didn't plan to, either.

Nan hummed to herself now as she thought about what we might do next. After a few moments, her face lit up and she said,

"That may be the only thing we can do about this particular problem, but there's more than one way to… Oh, dear, that is a terrible
expression, especially in light of current events. What I mean is
there's more than one problem that needs solving."

"The shelter?" I asked, my voice cracking on the first syllable of
that second word.

My grandmother nodded. "You mentioned how much they're in
dire need, and I just so happen to have some extra money left over
from selling the old house to Charles. Perhaps it's time I made a
donation of my own."

She was right. Donating had made me feel so much better
earlier that day, and at least the shelter wanted to be helped, unlike
Octo-Cat. *Hmm.* How late do they stay open? It's almost dinner
time now."

This didn't stop Nan, however. "I'll run down now and give it a
try," she said. "If they're already closed for the day, I'll head over
again first thing in the morning."

I stopped walking and put an arm on Nan's shoulder before she
could head down the grand staircase to the main floor. "Oh, no you
don't! There's no way I'm letting you go on your own. Remember
what happened last time you visited the animal shelter
unsupervised?"

"Of course I do," Nan said with an impish grin, lifting Paisley in
her arms and giving the little dog a kiss on her nose. "But was it
really so bad? I mean, look at this sweet girl!"

"Depends on who you ask," I said, then motioned back toward
my room with a beleaguered sigh.

"Be right back," Nan informed me as she turned away from the
staircase and shot down the hall to her bedroom. "I need a quick
change of costume."

When Nan joined me downstairs a few minutes later, she was
wearing a hot pink T-shirt that read *Dog Mom* across the chest. Both
*O*s had been fashioned to look like paw prints.

"When did you have time to get that?" I asked with a chuckle.

"Overnight shipping, dear," was her reply as she rummaged

about in the coat closet and extracted a matching pink leash for Paisley along with a…

"A spiked collar? For your five-pound Chihuahua? Really?" Now I was laughing in earnest. Just because I was never surprised by my grandmother's antics didn't mean they weren't hilarious.

Nan lowered herself to the floor and patted her lap. "Well, why not?" she mumbled while she worked on sizing the collar appropriately for Paisley's thin neck. "For all we know, the heart of a warrior beats within this tiny body."

I blew a raspberry. "Um, I can talk to her. Remember?"

"I'm a warrior!" the dog exclaimed enthusiastically, lapping up all the attention. "I'm a big, brave dog!"

I just shook my head. These two were clearly perfect for each other, and I was so, so happy for them.

CHAPTER SEVEN

I felt like the odd one out, given that my two companions had decked themselves out in a vibrant matching shade of pink while I wore a black polka-dotted blouse and flippy yellow skirt. On the way out the door, Nan had decided to pair her T-shirt with silver sling-back kitten heels, and I'd thrown on my favorite battered combat boots. As usual, we made quite the interesting pair. Throw in the Chihuahua, and we were practically a walking fashion show —or at least a reality TV show.

We reached the shelter a few minutes before six and were greeted with a firmly locked door.

"Crud," I muttered, rattling the handle just in case.

I looked toward Nan just in time to catch her ducking around the side of the building and out of view.

"What are you doing?" I whisper-yelled, chasing after her.

"Why, looking for another way in, of course," she said, tapping a long fingernail against the window and then turning to me with a devilish smile.

"This isn't one of your spy movies, Nan. We can just come back tomorrow. No need to sneak about. Now c'mon. Let's go," I hissed as I attempted to yank her back toward the parking lot.

Nan shook me off, then raised a finger to her lips and sank to the ground, motioning for me to get down, too. "Wait. Someone's in there."

Despite my better judgement, I did as Nan instructed.

We both carefully peeked our heads over the brick ledge and peered through the window. Inside, a thin blonde woman riffled through a tall stack of papers. She muttered something to herself, but I wasn't able to make out the words.

Nan pinched me. "Will you look at that? I knew there was something fishy going on here."

Sure she did. Really, she just got lucky this time and every other time she wanted to have herself an adventure. These days, Nan was never disappointed when it came to uncovering crime and drama in our once sleepy small town.

We both watched as the blonde woman inside pulled a sheet of paper from the middle of the stack with shaking hands and pushed it through a desktop shredder. For a brief moment, she glanced up as if sensing that someone—or rather, some*ones*—was watching her, then cursed under her breath and hurried out of view.

"C'mon," Nan said, duck-walking toward the next window.

I waddled after her, and Paisley pranced after me. What a merry band of spies we made.

We didn't see the girl again until we reached the very end of the building and the room I easily remembered as Mr. Leavitt's office. Once there, the blonde pulled open the bottom left drawer of his desk and shoved the remaining papers inside, took another quick look around, and fled.

"Shoot. Is she leaving?" I asked, short of breath from the excitement of our discovery coupled with the grueling physical task of the duck-walk. "She'll see our car in the parking lot and know that someone's here."

"Ooh, you're right." Nan popped up and sprinted back toward the main entrance, beating the blonde girl by a solid thirty seconds.

If she was surprised to see us waiting outside the doors for her, she did a great job hiding it. "Oh, hello. Can I help you?" the girl asked.

"Yes, dear. Thank you," Nan answered in her over-the-top grandmother voice that she took on whenever she wanted to appear extra frail or needy. "I've come to make a donation, but I'm afraid I may not be in the right place. Is this the Glendale Community Animal Shelter?"

The blonde smiled with what appeared to be relief. "Yes, that's us, but I'm afraid we're closed now."

"Oh, bother," Nan chirped, sounding far too upbeat given the words she'd just spoken. "Well, that's what I get for nodding off during my stories."

"Aww, it's okay," the girl said, shooting Nan a placating smile. "We open again tomorrow at eight. Or, if you prefer, I can take your check now and make sure it gets into the right hands tomorrow."

"Oh, bless you, dear," Nan said with a gracious smile. "That would be wonderful. Now what's your name? I want to make sure I can mention to my followers on the Facebook how helpful you were to me this evening."

"I'm Trish," the girl introduced herself with a laugh. "And thank you. We can use all the volunteers and all the donations we can get."

"Well, Trish." Nan extracted her checkbook from her purse. "It isn't much, seeing as I'm on a fixed income, but I hope it gives you the help you need."

"No amount is too small. Believe me. I don't have an extra two pennies to rub together, which is why I donate my time instead," Trish explained as she shifted her weight from one foot to the other.

"They're very lucky to have you," I said, when Nan didn't.

Trish and I watched in silence as Nan wrote out a check for one hundred dollars and tore it from her checkbook with a flourish.

"On behalf of the animals, thank you very, very much for your generosity," the girl said, holding Nan's donation close to her heart.

"Oh, it was nothing," Nan responded with a dismissive wave. "I just wish it could have been more."

"Every small donation makes a huge difference." Trish folded the check in half and stuck it in her front pocket. "I'll be sure this gets added to our coffers tomorrow. Good night, and thank you again!"

We returned her goodbye, waited for Paisley to take a quick potty break, then headed back to the car.

"Who was that?" the little dog asked. "I've never seen her before."

"Trish," I explained. "She's one of the volunteers. Are you sure you haven't seen her before? She's obviously not new if she's in charge of closing up."

"Nope, never," Paisley answered without the slightest hesitation. "She was really pretty, though. I like her."

"Wait," I said with a creeping grin as I thought of the early days with Octo-Cat back when he was simply upset about me providing him with the wrong brand of bottled water as opposed to threatening to murder a Chihuahua. "Do you maybe not recognize her because all humans look the same?"

Paisley's long pink tongue lolled from her mouth as she panted in amusement. "Why would you say that? Humans don't look the same at all, and you smell very different, too! Nope. I definitely would have remembered seeing—and smelling—her before."

I quickly caught Nan up on the dog's and my little side conversation.

"*Hmm,*" she said with a dramatic huff. "That's a bit odd."

"It is," I agreed. "What do you think Trish was doing in the shelter all by herself? Does she actually volunteer there, or no? And what did she secretly shred?"

"Good questions," Nan answered as she navigated the roads that would lead us back toward our home. "One thing's for sure, I'll be keeping a close watch on my bank account to see where that check actually ends up."

I nodded to show my agreement. "Smart."

"Maybe tomorrow night we can go back and try to break in," she added with a completely serious expression on her wrinkled face.

"Nan," I scolded. "We're trying to stop someone else from breaking the law, not break it ourselves."

"Well, you're no fun," she groused.

Maybe I wasn't fun compared to my wild grandmother, but one of us had to be the level-headed one in this investigation.

And with Octo-Cat out of commission, apparently that job would fall to me.

CHAPTER EIGHT

We returned home to find my boyfriend Charles waiting on the front porch. As soon as I parked the car, I ran up the short set of steps and straight into his outstretched arms.

"What are you doing here?" I asked after a quick peck hello.

"Well, I missed seeing you yesterday when the petaversary celebration got cancelled. And when we talked earlier today, you just seemed so down. You know I had to come by and cheer up my best girl." His eyes held mine as he spoke, making me feel weak in the knees. Even though we'd been dating for a few weeks now, I still couldn't get over the fact that we were finally together. I'd crushed on him for so long, and now? He was my honest-to-goodness boyfriend—and a really great one at that.

Once I had my strength back, I pulled away and studied his handsome features. "Your best girl?" I asked with a giggle. "That sounds an awful lot like something Nan would say."

"Okay. Fine," he confessed with a breathy laugh. "So maybe she did call and put me up to it, but the important thing is that I'm here now and I have something special planned for us tonight."

I hugged Charles tight and pushed my face into his chest in an attempt to hide my nervous expression. I was still pretty new to this whole relationship thing and terrified I'd do something to mess it up at any minute. We were especially tricky, too, given that we'd become such good friends before ever getting romantically involved.

Because of our unusual timeline, I feared we were dangerously close to the "I love you" stage even though we'd only been dating for a little less than a month. I also feared the "Will you marry me?" stage might quickly follow once the first three little words were out of the bag. And as much as I adored Charles, the thought of becoming somebody's wife—of living with anyone other than Nan —made me break out in goose bumps and a cold sweat all at once.

One day at a time, I reminded myself as I so often did. The now was very good indeed, and I needed to take some time to enjoy these early puppy love days of my first real adult relationship.

Swallowing down the last dregs of my anxiety, I asked, "Am I allowed to know what you have planned, or is it another one of your famous surprises?"

Charles kissed my forehead, then released me from his embrace. "This time, I'll tell you," he answered with a smirk. "But next time, I'm keeping whatever I plan for us a surprise until the last possible moment."

I nodded, still focused on the now and eager to find out what we'd be doing that night.

Charles put both arms around my waist and pulled me close. "There's a new day spa that just opened up on the edge of Dewdrop Springs, and they're running a special on couple's massages. I figured we could go check it out. What do you say?"

"I say, *sign me up for that!*" I squealed and gave a happy little leap into the air. I'd never had a massage before, but I'd heard good things—mostly from my grandmother. Truth be told, the whole idea made me a bit nervous, but I appreciated Charles's gesture too much to let him in on any of the hesitation or worry swirling through my mind.

"Bye, dear," Nan called after us as Charles led me to his waiting car. "Don't do anything I wouldn't do!"

I laughed so hard at that I almost choked. Nan would do just about anything with hardly a moment's thought first, definitely not the model for chaste behavior. Then again, maybe that was the point she was trying to make here.

"Thanks for getting me out of there," I told my boyfriend as he backed us out of the long driveway.

"Any time," he promised me with a smile that made me want to kiss him right then and there. "Is Octo-Cat still pouting about the new arrival?"

I sucked air in through my teeth. "That would be putting it mildly."

He chuckled at this. "Remember Yo-Yo?"

Ahh, Yo-Yo the Yorkie, the only witness to his owners' double murder. That was the case where Charles and I had first become good friends, even though the whole thing started with him black-mailing me and threatening to expose my secret to the world.

"Of course I remember Yo-Yo," I said with a smug grin. "I also remember how Octo-Cat never quite got used to him for that whole time they were together."

"That was only the better part of a week. Paisley will be around for the rest of his life. Even he can't wage his silent protest for that long."

"Oh, ye of little faith," I quipped, then rolled my eyes for good measure.

We drove for another half hour before reaching our destination. The swanky new spa was part of a run-down strip mall, which didn't inspire much confidence on my part. Once we pushed through the doors, however, we were greeted with a beautiful office space, painted in a tranquil green with a large stone fountain bubbling near the welcome desk. Soft classical music piped through hidden speakers, and the woman waiting to greet us wore all white from head to toe.

Her red hair shone even in the dim lighting, and her pale skin appeared flawless to my untrained eye. "Welcome to Serenity," she said melodically. "How may we improve your world today?"

I fought back any number of sarcastic comments that were teetering right on the edge of my tongue and gave this would-be world-improver a tight-lipped smile.

Charles, however, seemed far more in his element. Perhaps because he'd grown up in California. He forged right ahead in the direction of the woman and the desk, grabbing one of my hands and tugging me along as he went. "We're here for a seven o'clock couples massage," he informed her.

"Ahh, last spot of the day. Excellent." She paused for an unnaturally long time before adding, "You'll rest well tonight."

Another awkward pause.

Charles and I glanced at each other questioningly, then back toward the woman.

"Stone is just finishing up with his previous appointment, if you'll please have a seat." She floated out from behind the desk and guided us toward a pair of giant exercise balls set around a small area rug.

"Um, thanks." I sank awkwardly onto the dark green ball, leaving the tan one for Charles.

The welcome desk lady smiled at us for slightly longer than was comfortable, then let herself into the back room, leaving Charles and me by ourselves. Well, Serenity was certainly a strange place, if the greeter was any indication. This made me more nervous than I'd been before. Of course, Nan would like this whole dog and pony show. She liked everything, the weirder the better. Me? I preferred to stick to what I already knew and loved.

"You don't think Stone's that guy's real name?" Charles asked, making a funny face.

I was about to ask him the exact same thing, but instead I hit him playfully and giggled. "It all contributes to the *ambience.*" I over pronounced that word so much it sounded like it belonged to another language. French, maybe.

"It's all part of improving our world," he added with a quiet chuckle as he bumped his giant exercise ball seat into mine.

I rolled back to gain some momentum, then nudged his even harder than he'd bumped mine. A flirtatious game of bumper balls followed, each of us making up the rules as we went along.

We didn't even notice at first when the attendant returned—not until she cleared her throat loudly and stared unforgiving daggers our way.

"Stone is ready for you now," she alerted us, forcing a smile for Charles's benefit, I would guess.

Just then, the door to the back swung open and a lithe, blonde figure emerged.

"Trish?" I asked, unable to believe I'd managed to run into the shelter volunteer twice within the span of about an hour—especially considering the distance we'd all had to travel to arrive at the shopping center from Glendale.

Trish blinked over at me, then smiled. "Oh, you came with your mom today to make a donation. Right?" she asked sweetly, so sweetly that it seemed very, very fake.

"My nan, actually, but—yeah—that was me." I smiled graciously to show I meant her no harm. "What are you doing here?"

"N-n-nothing," came Trish's shaky reply. "Just headed home."

And before I could ask anything else, she flew out the door.

Well, so much for making small talk.

CHAPTER NINE

I'm not exactly sure what I'd expected from Stone, but it wasn't the new-age Irish lumberjack who greeted us a short while later.

Though he wore all white like the front desk attendant, he had a completely different vibe. A gigantic toothy smile peeked out from behind his thick red beard. "Good evening," he said as he pushed through the room, his long arms dangling as he moved toward the cabinets that lined the back wall. On his way, he turned up the music track; the soothing sounds of an exotic stringed instrument filled the room, adding to the otherworldliness of this whole experience.

"I'll return in five minutes to begin your massages." Stone handed us each a fluffy white robe, then left to give me and Charles the chance to change into them privately.

Whoa. He'd hardly exchanged five words with us before instructing Charles and me to take off our clothes! It's not that I was a prude, but I'd always been modest about my body.

I'd never even been naked in front of Charles before, but thankfully he was a gentleman about the whole thing. He turned his back to me and promised not to look until I told him it was okay. Still, I tore off my clothes and yanked on that thick robe with record speed.

The unfamiliar garment seemed to swallow me whole, but at least it was comfortable against my bare skin.

"You can turn around now," I called sheepishly. In fact, I felt like a sheep, too, as I stood swaddled in that overly fluffy cotton robe.

And if I was a sheep, then Charles was definitely that cartoon wolf, sizing me up. He let out a low whistle and remarked, "You look extra cuddle-able right about now." Closing the short distance between us, he then wrapped his arms around me and swayed to the meditation music in a ridiculously misguided romantic gesture.

"I'm naked under here," I whispered, embarrassment setting in.

He just laughed and continued to dance with me until a soft knock sounded on the door.

"Come in," Charles called as I clutched my robe even more tightly.

Stone had returned with the front desk attendant in tow. "This is my colleague, Harmony. We'll be massaging you together. Please make yourselves comfortable."

Charles widened his eyes playfully and rubbed his hands together, then made his way to the first of the leather massage tables, slowly lowering himself and lining his face up perfectly with the hole at the top.

"Now you, Angela," Harmony coaxed. Her voice sounded different than it had upfront. Perhaps it was the different acoustics, or maybe she truly had a different voice for working the front desk versus working on a client. Whatever the case, it seemed mighty weird to me.

Apparently sensing my discomfort, Charles reached out and touched my arm as I passed. He was such a good boyfriend, and so much more cultured than me.

I took in a deep breath, vowing to give this whole experience a fair chance before deciding it wasn't for me. After shooting quick smiles to Stone and Harmony, I at last positioned myself on the table—far less gracefully than Charles had, but at least the deed was done.

"Lavender for relaxation," Harmony said, spraying something all around the room.

"Our own proprietary blend," Stone added fondly.

The two took turns speaking to us in quiet, even-tempered voices. Their words blended together perfectly, and I imagined this whole opener had been rehearsed many times to get it just right.

When they had finished, Harmony placed a soft, warm hand on my neck and began to tug gently on my robe.

My heart sped to an uneven gallop. Weren't massages supposed to be calming? Because my anxiety had officially been kicked into overdrive here. "Can I keep the robe on?" I mumbled, hoping it was loud enough for her to hear me.

"No," she said in a voice that brooked no argument, lowering the robe farther and farther until at last she stopped at my hips.

"It's okay, Ange," Charles said from beside me. "It's normal to be nervous the first time. Just keep talking until you relax."

The first time? Had Charles done this before? Had he done it with his ex, Breanne? Yuck, I sure hoped not.

Still, by the time my masseuse had begun to rub oil into my upper back, I'd decided to take Charles's advice. At least talking would make the time go by a bit faster.

"Nice place you've got here," I mused. "Of course, I can only see the floor right now, but the stuff I saw when coming inside was nice, too. Haha."

"Relax," Harmony cooed, sweeping her hands gently along my spine. "Relax."

That did not help me relax.

"So, you guys are new around here? Right? What made you decide to set up shop in Dewdrop Springs? And why is it called Serenity? And are your names really Harmony and Stone?"

"Relax," Harmony said again, a sharp edge working its way into her previously calm voice. What would happen if I didn't relax? Would they call the whole thing off? I didn't want to do that to Charles, especially knowing how hard he worked as the only partner at Glendale's most infamous law firm.

"Sorry, I'm just nervous." I took several slow, shaky breaths, trying to match my breathing to Harmony's, hoping that's what would ultimately help me get into the right headspace for this experience.

"You'll enjoy our work more if you let your tension go," Stone suggested rather unhelpfully.

"This is her first time," Charles explained. "Can we all just talk a little to help her ease in?"

"We won't be going over the allotted appointment time," Harmony warned. Each time she spoke, her voice lost some of that ethereal quality. I wouldn't be surprised if she worked her way up to screaming at me before long.

"We don't need to," Charles was quick to respond. "But she's not going to have a good experience if we don't help her relax."

"Fine," Harmony spat while Stone just chuckled good-naturedly. Of course, I got the ice queen masseur, but I suppose it was better than having the unknown man's hands all over me while I lay there exposed and helpless.

"We're called Serenity because that's the aura we try to create for all who pass through our doors," Stone said.

"What about Trish?" I asked, unable to help myself as I thought back to the startling encounter with the lithe blonde. "She didn't seem very serene when she ran out of here in a hurry."

"We don't discuss other clients," Harmony said, giving me a little pinch as she did.

"Clients? Was she here to get a massage?" I asked innocently.

"Yes," Stone answered definitively. "Yes, she was. And don't worry about her. Her experience definitely wasn't typical. She at least left us with less stress than she brought in with her."

Harmony let out a frustrated groan but said nothing more.

"Why is she so stressed?" I asked.

Although I certainly hadn't expected an answer, Stone provided one anyway. "Because the city cut funding to the animal shelter, and they're having a rough time over there."

"*Stone,*" Harmony hissed. "Remember our code of ethics, please!"

Everyone fell silent for a few minutes.

"Hey," Stone said, forgetting to use his soothing meditation voice. Rather than sounding irritated though, he came across more like a friend. "You know what helps me when I'm feeling nervous? I like to list all the things I'm grateful for. Let's all take turns as we focus on the positives in our life. I'll go first. I'm grateful for being able to do what I love for a living."

"Me, too," Charles piped up.

"Me, too," I said. "Well, sort of. I haven't been doing much of it lately, but—"

"No explanations," Harmony snapped. "Just state your thought, release it, and move on."

"Fine," I snapped back. "Then I guess I'm grateful for my cat."

But was I grateful for this experience? Certainly not.

Maybe next time Charles would let me plan date night.

CHAPTER TEN

"Did you enjoy your massage?" Charles asked after Harmony and Stone left us to change out of our spa robes and back into our street clothes.

"Yes," I said definitively, hoping that he would believe me. I appreciated the gesture but didn't find the actual act of getting touched all over by a stranger very relaxing at all. I'd much rather pet Octo-Cat or Paisley until all my troubles melted away. Or get in a few snuggles with my boyfriend. Or go on a sugar binge with Nan.

Basically anything other than being poked and prodded by an angry person fake-named Harmony.

"You're such a bad liar," Charles said with a chuckle. "And even though I couldn't see you, I could still tell your wheels were spinning that whole time. You were thinking about the shelter. Weren't you?"

Okay, he knew me eerily well, but I guess that was just part of his charm. "Don't you think it's weird that city hall would cut the shelter's funding when it's already struggling?"

"Maybe the shelter isn't the only thing struggling," Charles suggested. "This past year we've had a pretty high murder per capita. It could be that people are moving away, houses are sitting empty, and the local government has less money to spend overall."

"Maybe," I agreed half-heartedly. His logic made good sense, but my gut was telling me something else was to blame here. "But I don't think that's it. It seems like something fishy is going on with the shelter in particular."

Charles played right along. He, too, had learned to trust my instincts, and he never made me feel bad about needing to investigate—or obsessively discuss—a hunch. "And you think that woman we saw... Trish... is at the center of it all?"

"Of course I do." I accidentally turned around before Charles had finished getting dressed and caught an eye full of his bare legs and chest. "Oops, sorry."

"Don't worry about it. I'm not nearly as shy as you are."

I waited for that tell-tale sound of pants zipping up before turning around again.

When I did, Charles greeted me with a grim expression. "But I can't help worrying about you. Are you going to at least be careful about inserting yourself into a potentially dangerous situation this time?"

I shook my head and let out a sarcastic huff. "I'm always careful."

Charles laughed so hard he had to cough. "Yeah, we both know that's not true, so let's try again. Can you at least be more cautious than you usually are?"

"Fine," I acquiesced and let him wrap his arms around me. "Although you know I no longer work for Longfellow and Associates, which means you're not my boss anymore, either."

"Yeah, but you mean more than ever to me now. You think I'm only warning you off because I'm your boss? That hurts."

"No, I'm sorry. You're right. Any other demands, oh great and powerful boyfriend?"

"Now that you mention it." He placed a kiss on my forehead first, then my nose, and finally finished up with a lingering kiss on my mouth. "I do have one tiny request."

Even before Charles said anything more, I already knew I'd grant him any wish he wanted. I was a big pile of cotton fluff in his hands. *Literally.*

"Let me swing by city hall to see what information I can gather about the budget cuts. Once I do that, you're free to investigate to your heart's content."

"Fair enough." I pulled his face back down to mine and gave him another enthusiastic kiss.

"What was that for?" he asked with a smile once we'd pulled apart.

"For trying to make me feel better, and then actually doing it."

"So, you mean I shelled out for this fancy couple's thing when all I had to do was wave my lawyer card around a little?"

We both chuckled and then kissed again. Even if I kissed Charles every day for the rest of my life, I doubted I'd ever grow sick of it, sick of him.

Still, we had things to do, so I reluctantly pushed him away. "Now turn around and face the wall so I can get dressed in peace," I instructed, happy to put this whole experience behind me and get back to the real world where people went by their given names and spoke in their actual voices.

Buh-bye, Serenity.

Hello, mystery at the shelter.

I returned home to what could only be described as a war zone. Nan wore pink camo sweatpants to go with her pink *Dog Mom* shirt, and even her adorable sidekick Paisley had undergone a costume change. The shaking ball of sleek fur now wore a skull and crossbones tank top with a glittery pink bow affixed to one side of the skull.

Oh, brother.

In the dining room, a giant map of the Blueberry Bay region took up most of our large table. Nan had also brought out a fresh piece of poster board and a rainbow array of all her favorite Sharpies.

"What's going on here?" I asked, not entirely sure I wanted to know the answer.

Noticing my arrival at last, Nan marched straight across the room and put a hand on each of my shoulders. "The check was cashed," she informed me, eyes flashing with glee.

I frowned. This seemed like a ridiculously over-the-top way to celebrate a check being cashed. Of course, my head was all fuzzy from Harmony's massage, so maybe my synapses were still slow to fire.

"And you turned our house into a war room, because...?" I asked, anyway.

Nan pointed toward the desktop computer she kept set up in the far corner of the living room for her occasional use and said, "Remember how you taught me to pay all my bills online?"

"*Yessss,*" I answered slowly, not sure I liked where this was going. It was one thing for me to take risks for a case, but I hated the thought of ever putting Nan in harm's way.

"Look at this." She thrust a piece of computer paper at my chest.

Although the image was grainy, I could clearly make out the scan of Nan's check from earlier that day, along with the sloppy signature and the stamp that read First Bank of Blueberry Bay.

"Check out the address," Nan urged me with an eager smile.

"Dewdrop Springs, *huh,*" I read aloud. "But why would the Glendale Animal Shelter be cashing checks in Dewdrop Springs?"

"That's what I was hoping to learn from you. You were just over there, after all." She grabbed the paper back and waited for me to explain everything.

I didn't have the answers she was looking for, but I did have a bit of information that could help us get there. It was my turn to make a big reveal, and I relished it. "Now that you mention it, Charles and I did run into Trish at the massage place. Do you think she's the one who cashed the check?"

We both studied the messy scrawl of the signature, but it was impossible to decipher without knowing Trish's last name.

"Weird," I said at last.

"Definitely weird," Nan agreed with a nod.

"So what is all this about then?" I motioned around at the giant mess that had exploded in our normally pristine home during my brief absence.

"It's easier for me to think with all my supplies close at hand," Nan answered with a shrug.

This made me chuckle. "And what have you thought of?"

"That we definitely need to be investigating that shelter more for a start," she said without a second's hesitation.

"Yeah, I kind of have the same feeling, too. Ooh, let me catch you up on what I learned while I was out."

"Excellent, but first, tea," Nan declared.

She scurried toward the kitchen with a plucky Paisley in tow, then let out a sharp gasp. "Oh, dear. I think we've had another attack!"

I raced after her only to find a pair of coffee mugs shattered against the hard floor.

What in the heck?

Who was breaking all our things?

And how had Nan not heard all this racket from the next room over?

Sigh.

It seemed that we now had more than one mystery to solve.

CHAPTER ELEVEN

D espite my niggling dislike of Harmony, even I had to admit she'd gotten one thing very right: I slept like a log that night. It could have been the massage, or it could have been the fact that I'd decided to stop tiptoeing around my angry cat and had actually gone to sleep in my own bed when the time came.

I hadn't laid eyes on Octo-Cat before tucking myself in but knew he must still be somewhere in the tower bedroom. Not that I cared all that much at the moment. Honestly, I was so done with this tantrum of his. He could either learn to live with Paisley or he could make himself a prisoner in my bedroom until the very last day of his very last life.

I hoped it wouldn't come to that, but he'd made it quite clear that he wasn't willing to negotiate when it came to our new doggie family member.

Beyond exhausted, I didn't rouse that morning until my angrily ringing cell phone forced me out of bed.

"Ugh, what time is it?" I groaned in the general direction of the phone instead of saying hello outright.

Charles laughed on the other end of the line. "Wake up, Sleeping Beauty. Your prince charming has some news!"

"Sleeping Beauty has Prince Phillip," I corrected, wiping the sleep from my eyes.

"And you have Prince Charles. Oh, *hmm*, maybe not." He chuckled to himself, but I was still too groggy to join in.

"Anyway, I've got news," Charles continued. "And it's almost ten o'clock by the way, you should really get up and greet the day."

I groaned again, which only made my boyfriend laugh harder. "What's your news?" I asked, searching my nightstand for the gummy multivitamin I took each morning.

"Well, I started my day at city hall as promised. You can really learn a lot when you know the right people, I might add." He sounded quite proud of himself. Did this mean he had found something good? Something that would help Nan and I figure out what in the heck was going on with that shelter?

"And what did you learn today?" I asked with a smirk before popping the sugary vitamins into my mouth.

He sucked air in through his teeth, then explained, "That the animal shelter funding hasn't been cut like Stone said. In fact, it's increased year over year beyond inflation."

I yawned and tried my best to refocus. It was way too early for words like *inflation*. "Which means?" I asked, hating how stupid I must sound to Charles's educated ear. Granted, my seven associate degrees were nothing to shake a stick at, but they still weren't nearly as impressive as his one law degree.

Charles took a deep breath, then revealed, "It means that if the shelter has a money problem, it's not due to lack of funding."

"Do you think someone's stealing?" I asked, unable to think of any other possibility given the way that evidence had been stacking up the past couple of days.

"Stealing from a business—or in this case a nonprofit—is called *embezzlement*. And, yes, it does seem like that might be a possibility here." The fact that Charles had shifted into full-on attorney mode told me that whatever was going on, it was very, very illegal. I sincerely hoped the culprit would not only be caught, but also punished to the fullest extent of the law.

Rage flew through my veins, waking me up better than any form of caffeine ever could. "But it's not just money," I argued. "It's these animals' lives! They're already three to a cage… What happens if the shelter has to be shut down?"

"Maybe another shelter would take them in." Charles's whispered words betrayed his true beliefs. He felt just as hopeless as I did in this situation, and it didn't do anyone any good skirting around the issue.

"Or maybe they'd all be turned loose on the streets. Or worse, eu-eu-euthanized." I shuddered at that last word. It represented one of the most awful things I could imagine. Those poor sweet animals.

"That's not going to happen," Charles assured me. His voice came out stronger now, surer.

"But how? How can you know that for a fact?" Hot tears stung at my eyes, but I refused to let them fall. I needed to stay angry. Angry got things done.

"Because I know you, and I know you would never let that happen," my boyfriend told me.

"I gotta go," I mumbled into the phone, already halfway to my closet and ready to throw some clothes on in a hurry.

"I know you do," Charles said, and I could hear the smile in his words. "Stay safe and call me if you need anything. Got it?"

"Got it," I said, then pressed to end the call.

Never had I been so determined to solve a case—and to solve it quickly. Dozens of lives depended on it.

By the time I'd clambered down the stairs in my hastily assembled outfit, Nan was already dressed and waiting for me at the front door. "Finally," she said with a huff. "Ms. Paisley and I have been waiting all morning."

"Hi, Mommy!" Paisley cheered, wiggling her butt in merriment. "We're going for a car ride!"

"To the shelter?" I asked, just to be sure.

"To the shelter!" Nan called in a rallying battle cry, then flung the front door open so that the three of us could march into battle.

This time, we took Nan's little red sports car instead of my old clunker. "We want them to know we have money and that we aren't afraid to use it," Nan offered as an explanation.

"Is that the whole plan?" I wondered aloud. Once again, I was worried that Nan had chosen to view complex problems far too simplistically. The world inside my grandmother's head and the world as it actually was didn't always line up perfectly. God bless her.

Nan shot me a warning look as she twisted the key in the ignition. "Of course not!"

"Then fill me in already."

"You'll see when we get there," she said with a wink and then pushed down hard on the gas pedal.

Whatever happened next, I was ready for it.

Although I hoped Trish wouldn't be there this morning; otherwise, Nan's whole feeble retiree on a fixed income act from yesterday evening would fall apart the very moment she was spotted pulling up to the shelter in an expensive sports car. It seemed unlikely we'd run into Trish, given that Paisley had sworn up and down that she'd never seen the mysterious volunteer once in her entire life.

But, still, I had to wonder...

We got there quickly, thanks to Nan's penchant for driving at least ten miles above the speed limit wherever she went. And it wasn't Trish, but rather Pearl—the kindly, older volunteer I'd met on my own yesterday—who greeted us upon our arrival.

"Back so soon?" she asked with a warm grin. It took me a moment to realize that her smile wasn't intended for me, but rather Nan.

"You know me," my grandmother crooned. "I just can't stay away."

Turning to her side, Nan motioned toward me but continued to address Pearl. "This is my granddaughter, Angie, and of course you already know Ms. Paisley."

Paisley barked in acknowledgement.

I simply nodded and forced a grin.

"Hello, Angie," Pearl said as she regarded me with a blank expression. Did she really not remember meeting me only yesterday? "Now, what can I do for you, Nan?"

I found it downright hilarious that this old woman was calling my grandmother *Nan* of all things, but I at least managed to keep a straight face throughout their exchange.

Nan brought a hand to her heart and sighed. "I can't stop thinking about these poor animals and the trouble you folks are having."

"Oh, don't worry about us," Pearl answered with a sad shake of her head. "We'll find a way. We always do."

"Surely, there must be something I can do," Nan pressed.

Pearl rose to her feet and placed a placating hand on Nan's arm. "I promise we're doing all we can. It's just the funding's been cut, and we're still trying to find a way to work within our new budgetary constraints."

Nan chewed her lip. Whether she was honestly disheartened or just putting on a good show, even I couldn't say for sure.

"I understand, I do," she mumbled, "but—hey, I've got it!"

Pearl and I both waited to hear what Nan would say next, and she, of course, kept us waiting to heighten the anticipation.

"Well? What's your big idea then?" Pearl prodded.

Nan flashed a toothy grin before revealing her grand idea. "What if I were to put on a big fundraiser to help save the shelter?"

"We're not really at the point of needing saving, but your heart is in the right place. Tell you what, I'll take you to Mr. Leavitt, so the two—" She paused and glanced back toward me with a nervous smile. "—I mean, the three of you, can discuss this in private."

Nan gave a single affirmative nod. "Thank you, Pearl. That would be lovely."

The other woman smiled and led us toward the door that led deeper into the shelter. As we followed her back through the long room of kennels, Nan reached out and squeezed my hand. I was still flying blind here as far as her plan went, but at least we seemed to be making forward progress.

I only hoped that would continue…

CHAPTER TWELVE

Mr. Leavitt welcomed Nan, Paisley, and me into his office with huge smiles for everyone. And unlike Pearl, *he* remembered meeting me the day before.

"Welcome back, Angie," he said, clapping a hand on my shoulder as I passed through the door and into his office. "I'm starting to suspect you may be our own personal angel here at the Glendale Community Animal Shelter. You not only wrote us a generous donation of your own, but you came back the very next day with a new donor. Please, both of you, come right in."

That's right. I had given him a check. Had that really been less than twenty-four hours ago? And was it cashed at the same time and place as Nan's donation? So much had happened in that short span, I'd forgotten to look into it.

"I'm going to do so much more than write a check," Nan told him, lowering herself into one of the chairs opposite Mr. Leavitt's desk. "I'm going to put together a fundraiser so lots of people can write checks. How about that?"

Mr. Leavitt's eyes grew wide with the promise of a large cash infusion. "Well, now, I love the sound of that," he chortled. "Now, tell me. How can I offer you my assistance?"

"I'm glad you asked," Nan chortled right back. "I won't need much, I promise, but I *am* going to need some time to get a feel for the facility and the animals who live here. That will help me make sure I'm planning the right type of fundraiser. After all, why throw a bake sale when what you truly need is a gala?"

"Too true, too true," Mr. Leavitt said, bobbing his head as his eyes grew wider still. "It would be my privilege to give you a tour of our facilities. If you'll just give me a few moments to finish a few things first, I'll—"

"Actually," Nan interrupted. "I'd much rather walk around by myself, if you don't mind. I'm sure you understand. I need to feel the place out, not listen to a speech about its history." She crossed her legs and sat straighter, spoke more commandingly.

And Mr. Leavitt immediately fell under her spell. "Oh, of course. If you need anything—"

"Then I know who to come and find. Thank you," Nan finished for him, then rose back to her feet and walked out without waiting for me and Paisley to follow.

I had to power walk to catch up. "Now what?" I whisper-yelled as she strode confidently through the kennels.

"Now we're going to chat with some of the animals and see if they know anything." *We.* Yeah, right. It was my neck that was on the line here.

"Nan, what if someone catches us?" I asked fearfully, silently adding, *What if they overhear our suspicions and decide to hurt us to keep us quiet?* It had happened before. It could most assuredly happen again. One thing I'd learned well during all my months of sleuthing is that criminals hated being caught. Obviously.

Nan didn't seem worried in the slightest, however. "I'll stand guard, and if anyone catches us, you can just pretend you were talking to me or to Paisley," she explained with a no-nonsense expression. "But be quick, I doubt we're going to get another opportunity like this one."

Paisley, right.

I sure missed having Octo-Cat as the Watson to my Sherlock.

The little dog was nice enough, but I still didn't know how much Paisley actually understood about the mystery we'd uncovered.

Guess it was time to find out.

"Hey there, Paisley," I cooed, lifting the dog into my arms. "Wanna help me with a little game?"

"A game!" the Chihuahua barked. "Like fetch? Or keep-away? Or, or chase the cat? Yes! I love those games!"

"Not exactly," I hedged, biting my lip for a moment as I thought. "This game is called *Detective*. We play by trying to figure out a secret."

Paisley rearranged her face so that one of her lower canines overlapped her upper lip. She looked so stinking cute as she said, "I don't have any secrets. Can I still play?"

"Of course you can," I assured the tiny black dog. "In fact, we already know what the secret is, but we don't know who it belongs to. Do you think you can help me figure that out?"

"I will try my best, Mommy!" Paisley promised, shaking with newfound glee.

"Great, that's the spirit!" I gave the doggo a wet kiss on her forehead followed by an enthusiastic scratch between the ears. "Okay, the secret is that someone is stealing money from the shelter, but we don't know who is doing it."

"What's money?" Paisley asked, quirking her head to the side in interest.

"Forget the money," I said, backtracking fast. "What I meant to say is that someone at the shelter is being very bad, and it's up to us to figure out who."

"*Hmm,*" Paisley said, her ears twitching like miniature satellite receptors. "I bet it was a cat!" she shouted after a few moments' thought. "When these things happen, it's usually a cat."

This made me laugh. "Actually, I'm pretty sure a human is to blame this time."

The little dog whimpered. "But all the humans here are so nice," she argued. "They feed us and walk us and play with us and help us find homes. Nobody is bad, and definitely not *very* bad." She actually shuddered at the thought.

Oh, dear sweet Paisley.

She really did see the best in everyone. Even the cat at home who'd threatened to kill her and the people at the shelter who were stealing resources from the animals in need. As much as I wanted her help, I doubted I'd get her to see the truth even if it happened to come out and stare straight into her soul.

"Okay, tell you what," I said, changing tactics. "You keep Nan company, and I'll talk to some of the other animals and see what they have to say. Sound good?"

"Okay, Mommy!" Her tail wagged so fast it became a blur. Oh, to be that happy!

I set Paisley down, and she immediately bounded over to Nan and stretched her tiny paws in the air, begging to be picked up and cuddled. "Keep an eye out," I mumbled, then jogged to the last cage at the very farthest end of the room. Might as well be organized about my investigation.

An enormous wrinkly dog stared up at me with sad eyes. At his side sat a much smaller hound mix whose sole focus was biting and chewing one of his hind feet.

"Hey, there," I cooed, absolutely hating the air of sorrow around this place. These two at least seemed older and wiser than Paisley. Perhaps that would be to my benefit. "My name is Angie, and I was hoping you could help me. A very bad human is stealing from the shelter. Any idea who that could be?"

"All the humans here are nice," the big dog informed me with zero hesitation.

"Yeah," the hound added around a mouthful of foot. "If anyone is being bad around here, it's probably a cat."

"Oh, yes. Thanks for your help," I said, forcing a smile. We'd only just begun and already it was abundantly clear that I wouldn't be able to learn much from the dogs here. Still, I spoke to several more before finally giving up and heading to speak with the cats as suggested.

The cat area of the shelter was much smaller and offered no privacy, which wasn't a problem since every set of kitty eyes and ears fixed on me from the very moment I entered.

"Hi," I said nervously, even though I fancied myself a cat person. I loved Octo-Cat when he wasn't being needlessly cruel and dramatic, but the thought of twenty of him in one place scared the living daylights out of me. "My name is Angie, and I'm trying to find a very bad human who works at the shelter. Do you know——?"

"Darling," a flat-faced fluffball drawled, cutting off my question at the quick. "Look around. All humans are bad."

"They'd descend into chaos without us cats around to keep an eye on things," an orange tabby with an angry face insisted.

No wonder cats and dogs disliked each other so much. They were as different as two creatures could come. Still, at least they didn't blindly trust everyone's motives. Maybe they'd be able to offer some kind of clue if I asked my questions right.

I cleared my throat and tried again. "Is there one human that's worse than the rest? Maybe someone who is stealing money from the shelter?"

"That's like asking if there's one blade of grass that's greener than the rest," the flat-faced cat spoke again. "There are just so many of them, and they're all green besides."

The other caged felines meowed their agreement, and I officially gave up on finding any leads via the shelter animals.

It was time to do things a little differently.

Unfortunately, I didn't have any idea how.

CHAPTER THIRTEEN

O cto-Cat sat waiting for us in the living room when Nan and I returned home. I'd left the bedroom door open before we headed out just in case he might want a change of scenery, but I hadn't exactly expected him to take advantage of it.

Luckily, Paisley was already tucked securely into Nan's arms, so she couldn't be tempted to make a run for the ornery feline. Couldn't Octo-Cat see how much she already loved him? How much she wanted to be his friend?

Judging by the tabby's furrowed brow and tense posture, that was a hard no.

"Well, look what the cat dragged out," I quipped, part relieved to see him and part worried about what he might demand next.

"Hardy har har," he said dryly and then, "I see you're still playing house with that imposter."

Well, as it turned out, we'd made no progress at all. "You saw right. Now don't you think it's time for you to stop your pouting and rejoin the living?"

Had I made a mistake by kowtowing to his demands about the Fancy Feast and the Evian and the exquisite manor house? It had been easy to do regarding mere things, but now another life was involved. I refused to send Paisley back to that overcrowded shelter, especially when its future was so uncertain.

I knew it wouldn't be so easy, but still my heart ached when Octo-Cat responded with, "Bad things happen when good cats remain silent."

"But that's exactly what you're doing!" I argued. "Giving me the silent treatment. Haven't you had enough?"

"Haven't *you* had enough?" he shot back in a deep, ominous voice. Something told me there was no right answer here.

"Mr. Octopus Cat," Paisley squeaked, drawing both of our attention to her big black eyes and tiny pink mouth. "I know you don't like me, but I promise I'll do anything to make things right. I want to be friends."

"Aww, how could you say no to this face?" I cooed, scratching Paisley under her tiny, quivering chin.

Her whole body squirmed in response, and Nan had to make quick adjustments to avoid dropping her.

"Easily," Octo-Cat spat, unmoved by the show of love. "Very easily, indeed."

"Are they finally playing nice?" Nan asked, a hopeful sparkle in her eyes.

"Um, not exactly," I answered with a sigh. "But this is progress, nonetheless."

"Say, dog," my cat lisped, rising to all four paws. "Will you really do anything to make me happy?"

"Oh, yes!" Paisley cried, her shaking thus renewed. "Yes, I will do anything!"

I waited in silence for the big reveal. Would Octo-Cat's demand be one we could meet? I'd do almost anything to bring peace to our divided house.

The cat's large, amber eyes narrowed, and he spoke very, very slowly. "Then run far, far away and don't ever come back."

The Chihuahua whimpered, which made our evil feline overlord laugh. "Do I really have to, Mommy?" Paisley asked, a pathetic whine lacing each of her words.

Oh, that cat! He made me so angry sometimes!

"No, of course not. He's just being mean!" I scowled at my unruly pet, but he didn't look the least big apologetic.

"Hey, I know what I want." Octo-Cat flicked his tail in one direction and then the other. "And also what I don't want. The dog needs to go."

"Hush up, Octo-Cat. You've been outvoted," Nan said, even though she couldn't understand any part of the conversation other than mine.

Paisley wriggled and licked Nan's hands, whether to derive comfort or to agree with what had been said in her defense, I couldn't be sure.

"*Unbelievable,*" my cat mumbled as he hopped to the floor and skulked out of view. A few moments later, we heard his electronic cat flap lift open and admit him into the outside world.

"And stay out until you've had an attitude adjustment!" I shouted after him.

"Don't worry about him, you sweet girl." Nan kissed the Chihuahua's head and then set her on the floor. "Let's go make ourselves some lunch. Huh?"

We all moved to the kitchen, where Nan took out three chicken breasts to grill on the stovetop and I began working on the fixings for a Caesar salad. "I'm making one for Paisley, too," she explained with a grin.

Oh, the little dog would definitely love that.

We'd almost finished our lunch preparations when a loud crash sounded from the foyer. I glanced toward my feet and found that Paisley had left us some time ago.

"Why does everything keep breaking around here?" Nan grumbled as she removed her pan from the burner and marched out to locate the source of the disturbance.

I spotted the mess before she did. One of Ethel Fulton's antique Tiffany lamps lay in pieces by the entryway. A priceless heirloom. *Great.*

Paisley stood beside the mess, howling. "I'm so sorry," she cried. "I don't know how it happened. I was just minding my own business, and—crash!"

"It's okay, sweetie. We know you didn't mean to," I coaxed as Nan began to sweep up the mess.

"Unbelievable," Octo-Cat mumbled and then ran up the grand staircase, presumably back to his self-imposed prison in my bedroom tower.

Funny, I hadn't heard the electronic pet door buzz open even though we were standing directly beside it.

"Can you watch Paisley for me this afternoon?" Nan asked once the three of us had finished our mid-day meal. "I'd bring her with me, but I have a lot of errands to run and don't want her to get lost underfoot."

"Sure," I answered absentmindedly while logging into the bank's mobile app on my phone. I had to click around a bit to find exactly what I was looking for. When I did, I handed the phone to Nan and asked, "Hey, is this address the same as the one on the check you had cashed?"

Nan studied the tiny screen for a moment, then handed the phone back my way and rummaged around her desk until she found the printout she'd made the night before. "The very same," she said, holding the paper beside the phone screen so the two of us could compare.

I glanced between them a few more times, feeling more and more confident that we'd made a match with each new look. "The signature's a little different on this one, but it looks like it belongs to the same person. I think maybe it starts with a *D* or an *O*. Hard to say for sure."

"But that's not how you spell Trish," Nan said with a sigh.

"No, it's not," I agreed, feeling more confused than ever as I logged out of the app and set my cell phone back on the table.

"I'll think on it while I'm out," my grandmother promised.

"Where are you going, by the way?" I'd only half paid attention when she said she was leaving and was curious now that she'd brought it up again.

"To begin work on the charity fundraiser for the shelter, of course. I've decided to go with a gala. That will bring all the key players out better than any bake sale or car wash ever could."

"Good thinking." Or was it? I hated contradicting her, but had she really thought this whole thing through before deciding to jump into action?

"Nan, a gala takes a lot of prep work, though. What if it's too late for the shelter by the time you've finished the planning?"

She waved her hand dismissively. "Stop being such a negative Nancy. You know better than to doubt your nan. Now, you two be good. I'll be back in time to rustle up some dinner. *Ciao.*"

And just like that, she was into her shoes and out the door. Man, she moved fast. I often felt like a slouch next to my fit and active grandmother. Maybe one day I'd actually do something about it— but today was not that day.

"What would you like to do this afternoon?" I asked, searching the floor for Paisley. Normally, she clung to the closest human like a bur, but at the moment, I couldn't spot her anywhere.

"Paisley!" I called. "C'mere, girl."

"I don't wanna," came the muffled reply.

It took a few minutes, but I finally found her hiding under our antique Victorian loveseat. "Why so sad, sweetie pie?" I sat down on the hard, uncomfortable floor and waited for her to show herself.

"The cat doesn't like me," she sniffed while remaining firmly in place beneath the old couch.

"Oh, don't worry about him. He doesn't really like anyone."

"He doesn't like me *a lot*, though. And at the shelter, I couldn't help you win Detective. And now Nan left and didn't want to take me with her. What if she never comes back?"

The poor dear! I hated that she felt this way and that there was very little I could do about it.

"Paze, please don't cry. You did a great job helping with Detective, and—hey—the game's not over yet. We still have time to win. And I promise Nan will come back just as soon as she finishes her errands. We all love you very much."

"Even Octopus Cat?" she asked, raising her head slightly.

"Even Octo-Cat," I assured her with a chuckle. "He just doesn't know it yet."

CHAPTER FOURTEEN

Seeing as both Paisley and I could use a change of scenery, I leashed her up and drove us downtown to enjoy a bit of window-shopping.

"Have you been here before?" I asked my doggie companion as the two of us strolled down the narrow sidewalks that flanked the commercial heart of our small seaside town.

"Nope," Paisley answered, then stopped to squat beside a young tree that had just begun to change colors for the fall. "But I like it very much. So many excellent smells!"

Although I was sure our definition of *excellent* varied substantially, I smiled and nodded my agreement. Paisley was happy again, and that's what mattered most.

"Which smell is your favorite?" I asked conversationally.

"Oh, definitely all the pee!" she squealed, happier than a pig in number two as she enjoyed the apparently intoxicating aroma of number one.

I didn't ask any more questions after that. Instead, the two of us continued on our way, stopping frequently to allow the Chihuahua to sniff anything that caught her fancy.

"Oh, hello there, Angie!" Mr. Gable, the owner of the nearby jewelry store, called from the spot where he was idling with a steaming mug of coffee. The old man had become something of an institution here in Glendale, and it was no wonder he'd recently been voted head of the downtown council.

"Hello, Mr. Gable," I called, quickening my pace to join him.

"And who might this little fella be?" The smiling, white-haired man carefully lowered himself to the ground and let Paisley sniff his hands. His coffee, too.

"This is Paisley," I announced proudly. "Nan's and my newest addition."

He laughed good-naturedly. "Oh, I bet the cat doesn't much care for that."

"You bet right," I answered with a laugh. Hopefully, Mr. Gable's well-meaning comment wouldn't turn the dog into a nervous, shaking mess all over again.

In the end, she appeared too taken by the kindness of this new friend to worry about the unkindness of the hostile feline back home.

Mr. Gable and I chatted amiably for a few minutes about the upcoming holiday spectacular. We were a good three months off, but it was widely known that the downtown businesses started planning on December 26 of the previous year. The yearly festival got bigger and grander with each run, and I couldn't wait to see how it would look this Christmas.

Mr. Gable, however, refused to give anything away. "It's better as a surprise," he promised with a Santa-like wink.

Just as I was about to press a little harder for details, an unexpected movement down the street caught my eye. Mind you, we were in downtown Glendale, which meant lots of people, dogs, and vehicles came and went—even in the middle of the day.

Somehow, though, I knew the sudden pale blur wasn't a part of all that. I guess you could say my kitty sense was tingling.

Paisley felt it, too, because she nudged my foot with her nose and said, "It's that nice lady we smelled the other day. Remember at the shelter?"

And she was right. Suspicious Trish had made yet another appearance in my life, and I wanted to know why.

"Well, nice chatting," I told Mr. Gable with a brief wave good-bye. "We'll see you soon."

I picked up Paisley, even though I knew she'd probably rather walk, and hurried back in the direction from which we'd come. I needed her close so that I could whisper to her about what would happen next.

"We have to be very, very quiet," I told the little dog, channeling my inner Elmer Fudd. We weren't hunting wabbits, though, we were stalking suspects—and that was way more dangerous.

"If we can stay quiet and hidden long enough, I think we might just win Detective," I promised with a quick grin.

Paisley gasped but said nothing in response. Good dog.

Trish cut through an alley, and I raced faster to catch up, making sure I remained far enough behind to avoid letting her spot me. She stopped in a parking lot and stood, waiting.

Paisley and I hid ourselves behind a nearby dumpster. Neither of us spoke a word.

Then I spotted it, a giant, beat-up Cadillac crunching onto the gravel lot. The driver was most definitely male, but I couldn't make out much more than his wispy frame and deep voice. He and Trish spoke for a few minutes and then he hopped out of the car and popped the trunk open.

Inside, the spacious trunk was filled to the brim with pet supplies, still in their packaging. If the mysterious man was here to make a donation to the shelter, he was sure acting shifty about it.

I didn't have long to puzzle over this, because the very next thing I knew, Trish had pulled a wad of bills from her front pocket and handed it to the driver.

And that was more than enough to make me finally spring to action. First, I grabbed my phone and zoomed in on the license plate, so I'd have it for later. Then I placed a call to my good friend Officer Bouchard and told him he needed to come down straight away.

"Did we win Detective?" Paisley asked, staring up at me with glistening dark eyes.

"Yeah, I think we did," I told her, offering an enthusiastic petting for the job well done. "But we need to be quiet just a little longer before we can know for sure."

We watched as Trish and the man had some kind of argument, and then he drove off with both the cash and the pet supplies. Trish groaned and stalked back toward the alleyway, where Paisley and I still stood crouched behind the dumpster.

Uh-oh.

I needed to think fast, so I set my dog on the ground and cried, "Oh my gosh, Paisley! There you are! I've been looking everywhere for you!"

"Yes, I'm right here, Mommy!" the little dog barked, not quite catching on to the ruse.

Trish walked by us without so much as a nod of recognition, so I called after her. "Hey, Trish. Is that you? Three times in less than twenty-four hours! What are the chances?"

She grimaced but stopped moving at least. "I'm sorry, I can't really hang around and talk. Nice to see you, though." Without waiting for my response, she quickened her pace again and continued down the alley.

Oh, no you don't. You're not getting away that easily.

She must have had an awful lot on her mind, because Paisley and I easily trailed her without her discovering us. She moved fast, and I wished for the second time that day that I was in better shape. Somehow I managed to keep up, though, as Trish led us to a second parking lot on the other side of downtown Glendale where the same man from before sat waiting in his idling car.

"Bingo," I whispered, then sent a quick text to Officer Bouchard to let him know we'd relocated to the north parking lot.

Trish unlocked a dirty white sedan and popped its trunk, then together she and the man began to move the contents of his vehicle into hers. They'd managed to clear about half of the goods by the time Officer Bouchard's police cruiser joined us on the scene.

My excitement mounted. My cop friend had made it on time, and now this was it. Somebody was going to be in big trouble.

CHAPTER FIFTEEN

The man pushed his trunk closed, but not fast enough to escape the notice of the officer who'd just arrived on the scene.

I took this as my cue to come out of hiding. This time there hadn't been a dumpster, so I'd had to resort to pressing myself flat against the brick wall in the alley. I strode into the parking lot with confidence I didn't quite feel—and wouldn't until I knew for sure we'd caught the crook who was embezzling money from the animal shelter.

Officer Bouchard saw me first and reached his hand overhead in a wave.

Both Trish and her accomplice spun in my direction, and the moment she spotted me, her eyes filled with disdain. "You followed me!" she cried.

"Now, now," Officer Bouchard said peaceably. "We don't want any more trouble than is already here. Go ahead and open up the trunk, young man."

I was close enough now to make out our mystery man's features. He was tall and lanky with light skin and even lighter hair. As far as I knew, I'd never seen him before in my entire life.

"Hey, wait just a minute," Trish argued, pointing a shaky finger my way. "She followed me. Isn't stalking, like, illegal?"

"Not *like* illegal. It is illegal, but something tells me there's something even more illegal in that there trunk, and that Ms. Russo was just doing her civic duty by calling it in and keeping an eye on you until I could show up to officially handle things. Now open that trunk."

Trish's accomplice did as he was told, once again revealing the trunk filled with brand-new pet supplies.

"And that one, too, please." The cop pointed to Trish's filthy white car and waited until she complied with his order.

"Well, well, well," Officer Bouchard said with a chuckle. "These wouldn't happen to be the pet supplies a shop in Dewdrop Springs reported missing earlier today." He raised an eyebrow and glanced at the younger blond man. "Or would they?"

"Whatever, man. I'm just the go-between. She's the mastermind."

If he was sorry, he didn't look it. I had to wonder if perhaps this man was from out of town, if he'd thought no one would notice some missing pet supplies. Apparently he hadn't counted on the fact that everyone notices everything in a small town like ours.

Trish stamped her foot on the ground. "How dare you try to pin this all on me!"

"Enough bickering," the officer warned. "Who's stealing and why?"

"I didn't steal anything," Trish ground out. "I bought these supplies fair and square."

The policeman crossed his arms and stared down the bridge of his nose at both culprits. "Well, *I'm* not buying it, little miss. Why buy pet supplies from the back of some guy's trunk when it's just as easy to go to the store and purchase them there? You know, like you're supposed to?"

"He was giving them to us at a discount. We needed the savings. The shelter isn't doing so good, and… And I was just trying to help the animals!"

"Let's go," Officer Bouchard said, uncrossing his arms and

making a sweeping gesture toward his waiting car. "I'd love to hear more about this down at the station. And you're both invited."

Trish scowled at me as Officer Bouchard nudged her toward the police cruiser. He hadn't cuffed either her or the man with the trunk full of stolen goods, but he had called for backup to come clear the scene while he dealt with the suspects.

"Thanks, Russo," he said, returning to my side. "But I've gotta ask, what made you decide to follow her?"

I quickly caught him up on Nan's and my suspicions, ending with a dramatic, "And she doesn't even actually work there. At least I think she doesn't."

"Oh, you and your nan. One of these days we should formally hire you to work for the county. I can promise you this, though. We're going to find out what's going on at that shelter. Stealing from animals in need is a level of despicable I don't like seeing in our town. Both of my cats were adopted from that very shelter, come to think of it."

"Officer Bouchard," I said with a grin, bumping my shoulder into his. "I had no idea you were a cat person."

He put his tough cop face back on and sniffed. "Yeah, well, don't let word get around. I already get more than my fair share of guff from the other guys at the station."

"Your secret's safe with me," I promised, loving this new detail about him. I was a cat person, too, after all. Well, most days at least.

"I've got things from here," he informed me. "Now go try to enjoy the rest of your day." The cop gave me a firm nod, which I took to mean I was formally dismissed from the investigation. Hopefully, the county would be able to finish strong from here, which meant Nan and I could focus on our little mystery at home. Namely, why so many fragile things kept breaking.

"Did we win?" Paisley asked as the two of us headed back down the alleyway.

"Yes, the bad guys have been caught, and all is right with the world again," I assured her. I missed having Octo-Cat's assistance, but Paisley hadn't been such a bad crime-solving companion this time around. With time, she could learn. The three of us could work together… That is, if Octo-Cat ever got over his ridiculous aversion to dogs.

Then Paisley asked a question I hadn't been expecting. "They seemed really nice to me. How do you know that they're bad?"

"Because they did bad things," I answered simply, honestly.

She appeared to think about this for a moment, then asked, "So if I do bad things, am I bad?"

"No, that's not the same."

"Why not?" Paisley's ears lowered, giving her an even more puppy-ish appearance than usual.

Clearly, I had a choice to make. I could let the Chihuahua keep believing the best of everyone, or I could destroy her innocence by explaining how mean the world could be sometimes.

At the end of the day, I liked my new dog daughter exactly as she was, so I said, "You know what, Paze? You're right. It was just a game. Now let's go see if Nan's back home yet, huh?"

"Oh, yes! We've been apart forever! I miss her so much!" Paisley cried, our deeper conversation about ethics and morals all but forgotten.

Maybe it was time for me to go back to Blueberry Bay Community College and grab an eighth associate degree. This time in Philosophy. Next time Paisley hit me over the head with questions like this, I wanted to be ready.

I sent Nan a quick text to let her know we were on our way home and to ask if she could meet us there, then I let my sweet little dog take all the time she needed enjoying her scenic scenting tour through downtown.

And she made sure to tell me each time she found a new one, too. Especially if it was pee.

Dogs were so weird.

CHAPTER SIXTEEN

N an beat me and Paisley home, which was probably a good
thing considering what we found when we got there.

"There's poop everywhere!" I cried with a disgusted groan.

"You should have seen this place before I started cleaning up."
Nan squirted another shot of all-natural cleaner on the rug and
gave the smelly stain a good, solid scrub.

"This is gross." I crossed my arms and surveyed the damage
with a frown. "Do you even think it will come all the way out of the
area rug? This was original with the house."

Nan paused and studied me with a furrowed brow. "What
worries me more is that one of the animals has to be very sick to
make such a huge mess."

Paisley kneaded her front paws against my leg and begged for
me to pick her up. "It wasn't me," she said in a soft, sad voice.
"Honest."

"It couldn't have been Paisley," I relayed to Nan, setting the dog
back down and then slipping on a pair of thick yellow rubber gloves
to help clean up the mess. "She was with me the whole time you were
out, and this mess wasn't here when we left for our walk earlier."

"Even still." Nan moved to another spot on the carpet and scrubbed vigorously. "We should take both of them to the vet. Maybe she'll have some tips on helping them adjust to their new living arrangements."

"But Paisley isn't the problem," I reminded her. "Octo-Cat is just being stubborn."

"Well, we have to do something." Nan frowned at the spot and sprayed some more cleaner. "What if Octavius isn't just being mean for meanness's sake? What if he's seriously ill?"

That thought hadn't occurred to me before, but now that Nan had mentioned the possibility, it was all I could think about. As much as Octo-Cat had irritated me the last few days, he was still my best friend and I couldn't picture life without him.

"I grabbed a doodie sample before I started cleaning up, so the doc will have that to test. I've already called and let her know we'll be coming in shortly."

"Then let's go," I said, peeling my gloves off, then picking my purse back up from the coffee table. "We can clean the rest of this up after."

Nan followed suit. "I'll wash up real quick, then grab the sample and get Paisley and myself settled in your car. You go on upstairs and get Octavius."

Right.

My cat didn't like car rides under the best of circumstances, but now that he was sick and expected to take today's ride with his sworn nemesis, it would be downright impossible to convince him to come willingly.

I briefly considered my options as I jogged upstairs to collect him. I could try asking nicely, but that would alert him to my intentions and ultimately make catching him so much harder after he refused to come peacefully. I could also try forcing him into his walking harness, but I knew well enough from experience that this was more of a two-person job. That left only one option, and it was the one I knew he would hate most of all: the cat carrier.

I hadn't ever used it before, but the very fact I kept it in the house for emergencies was a constant source of discontent for Octo-Cat.

Well, at least we'd finally have the chance to make use of the thing.

I grabbed the greatly despised carrier from storage and blew off the thin coat of dust that had settled on top of its plastic shell. Climbing the stairs to my tower just as quietly as I could, I let myself into the bedroom while attempting to hide the bulky carrier behind me.

It didn't work.

"I see you," my cat hissed from beneath the bed. "And whatever you want from me, the answer is an emphatic no."

"I'm sorry about this," I answered, pulling my bedframe away from the wall with a series of grunts and tugs. "But I can't let you waste away in here any longer, especially seeing as you're sick."

Octo-Cat moved with the bed, remaining dead center, which made him incredibly difficult to reach. Even when I dropped to my belly and extended my arms at full length, my fingertips just barely brushed the tip of his tail.

"I'm not going, and you can't make me."

Ugh. Why did he have to be so difficult?

I didn't want to manhandle him given his upset belly, but bribing him to come out wasn't exactly a possibility either. Some things about our relationship were easier because of our ability to talk to each other, while others were infinitely more difficult. This was one of those infinitely more difficult things.

Think, Angie. Think!

And then I had an idea that I was about ninety percent certain would work. I moved to my desk and grabbed the small keychain I kept in my top drawer in case of an emergency, then I gathered my comforter from the bed and bundled it up in my arms. Holding tight to the wad of blanket with one hand, I used the other to activate the keychain light.

And the red dot came to life on the carpet before me.

One of our past acquaintances had used the power of the red dot to trick two unwitting cats into doing something very bad. At the time, Octo-Cat had explained to me that while most cats logically knew the dot was just a result of a laser pointer, they also couldn't resist pouncing whenever that little sucker made an appearance.

That's precisely what I was counting on now.

The dot danced when I wiggled my hand—and when I flicked my wrist, it jerked wildly to the side.

This sent Octo-Cat shooting out from beneath the bed at lightning speed.

Thankfully, I was just fast enough to toss the blanket on top of him as an impromptu net, and—gotcha!

He was captured and spitting mad about it, too. "I will never forget this betrayal, Angela. Never. Not in all my lives."

"I'm sorry," I muttered again, picking up the blanket with him in it and then releasing him into the plastic carrier.

There.

I'd done it, and by some miracle neither of us had managed to get hurt in the process.

"Don't worry," I cooed softly even though my breathing was now labored from this whole debacle. "We're going to get you all patched up at the vet. You'll be feeling like yourself in no time at all."

"But I'm not sick," he argued before coughing up a hairball right inside the carrier.

CHAPTER SEVENTEEN

Our usual veterinarian wasn't at the office that day, but the newest member of her practice was able to squeeze us in for an emergency visit. From the looks of her smooth skin and perky posture, Dr. Britt Lowe had only finished veterinary school quite recently. If her supposed lack of experience caused me to worry, though, her friendly demeanor and knowledgeable speech instantly put me back at ease.

"On the phone you said one of the animals—probably the cat—is experiencing a bout of diarrhea. Anything else to add?" she asked looking from her chart to the place where Nan and I sat in twin bucket seats inside the cramped exam room.

Octo-Cat growled in the carrier that I'd set on the floor beside me.

"Oh, he does not sound happy," Dr. Lowe added with a frown. "Do you mind if we take him out while we talk? When animals get this worked up, it's best to get things over with as quickly as possible. Poor guy."

"Sure, if that's how you want to do it." I lifted the carrier onto the metal table between us, then allowed the vet to open the latch.

Octo-Cat immediately tried to make a run for it, but she caught him without much trouble and used her hold on the angry feline to examine his eyes and teeth.

"There's a good man," she said soothingly. My guess is the only reason she managed to avoid getting bit was the fact she hadn't referred to him as kitty. Something about the vet's skilled hands calmed him a bit. Perhaps he knew that she was on his side in all this. That she just wanted him to be happy and feel better.

Not that I didn't want those same things, but…

Dr. Lowe set him on the table, keeping one hand on Octo-Cat's back as she motioned for me to join her. "Now hold on tight to him. Most cats don't like this next part."

Before I could ask any questions, she stuck a thermometer up his backside.

Octo-Cat's eyes widened to a comical size, but he didn't make a single peep until she'd finished. "I feel so violated," he moaned.

"You can let him go now," the vet informed me, and as soon as I did, Octo-Cat hurled himself back in the carrier he had loathed only minutes before.

Dr. Lowe frowned. "His temperature is normal, and he seems very healthy. Are you sure it wasn't the dog who made the mess?"

"We're sure," Nan piped up. "But I did bring a sample in case it helps." She handed Paisley off to me and then fished around in the disposable shopping bag she'd brought with her until she found the triple-bagged fecal sample.

"Oh, dear," the veterinarian said with a laugh. "I think I see the problem."

"Don't you need to test it first?" I asked, unable to see what was so funny about this disgusting situation.

"No, I don't think I do. That's not cat feces. It's not dog, either."

"I told you I'm not sick," Octo-Cat pouted from inside his carrier.

"Then what is it?" I asked, completely at a loss for ideas.

Dr. Lowe held the sample up to the light, and we all stared at it as she explained, "This definitely came from a wild animal. Judging from the size, I'd guess a raccoon."

Raccoon!

Now it all finally came into focus. Octo-Cat had been able to be in two places at once by employing the help of his biggest fan, the raccoon that lived under our porch. His name was Pringle, and he worshipped the ground my spoiled cat walked on.

"Could you maybe give us a moment?" Nan asked politely. It seemed she too had figured out exactly who was to blame for all the strange happenings around our house as of late.

"Of course." Dr. Lowe nodded, then let herself out through the back door.

Once we were alone again, I bent forward so I could look Octo-Cat straight in the eye. "Please tell me you didn't really hire your raccoon fanboy to frame Paisley for your bad behavior."

"I didn't," he said, but even he didn't seem to believe it.

Placing both hands on my hips, I narrowed my gaze and waited.

My cat came to the edge of the carrier and laid back down with a sigh. "First off, hire would imply that I paid him. He did it for free. Secondly, it's not my bad behavior. I didn't do anything."

"But you're the mastermind," I pointed out.

And then it occurred to me... "Why would you break your own teacup?"

He let out another heavy sigh. "Pringle isn't the best at following instructions. He grabbed the wrong cup by accident. Believe me, I'm quite upset over it. We haven't even had the funeral yet."

"How could we have when you've been either hiding or scheming all day?" I asked, shaking my head with fury.

"You make a decent point," Octo-Cat conceded. "But my point also remains. I don't want the dog to live with us."

"Why not?" I demanded.

"I don't like dogs," he groused.

Oh, no. He was not pulling this one again. If he really hated Paisley, then he needed to be able to tell me why. I doubted he could, and I was more than ready to call him on that bluff.

"But why don't you like her, specifically?" I asked, raising an eyebrow in suspicion.

"Because she's a dog. Duh."

"Mommy, can I try talking to him?" Paisley asked from my arms. She was so light I'd almost forgotten I was holding her.

At the Chihuahua's request, I gently set her on the exam table so she and Octo-Cat could sit face-to-face. It struck me then that she'd never once had this kind of opportunity with him. The cat had always yelled, complained, and then run away to hide. But would he actually have a conversation with her now that he was stuck inside this tiny room?

"Hello, Octopus Cat," Paisley began with a reverential dip of her head.

"My name is not Octopus Cat," the tabby growled. For a moment I worried that he would take another swipe at her, but he kept his claws under control.

Brave little Paisley either didn't know that she was talking to an animal on edge or she was ready for whatever consequences she reaped as a result of this conversation. "Oh, then it seems I might have misheard," she said, blinking slowly. "What is your name?"

"My name—and you better remember this, because I'm only going to say it once—is Octavius Maxwell Ricardo Edmund Frederick Fulton Russo, Esq. P.I." He rolled each of the Rs as if doing so were required to pronounce the monstrous moniker properly.

I put a hand over my mouth to keep from laughing. Every time Octo-Cat gave out his full name, he added something to it. I was starting to doubt he'd ever been given any middle names at all.

"It's very nice to meet you, Octavius Maxwell Ricardo Edmund Frederick Fulton Russo, Esq. P.I." The Chihuahua said, carefully mimicking the cat's pronunciation and causing my mouth to fall open in shock. I'd known this cat for over a year and still didn't have all his names memorized. Had the young dog really picked the entire train wreck of a name up after hearing it just once?

"My name is Paisley Lee," she informed him with another slight bow of her head. "When Nan adopted me, she gave me her last name, so I guess we aren't really brother and sister. I'm sorry if my calling you brother upset you. I know now that I was wrong."

"It's all right," Octo-Cat mumbled, obviously charmed by the little dog's impeccable manners even though he most certainly wished that he wasn't.

"I really would like us to be friends, but if you don't want that, I understand," Paisley squeaked. Tears lined each of her large black eyes, but she continued on bravely. "I will try my very best not to chase you anymore or to make you unhappy in any way, but please can I stay? This is my family now, too."

"I guess that would be okay with me," Octo-Cat said and then retreated deeper into his carrier.

The conversation had reached its natural end, and somehow everyone had managed to survive.

We really were going to be all right, after all.

CHAPTER EIGHTEEN

True to his half-hearted words, Octo-Cat quit hiding in my bedroom non-stop and started to rethread his life with ours. He didn't even leave the room when Paisley entered anymore, which I considered a huge step in the right direction.

Paisley adopted the practice of not speaking to him unless he spoke first, and occasionally he actually would initiate a brief conversation with her.

Several days passed, each better than the last.

Now that we'd solved the mystery of the broken household items and both pets were on their way toward forming a lasting friendship, my thoughts returned to Trish.

The county police had found enough evidence to charge her with Class C Theft after a bank teller in Dewdrop Springs identified Trish as the person who had cashed Nan's and my donation checks the week before. She'd then used that money to purchase several hundred dollars in stolen pet supplies. Together, the stolen cash and goods tallied up to just over one-thousand dollars, which marked her actions as a felony in our great state of Maine. She was still awaiting her trial at the moment, but Charles had informed me that the punishment could be both a hefty fine and possible jail time.

I still remembered how kind she had been to Nan and me outside the shelter when we first met her and how she'd mentioned not having much money herself. But was she really the type to steal from animals in order to line her own pockets? And if so, then why did she use the cashed checks to purchase supplies for them?

Something wasn't sitting right about the whole situation, but I couldn't quite figure out what. At a loss for answers, I let my questions about Trish and the embezzlement at the animal shelter simmer at the back of my mind as I worked on building a website for Octo-Cat's and my new P.I. company. Eventually we'd have customers, and I wanted to be ready to wow them when they finally came calling.

Maybe someday soon, he'd agree to let Paisley join the investigative team. I, for one, knew the little dog would love the chance to play—and win—Detective again.

That morning, Paisley decided to celebrate her new kind of sort of friendship with Octo-Cat by bringing him a present. We'd just finished tea when the little dog skittered in through the electronic pet door. Her collar was now outfitted with a coded chip, too, which meant she could come and go as she pleased—just like her new hero, Octo-Cat.

Our raccoon friend Pringle, on the other hand, had been given a massive lecture and a warning that we were to never, ever see him in the house again, no matter what Octo-Cat said was or wasn't okay.

"Hey, girl," Nan called when she saw the dog's small, dark form traipse through the foyer. "What have you got there?"

Sure enough, Paisley had something large stuffed inside her mouth, which she brought straight to Octo-Cat and laid at his paws, her tail a waggly blur of joy. Thank goodness, the tabby had been laying on the floor rather than the couch, because the gift in question was a very large and slightly bloody mouse.

Dead, of course.

Octo-Cat studied the corpse before him, then looked back up at Paisley. His eyes softened as he asked, "For me?"

She blinked and shivered and wagged. "Cats like mice. Right?"
I think Octo-Cat surprised us all with his genuinely large smile.
"Yes, and the deader the better. Good job, kiddo."

The sight made me want to throw up, but I felt too happy to let
my roiling stomach stand in the way of this important bonding
moment. "You know cats are supposed to be the ones to catch
mice," I informed them both.

"That's old-fashioned thinking," Octo-Cat protested. "Besides,
she caught this mouse for me, which kind of means I'm the one who
did it, anyway."

Paisley beat her tail against the ground, hanging on every word
that spilled forth from Octo-Cat's lips.

"Nice try," I said with a sarcastic chuckle. "But you can't just
take credit for someone else's..." My words trailed off, and I looked
toward Nan.

"What is it, dear?" she asked, then took another sip of tea.

"Trish," I said, thinking back to how sure I had been that we'd
caught the bad guy and put the mystery at the shelter to rest. Too
sure. The evidence was too neatly wrapped up in a nice little bow.

"What about her?" Nan said as the animals continued to share
their gross bonding moment separate from us.

"Well, what if she wasn't the one stealing money? What if
someone else was doing it but let her take the fall?"

"You think she was framed?"

Nan's even tone bothered me. Did she really not believe that I
was on to something here?

"I'm not sure, but it's a possibility. All the evidence was too
neatly stacked against her," I explained, using the same wild hand
gestures my Italian-American father often used while trying to make
a point. "Either she's a terrible criminal, or she's not one at all."

"Interesting," Nan said and dipped a cream-filled cookie into
her tea.

"Think about it. She was the one sneaking around after closing
time. She's the one who shredded that paper. I saw her in Dewdrop
Springs the same night our checks were cashed there, and she wasn't

exactly subtle about buying those stolen pet supplies in broad daylight."

"But didn't she also tell those massage people that the shelter had its funding cut?" Nan pointed out as she stared deep into her teacup. "Charles checked and said that wasn't true."

"Yes—but oh! When we went back to the shelter the next day, that old woman, Pearl, also said the funding had been cut."

"Who you calling old?" Nan's voice finally picked up some passion. "She's at least fifteen years younger than me."

"Sorry, Nan," I muttered. "But how well do you know Pearl? She seemed to know you quite well but couldn't remember me."

"She was in my community art class over the summer. Remember that?" She finished her tea and set the cup and saucer on the coffee table, then leaned back in her chair.

"Would you say she's the type to steal money from the animal shelter and then lie about it to others?"

"Certainly not. She was always on and on about her volunteer work with the shelter. She loves those animals as if they were her own."

"Then who else would have the means, opportunity, and motive to take that money?"

"Trish did mention being short on cash when we bumped into her outside the shelter," Nan reasoned. "Then again, money is its own motive, whether you have it or not."

"It has to be somebody inside. Somebody with access to the finances." I picked at a hangnail as I thought, a bad habit I'd thought I'd seen the last of. Apparently not.

"And somebody who could weave a narrative about funding cuts that others would willingly believe." Nan nodded and bit her lip. What a pair we made.

We both thought a little while longer, and then suddenly we had it.

"Mr. Leavitt!" we cried in unison, turning toward each other in excitement.

"Oh, he is going down," Nan promised the universe.

"We need to get him to confess somehow," I said, because apparently it was up to me to state the obvious here. "Any ideas?"

"Excuse me," Octo-Cat said, still beaming proudly from behind his unsettling gift. I hadn't even realized he was paying attention. "I think I might have an idea," he said and then let out a contented chuckle.

He was back, baby!

CHAPTER NINETEEN

One week later...

My mom held a microphone to Nan's face, beaming at her with daughterly pride. "And to think, it only took you two weeks to plan this gorgeous affair."

My grandmother wore her hair in a French twist and sported a bold red lip. She'd even commissioned a special gown to wear to the gala. Silver beaded pawprints lined the neck and sleeves of her pink satin dress, creating a stunning effect.

Despite the quick event planning turn-around, it seemed all of Glendale had shown up to support Nan's fundraiser for the Community Animal Shelter. Half the people from our neighboring towns, too. My mother and her cameraman had also shown up to film a human-interest piece for the local news.

Yeah, it was a pretty big deal.

While Mom interviewed Nan, I did another round through the house. Yes, we'd decided to use our own home as the location for the event tonight. Mr. Gables from the downtown council also helped to secure a series of large, impressive-looking tents, which we'd set up outside to expand the venue's workable space.

The charity gala included a catered dinner, silent auction, and the chance for attendees to write generous checks to support our shelter. We'd arranged to have all the VIP players inside the house so that it would be easier to keep an eye on them. If all went according to plan, we'd be able to oust a weasel before the night was through.

I'd chosen to wear a little black dress, so I could sneak around if it became necessary. A hands-free communications device had also been tucked into my ear so that Octo-Cat and I could keep each other updated throughout the evening. As long as I made it look like I was discussing something related to the gala, then I could speak freely and without question.

We'd blocked off the upstairs to discourage guests from exploring the upper floors and also to help hide Octo-Cat where he sat perched near the spindles that lined the hallway. His job was to watch the guests below and report what he saw via our FaceTime voice call.

He'd actually been the one to come up with the idea for tonight's ambush. Nan and I had just seen to the details. Paisley, too, by keeping everyone's spirits up with her constant optimism and kindness.

She believed the bad guy would be caught and that we would all win Detective once and for all.

And I chose to believe that, too.

"The eagle has landed," Octo-Cat rasped in my ear. He'd been joining Nan for her spy movie marathons lately and had picked up the lingo quickly. Since no one could understand him but me, I preferred he speak plainly—but I guessed whatever made this fun for him was okay by me.

I turned toward the foyer just in time to see our target, the shelter's Community Outreach Coordinator, Mr. Leavitt, enter my home. He wore a very becoming black tux and an enormous grin that stretched from cheek to cheek.

"Hello, stranger," I said after I made my way over to him, hating the taste of those flirtatious words in my mouth. My heart belonged to Charles and Charles alone, but still I needed to get our prime suspect to play straight into my hands and was willing to do whatever it took.

Well, within reason, that is.

"You and your grandmother have really outdone yourselves," he exclaimed as I led him toward the cash bar we'd set up in the dining room. "This place looks fabulous!"

"It doesn't just look fabulous. It *is* fabulous," I responded right on cue. Nan and I had practiced my role in this charade many times, and while I didn't have an exact script, I knew all the points I was expected to hit as quickly and naturally as possible.

"We've already raised over twenty thousand dollars just from the table reservations alone. By the time the silent auctions and donations come in, we could be over one hundred thousand. Not bad for one night's work, huh?"

There, I'd said all the most important things. Nan would be so proud if she were here to witness my debut performance.

Mr. Leavitt's eyes widened with poorly concealed avarice. If he'd been carrying a drink, I imagine he may have choked on it. Instead, he merely stuttered his next words. "O-o-one hundred thousand dollars? You don't say."

"Oh, but I do." I placed a delicate hand on his shoulder and laughed. "It turns out people are very generous when it comes to saving the animals."

"Yes, I've always thought so."

The bartender handed him a glass of white wine and refilled my seltzer and lime. I wasn't much of a drinker under normal circumstances, but tonight I needed all my wits about me. I also needed to redirect Mr. Leavitt to the foyer so that Octo-Cat could keep an eye on things as they went down.

"Excuse me for just a moment," I said, drawing my phone out of my strapless clutch and pushing send on the message that I had already composed earlier that evening.

Smiling up at Mr. Leavitt, I said, "There. Now that that's done, let's enjoy the party. I have so many people I'd like to introduce you to. Did you know Nan was a famous Broadway actress back in her glory days? She has many wealthy friends from her time in the city,

and several of them came out to support her—to support the shelter
—tonight."

"Fantastic," Mr. Leavitt said and took another sip from his glass.

A loud tapping followed by a burst of microphone interference
filled the room, causing everyone to fall silent.

"Excuse me, excuse me, ladies and gentlemen," Nan cried into
the mic. "I just wanted to say a huge thanks to a donor who asked to
remain anonymous. She just gave us a fifty-thousand-dollar donation, single-handedly putting us over our fundraising goal for the
evening. Thanks to her big heart, the shelter can stay open for
another two full years and we can help all of Glendale's stray pets
find their forever homes."

Everyone clapped politely. Some even gasped in awe.

What an amazingly generous gift... had it been real.

"Oh, this night has already exceeded our wildest expectations," I
gushed to Mr. Leavitt, continuing the carefully planned facade.
"Nan and I had hoped our little gala would be a success, but we had
no idea it would raise *so much* money."

Nan snaked through the crowd and joined the two of us in the
foyer. "Mr. Leavitt," she enthused. "I wanted to hand you this check
personally. A fifty-thousand-dollar donation. Can you believe it?"
She pressed the check into his hand, which was my signal.

"A problem with the vegetarian dinner option?" I shrieked into
my headpiece. "No, no, no. We can't have that, especially not at a
fundraiser for animals. I'll be right there."

I pressed my Bluetooth device to imitate ending a call and then
turned toward Nan with a panicked expression. "C'mon, I think this
one might require both of us. It was nice seeing you again, Mr.
Leavitt. Enjoy the rest of your evening."

"It's all you, bud," I mumbled into the headpiece as Nan and I
rushed outside. "Operation Red Dot is in full swing."

CHAPTER TWENTY

A s much as Octo-Cat had hated being tricked by the red dot when I had to capture him for our vet visit, that little moment of treachery served as the entire basis for our plan to catch Mr. Leavitt red-dot-handed.

"It's not about the red dot," Octo-Cat had waxed philosophically. "It's about what the red dot *represents.*"

He'd gone on to explain that, for cats, the red dot itself is irresistible and basically impossible to ignore. My cat then urged us to find Mr. Leavitt's red dot, and by that time Nan had already said it best: *Money is its own motive, whether you have it or not.*

From there, we flew full force into planning the charity gala and, with it, our master plan. So, the fifty-thousand-dollar donation was a total fraud. We had fake checks printed with a fake name and fake address and even a made-up account number, counting on our bad guy to do the bad thing and steal it.

Officer Bouchard had gone undercover in plain clothes to stake out the bank in Dewdrop Springs. At the end of the day, Mr. Leavitt had a decision to make. He could either continue to slowly embezzle funds from the failing animal shelter, or he could grab the big check and make a run for it. Our hope was that the fifty-thousand-dollar carrot—or red dot, using Octo-Cat's preferred analogy—was enough to encourage him to do the latter.

"He's leaving! He's leaving!" Octo-Cat cried inside my ear while I pretended to be busy examining a tray of broccoli florets.

"Text him," I told Nan, who had a text to Officer Bouchard ready to go on her phone. As much as I hated being left out of the action, my role in this ambush had officially ended.

"Good work, Octavius," I said before removing my headpiece. After that, I pulled my phone out of my clutch and sent a quick text to Charles.

May I have this dance?

He found me a short while later, and together we swayed on my front lawn until the stars came out...

Actually, that would have been incredibly romantic, but we did have to face one minor distraction first.

"He's got him." I heard Nan's words only moments before I felt her arms wrap around me from behind. She joined Charles and me in our dance as she whispered in my ear. "That fool went to the same exact bank as before. Turns out it had been him the whole time, except for the last two checks, of course. I'll tell you more when I know more." She gave me a kiss on the cheek and then wandered off.

"Your nan just pinched my butt," Charles told me with a laugh.

"Nan's gotta Nan," I responded, rolling my eyes. She and I could have a talk about boundaries later. Right now I wanted to enjoy my evening held tightly in Charles's strong arms.

"How'd you know it wasn't Trish?" he asked me.

"It was too perfect," I murmured, ready to put this whole thing behind me and enjoy the rest of the gala as best I could.

"Kind of like you," he said, giving me a quick kiss on the cheek.

"Yeah, sure," I joked, but snuggled closer to him all the same. If he wanted to believe I was perfect, then I refused to stop him.

I t was Harmony of all people who finally gave the info that would solve the case. Remember that mean masseuse? Yeah, her.

Turns out Trish had visited Serenity day spa because Stone—whose real name was Declan—also worked at the Dewdrop Springs branch of the First Bank of Blueberry Bay. He'd helped Mr. Leavitt cash his stolen checks and then frame Trish for it.

And Harmony—whose real name was truly and legitimately Harmony—heard enough to testify against him. From there, he cracked wide open and confessed everything.

Paisley hadn't seen Trish before because Trish didn't technically work for the shelter. The sweet but forgetful front desk attendant Pearl was her grandmother, and for weeks Mr. Leavitt had been threatening to let her go due to her age and the suspicion she had early onset dementia. He'd used that threat along with a few carefully constructed lies to con Trish into carrying out his dirty work.

And when he sensed me and Nan hot on his tail, he set Trish up to take the fall for all of it. He'd sent her to cash the checks with Stone. He'd also sent her to buy the stolen supplies, instructing his lackey to purposefully end up in the wrong lot and force her to walk all about town with the hopes someone would discover her suspicious behavior.

And, yeah, I'd played right into his hand.

If it weren't for my pets and that disgusting dead mouse, I may have never realized that we'd accused the wrong person.

Luckily, my pets *were* gross, and Mr. Leavitt—whose first name is Alex, by the way—would be going away for a long, long time. Now someone who really believes in the animal shelter's mission will be taking over as the Community Outreach Coordinator.

Pearl.

A doctor quickly dismissed the dementia diagnosis and ruled her completely in good health and of sound mind. So now, she runs things, and her devoted granddaughter Trish has taken over as the first face you see when entering the facility.

Nan and I, for our part, plan to continue organizing fundraisers to help the shelter get back on its feet.

So I guess you can say we all lived happily ever after.
Well, until the next case anyway...

WHAT'S NEXT?

Taking crazy cat lady to a whole new level... Binge read books 7-9 with this special boxed collection!
Ever since Angie Russo woke up from a near fatal run-in with a coffee maker, she's been able to talk to—and even worse, understand—one very spoiled tabby named Octavius.

This collection includes *Raccoon Racketeer*, *Himalayan Hazard*, and *Hoppy Holiday Homicide*. Read along as surprising family secrets are uncovered by a gossipy raccoon, murder happens on board a train, and Octo-Cat even finds love. Add in a double homicide and a kidnapping on Christmas Eve, toss on your favorite deerstalker cap, and let's go sleuthing!

If you love kitty detectives and quirky humor, then you do not want to miss this USA Today bestselling series and your chance to binge read books seven through nine with this special boxed collection... Enjoy!

PET WHISPER P.I. BOOKS 7-9 SPECIAL BOXED EDITION
is now available.

CLICK HERE to get your copy so that you can keep reading this series today!

MORE MOLLY

ABOUT MOLLY FITZ

While USA Today bestselling author Molly Fitz can't technically talk to animals, she and her doggie best friend, Sky Princess, have deep and very animated conversations as they navigate their days. Add to that, five more dogs, a snarky feline, comedian husband, and diva daughter, and you can pretty much imagine how life looks at the Casa de Fitz.

Molly lives in a house on a high hill in the Michigan woods and occasionally ventures out for good food, great coffee, or to meet new animal friends.

Writing her quirky, cozy animal mysteries is pretty much a dream come true, but sometimes she also goes by the names Melissa Storm and Mila Riggs and writes a very different kind of story.

Learn more, grab the free app, or sign up for her newsletter at **www.MollyMysteries.com**!

PET WHISPERER P.I.

Angie Russo just partnered up with Blueberry Bay's first ever talking cat detective. Along with his ragtag gang of human and animal helpers, Octo-Cat is determined to save the day... so long as it doesn't interfere with his schedule. Start with book 1, **Kitty Confidential**.

PARANORMAL TEMP AGENCY

Tawny Bigford's simple life takes a turn for the magical when she stumbles upon her landlady's murder and is recruited by a talking black cat named Fluffikins to take over the deceased's role as the official Town Witch for Beech Grove, Georgia. Start with book 1, **Witch for Hire**.

MERLIN THE MAGICAL FLUFF

Gracie Springs is not a witch... but her cat is. Now she must help to keep his secret or risk spending the rest of her life in some magical prison. Too bad trouble seems to find them at every turn! Start with book 1, **Merlin the Magical Fluff.**

THE MEOWING MEDIUM

Mags McAllister lives a simple life making candles for tourists in historic Larkhaven, Georgia. But when a cat with mismatched eyes enters her life, she finds herself with the ability to see into the realm of spirits... Now the ghosts of people long dead have started coming to her for help solving their cold cases. Start with book 1, **Secrets of the Specter**.

THE PAINT-SLINGING SLEUTH

Following a freak electrical storm, Lisa Lewis's vibrant paintings of fairytale creatures have started coming to life. Unfortunately, only she can see and communicate with them. And when her mentor turns up dead, this aspiring artist must turn amateur sleuth to clear her name and save the day with only these "pigments" of her imagination to help her. Start with book 1, **My Colorful Conundrum**.

SPECIAL COLLECTIONS

Black Cat Crossing
Pet Whisperer P.I. Books 1-3
Pet Whisperer P.I. Books 4-6
Pet Whisperer P.I. Books 7-9
Pet Whisperer P.I. Books 10-12

CONNECT WITH MOLLY

You can download my free app here:
mollymysteries.com/app

Or sign up for my newsletter and get a special digital prize pack for joining, including an exclusive story, Meowy Christmas Mayhem, fun quiz, and lots of cat pictures!
mollymysteries.com/subscribe

Have you ever wanted to talk to animals? You can chat with Octo-Cat and help him solve an exclusive online mystery here:
mollymysteries.com/chat

Or maybe you'd like to chat with other animal-loving readers as well as to learn about new books and giveaways as soon as they happen! Come join Molly's VIP reader group on Facebook.
mollymysteries.com/group

MORE BOOKS LIKE THIS

Welcome to Whiskered Mysteries, where each and every one of our charming cozies comes with a furry sidekick... or several! Around here, you'll find we're all about crafting the ultimate reading experience. Whether that means laugh-out-loud antics, jaw-dropping magical exploits, or whimsical journeys through small seaside towns, you decide.

So go on and settle into your favorite comfy chair and grab one of our *paw*some cozy mysteries to kick off your next great reading adventure!

Visit our website to browse our books and meet our authors, to jump into our discussion group, or to join our newsletter. See you there!

www.WhiskeredMysteries.com

WHISKMYS (WĪSK′MƏS)

DEFINITION : a state of fiction-induced euphoria that commonly occurs in those who read books published by the small press, Whiskered Mysteries.

USAGE: Every day is Whiskmys when you have great books to read!

LEARN MORE AT
WWW.WHISKMYS.COM